SUBTLE POWERS

SUBTLE POWERS

THE LAND OF BROKEN ROADS
BOOK THREE

Ryan English

Podium

SUBTLE
POWERS

CHAPTER ONE

A PPROACH, *said Father.*

Socks lowered his head, ducked his tail, and crept forward on unsteady paws.

Dirt held his breath from the top of the tree, trying to push a few more of the red-and-yellow leaves out of the way so he could get a better view. This was it. For the first time, he was returning to appear before Father, and Socks would live or die based on the giant wolf's approval.

One of Socks's older siblings, a female, reached her nose forward as he passed her, and he shyly touched it with his, his tail twitching in a hidden wag. But he didn't stop moving forward, and the other three ignored him, pointedly looking elsewhere. Dirt suspected they'd be more friendly after seeing whether Socks would get eaten.

Socks reached Father, who towered over him like a mountain. From where Dirt was watching, little Socks looked like a pygmy species compared with his sire, not just a child. They had matching scars across their faces, except Father's was much larger and more vicious, from a more brutal wound. And Socks was still just a darkening gray, where Father's coat was so black it seemed to swallow the light around it.

Father leaned down his great head to sniff his pup, and Socks whimpered, a heart-wrenching, pleading sound that Dirt almost never heard. The pup gave a timid, playful little hop with just his front legs and reached his nose up to meet Father's, licking his snout, then fell to his back to expose his stomach. *I love you, please accept me, I submit to you,* Socks was saying in the language of wolves.

Father growled and bared his teeth, and Socks whimpered, pawing at the air. The sound of Father's growl was so shocking to Dirt's basest instincts that he nearly lost his grip on the branch and fell out of the tree.

GET UP AND GIVE ME AN ACCOUNTING OF YOURSELF, commanded Father. Socks rolled over to his belly and sat up, head still halfway to the ground as he looked upward with pleading eyes.

Socks must not have started quickly enough, because Father said, *ARE YOU TOO COWARDLY TO SPEAK WITHOUT YOUR PET?*

-That's not it,- said Socks. From across the valley, his mental voice was on the quiet side, but Dirt could still hear it. The pup was probably doing that on purpose. Dirt didn't dare open his mental sight right now, not with Father so close.

WHAT IS THAT YOU HAVE ON? HAVE YOU BEEN TAMED? asked Father, his voice more threatening than lightning strikes.

-I wanted it, so some humans made it for me. I am wearing a harness, but I am not harnessed. Its purpose is to give me pockets because I like to carry things,- said Socks, sounding gentle and conciliatory.

SHOW ME WHAT YOU HAVE IN THERE.

Socks's ears twitched eagerly, and he turned his head to look at the pockets on either side of his harness. He pulled out their contents with his mind, circling them around himself in the air. He couldn't help but wag his tail as he explained, *-This is a big bone that I like to chew on. It's from a bull. This is a ball of metal the humans gave me. It's called iron, and I use it to hit things. This is a rock I found, and I like it because it's so square. I wear it on the other side to balance out the metal ball. The duchess gave me this necklace, and it has a special rock called an emerald. This is Dirt's backpack, and it has his clothes and a scroll in it. I only carry it sometimes. This is a flower that had lots of bees on it, and I wanted to see if they would follow it. They didn't. It's drying out now. This is a red leaf, which I kept because I didn't know they turn color when autumn comes. This is a rake that Dirt uses to brush my fur and scratch me whenever I want.-*

WHY ARE YOU CARRYING AROUND GARBAGE?

-None of this is garbage.-

A WOLF NEEDS NONE OF THOSE THINGS.

-I still want them anyway. They are fun. You should let Dirt rake you.-

The pup didn't seem to be taking this as seriously as expected, which made Dirt increasingly nervous. Dirt couldn't tell from Father's body language whether he was impressed or not, but at least Socks was still alive, so that was something. If it'd help, Dirt would certainly rush all the way across the valley in an instant to grab that rake.

-*Watch this!*- said Socks. He shoved everything back into the big pockets except the iron ball, just larger than Dirt's head, which he flung in a smooth arc against a nearby tree. The poor thing's trunk exploded with a resounding *CRACK*, splitting in half and sending splinters whistling in every direction. Socks yanked the ball back and made it slowly circle over his head, tongue out and looking quite pleased with himself.

Then he suddenly shot it at another tree, shattering it like the first. Before the sound had even reached Dirt's ears, Socks had retrieved the ball and held it ready for another fling.

YOU ARE ACTING TOO HUMAN. WHAT USE HAS A WOLF FOR TOOLS?

-*I am not too human. You would use tools too, if you had pockets. With this, I can hit something over there, even if I am over here.*-

YOU CAN ALREADY DO THAT. YOU DON'T NEED AN IRON BALL.

-*I know, but I figured this out. When you lift something with your mind, the force has to go back into your body. But that works both directions. If I brace my feet, I can use all my muscles.*-

YOU DO NOT NEED AN IRON BALL. WATCH. Father turned his gaze toward a tall, thick pine and a sharp thump sounded across the field, a strange noise too quiet to echo. The tree remained standing. Then another high-pitched thump, and another.

LOOK, LITTLE PUP.

-*Those holes are as small as Dirt's fingers. How did you push them all the way through the trunk? Is it because you're so big?*-

NO. THINK OF THIS SHAPE.

-*Oh, you start big and then funnel it down, like water going in a hole. Let me try,*- said Socks. His posture had perked up a little, even if he made it obvious how he leaned toward Father, never looking away from him for long and frequently reaching up with his nose. He nuzzled his sire's front leg in a way that wasn't subtle at all, then braced himself and tried to hit the tree with his mind the way he'd been shown.

The thump was so quiet from this distance that Dirt thought he might have imagined it, and Socks ducked down in dismay at his failure. But Father didn't bite his spine in half, so he hurriedly tried again. The second try made a slightly louder sound, and a third.

I DID NOT CALL YOU HERE TO WATCH YOU PRACTICE.

-One more try. I think I've . . . - said Socks, trailing off. He braced himself, digging in with front and back claws, and smacked the tree with his mind. Dirt heard the thump, faintly, but it sounded right. The pine swayed a bit at the top, which it hadn't done for Father. *-Well, I made a bigger hole than you did, so I didn't hit as hard. But I still made one. See, Father? I am strong. I am not getting weaker running around with Dirt.-*

PINE WOOD IS SOFT.

-Can my siblings do that?-

The great wolf hesitated to answer, giving away the answer before he replied. Dirt grinned to himself to see such an overwhelming presence give pause, and Father shot Dirt a look, just the quickest of glances, to tell him he was watching. Dirt's smile vanished.

NO, said Father.

-How about—-

MOST OF MY CHILDREN ARE ADULTS BEFORE THEY GAIN THAT LEVEL OF MENTAL CONTROL.

-Then I bet they can't do this either. Watch closely, everyone.-

Socks turned and stepped backward to be alongside Father, then pulled the emerald necklace back out. Even from here, Dirt could see the pup's entire body focus on the necklace. Not quite well enough to know for sure, but Dirt could guess what was happening—the pup was unlatching it. That was hard enough for Dirt, who had fingers; it was near impossible for a giant creature like Socks. The necklace's band was so thin it looked like a thread instead of gold links at first glance, even up close, and the clasp operated by a tiny lever that Dirt had to use a fingernail to open. It had taken Socks four straight days of practice before he'd gotten it.

The other pups all startled at the same time, indicating that Socks had succeeded. They crowded in for a closer look, perking up their ears and wagging their huge tails.

YOUR PET'S FIDDLY LITTLE FINGERS HAVE BEEN GIVING YOU IDEAS. YOU SHOULD NOT IMITATE SUCH BIZARRE CREATURES.

-They look funny, but mine is cute. And they can be useful.-
PERHAPS. SHOW US WHAT ELSE YOU HAVE LEARNED.
Socks thought about that for a moment. *-Okay, no one move.-*

The area filled with sparks, around and under all the other pups and even Father, surrounding them all in a cloud of glowing embers. Each spark burst into a short-lived flame, creating a giant ball of white and yellow fire that burned out almost instantly. Socks's four siblings yelped and jumped back, and Father growled sincerely, creating a menacing low rumble that Dirt could feel in his chest. Fighting back against his instinctual panic got no easier.

-Look, I didn't burn you. I didn't even singe your fur. See how careful I am?- said Socks. He stepped from sibling to sibling, making that squeaky whimpering sound, giving their faces little licks. Only once they were sure all their fur was intact did they return any of the affection.

Dirt gripped the branch ever tighter. What was Socks doing? How could he possibly dare do anything to aggravate Father?

HOW HOT CAN YOU MAKE THE FIRE? asked Father, sounding unimpressed. Still, some of the carnivorous edge had faded from his voice, which gave Dirt hope.

Socks stood straighter and wagged his tail. He skipped halfway across the field, then looked around to make sure no one had followed. They knew better.

He lifted his face upward and created another field of sparks about a body length above himself, then brought them all in together in a small ball. More sparks appeared and fell into it, looking very much like it was drawing them in, then a third batch. The ball swirled.

Socks strained, stretching his focus to its limit as he brought in more and more sparks. All at once, it became too many and exploded in a flash of white light. A searing wave of heat hit Dirt's face and made his eyes water, followed by a gentle press of wind.

Dirt almost jumped out of the tree to go pat Socks's fur when he saw it smoking, but the pup rolled on the ground and put it out, then hopped back to his feet, looking pleased with himself.

-I can make it even hotter if Dirt helps.-
DIRT IS NOT ALLOWED TO HELP RIGHT NOW, said Father. The great wolf moved over to Socks, only needing a few steps to cover that broad distance, and leaned down to sniff him. Socks rolled to his

back again and raised his paws, reaching for his sire's face. Father lifted his head just high enough not to be reached and gave another quiet growl.

Then Father turned and stepped back to where he was before. *COME FORWARD,* he said, indicating with a thought which wolf he meant. It was the female who had greeted Socks, his sister one year older.

She stalked out into the meadow, all playfulness gone. She approached like a predator, not a friend, half again Socks's size or more with almost none of the fuzz and gentleness of puppyhood. The gray fur of her birth had almost all darkened to black, indicating her maturity. Her orange eyes lost all their affection, and she began to regard her little brother as prey.

TAKE OFF THAT HARNESS, PUP. IT WILL NOT HELP YOU HERE, said Father.

Socks grabbed the harness with his mind and stepped backward to slip out of it, then deposited it carefully on the ground beside a thin pine at the edge of the meadow. He shook himself to loosen the lines of flattened fur that had been under the straps. Then he stood straight, looking ready.

KILL HIM. IF HE SURVIVES LONG ENOUGH, I WILL TELL YOU TO STOP.

Socks wagged his tail for just a moment, glancing across the field to the tree where Dirt was watching, which filled the boy with panic. What was he thinking, losing focus at a time like this? Please, please live, he begged to no one, still keeping his thoughts to himself.

The pup looked back at his older sister and said, *-I have fought scarier things than you.-*

She snarled and stepped forward, circling to look for an opening. And immediately lost her balance and bit the grass. Socks had tripped her with his mind. She tried to rise but took a ringing blow on the head, pushing her back down.

That was only temporary, however, because she redoubled her strength and surged forward, shrugging off blow after blow. She kicked forward through another mental trip attempt and lunged, teeth and claws ready. Socks ducked under it and hoisted her right over himself, then stepped away.

For her second attack, she charged straight through, and none of Socks's mental attacks could stop her. Socks was over fifteen feet at the shoulder already, but she was half again his size and probably twice his weight, and that was before she strengthened herself with mana.

They became a tangle of twisting limbs and vicious roars. They bit and tore at each other, growling and snarling the whole time. She had the clear advantage, but Socks was wily enough to keep his throat out of her teeth. More than once she got her fangs into the fur around his shoulder, and he tore himself away, opening bloody flaps of skin to keep from letting her do even more damage. The blood slicked his fur and made him harder to grab.

Dirt whimpered and clenched his teeth to keep from crying out.

Socks raked her belly with his rear claws, opening long, bloody lines, but it wasn't deep enough to let her guts out and end it. She roared in fury, but Socks twisted out from below her grasp.

They stood apart, then lunged at each other, trying to sink their fangs into whatever they could grab. They split up and lunged again. And again. Her attacks were stronger and more direct, and each time Socks had to pull himself out of her teeth. Not every attack drew blood, though—sometimes she came away with just a tuft of fur.

The fight raged from one end of the meadow to the other, and beyond it. They crashed into trees, uprooting the smaller ones and shaking the birds from the others. It was so fast, so bestial and chaotic, that Dirt could hardly stand to watch. He had to, though, despite how hard it was to see. He and Socks had come mentally prepared for the worst, but that didn't make it easier.

Socks shifted his strategy again, spending more effort dancing away. Invisible hands pushed his sister's jaws aside, or caught her foot at just the right moment to make her stumble, or some such thing. Never enough to stop her—he couldn't—but always sufficient to slow her down.

He began to look like he was enjoying himself, despite Father's judging eye, which filled Dirt with desperation. The whole field was torn up, trees broken, earth and blood and bits of fur everywhere, but Socks was wagging his tail like he was playing tag with children.

That enraged his sister more and more, but there wasn't much she could do about it. If Socks turned to run, she'd be on him in an instant. If he faced her directly, she'd overpower him. But this dance of dodging and misdirection was something she couldn't outmaneuver.

Until she grabbed him with her own mind. Dirt watch Socks's movements slow as her mental grip tightened around him, and although it seemed she had much less control, her strength was more than he could resist. Finally she held him secure and lunged in one final time to rip his throat out.

But she didn't. She snapped her jaws shut and buried her muzzle in his neck instead, looking completely confused. She stepped back and waved her snout in the air, twisting in every direction and Dirt quickly realized that Socks had clamped her mouth shut. No matter how she struggled, she couldn't get him to let go.

She still had her claws, and she still held Socks in her grasp. But she was so surprised by her inability to get her mouth open that it seemed she'd forgotten all that. Dirt quickly removed those thoughts from his mind lest she happen to see them.

ENOUGH, said Father. Both pups let go of the other, and Socks quickly stepped over to lick his sister's face affectionately. Despite his injuries, he seemed in a great mood. Dirt, on the other hand, couldn't hear the birds anymore over the sound of his own terrified, beating heart.

Father lifted both pups and placed them before himself, rather than step over where they were. The great wolf huffed in annoyance and looked over to Dirt, who ducked down instinctively, as if that would do any good. Then Father looked back down at Socks and said, *THIS IS NOT WORKING. YOU ARE SUPPOSED TO BE FRIGHTENED AND TIMID. DO YOU NOT THINK I WILL KILL YOU?*

-She gave it away on accident. I am very good at seeing thoughts someone is trying to hide, because Dirt and I play a game like that. But not just her. She was the first, but they all did,- said Socks, sounding proud. *-I saw as soon as I got here, and then I hid it from you so you wouldn't find out.-*

AND I DIDN'T THINK TO LOOK. I AM GETTING LAX, AND YOU ARE A RASCAL. THE GAME IS OVER. LICK THEIR WOUNDS, said Father. He lowered his huge head and finally rubbed faces with Socks while the other pups came and licked the wounds of the combatants.

Dirt could hardly believe what had just happened. Socks had known he wasn't going to die, all the way from the start? He edged closer and closer to the end of the branch, wondering if he was allowed to come down there yet or if he even wanted to. It really did look like the trial was over, because now he couldn't detect even a hint of hesitation or coldness among them.

Indeed, it was nice to see Socks finally smothered in the affection he deserved from his own kind. Maybe Dirt could wait until his heart stopped pounding so hard before he went down. He finally let his mind open to their thoughts so he could watch what was going on, though.

Socks and Father had been speaking in words, but the other pups didn't care to. They probably could, but why bother? The air filled with their thoughts, pure emotion and scent and complex ideas all jumbled together in a way Dirt had nearly forgotten about, it'd been so long. Affection and admiration, mostly, speaking so loudly there was no chance he'd miss it. They were curious about Socks's adventures and the things in his pockets, and Dirt relaxed onto the branch to watch and flush the anxiety from his system.

Father's voice nearly startled him from his perch, though. *GET DOWN HERE, HUMAN. I HOPE YOU ARE PROUD OF YOURSELF. THEY ALL WANT POCKETS NOW.*

Dirt jumped right out of the tree rather than waste an instant climbing down. He strengthened his legs and back with mana and rolled when he hit the ground, then sprinted over and lay down on his back right next to Socks. He pulled up his shirt to expose his belly and looked away, in a posture of complete submission.

I SEE YOU FOUND SOME CLOTHES, said Father.

-He wears them most days now because it gets cold in the morning and he doesn't have any fur,- said Socks, adding ideas and pictures to the words. Dirt shivering after waking up, his teeth chattering in the cold wind while Socks ran, the city full of humans and all of them dressed.

Dirt said something as well, trying his best to speak in the way of wolves. A bundle of ideas and scents—familiarity and relaxation, the comfortable feeling of cloth on his skin, the bite of cold air and his need to stay warm. An image of himself leaving the human city and the reassuring scent of Socks's fur as he lay down for the pup to run. Their affection and Dirt's choice to stay with him.

The other wolves were amused, all of them opening their mouths to show their tongues. *-You speak like an infant,-* said one of the younger males. Dirt grinned before he remembered that baring your teeth was different for them. Fortunately, though, they understood.

Of the four pups, Dirt recognized two as being from Socks's litter. He'd met them before, and even spoken a bit. He sent them puffs of affection and recognition. To the two older pups, he sent respect and greeting. And, foolishly, to Father he sent complete humility and gratitude, the kind that expects nothing in return. He still did his best to avoid looking at Father's mind, though, which glowed like the burning summer sun at midday.

GET UP OFF THE GROUND, HUMAN. THAT IS NOT HUMAN BEHAVIOR.

Dirt hopped instantly to his feet and bowed, like people did for the duke.

THAT'S BETTER. NOW, PICK UP THAT RAKE. AFTERWARD, WE WILL DISCUSS WHAT YOU TWO WILL BE DOING OVER THE WINTER.

Father lay down, his bulk shoving trees aside rather than moving to where there weren't any. He rested his chin on the ground and looked at Dirt expectantly with eyes as big as the boy was.

CHAPTER TWO

Dirt wasted no time. He grabbed the rake in both hands and used mana to jump atop Father's head, right up between his ears. It was a close thing—the rake caught the wind and slowed him down, and he almost missed his target, landing on the slope of the skull and only barely keeping his balance.

But he still made it up there and immediately got to work, doing it like Socks preferred. Rough and deep and scratchy first, really digging in, then smoothing it out to leave it flat and handsome. Dirt had enough practice by now to know where the skin was thin and tender and not to scratch as hard there, but that wasn't as important atop Father as atop Socks. Father was so big it didn't feel like he was standing on a living creature, more like a strangely shaped hill covered in rough black fur.

Father gave no reaction beyond a deep, cavernous huff, which sounded to Dirt like a satisfied sigh. The pups, Socks included, watched for a moment with eager curiosity, expecting their turns to come next.

And they were right, but it wouldn't be soon. Father was enormous. Just his head had more fur than Socks's whole body.

After Socks and his siblings got tired of waiting, which wasn't long, they began to play, hopping around and exploring, chasing and play-biting at each other, rubbing up against trees to scratch themselves, and generally having a good time. Their games were all physical, all causing frequent contact with each other, and none of them were serious. Half-hearted races ten paces away, or wrestling someone to the ground, then panting proudly for a moment before he or she twisted away.

When a gust of wind filled the air with red-and-yellow leaves, they chased them, snapping their jaws in the air. If they managed to catch a leaf, they regretted it and had to wipe it off their wet tongue with a paw, but that didn't stop them doing it again.

Dirt couldn't pay too much attention to them, having a much more important task to complete. But he did notice that when it came down to it, Socks wasn't visibly stronger or faster than the two his age, and certainly not than the older two. Those two bowled him over just running past. It looked a lot different when they weren't using mana, he decided. Probably much like humans in that regard.

It really was nice to see Socks finally get to play with creatures his own size. Dirt hummed happily to himself, content for it to take as long as it took, and let Socks be.

Once Dirt got down to the neck and beyond, Father's fur was full of tangles—nested twigs or vines with thorns, or hardened grime that Dirt suspected was old gore from something Father killed. Tufts of fur matted around briars, other such things. He didn't dare just yank, lest he cause the great wolf the slightest discomfort, so when he couldn't gently rake something out, he got down with his knife and carefully trimmed it away.

Truthfully, what Father needed most was a good soak, but where was a lake big enough? The deepest water Dirt had seen anywhere was that stone basin with the tentacle monster, but Father could probably stand in that without getting his belly wet. Maybe he could lie in it for a while with just his nose out to breathe.

But if not a soak, then Father needed his own team of humans to tend him, well-dressed servants like the duke had, who were nimble and could use mana. And had some longer rakes.

I HAVE HAD HUMANS TO TEND ME AT VARIOUS TIMES, WHEN THE FANCY STRUCK ME. THEY DO NOT LAST.

Dirt hesitated, dread gathering in his heart, wondering if he should reply. But Father seemed to be making conversation, reading Dirt's thoughts and commenting on them. So Dirt replied, just thinking to himself and not speaking to Father directly. *"Because we're short-lived? If you let them have children, then they could tend you for a long time."*

NO. EITHER THEY GROW RESENTFUL AFTER THREE OR FOUR GENERATIONS, OR THE GODS GROW JEALOUS. THEY NEVER DID LIKE TO SHARE.

"Oh. Well, I'm glad I can do it this time," thought Dirt. Did he dare ask about the gods, and what happened to them? He had a growing belief that he'd directly caused whatever it was, and Father didn't seem too keen on having them return. Father had said once he was freer than he ever had been, now that they were gone.

On second thought, what could it hurt? Dirt was utterly insignificant to a being like Father, and it was obvious Dirt had no intention of giving any offense or disrespect. Most likely, Father would simply ignore anything he didn't care to answer.

So Dirt asked, "What happened to the gods? What are they?"

Father raised his enormous black head to look at Dirt with one yellow eye, and Dirt ducked his head down and got to raking twice as hard, his heart beating heavily against his ribs.

YOU MAY SPEAK TO ME DIRECTLY. WATCHING YOU TRY TO AVOID IT IS TIRING. SPEAK TO ME AS YOU SPEAK TO THE OTHERS. AS FOR THE GODS, YOU WILL FIGURE IT OUT EVENTUALLY. FIND ME ONCE YOU HAVE THE ANSWER TO YOUR FIRST QUESTION, AND WE WILL DISCUSS THIS FURTHER.

"Yes, Father," said Dirt, sending the thought as directed, instead of just thinking it. Then, for no reason beyond reckless daring, he turned his mind-sight onto the blinding sun of the great wolf's thoughts. Father had most of his mind hidden so tightly and perfectly that Dirt realized just how sloppy he and Socks were, but there was one thing he recognized—Father wanted to be scratched over by the shoulder.

Dirt raced over to the spot and raked it well, finding and then cutting out a stick the size of his forearm. His lips drifted into a smile that spread while he worked, his excitement too great to contain. Not only was Father showing him an unbelievable level of tolerance and condescension, but the answers really were out there, and Dirt would find them.

"Can I ask you a few other things?" asked Dirt, raking just a bit faster to show he was still fully engaged in his task.

ASK.

"What was that big purple smoke thing in Ocriculum? We heard it tapping on the door, so it was still alive, but it must have been there for a really long time," said Dirt.

IT WAS PART OF A PARASITE. EVEN DIVIDED IT CAN PROVE AN UNFAIR THREAT TO MY PUPS.

"A parasite? So it would have attached to something, maybe? Like a leech?"

Father sent him a vision of a vast, skeletal being, the size of a mountain, bigger even than the trees. Parts of it looked human, but it wasn't. Not even close. A skull and shoulders, like Dirt remembered, and a skin of dark-purple fog inside which swirled countless bones and other remains of death, but indefinite and worm-like below that, with too many arms, each having too many joints. Its finger bones were tendrils that sank into the earth as it leaned down, jawbone open in a wretched scream that twisted Dirt's soul, even in so distant and abstract a vision. He'd heard that scream, once, and it sickened him even now.

Every living thing its bony tentacle-fingers touched was drained of all color and became a husk, still moving but empty. Skeletal. Drained and dead. Dead but still moving, until whatever motive force kept it going ran out, at which point it collapsed. Deer, wild cattle, a gryphon, and even some humans fell prey to it, wandering like walking corpses, which is what they were.

The abomination itself remained floating in the air, fading in and out of visibility, drifting patiently as it looked for more prey whose life could feed it. The walking dead gathered below clutched anything they found with their arms or claws until the abomination's snaking fingers found it and drained it of life and color.

The sun crested over the distant horizon, and rays of light found the hateful thing. It squirmed as its dark-purple skein of fog absorbed the light, bulging in odd places and making it bloat like a corpse that'd been out too long. After several minutes of slow suffering, all while it kept feeding wherever it found life, it exploded, sending flecks of itself great distances in every direction. Most flecks fell on barren ground or on plants too small to provide any nourishment, and all those soon vanished like sticky bits of fog, wisping away into nothing. But some fell onto humans or other animals and sank into the skin, causing large purple lumps to appear, diseased and painful. The unfortunates grew crazed and confused, lurching away from dens and homes to wander in search of dark, quiet places to lurk.

Places like the tombs beneath Ocriculum, where one cursed human cowered behind the statue of the Shepherd of the Dead, before that god was damaged and fell from his place. Hiding in burial nooks alongside the dead when the living brought in life, waiting mindlessly until they left. The diseased woman cowered long in the dark, feeding on corpse flesh, waiting. Until disaster drove hundreds to hide in the tombs. The door closed, leaving so many hapless souls trapped in there with her. With *it*. The vision faded when the first of them screamed.

Dirt realized he'd stopped combing Father's fur, deeply unsettled by the vision, the worst parts of which lingered. He shook his head, took a deep, calming breath, and resumed.

"Can Socks and I fight it if we find another piece of it someday? What should we do?" he asked.

IF IT IS NIGHT, HIDE. IF IT IS DAY, RUN OR CONCEAL YOURSELF AND LET THE SUN BURN IT AWAY. IT WILL TAKE A GOOD PORTION OF THE DAY. THEN DESTROY ALL THE PIECES.

"How do we destroy the pieces?"

BURN THEM WITH FIRE, AND ANY INFECTED HOST. IF IT ATTEMPTS TO INFECT YOU, YOUR ONLY CHANCE OF SURVIVAL IS TO THRUST IT AWAY WITH THE RADIANCE OF YOUR OWN LIFE. MY PUP WAS YET SMALL. THE DAY WILL COME WHEN IT FLEES HIM, AS IT DOES ME.

By now, Dirt had gotten most of Father's fur scratched and combed on this side, and Father gave him no warning before rolling over. Dirt had to sprint to keep up, moving from Father's left to his right by running straight across his stomach. Dirt giggled, thinking Socks would probably have done the exact same thing and found it funny. And it was.

Between Father rolling over and the pups' wild play, the meadow was twice as big now as when they first arrived. Countless trees had been knocked over or broken. There were only three kinds here: tall dark-green pines that grew so close together only their top third had any needles; short, white-barked birches whose circular leaves had mostly turned yellow and fallen everywhere; and smaller, scrubby trees that were too tangled and messy for even Dirt to want to climb through. Those had handsome red or orange leaves, and most of them were still attached. Until a pup crashed into one, at which point the leaves were flung up into a cloud and drifted quickly down to get caught in any fur they found.

As such, the pups were making quite a mess. Their fur stood up with static, which made the leaves stick even more, and Dirt found it too comical not to laugh once he got a good look.

"Can I ask another question?" said Dirt. *"I'll try not to get distracted by the answer this time. Sorry."*

ASK.

"What was the eyeball monster thing that came out of the sky at Ogena?"

THAT WAS THE GREAT ENEMY OF MANKIND. IT SEEKS TO MAKE YOUR KIND EXTINCT. HUMANS ARE TOO SHORT-LIVED AND LIMITED IN PERSPECTIVE AND EXPERIENCE TO COUNTER IT, AND ITS VICTORY DRAWS EVER CLOSER.

Dirt shuddered, or perhaps trembled. His arms felt like empty cloth, but he made himself keep raking anyway. He knew what question he wanted to ask next, but lacked the courage. Except that was silly. Father already knew what he wanted to ask, and what the answer was. So he asked, *"Why did it have my face?"*

YOU WERE THE FIRST THING IT SAW WHEN IT PEEPED UPON OUR WORLD. I WILL TELL YOU NO MORE ABOUT IT UNTIL YOU FIND THE ANSWER TO THE FIRST QUESTION YOU ASKED ME.

"Okay. Well, thank you for answering so much. You know I'm grateful. You can see it. And I am. And thank you for letting me be with Socks," said Dirt. He got back to raking, and all it took was to think about how happy Socks was, over there at the bottom of the puppy pile, to fill his heart with warmth, so much it choked him up a little if he let it. This time, he did. He truly loved the pup, and his siblings, and even terrible, magnificent Father, the mere thought of whom filled him with immeasurable, wordless awe. How could anyone be happier than Dirt was?

THAT IS ENOUGH FOR NOW. GO PLAY BEFORE THEY GET TIRED.

Dirt nodded and slid down, landing hard and rolling since it was so far up. He even had to reinforce his legs with mana to keep his ankles from breaking. But he tossed the rake aside and looked at the pups, considering how to approach this. He quickly stripped his clothing off, since there was no chance it'd survive what he had in mind, and ran into the tangle of pups, right into the middle, making them all freeze for fear of crushing him.

"Whoever catches me first gets raked next! And no using your mind! You can use your claws or teeth, since I'm sturdy. But not too hard. Okay, go!" Then with a wild laugh, he raced with mana-infused legs under Big Sister, swatting her tail with his hand as he passed. She nearly flipped over trying to chase him.

It turned out to be easier to avoid them all at once than one at a time, since he was so small and they kept crashing into each other. It took no time at all for them to watch Socks and see how much force was safe to use, which was more than they were expecting. Dirt was no mouse, and they could step on him if they had to. If they could catch him.

Dirt hooted and squealed as he darted between them, jumping over their heads when they lunged in for a bite or rolling to one side when they tried to pin him with a paw. The game was rough enough he was glad his broken arm had had plenty of time to heal; wearing the Home-staff as an arm brace was a convenience now, rather than a necessity.

And the pups were certainly not going easy on him. Big Brother tried rolling on top of him, and that almost worked until Little Sister got in the way and gave Dirt a space to squeeze out, where he only barely rolled away from Socks's paw trying to hold him in place.

The game got more serious the longer it went on, which made it outrageously fun. The pups snarled and growled at him and each other, with Dirt screaming gleefully each time he saw an attack coming. Finally, Little Brother got him by smacking him out of the air with his tail when he tried to jump out of Big Sister's way. The pup spun and snatched him right out of the air, getting his teeth around one of Dirt's legs, leaving him dangling awkwardly.

"Okay, you got me. Put me down!" said Dirt, laughing. Little Brother was biting him just a little hard, and Dirt could feel the mana tingle as it burned away to protect his skin.

Then it turned out Little Brother would rather keep playing than get raked. He could get raked later, and this was too good to pass up. Hunting a prey like Dirt, who you could bite semi-gently without killing, and who was just as quick and wily as a wolf, was not an opportunity to miss.

Dirt had to use every trick he had, then think of new ones. The pups were quick learners, and after Dirt had been caught twice more, the real trick was catching him without moving him into a position to be caught by someone else. For his part, Dirt ran on all fours, or clung to their fur on a spot they couldn't reach, or anything else he could think of. Socks caught him once, then Big Sister, then Little Brother again, then Little Sister. Finally Big Brother managed to catch him by snatching him off Big Sister's neck when he thought he was safe.

Dirt's mind wore out before his body did. Staying that wary, watching in that many directions at once, was incredibly tiring. He called a stop to the melee and lay down, arms and legs outstretched while he caught his breath. The pups all licked him at once, all five of them, covering him from head to toe with their huge tongues and leaving him almost sopping wet when they were done. Then they curled up around him with their noses inward so they could keep sniffing him while they all relaxed.

Big Sister licked him again, just slightly with the tip of her tongue. She said, *-Where can I get pockets?-*

Socks answered for Dirt, since he could tell her the way. He shared his sense of direction and location, showing her the feeling that would guide her to the exact center of Ogena. Then he said, *-Tell them you are my sister and Dirt's friend, and hunt some goblins for them, and they will make you pockets. Humans are not dangerous, but be careful around them because the father of their den is our friend. He is called the duke.-*

Dirt added, "We have other friends there, too. The duke's children and his mate, who are called Èlia and Màxim and the duchess, and a man named Ignasi is still there. And Hèctor. Marina is our other friend, but I don't know if she went to the forest yet or not. She was looking for a mate."

I AM NOT PLEASED AT THE THOUGHT OF ALL MY PUPS RUNNING AROUND WITH HARNESSES ON SO THEY CAN CARRY GARBAGE, said Father. He only sounded half-serious.

-We will grow out of it. We are still just pups,- said Socks.
GROW OUT OF IT NOW, THEN.

-Soon. I promise. Very soon,- said Socks. His siblings all gave him amused looks. Dirt was sure that if Socks thought Father meant it for real, that'd be the end of it. Socks was being sincere when he submitted and begged for affection from his sire. And while it seemed like they had all been selected to grow up, who knew? Getting eaten might still be a possibility. Either way, the pups didn't seem too worried about it.

Father rose, and a few steps placed him above their heads. He leaned down, and the pups all whimpered and leaned back up at him, licking his maw and pressing their noses together in a bid for his attention.

IT IS TIME TO DISCUSS WHAT YOU WISH TO DO OVER THE WINTER. I WILL GIVE YOU TWO OPTIONS, said Father.

The great wolf gave his pups their options in two complex bundles of thought that arrived all at once. It took a moment to contemplate and consider them, and for a moment, no one said much.

The first option was to stay with him over the winter. They would journey through the mountains in the bitterest cold to hunt the choicest prey. Great beasts with long tusks, humanoid creatures that bellowed like warhorns, rocks and wind and storms and violence, but always a safe refuge at the end. Gentle caves to hide from wind or warm dens Father himself had dug would mark their journey across the great expanses of mountain and plain. They would learn the ways of wind and earth, about rocks and weather and the rotations of the skies. Father would protect them from the Devourer as well as could be expected, as he had been doing thus far. Dirt, however, would almost certainly freeze to death. If Socks went with Father, Dirt would have to spend the season somewhere else.

The second option was to wander south, all on their own. It would be the first time for the other four pups, but Socks had managed to avoid the Devourer over the summer, so perhaps it was possible as long as they all kept moving. They should wander south far enough to avoid most of the snow, into the warm, desolate lands of sand and cactus and gray brush, with black hills and red mountains and hardly any prey at all. They would teach themselves to hunt and find water in scarcity. Dirt would be forbidden from giving Socks any sap or water if Socks chose this option.

-Are there any humans in the south?- asked Socks. *-Dirt wants to find more scrolls, so we were going to the kingdom to find the king before we got distracted and went another way.-*

THERE ARE SOME, BUT I DOUBT THEY HAVE ANY SCROLLS.

"Socks, you shouldn't make the decision based on me. Father, what do you think would be best for Socks? I don't want to be left anywhere for a whole season, but I think if I was a reason Socks didn't become the best he could be, I'd be even sadder."

THE CHOICE IS NOT A TEST. I WOULD NOT GIVE TWO OPTIONS IF ONE WAS CLEARLY INFERIOR.

-I will go north into the snow,- said Big Brother. His thoughts shared his enjoyment of the cold, preferring it to the heat. In that regard, he was just like his sire.

-As will I,- said Big Sister, thinking of the grand exploration promised by the mountains.

-I will go south. I might find my own human,- said Little Sister, not without a hint of envy for Socks.

-And me. I want to explore on my own for a season, if Brother did it and survived,- said Little Brother.

AND YOU, CHILD? asked Father.

-I'm still thinking.- said Socks. *-If I go south, can I still spend another season with you someday, before I'm all grown?-*

YOU CAN. AND PERHAPS I WILL TOLERATE YOUR PET.

-Then I will miss you. I miss you and Mother and my siblings a lot. But I will go south this time.-

CHAPTER THREE

Father leaned down and sniffed his tiny pup, then the others. Satisfied at whatever he was checking, he said, *VERY WELL, THEN. THE DEVOURER IS NOT CLOSE, SO WE SHALL REMAIN HERE FOR A FEW DAYS FIRST.* He turned his terrible gaze to Dirt and added, *EXCEPT FOR YOU. GATHER YOUR THINGS.*

Dirt looked down, trying to hide his sudden disappointment, and ran to gather his few belongings. He pulled his clothes on so hastily he put his shirt on backward the first time, to the amusement of the pups, who loomed over him to watch. Once he had his shoes on and everything was proper, he slung his backpack over both shoulders and said, *"Okay, is there anywhere in particular you want me to go? Or just . . . away."*

He didn't conceal his feelings of disappointment and rejection, or make himself feel something else to be diplomatic and inoffensive. That was probably pointless anyway, and better to hurry than be tiresome. Socks noticed and sent him a little puff of sympathy.

Father didn't reply. He just huffed and looked away, making Dirt wonder for a moment if the great wolf was amused or annoyed. Before Dirt could pick a direction on his own and start walking, however, the world vanished around him.

Dirt hurtled at incomprehensible speed, sharply slamming this way and that, unable to see or hear or smell anything. By the time he realized what had happened, he landed on soft ground in a daze.

Root travel! Hitting the ground that hard knocked all the bad feelings right out of him, since he instantly knew where he was. There was no mistaking this damp, black soil. How silly he'd been, doubting Father. When had the great wolf ever shown him the slightest cruelty? Never. "Thank you!" he muttered, his mouth barely working, just in case Father was watching.

He shot to his feet so fast he almost fell over and braced himself by clasping Home in a tight hug. He found her more by feel than sight, since his eyes refused to focus that quickly. She hugged him back, not too hard, and he inhaled deeply to smell her subtle scent of bark and leaves. He was finally back! It'd seemed like so long, most of the summer and a good portion of autumn as well. It was warmer here, he noticed. The same temperature it always was. The perfect temperature.

"Hello, Home. How did you know to bring me?" asked Dirt.

"The Father of Wolves told us to summon you. The part of me that is your brace, or staff, or armor, will remain there until it is time to send you back," said Home, smiling warmly. Now that Dirt had more experience with humans, her body language and posture reminded him of the duchess, even though her dryad was still his size.

Dirt held out his arm and pulled back the sleeve, and sure enough, the brace was gone. "Oh, it's everyone!"

Now that Dirt was regaining his equilibrium enough to actually look around, he found himself surrounded by a huge crowd of dryads, all those he recognized and plenty more he didn't. They looked different, though, and it took him a moment to realize why. Clothing. Many—though not all—had clothing on now, not just the fuzzy carpet of leaves they used to have. It wasn't fine cloth like the duke and his family wore. No vibrant silks bedecked with jewels. Not regular cloth like the others in Ogena had, either, with colorful patterns and layers. No, it was laborer's clothing, simple and brownish gray in color. Undyed fibers spun into thread and woven.

"Welcome back, friend Dirt," said Callius, spinning in a circle and then planting his hands on his hips. "What do you think?"

"Did you make those yourselves?"

"We did! Do you want to see?" said Callius, face bright with eagerness.

"Of course I do," said Dirt.

"Great! I'll show you how we make it later," said Callius.

"Oh," said Dirt. "So, until then, I guess we can—"

"Look around you, silly Dirt," said Callius. "Look."

Dirt looked at all the dryads, not sure what else he was supposed to notice. Hundreds of gray-skinned, green-haired girls his age. Those who had clothing on wore it short, never past the knees, whether a skirt or pants, so it wouldn't get dirty walking through the black soil. Come to think of it, Dirt should probably take his shoes and socks off and roll his pant legs up, at a minimum. Maybe he should take everything off, in fact. There'd be no way he'd be able to play with the dryads without getting nice and filthy. No need to ruin his clothing. Although, maybe if they were all dressed, he should be too? Or did they . . .

His thoughts trailed off into a stunned stupor when he noticed the buildings. They were everywhere, in perfect rows just like he remembered. Gray stone stained with black soil rose from the ferns to stand silently beneath the trees. Where stones couldn't be found to patch the building back together, wooden vines filled the gaps. The roofs had almost no tiles and were covered instead with wide, five-pointed leaves bigger than Dirt was. Most of the paint and stucco was gone after so long, but he still recognized them. He knew exactly where he was.

"Turicum," he said quietly. This was Vicus Salutaris, a street he knew well. Over there was one of the nicer hostels in the city, busy at all hours. And next to it, Clavii Caupona, with the good lamb and vegetables, always hot and ready. Avitus had known Clavius well after eating there so many times. He could almost picture the man. Almost.

The streets weren't completely paved, leaving gaps for bare soil already growing in with baby ferns, but they were there. The original stones. So much of it was just how he remembered, even if the colors were faded, the stucco lost forever and the paint worn away to nothing. Flower pots and sculpture remained, and partial façade over doorways. Most of the buildings were missing their shady wooden awnings, but the dryads probably didn't know about those, and there wasn't much need for shade now anyway.

Dirt—no, Avitus—walked up the street in a daze, his posture straightening and growing dignified. This was his city, once full of his people. It wasn't like the ruins of Ocriculum, where, for most of the city, nothing but footings and foundations remained. Here, entire buildings had been fully resurrected, although the city wasn't completely rebuilt. Some buildings were only partial, one story instead of seven, but the upper floors had all been wooden, and the trees couldn't have known that from the ruins. And some buildings hadn't been raised from the ground at all for whatever reason. Perhaps not enough of them remained to bother, or maybe the dryads needed to leave room for the ferns and grubs and all the little bugs that lived in the soil.

Furthermore, Ocriculum had seemed like an old skeleton falling to dust. The remains of a place, not the place itself. But here, dryads occupied the buildings, waving at him from inside the windows and doorways and resting on benches to chat. They smiled as he walked past.

For him. All of this was for him. So much effort and time and care. They were wearing clothing because that's what humans did, and they were resting or chatting or walking about just like they'd seen humans doing in Ogena, through Home's staff. All for him.

It was too much. The precious familiarity became mixed with his gratitude for their love and overcame him. He turned with tears in his eyes and embraced Callius, who had been the closest. "Thank you!" he whispered, his chest shaking. He reached an arm out for Dawn, who was close by and pulled her in as well.

A stray but powerful thought interrupted the moment and he shouted, "Oh! Wait, I remember . . . I remember where it is!"

He couldn't contain himself and pulled away, blinking away the tears. He patted Callius and Dawn apologetically, then spun and ran down the street, turning at the five-way intersection. He passed the small theater and the apartments where Drucus and Ecidia lived. Past the brassworker's shop and the two cheap potters. He ran past the old shrine and several more row houses, past the enchanter's shop where some of his apprentices had worked, past the justice's outpost. One more turn, then down the street, and there it was.

His stone fence, mostly reconstructed, walling in his private villa. And inside it, his home. The walls had been fully restored, and the roof was the right shape, although it was replaced by the standard vines and leaves. Nearly all the pillars were back as well, although most of them had cracked and were held together with vines. They lined the walkways, holding up nothing since the awnings were missing. Well, he could fix that himself later.

"This was my house," said Avitus, staring in awe. Dryads were pouring into the villa, standing on the walkways and the empty garden areas, all walking in with eager faces.

"Then I am glad we dug it up. You must go inside, friend Dirt," said Callius warmly.

His villa felt alive, even though it was dead. It was a ruin, but not truly, not anymore. Those were the original stones. The original concrete patched back together. He stepped to the doorway of the living area and traced his fingers along a crack in the wall, then walked inside, anticipation stealing his breath.

He walked down the short hallway into the large atrium, just as he left it, minus all the wooden furniture. It felt so *familiar*. The interior fountain was empty, and they didn't leave an opening in the roof over it, making the whole room much darker than it was supposed to be. The shadows hid what remained of the wall paintings, but most of the beautiful, tiled floor was back, and in the right place. The statues were there, the youth pouring water into the pool and the woman with a bird resting on her finger.

"I used to receive guests here. There were couches and divans once, with cushions. In fact, this corner was my favorite spot to read. Hilaria liked to sit by the fountain and embroider. I remember that," he said, his voice quiet. He was having difficulty remembering the dryads were still here, despite how they crowded in to watch. His mind was too distracted with enjoying the feeling of familiarity and trying to claw some of his lost memory from the void.

He remembered the sense of people, but little more than that. A name or two, but no idea who they'd been. A strong man used to stand here, reassuring and friendly. And over there, a gossipy group of women who laughed and sang. Were they his brood? Was one of them his mate? He had no idea. But he felt drawn to his corner, to being the man who had occupied this space and whose faded memory now haunted it.

Avitus sighed and entered a different doorway, following a wider hall to the left. He passed the hot bath, now empty and cracked and unlikely to hold water again, and the cool bath, much the same. A storage room where he'd once put . . . well, it was empty now, not even shelves remaining. Another storage room, just as small, but with a larger doorway. Ah, right, clothing and towels and things. That's what he'd stored there, with no door to allow easier access.

Then, finally, at the end of the hall, his bedroom. It was built against the exterior wall, sporting windows to the front and side, and was grimy and dark now. Dark soil filled all the lines between the floor tiles, drawing out the patterns. The stove for heating had been restored and looked like it probably still worked, although the metal grate was gone. And there was nothing to burn, and he'd have to fix the chimney, which was sealed. It seemed like he'd never used it, now that he thought about it, but couldn't remember why.

The first thing he'd have to do was make a new bed, though.

"We didn't know which house was yours, or we might have taken more care for it," said Dawn. She was a little taller now, he noticed, a bit rounder and more feminine. She reminded him of Èlia, in fact. She still had that girlish cheer, though. It was unmistakably her.

"It's fine. I wasn't expecting any of this. I forgot this place even existed. I used to sleep right there, on a bed. Three thousand years ago," said Dirt. "I can clean it myself, if I can get someone to make water for me."

"We know you were not expecting it, which is what makes it a surprise," said Callius.

"It's a good surprise! I love it. Truly, I really do. Do you have any plans for the city, or did you just do it for me?" asked Dirt.

"You gave us an entire world, friend Dirt. We can give you one little city in return," said Callius.

"Come, we have something more we wish to show you," said Dawn, grabbing his hand and giving it a gentle tug. "It is in the schola, where the cursed dead captured you. Or will you be too troubled to see that place again?"

"Oh, did you rebuild that place too? It's fine, it won't bother me," said Dirt. He remembered it being mostly intact, but to be fair, he hadn't spent much time there, and he'd been preoccupied.

"Then come," said Dawn, tugging his hand more urgently, her dry, glassy eyes almost sparkling.

"I know the way," said Dirt with a half-smile. He inhaled mana and leaped out a window, then ran up the street. He dashed to a main road and followed it out of the city, marveling at just how large it was, and how much had been restored. It was larger than Ogena and Llovella together, easily. He passed by more than ten trees before they reached the exterior wall of the city, and they were hundreds of paces apart.

Out the gate and into what had once been the countryside, with large sections of the highway restored, as well as whatever stone or concrete buildings had been found along the road. Mostly farmer villas. It was a good distance from there to the schola, and they traveled through two different villages, Iguvium and Dullu, which were in much worse condition now, due to having been constructed from a lot more wood.

Then the side road off the main highway, where a signpost had once stood, and a well for travelers to water their horses. Neither were there now. Dirt turned, followed by the crowd of hundreds of happy dryads, and sped along the path until it came into view.

Prisca's schola, just as he'd left it. Except the ornate gardens were in better order now, fallen stones stood back up, and walkways and walls and such all restored. Even the pillars in the front of the building had been pieced back together, and much of the façade. He could read the name now, which had been carved in fascia stone that had been missing before: SCHOLA SAPIENTIAE ANTIQUAE, the school of ancient wisdom.

He smiled at that. Most of what they'd taught there hadn't been quite so ancient. Or was it ancient in a different sense? Something about that word tugged at him, but it never snapped into place. The ancients. Oh well. A question for another time.

Dirt stopped at the little basins of water, pleased to see they were working now, all full of cool, pellucid water instead of just the one. He bent down and plopped his face in to drink his fill, then stood again and wiped the water off. Some of it dripped onto his shirt, giving him a little chill, but even with that it wasn't as cold as where he'd left Socks, so he found it pleasant.

He paused at the entrance to the schola, though. It was dark as night inside, just as before. The memory of terror wafted from the place and sank into his skin, leaving him clammy.

Home took his hand and held it tightly. "Do not be scared, dear Dirt," she said.

"I'm okay. I like how well you put this place back together. Should we go inside?" he asked, gathering his courage. It'd be fine. Surely.

He snapped with his other hand and made a light, then split it into several more and sent them ahead, then followed them in.

The yellow glow of his lights made the lecture hall feel warm and inviting, as if by gentle fires on a cool night. They flickered as he pushed them mentally into the farther reaches of the huge room. Ancient wooden benches stood in their proper places, and some new ones, paler in color, which the dryads must have made. The frescoes and statues brought extra life to the place, and Dirt's fear faded, replaced by nostalgia.

Such a charming thing, the schola, and this was one of the greatest ones. And the most expensive, which still showed, all these years later. Tiles and decorations everywhere, exacting architecture that carried sound perfectly from the front into every ear. Any ruined furniture had been removed and generally replaced with passable reproductions, everything from chairs and tables to shelves and candelabra and lamps. Dirt was sure that if he looked close, he'd find the lamps solid and unusable. That and other clues would indicate that the dryads didn't know what most of this stuff was for. But even so, to Dirt's eyes, it rivaled the duke's palace.

"This is incredible," he said. "You restored so much of it! Is it because this place never sank, so lots of the wooden furniture remained?"

"This is not what we wanted to show you, friend Dirt," said Dawn, taking his hand from Home and tugging it. "Come. This way."

"What? There was more?"

"Come!" said Dawn, insisting. She was practically bouncing.

She dragged him toward a side door, out into the hallway that led to other rooms of the schola. He stumbled trying to keep up, but she didn't relent. Her steps were a dance as she tugged him onward, past two empty doorways and stopping in front of a third, on the other side. "Go in," she said, pointing into the shadows.

Dirt snapped again, summoning another bright spark, and sent it in. Dawn pushed him right behind it, almost knocking him over. Callius laughed. "Be gentle with our little Dirt, my dear," he scolded. "That is the wrong place to fall and break something."

He couldn't believe what he saw. The room had started as a library, with hundreds of nooks for scrolls, and every single one of them was full. Overfilled, even, stuffed beyond what they were ever meant to hold, and spilling out onto the floor where they could.

In front of the shelves, covering nearly every inch of floor from wall to wall, were baskets and chests of every conceivable thing, all stacked on top of each other from floor to ceiling, leaving almost no room to walk despite the size of the room. He saw silver and gold and cups carved from precious stone, beautiful works of old, yellow ivory, amber, and more. He didn't even know where to start.

Wealth. The word for this was wealth. Riches. Each piece a treasure, and worth looking at by itself.

"This is all the stuff we found digging up the city," said Callius. "We brought any preserved scrolls to put here with the others, but we didn't know where else to put everything. We put it all here because this is a room for storage."

CHAPTER FOUR

irt had no idea where to start. The room was too full to get around in, and he couldn't climb over because most of it was stacked all the way to the ceiling, more than twice his height. All the silverware and gold cups and carved stone trinkets and so on were impressive, and they'd be fun to sort through later, but what he really wanted were the scrolls, and he'd have to climb to get any. He *really* needed to figure out how to move stuff with his mind like Socks did.

"How did you find all this stuff? I'm guessing you found the stones of the city sunk into the ground and pulled them back out and put them together. But how did you find little stuff, like this quill stand?" asked Dirt, lifting the first thing his hand rested on. In fact, that box was full of them, and inkwells.

Callius gave him a smirk. "The answer would be more complicated than it's worth. Let's just say we felt around for it."

"I guess that makes more sense than just digging everywhere to see what you find," said Dirt. They must have used their roots and grown something like a net. That was his guess. "Okay, let's see if I can . . ."

Now that he got a closer look, the boxes looked like the dryads had grown them all of one piece. They would be sturdy, for certain. But they were all different sizes and not quite flat around the edges, so they didn't stack very well and had to rest against each other to stay upright. Dirt stepped up on the rim of one and wondered if he dared pull himself up. Could he fit through the opening up there? If it fell over on him, then he'd have a mess and no progress.

"Okay, everyone, I don't think that'll work. If I try to climb over, I'm just going to break something, so let's move all this stuff to the lecture hall. Maybe we can build shelves in one of the villas or public buildings and humans who visit can look at it. But the thing I want the most is the scrolls," he said, "and they're the farthest thing in the back."

"At least we organized it all first," said the dryad, shrugging.

"You did? How did you know what everything was?"

"We had someone to show us many human styles and dwellings, dear Dirt. We saw similar things being used. Did we not?" said Home. She meant him, of course.

"Right, I guess that was a silly question. You probably noticed more than I did, since I can only look in one direction at a time," said Dirt.

"Just so," said Home. Her demure half-smile gave her a truly dignified air. Dirt was sure that if she made an adult-sized dryad, it'd be like having a second duchess around.

"We don't know what all of it is, though," said Dawn, picking up a gold ring from a basket on the floor and slipping it onto her little finger. It was far too big, and she spun it around like a toy. "I know what this is. But some things, we organized by shape."

"So what do you want to do?" asked Callius, hands fidgety like he wanted to go play. "Do you want us to move all this now?"

"At least enough to get to the scrolls. I can read them later, but I want to find out what they are."

With that, Dirt handed the box of writing tools to Dawn and waved her out. She took it in one hand like it weighed nothing at all, and Dirt placed a second box on her other hand, one full of . . . bathing implements, it looked like. Out she went.

Callius was next, and he slid around Dirt, stretched his arms out to an absurd length, and grabbed the top box, which he handed to Home. Dirt stepped farther out of the way and left them to it. He'd given names to many of the other dryads in the weeks he and Socks stayed here before they left for the summer, and those ones all came next.

Sunset, a quiet girl who was always hanging around near Dawn; Dancer, a flighty girl who seldom looked like she was paying attention, even though she always was. Votorla, who had made up her own name from random sounds and wore a longer rough-spun tunic than anyone else, black with dirt along the bottom hem. Tooth, a boy who only interacted with Dirt if Callius wasn't around, since apparently one male was enough. Starwatcher, another girl. Chaser. Pathway. Gift.

Dirt thought progress would be faster than it was, since another dryad appeared with arms outstretched as fast as one got out of the way. But there was simply too much. Surely this was more gold than the duke had, by far. And more silver.

And it wasn't all things for daily living. A chest, complete with a lid, held spearheads, some in surprisingly good shape. A container that was more like a barrel held swords, one of which was in perfect condition, gleaming like it had been made yesterday. But most were things like jewelry, lamps and candlesticks, cutlery, cooking implements, and so on. Objects of gold or silver that a normal household might only have a few of, to bring out on special occasions. But with a city the size of Turicum, it was wealth to fill a temple's treasury several times over.

A few boxes held hammerheads and similar tools, but they were so rusted, cracked, and flaking, that they'd never be restored. Someone might want to look at them for ideas, though, so it couldn't hurt to keep them around. Scissors. Dirt had forgotten all about scissors. He grabbed a lock of his dark brown hair and wondered if he needed a haircut. No one in Ogena had said anything, so probably not.

Finally, Dirt could climb over the last few things and get to the scrolls. The dryads continued clearing the room while he rubbed his hands clean on his pants and gently looked them over to see what they were.

Every single one of them had been magically preserved, no doubt by Prisca. She'd had plenty of time for that. Some of them looked like the protection had only been applied once they started wearing out, preserving fading ink and small rips and tears, but most of them were as pristine as the day the scribes completed them.

The library was a treasure greater than anything else in the world, to his eyes. Things Avitus might have known once, but which were likely completely lost to the world. Biographies and genealogies of emperors and noble families. Accounts of wars. Medical treatises, natural philosophy documenting birds or plants, mathematics and geometry and engineering.

Each scroll he touched filled him with a sense of recognition, but incomplete, which longed to be fulfilled. Each one was harder to put down than the last. Each subject reminded him of something he had once known but had since forgotten. He had known all about cattle husbandry, once. And olive horticulture. And arguments on the nature of Being.

The nostalgia was so powerful that he was almost surprised at the size of his child-sized hand as he held the scrolls. Avitus yearned to stop and pick one—any one at all—and race to his villa, plop down in his favorite divan, and read it the whole way through without moving, even if it took all night. Fabia was young enough to stay up with him and keep the lamps lit, and she enjoyed hearing him read. She was wasted as a handmaiden. He probably ought to sell her to . . .

Dirt tried to hold on to the memory, but of course it slipped away. It had never really been there, just the outlines, like everything else. A name with no face. Empty lines with no color inside them, lines made of ash that blew away if disturbed.

Then he found a scroll he couldn't pass up, and his hands trembled so much at the recognition that he almost dropped it. *Pomponius' Nativitas Deorum.* The birth of the gods, giving the most accepted account of how all things came to be.

Fear kept him from unrolling it any farther at first, not even far enough to read the first line. Avitus knew he loved the gods, whatever they were. They were no longer recognized or even spoken of, leaving a strange gap in public life among the duke's people that everyone pretended to ignore. Even so, there was still something there, a shadow resting in the undercurrents of human thought and society. The duke had claimed to know nothing of it. Avitus suspected, however, that it was more out of duty than conviction.

And furthermore, Avitus had a strong suspicion that he himself had harmed the gods, or cast them out somehow, or even killed them. From the scraps of information he'd been able to gather so far, that seemed the most likely cause of the death of the empire. The rise of the great trees, the freedom of the great wolves, and his own face on that great enemy—how much had Avitus caused, for good or ill? Mostly ill.

It almost seemed blasphemy to him, who was perhaps the gods' enemy, to read of them now, so long after their calamity and ruin. But despite that, he unrolled and read:

Due to increasingly popular beliefs now spreading amongst us, by which unthinking men are led into folly by fools, it is appropriate to lay out at the first what the truest cause of these things is. For many say that all things were once a single, raw, confused mass, which they call chaos. But this is not the case. For if there were matter in that eternal before-time, even unformed and immeasurable, then there must also have been thought, and time, and space, and knowledge, and truth, for those things are as fundamental as matter, and indeed, more so, for they measure it. And if there was a mind to measure chaos, then it was never chaos.

And if there were never truth, or thought, or knowledge, in the beginning, then whence could these things come? The Critians say the Great Primeval is he who brought himself into being, but he could not have done it, for before he existed, he did not exist to cause anything, even himself.

No, if a world there is, a world there must always have been. This earth, speaking only of itself and its form and not any particular thing that was ever found upon it, is perfectly eternal. For although we poor creatures farm our grain from the dust only to rot away into dust in the end, the land itself always remains, sometimes above water, and sometimes beneath; sometimes rich and sometimes poor, once rock, then sand, then soil, then sand again, which blasts away in the wind to reveal the rock.

The gods are the mighty ones who take possession of a part of it, as a man claims a field. This one claims the clouds and rain, and that one claims the farmland; this one claims the men of war who conquer, and that one the peaceable women who nourish.

They must be eternal to claim lasting dominion over that which is eternal and reshape it to their will. Thus we—

WHAT YOU ARE READING IS NONSENSE, said Father, his voice piercing Avitus's growing reverie so strongly that he became Dirt again.

Dirt blinked and lowered the scroll. Home was watching him patiently, a soothing, placid look on her face. If she'd heard the great wolf, she gave no sign of it.

SKIP TO THE LISTS IF YOU WANT TO KNOW THEIR NAMES, BUT MOST OF WHAT THE HUMANS SAY ABOUT THE GODS IS NONSENSE. NONE OF THEM WERE THERE.

"Thank you," said Dirt.

YOU ARE FILLING MY SON'S HEAD WITH TOO MUCH NONSENSE ALREADY.

"For what, dear Dirt?" asked Home.

"Nothing. Never mind," he said. It was a strange feeling, having so much cast into doubt before he'd even had a chance to digest it. Was he relieved, or annoyed? He couldn't tell. But if there were false things in here, then he didn't want to believe them, and if Father was going to offer him the slightest bit of help, then Dirt wasn't going to be anything other than grateful.

So he put a smile on that quickly sank into the rest of him, and rolled through the scroll, skipping the long discussions about the nature of matter and so on. It didn't take long for the smile to be completely sincere, either, because how lucky was he to know a falsehood from the start, especially such an important one? It didn't take long to find the lists.

Above them first is imperious Caelpater, whose vastness outstretches all things, who is the unending sky of Day, beneath whom even the conquering sun rides in obedience.

Those who rule are called by the name of his wife, Domina, who is Domina Noctis. The stars are her jewels, more glorious than every other creation. She joins hands with her husband to encircle all things in the cycle of dawn and dusk.

Just the names, remembered Dirt. Whatever was said about them might be wrong. So he had two so far, a father and a mother, Caelpater and Domina, rulers of day and night.

Next was their daughter, Lucina, a goddess of lamps and indoor light, and also of midwives and childbirth. Then a son, Pastorus, the shepherd of the dead, whose twisted statue Dirt had encountered in that giant tomb.

He started skimming, his eyes searching for a particular name without understanding why. He could come back and memorize the others later, and there were plenty, but there was one he was looking for. Soon he found it:

Least of these is bright Melodia, also called Mistress of Song, whose daughters by Oraculus are the Muses, inspirers of art. The Muses could inspire nothing without her, for she is the truth behind them all, the harmony of many voices and the rhythm of life and movement. The steady drumming of footsteps upon the earth is hers, and thus it is she who watches over travelers by day and night, eager for the cheer they know at journey's end.

Avitus lowered the scroll and stared at nothing, wondering at the affection he felt toward the name. No, not affection—reverence. Melodia. Why did that name hold such meaning for him? It sounded like gods were people, of a sort, so maybe he had known her? Or was it because he was a traveler now, and she was a goddess for travelers?

"Home, do you know anything about the gods?" he asked.

"I do not. But I am sure you will find what you wish to know among these writings," she said.

Now that he looked around a bit more, the room was nearly empty now, only a few stray baskets or pots here and there. He'd been so focused looking at all the scrolls that he'd missed all the work.

"Oh, was there a collection of little figures? Little statues of people?" he asked, quickly rolling the scroll back up and setting it in its nook.

"There was. Come," she said, holding out her hand. He took it, and she led him out of the library, down the shadowed hallway, and back into the main room, the lecture hall. The dryads had set all the boxes and chests and baskets out in an orderly grid, with just enough space to walk between them. Seeing the whole floor filled with treasure reminded him once more just how much it was.

Home led him right to what he was looking for, a wide box full of figurines of gold or tarnished bronze or silver. Dirt pulled them out one by one, hoping he'd recognize the one he was looking for. A soldier in armor. A nude boxer. A woman carrying a jug. A man captured by writhing snakes. A shepherd and a wolf. A boy sitting and pulling a thorn from his foot. A woman with bird wings in a flowing dress. A nude young man with bird wings. A nude woman bathing.

A woman with a crown of stars caught his eye. That must be Domina, the goddess, judging from the star shapes all over her dress. In the statue, her legs had been broken and she was kneeling on raw bone, weeping upward. It made him feel sick, and he quickly put it back and kept looking.

Then he found another god, which he recognized only because of how deformed and injured it was. It was a nude man leaning on a staff, but his whole body was punctured by swords and arrows, and one of his shoulders was dislocated. A shirtless goddess on her knees trying to gather

her guts back up, a god holding his own severed leg against his chest, face twisted in despair.

He found her. Melodia, the Mistress of Song. He knew it was her at once but couldn't say how. She was nude except a crown of flowers in her hair and shoes that made him think of dancing. Both arms had been severed at the elbow and lay on the ground near her feet. Her eyes had been stabbed out, complete with trails of gold to mimic the blood leaking down her face. Her ears and nose had been cut off and were nowhere to be seen, and her mouth was open in an eternal scream.

Avitus knew he'd feel something when he found her, from the first moment he'd thought to look. But he wasn't sure what it'd be. Sadness, perhaps. Revulsion, terror, relief. Perhaps all or none of those. He had not expected guilt, though, and guilt was all he had in him. Terrible guilt, like the reckoning of Heaven standing over him awaiting the merest whisper of Justice to come and crush him.

He had caused this somehow, either directly or indirectly, and if anything still remained of the gods, surely it was the curse of their wrath, waiting only until it found him to give him suffering greater than their own.

Guilt like physical pain racked him, coupled with cruel dread and fear of vengeance. He couldn't escape it, nor could he find relief in tears or laughter. He was sick with it.

Avitus had wondered somewhere in the back of his mind whether he might someday undo what he'd done. Now he trembled to think he might actually succeed and bring the gods back into the world in the fullness of their power and glory. He was a living sacrilege. The idea of facing them, revived and whole and angrier than storms, made his fingers tremble so bad he dropped the little golden statue of Melodia. It clattered as it fell among the others in the box.

"Dirt, are you all right?" asked Home, her face now full of worry.

CHAPTER FIVE

The dryads looked at him with mixed expressions, some confused and curious, others concerned. He gazed back, wondering how much of his inner horror was showing on his face.

"Dear Dirt, I see you are troubled. Please tell us why," said Home, in a voice that was probably meant to sound tender, but didn't. Not quite.

"I'm . . . Well, I'm not sure how to say it. I guess . . ." he said. Guilt scalded him, leaving him raw inside. It was all the more frustrating because despite knowing he was responsible, he didn't know precisely what he'd done, or why. He finally said, "I think I did something horrible a long time ago, and I don't know what to do about it."

"What do you think you might have done, since you do not remember?" asked Home.

"Broke the world. I don't know how, but Mother says I'm responsible, and when I see these little god figurines, I can tell it's true," said Dirt. "Look what happened to them."

The dryads regarded him calmly, and he noticed them pausing and holding still more than usual, indicating they were deep in thought. They were so eager to console him, the darling things. But all that eagerness looked desolate to him, since he knew they didn't really understand. Couldn't. They knew nothing of pain and very little of fear. They lived lives of unbroken joy, dancing in worlds he couldn't perceive. What could they know of guilt?

Home wrapped him in a slow hug, resting his face against her shoulder, and he began to relax slightly. His body, his creature, knew the feeling of comfort even if his mind couldn't justify accepting it. She felt perfectly lifelike, from the tickling strands of her green hair to the softness of her wooden flesh, even the bones underneath it. It wasn't easy, he knew, putting so much detail into a dryad. She might not understand, but she was sincere, and she really did love him. That was worth something.

"I do not know how best to comfort you. Are you miserable, and will it last?" she said.

"It won't last. I'll feel better soon," said Dirt. He didn't add that he suspected his mind would never rest easy about this ever again.

Callius patted Dirt's head and said, "Would it help if we gave you something else to think about?"

Dirt grinned slightly, despite himself. What silly creatures they were, he thought. They really had no idea what to do with him. They were like a bunch of humans trying to figure out why a bird was angry.

"Come with us," said Dawn. "Let us walk and run and play until you feel better. And if you wish, we will bury this place and never mention it again."

"Oh, no, keep it intact. I still want to read all those scrolls and look through all this stuff. And see the rest of the building," said Dirt.

"Come, then," said Callius, taking Dirt's hand and pulling him away from Home.

Starwatcher took his other hand. "I am close," she said. "Come to me." She was thicker now than when they first met, and it reminded him of a plumpish girl he'd briefly talked to in Ogena. Her face was still about the same, though, and her hand didn't feel any different from the rest. He wondered if she wanted to have another footrace, like she had so many times before.

Callius and Starwatcher led him out the wide doorway of the schola and onto the old marble pathway. He let his lights wink out behind him and felt the tiny trickle of mana cease. They walked while holding hands and swinging their arms like the children of Ogena did, and it helped him soothe away the turmoil inside him. Partially, anyway. Enough to keep it off his face.

Before they stepped off the path and into the ferns, Dirt stopped and rolled his pant legs up past his knees. They were already getting dirty around the hem, but since the dryads had made so many tunics, skirts, or shorts for themselves, he felt awkward just stripping like he might otherwise have done.

The walk was increasingly adventurous the farther they went, with all the dryads walking at differing speeds or showing variety in some other way. Some played games with each other, racing around at top speed and filling the air with laughter. It lent the forest a very different atmosphere than he was used to. Before, the trees tended to be quiet unless they were talking to him and preferred to walk behind him instead of in front. Usually. Now they were everywhere, acting like the crowds of children Dirt had met in Ogena.

He wondered if they would age alongside him, all their dryads growing up at the same rate he did, or if they would prefer to stay as children. And now that he thought about it, would he actually grow? Mother had said his "time" was one of the things he'd lost in the void, so did that mean he'd get more? Would he grow up a second time? Or stay this size forever? Or just fall over dead any day now, since he'd already been old before?

"I have a question. Are you all going to make your dryads grow up at the same speed as me?" he asked. "What about when Marina comes? Will some of you be adults around her?"

Callius was the one who answered. "At first, we all wanted our dryads to be like you. But now we understand that humans at different ages have different roles in society and interact with each other in different ways, and it is more complicated. We think it would be interesting to explore. What do you prefer?"

Dirt had to think about that for a moment. How would he have viewed Callius if he was an old man, or Dawn if she was a little girl, younger than him? Or any combination other than what they were now? "I was about to say, you should be whatever best fits how you think of yourself. But then I remembered most of you are thousands of years old, and I don't want to be surrounded by only old people."

Callius laughed. "Just because I am ancient does not mean I view myself as old. There's a small chance you're older than me, anyway. I first grew only a few years before the departure of the Gardener."

"Really?"

"Yep. And if she were still here, I would be much smaller and mostly oblivious. We were lesser beings then," said Callius. He squeezed Dirt's hand and added, "Consider this when you are tempted to feel guilty again, by the way. Even if you did something worthy of guilt, it wasn't all bad, was it?"

Dirt nodded. "Father mentioned once that the gods used to limit him and Mother, too. I think the world would be less wonderful without you all in it," he said. "But I still feel guilty about destroying my own kind."

Behind him, Home said, "Dirt, how do you view me now?"

He turned and found her in adult form. The skirt she had on hadn't grown with her and now looked like more of a long loincloth, tied in the back. Her childish face had filled out into one full of patient grace, with features of angular beauty that still seemed motherly, like a sculpture. All of her looked like a sculpture, round and feminine. She seemed about average height for a woman, a head taller than he was, maybe a little more. Dirt smiled and said, "Honestly, about the same. It suits you."

"Come, embrace me, dear Dirt. I am curious," she said, holding out her arms.

Dirt let go of Callius's and Starwatcher's hands and hugged her. His head rested against her bosom, on the flat space between her breasts and her chin. She still smelled the same, that gently earthy plant smell, and her body was the cool temperature of the air and soil. She was not a mother or a big sister, but she was not unlike those things.

He stepped back and looked her over once again, then said, "It suits you perfectly. I like it."

Home smiled in a way that was more girlish than womanly, with a hint of mischief in her eye. "You look different from up here," she said. "I can see how messy your hair is."

"What?" he said, feeling it to decide how bad it was. Callius laughed.

"I will fetch a comb later, and you will bathe," said Home.

A bath might be nice, but Dirt had a sinking feeling that Marina had been telling them things, things he'd rather not have them know.

"I guess. Let's keep going for now, though," he said.

They led him to Starwatcher's tree, which was one of the closest to the schola. Tooth's tree was the only one closer, and he was nowhere to be seen. Her roots twisted into a swirling shape, and she'd said it was a coincidence, but he didn't completely believe her.

"You have reached me. Now it is time to go up," she said. Her eyes had an eagerness in them that didn't make it to her voice.

"Oh no, I'm not doing this again!" he said. "I'm feeling a lot better already. I don't need to do that to recover."

Callius laughed again. "I knew he'd say that. No, silly, we're not going to try and kill you. It's time to show you what's in the branches."

"So there really is something other than just birds up there?" asked Dirt, growing excited. He stared upward, imagination sparking into motion.

"It was not the Mother of Wolves who gave us your language like she did her pups. Nor was it you we learned from. The physical process of speaking, yes, but the words themselves? You'll have to go up if you want to find out," said Callius. "I'll come so I can catch you if you fall. The others will be waiting at the top."

All around him, the dryads popped right out of existence, vanishing instantly without so much as a wave goodbye. It seemed like it should make a sound when they did that, but it didn't.

Starwatcher's dryad didn't disappear. Instead, it went completely inert as she withdrew her control of it. Dirt glanced at her mind and found her already working to create a winding set of steps to ascend her trunk.

And just like that, the forest was how it had been at first. If he didn't look at the schola behind him, there weren't many other buildings around. The scenery was as flat and empty as it had been that first day. An ocean of dark-green ferns, broken only by the impossibly giant tree trunks. The air grew still without anyone speaking, the silence growing until it encircled him like a blanket. Overhead, the gentle dappled greens of the canopy still hid the entire sky, letting not a single ray of sunshine through. The forest was eternal again. Quiet and sacred.

Callius clapped him on the back and pushed him forward. "Go, friend Dirt. You can take as many rests as you want."

"I'm going," said Dirt. "Actually, why can't you take me up there with root travel?"

"Because we don't want to," said Callius.

"Any reason why?"

"Nope! Let's go."

Dirt sighed sarcastically and hopped onto the nearest pale gray root and ran up to the trunk, enjoying how his bare feet slapped on the flat bark. He remembered that, too. Did that even count as nostalgia? Especially today, when he'd been nostalgic about things buried for thousands of years? Why not. Sure it did. It was a day for nostalgia, recent or otherwise.

Dirt kept the mana cycling inside as he hurried up the stairs, hundreds and hundreds of them winding around and around Starwatcher's trunk. They were regular and closer together this time, so it wasn't a struggle. Still, he kept a careful eye out for some trick. The height started making him nervous around two hundred paces up, when he stopped being quite so sure he'd be able to land uninjured if he had to.

It's not that he didn't trust the dryads, not quite. It's just that their idea of helping him didn't always coincide with his. So he slowed a bit, stepping carefully and listening for sounds in Starwatcher's trunk that might indicate she was about to do something sudden.

Fortunately, mana made the actual walking a lot easier. Callius said nothing, just followed him closely. Close enough to grab him if he slipped. And if they both fell together, what then? Would he turn into a giant fluffy bed before they hit the ground? Grow wings and fly like a bird? Dirt was almost tempted to fall and find out. Almost. He didn't want to find out the plan was for him to shatter every bone in his body. For his benefit, of course.

Halfway up, the forest seemed unrecognizable. The trunks faded against the deep green ocean of ferns, their huge roots hardly visible now. Above, Dirt could make out separate groups of leaves in more detail than he'd ever seen. Where one tree's branches met another, they wove together, sharing the space and brushing gently in the high winds that never made it down below the canopy.

Surprisingly, the air got warmer the higher he went, not colder. That was the opposite of going up a mountain. It stayed just as humid, though, and by the time he was three-quarters the way up, his shirt was starting to get drenched in sweat.

Time for a rest, he decided. A steady flow of mana kept his legs moving and energized, but it was still effort, and it was getting tiring. He turned and sat, then pulled his damp shirt off over his head and set it on a stair.

"You're leaking a lot of water," said Callius.

"It's sweat. It happens when I get too hot, or exercise too hard," said Dirt.

Callius smirked. "I know. I can also tell you all the substances it helps purge from your body."

"Really? Like what? Salt and water?"

"More than that. Perhaps the most surprising thing would be metal. There is a tiny amount of metal, more than one kind, in your sweat."

"Metal? Really?" asked Dirt, looking at the clear drops of it on his forearms.

"Really. Zinc, copper, iron, and two others that don't have names in your language. Those are the most prominent ones," said Callius. "Here, let me take that shirt. It's not drying out anytime soon."

Dirt wrung it out, curious to see if any liquid would drip out. None did. He handed it to Callius, who acted like he was tossing it down, but it disappeared before it left his fingers. "We'll leave it in your house."

"Which one?"

"Which one do you want to use?"

"Would Home be offended if I wanted to use my old villa?"

"Friend Dirt, what do you think my answer is going to be?"

"Well, I just don't want her to be sad. But I want to sleep in my villa tonight."

"Then so it shall be," said Callius. He ran a finger across Dirt's forehead, then licked the sweat off his fingertip. "Mmm, metal," he said.

"Is that a joke? Do I really have metal in my sweat?"

"No and yes."

"Does Socks have it in his?"

"Socks doesn't sweat, but his urine is similar to yours."

Dirt tried to remember. "I thought he did, after I sat in one place for a long time."

"Maybe, but it wasn't sweat."

"How do you know?" asked Dirt.

"Because we would have detected it on his fur, either when he sheds or when we touch him. We would smell it evaporating or see it in his pawprints. The Mother of Wolves will not let us analyze one of her pups properly, so we infer more than we can verify. But I am certain he does not sweat. He cools himself by panting," said Callius.

"It bothers me that you already know more about the physical world than I do, and I live here," said Dirt jovially.

Callius snorted and gave him a good-natured smirk. "Look down. Can you see Starwatcher's dryad down there?"

Dirt leaned over, just barely, and looked down. It was a long, long, way down. Far enough down he put a hand on Callius to keep his balance, just in case. "Nope."

"Exactly. You are very small. Now come on, we're almost there."

They stood and kept going. It was only two or three hundred paces now, close enough Dirt thought he could start to make out individual leaves. They were probably huge, but it was still a long way up. There wasn't much else to see yet, other than a vast network of branches. And as badly as he wanted to keep his neck craned upward, he had to look at the steps or risk missing one and slipping. And finding out what Callius's emergency plan was.

He looked with his mind-sight and froze in his tracks. There was something nearby. Something plural. Things. And they weren't trees, or even plants. They were something else, their minds full of patterns and flows and streams rather than discrete observations or ideas. And they were having fun. They were playing, whatever they were.

That was enough to get Dirt moving. He practically raced the rest of the way up, mana flowing freely and all his focus going to making sure his feet landed where they should. Before he knew it, he reached the end of the steps and stepped out onto a branch, the lowest one, just as wide as the roots so far below.

Too far down to make out, now that he looked. The dark green of the ferns camouflaged the forest floor to the point it looked like it didn't exist at all. Just emptiness down there. Empty green. It was more unnerving than when he saw the open blue sky for the first time.

"Higher up," said Callius. "We're not there yet."

There was at least another hundred paces of tree above him, but from here, at this angle, he saw spots of blue peeking in. He also finally got a good look at the leaves, which were bigger than he was, wide and round and full, with a series of small points jutting out.

The mysterious minds had a sense of anticipation to them, which he supposed was related to him. He hurried faster.

Up they climbed, sometimes using steps and sometimes hopping from branch to branch or simply climbing. The foliage got smaller and thicker the higher they went, making it easier to keep scrambling upward.

They ascended until Dirt's head poked up from the highest crowning leaves and they could go no higher. The sky was brilliant overhead, the sun startlingly bright against the deep blue. He'd never seen anything like this. The top of the canopy rose and fell like immense hills, leaving no hint of the cavernous emptiness beneath them. It was serene, but not somber and sacred like the forest floor. There was motion up here, vibrant activity.

One slip and he'd fall so far he could take a nap before he hit the ground, but it didn't seem that way. It seemed like he'd found a whole other world and he could climb out and race across the leaves to find new horizons. And honestly, maybe he could. The leaf stalks were as thick as his leg.

The birds were having no trouble, certainly. There were birds everywhere, mostly noisy little white ones that chirped and darted around with great excitement. A flock of larger ones in the distance flew over the forest in a V pattern. Another surprise was the variety of insects. One crawled across a leaf near his hand, smaller than a fingernail, and several more flew on wobbling paths nearby. None of the minds he was looking for belonged to birds or bugs, though. Now that he thought about it, the feeling of activity here had more to do with the mysterious invisible minds than the chirping birds.

"Do you see them yet?" asked Callius, popping up so close to Dirt the dryad's hair tickled his cheek.

"See what? I see a bunch of minds, but nothing with my eyes. What are they? I've never seen anything like them."

One was larger than the rest, full of countless threading pathways that rushed through and around each other like a vibrant knot of pure being. Dirt couldn't tell if he was looking at one long, tangled stream of thought, or hundreds all messed up together. There was absolutely nothing he recognized.

"Look closer. They might be hard to see," said Callius.

"What am I looking for?"

"Elementals."

The large mind reached out to him, but instead of a mental connection or something heard with his ears, he felt an electric shock. It tickled his mana vessel, reacting with the mana he still held inside him. A visible ripple appeared in the air around him, and for a moment he was worried that it was the great eye again, but it wasn't. Gray fog, thin and pale, filled in the ripples and from one moment to the next, a huge face appeared directly above him. A woman's face, round, with wide eyes. She opened her mouth, and a rush of wind washed over him; not strong enough to shake him out of the tree, but strong enough he held on tighter.

"We've been wondering this whole time how you two would communicate. She lives mostly in the world of magic, like us. Good luck," said Callius. He circled around to the other side of the last thin branch, turned his feet into hands to hold on better, and relaxed to watch.

CHAPTER SIX

The wind ceased, but the huge face's mouth remained open, unmoving, like a cheap carving on a fountain. The faint fog that composed her form waxed, waned, then waxed again, and Dirt felt the temperature shifting around him as it happened.

"Hello?" he asked. There seemed to be a minor reaction in her mind, but it was lost in the tangle too quickly to tell what it was.

Another gust of air blew over him silently, despite his expectation her mouth would make some kind of whistling noise. It didn't, and that made the gusts of air seem to be blowing in from anywhere. Normal wind, instead of whatever this was.

"I'm sorry, do you know how to speak using words? Or maybe you can think something really clearly for me?" he said. She seemed to be hearing him, but without any understanding that he could tell. He tried to follow her thoughts, but the tangles weren't anything concrete. They were a representation of a being comprised largely of motion itself.

At the next gust, he thought he recognized something in her thoughts. A trace of himself, but not as a whole person—it was a process, rather, a sensation like the wind itself would have as it passed over and around him. The smoothness of skin and the roughness of cloth. That gave him the insight he needed: It was his shape, perceived as a progression, as motion. Front, then sides and arms, then his back, as it washed over him. That perception then slid wildly throughout the twisting threads of thought, chased and led by many, many others.

Now more of what he saw in her mind started making sense. It contained more information than the trees' minds, startling amounts, even if less of it was . . . analyzed? Acted on? It was the shapes of things, but not the meaning of their forms, perhaps. No, there was no use trying to compare it to human ideas. It was simply what the wind felt, and that was all.

There was no use trying to put the images together into something he could recognize, not with so many moving this quickly. But if he held his attention on a single spot and simply tried to *feel,* to let it wash over him and experience it, he could almost understand.

Dirt opened his eyes and took in the scenery again, enjoying how the brightness of the sun gave the greenery a hint of cheerful yellow, making it feel active. Very different from the darker greens far below in their quiet shadows.

The gentle sound of rushing wind that stirred the leaves across vast distances in every direction filled his ears, punctuated by happily chirping birds. The flat face watched down from above, expressionless, and Dirt decided that wasn't really her. That was just an attempt to be recognizable, to let him see that she existed. No, the elemental had no body at all. She was alive all the same, though, a living band of motion that stretched past the horizons.

"What's her name?" he asked Callius, whispering at first. The rushing wind drowned him out, so he said it again, louder.

"I'm afraid I can't tell you," said Callius.

"So I just have to guess?" said Dirt.

"No, I mean I can't tell you. I have to show you. Gaze with your mana body. Are you ready?"

"Oh. Yes, I'm ready, go ahead," said Dirt.

Dirt strained to place his mind into his mana vessel and gaze outward into the strange and imperceptible world beyond. Even now, it was only possible because of all the practice he'd had going through the basic spells in the primer. On Socks's back he had no candles and chalk and daggers and a table, after all. Any magic he wanted to practice had to be done directly.

Just as Callius was doing now. The tree's magic pressed gently against his mana vessel, giving Dirt the impression of strings of shapes and signs and patterns, each more arcane and bizarre than the last.

Dirt apprehended it well enough, although he didn't recognize a single part of the name. Every symbol Callius had manifested was more complex than what was in the primer, or the simple spells for shaping wood or calling wind.

The name of the elemental didn't appear all at once, either, like a normal name would. Her name was a process, not a discrete signifier. It would be like having a complete dance for a name, or a song, and if any part was left out or changed it wouldn't be the name anymore.

"One more time, please?" asked Dirt, doubting his ability to remember it even after twenty times. The dryad obliged, manifesting the magic once more. Each section of it wove into something new until the process was complete. Perhaps he could recognize it contrasted against similar things, but he certainly couldn't reproduce it.

"I guess the reason I need to be careful with her name is if I say it with mana and get it wrong, something weird will happen? What'll happen if I do that and get it right?" said Dirt.

"Dirt!" said Callius.

"What?"

The dryad just looked at him with a blank expression.

"Oh," said Dirt, breaking into a slow smile.

"The difference is it'll work from anywhere, as long as you're outside and touching air," said Callius. "So, do you have any ideas?"

Dirt watched the gentle breezes shake the wind as far as he could see. Whether the elementals were the wind itself or simply partakers in it, he couldn't say. But they were not separate from it. While most winds returned to the sky and journeyed onward, some smaller currents of air twisted down into the branches and were lost, and the minds associated with them faded. They didn't seem to be dying, but perhaps they were. How long did wind live?

The round face hovering above him was only part of the great current of wind flowing across the treetops, and Dirt's body was hardly more than a tiny curiosity, a unique shape among so many things. The elemental knew where he was, though, and perhaps her face with her mouth that blew air was more like hands, trying to feel him in more detail.

He searched the many pathways of her mind until he found himself again, the sensation of his skin and pants against the wind. It took great mental focus to follow it as it flowed through her thoughts, but into that spot he sent a wordless feeling of warm greeting. *Hello.*

She touched his mana body again, the wind of her mouth causing electric sparks that danced all through him. He had no eyes for the world of magic, but he could sense the creation of shapes and patterns all around him as they manifested and faded.

Starwatcher's face appeared on a nearby leaf, down a step or two away from his foot. She said, "She is trying to play with you." Dirt looked around for other faces, but didn't see any. Still, he had no doubt they were watching.

Dirt closed his eyes and used all his mental focus on his mana vessel, doing his best to perceive what the elemental was doing. The area was suffused with her magic now that Callius had stopped, but there were two problems. First, his mind kept trying to turn what he experienced into something more familiar, like a feeling of touch or an image of sight. But that's not what it was. The more it became like something in the physical world, the less true it was.

The second problem was that none of the magic happening around him was *doing* anything. It was all just potential, none of it made real.

After a time spent in earnest focus it got a little easier, but the elemental seemed to be losing interest. She was trying to interact with him, and he was acting like a statue.

Was there a bit of magic he could do without completing it? A potential with no actualization? There was, and it was so instinctive to him he hardly even thought about it.

He raised his hand to snap and create a small light, but he left his fingers pressed, hovering in that moment between preparation and completion. The sigil manifested in the world of magic, just like the diagrams, just like he knew instinctively. Light.

The elemental's mind pulsed with sudden excitement and drew around the magical symbol for light with patterns of her own, expanding it into poetry. Dirt watched in awe, holding the inchoate light with all his strength as she worked. One piece of her efforts stood out to him somehow. Just that one part, but something about it seemed familiar and tickled his curiosity fiercely.

Then it hit him—it was far better drawn, and the shape was slightly different, but he knew it from the magical primer scroll. He'd just seen it yesterday, in fact. It meant "growth" in the sense of expanding within prescribed limits.

That was it! He wasn't sure whether to be proud of humans for getting it so close, or ashamed at how inadequate it was. Was that the limit of human magic? Scrawling out half-understood magical ideas and fueling them with power and hoping they worked?

No, proud. He should be proud. How had they even done it, without any real guidance? If only he could go back in time and ask himself.

Dirt shook off his focus, and his awareness returned fully to the world, almost like waking from a dream. "I figured it out! Callius, can you tell her I'll be back? I need to read some more. I need my scroll in my backpack, too, wherever that ended up. Can you send me to the schola again? No, wait, I'll tell her. I'll try," said Dirt, so excited he was in danger of babbling.

He quickly sent the elemental two emotions, one of growing affection and one of temporary farewell. Hopefully she'd understand, or maybe the trees could fill her in. He doubted she'd go anywhere, since she was in so many places already.

There were so many things he needed to try! He almost jumped out of the tree and risked his mana being insufficient to keep him from going splat when he hit the ground. Best not to risk it, though. Breaking your bones hurt. "Can you send me down with root travel, Starwatcher? Please?"

"I think our dear Dirt is excited," said Callius, glassy eyes sparkling with shared amusement. "What did you figure out?"

"Oh, well, I think if I take another look at the—" He vanished into pure speed, bouncing this way and that, and landed with a sudden thud near the colonnaded entry to the schola. He laughed into silence and jumped to his feet. They had done that on purpose! Dirt really needed to come up with a way to play a joke on a tree.

Dirt took deep breaths to wash out his dizziness, but it wasn't so bad this time since he hadn't come far. It was still quite a marked difference from above, though. Up there, it was warm and bright and windy, full of noise and motion. Down here, it was dim and silent and pleasantly cool.

He wasted no time and snapped a couple lights into existence before any dryads had even appeared. They were just starting to arrive, some forming anew and others popping into existence, probably sent by root travel. Dirt ran inside, ignoring all the boxes in the main hall, and turned down the hallway to the right, his bare feet slapping the stone and echoing loudly.

Dirt was running so fast he slammed into the ancient wooden door frame to slow himself down and bounced into the room. He checked each scroll as fast as he could without damaging them, looking for texts on magic. *For the Prosperity of Cattle.* That was one. He gently set it near his feet. *Scrying and All Useful Implements.* That was another. *The Hand.* He put that one with the others.

It would take forever to sort through everything, but before long he'd found several dozen magical treatises of varying usefulness. *The Measurements of the Heavens,* for one, had more geometry in it than magic, but it had some divination constructs that should prove useful. He stopped there, lest his pile get too large. It already was; he wasn't sure how much daylight there was left, but it had already been a long day.

The room had about thirty dryads in it now, too, and Dawn in particular kept reading over his shoulder. He could tell from how they shifted about that they were curious, or at least that they wanted him to think they were.

"All right, see these drawings? They're like how a human perceives the world of magic. Our minds turn it into patterns like this. That's why I have such a hard time copying Socks. He does it differently than I do. But this is how humans used to do it, long ago. We'd gather the right patterns, draw them on something in the right configuration, and then feed them mana. It's crude, but I guess it worked. It feels so primitive after seeing the elemental!" said Dirt, rolling through the text to find the next diagram.

"And how does that help you now?" asked Dawn, almost into his ear.

"Well, because she talks in pure magic. So if I can find the meaning behind more of these symbols, then I should be able to understand hers. I already know a few, and there are others that I'm remembering as soon as I see them from when I was Avitus," he said. "I just need to speak with her well enough to learn the rest as I go."

"And speak with us too. Human language is so *weird*," complained Dawn.

"Maybe, but it's pretty good at expressing human thoughts," said Dirt.

"Then your thoughts are weird, too. Soft folds of flesh, and you blow air over them to make them vibrate, then shape the vibrations with a wet tongue and teeth and lips, and somehow that's your *thoughts*," said Dawn.

"No, the thoughts are the words, not the flapping tongue itself. It's not that different. How is this," he said, manifesting the word for *light* in the magical world, hoping they could detect it, "any different from just saying 'light'?"

"Because the first one will make a real light appear, and the flappy flesh sound won't," said Dawn.

"Do not be distressed, friend Dirt," said Home. She remained in adult form, but had changed her attire to a dress that now covered her breasts, which Dirt supposed was the human custom. "You are strange, but we also adore you."

"Oh, I know. You're just teasing me. But Dawn has a point. Humans have a bunch of words for light, like in my language and the language of the Camayans. Different words for the same thing. So the words signify a thing, but they aren't the thing itself. I think the difference is, maybe the magic world's word is the thing itself. Or close to it," said Dirt. Now his mind was spinning with too much at once, when all he wanted to do was focus. Why did they have to bring up philosophy?

Home gave him a warm, motherly smile, which he suspected she was actively practicing, whether it fit or not. She said, "That magic symbol for light is not the light itself. It is the action of a will on the world of magic, suited to a specific purpose. Here, watch."

She created a ball of wood in her outstretched palm and tossed it into the air. "It is like my hand, tossing the ball. It is not the ball; it is the cause of the tossing. We know all things by the processes that create and comprise them."

Dirt nodded and said, "Okay, that might be helpful to know, actually. So if . . . hmm. Okay, let me read for a little bit. Is that all right?"

"Do as you wish, friend Dirt," said Dawn. She draped herself across his back and rested her chin on his shoulder so she could read along, and he decided to let her be.

He shuffled through his pile and picked up *The Hand*, since that looked like it'd be the most informative. And it was. It was an advanced guidebook on magical functions used in construction, like making things slow down or speed up, helping lift heavy objects, and so on.

It felt more and more familiar the more he read it, but strangely, it filled him with dismay instead of nostalgia. Avitus had known this text, or the author of it, perhaps, and disagreed strongly with some points. That feeling of frustration still lingered, and it made him second-guess everything.

And justifiably so, because at least a third of the diagrams in the scroll didn't look like they did anything at all. For example, this spell here had a complex set of diagrams and contained several words that Dirt was sure were correct. *Lift* was one, and *delay* was another. But the author had labeled a tangled scrawl as "This gives stone the weight of wood," and Dirt was almost certain it was made up.

Indeed, if he thought about each word and let it manifest into the magic world without giving it any power, many of them slid into proper shape. Others came apart, and that one—the one about weight—couldn't be manifested at all.

Not long after, the dryads made him stop to eat and drink. It was a good thing they did, too, because he needed it after all that sweating. And now that he thought about it, he hadn't eaten anything since this morning, with Socks. After that, it was back to studying.

Avitus felt just like his old self, but without all the joint pain. Here he was, sitting on a flat stone floor like it was nothing, reading. What a delight that was. How old had he been, before? Old enough just sitting could be troublesome. No longer, though. And what pleasure could there be like a new text? Especially one that proved useful somehow. And these were *all* new texts, in every way that mattered.

He struggled to take in as much as he could with the remaining daylight, speeding through scroll after scroll much faster than he probably should. The most gainful things he learned were the new diagrams, or seeing how one might be modified. After one text he suddenly jumped to his feet and snapped his fingers to make a new light, this one blue instead of candle-yellow, because he was able to recognize the part of it that gave it color and change it. Then another, green. And another as a ball the size of his fist instead of a tiny glowing spot, by adding two new symbols that spoke of shape and size. Shape, as expressed in the world of magic and then brought to being in the physical world, proved to be the single most complicated part of any magical word.

The relations that these humans had known were diagrammed in their proper places, but Avitus wondered if they'd ever done much magic directly. Well, there was one thing, he supposed. Snapping his fingers to make light. Perhaps that had been used as much to prove his mastery as to see in the dark.

After all, every text agreed on the methods. Drawings, using chalk or paint or whatever else, various ceremonial implements like daggers and candles and gemstones and bones. Rituals to follow, invocations of names and powers. Some were simple, but most were complex. And, as far as Avitus could tell, mostly pointless.

For example, this spell was supposed to help a newborn calf who was failing. The explanation said it helped generate blood and strengthen bowels and sinews, but in reality, he figured it just infused the poor creature with a bit of mana to help it get up and walk around on its own until it started feeling better. Why go through all the trouble, when you could just do like Socks did and shove in a bit of mana directly?

So much of it was wrong, too, not just pointless. It made Dirt start to wonder just how much magic anyone had actually been able to perform. Some, surely. But they didn't have the benefit of being suffocated in a tree to learn to gather mana. They had to learn it the slow way, whatever that was, so perhaps there was too much room for error for anyone to be sure.

Home patted him gently on the head and said, "Dear Dirt, you must retire. We will sleep soon. If we do not send you to your bed now, we will be unable."

Dirt stood and stretched, exhausted and stiff. He picked up his magical primer to read again in the morning. "Sorry. I hope you weren't too bored just watching me."

"We do not get bored. If you are ready to return, then let us step outside," said Home, taking his hand.

Many of the remaining dryads, including Callius and Dawn, had already gone inert and fallen asleep. They stood perfectly still, lifeless in a way that made Dirt glad he knew they weren't really human. No sooner had Home led him out to where he could touch a fern than he was tossed through the roots again.

He landed just outside his villa, where a few other inert dryads had been waiting by the gate. He patted their shoulders as he walked past, even though they couldn't sense it, and stepped lightly through the garden. He walked through the villa in the dark by feel, tracing his fingers on the wall. Slowly, to keep from running into anything he'd forgotten about.

In his bedroom, his shins bumped against a bed they'd placed here for him, just like the one he'd slept on underneath Home. He plopped into it with a contented sigh and snuggled down to sleep. What a day it'd been. First Father, then the schola, then the elementals, and all that reading. He was ready. Tomorrow, he'd talk to the wind.

Dirt dreamed of Socks that night, but it was a weak enough dream that he wasn't sure if it was really him. The pup kept trying to speak with his mouth, but all his words were barks, causing severe frustration for both of them.

The other dream of the night was a tree dream, full of their thoughts and experiences, only the tiniest portion of which he understood. But when he woke, he could remember a little more of it than last time. Enough to recognize some of it as the eternally shifting world of magic, all its patterns and shapes. More than anything, it humbled him. He'd never really expected to fully understand their world, but seeing more of its size and majesty gave him a lingering sense of inadequacy.

Well, that just made him appreciate them more. He rolled out of bed and stood up, stretching with a squeak that sounded out of place in the solemn silence. It was only barely beginning to lighten, just enough to find his way around. The early morning fog hadn't gotten down through the gaps in the roof and into the room, but it left all the openings misty and gray. The air was cool—cold, even—and he felt it keenly after being used to waking up on a warm puppy.

But it was *his* cold, in the middle of *his* forest, caused by *his* humidity dampening his skin and everything else. He had spent more time outside the forest than in it, but he still thought of this place as home, and that made every part of it his.

They'd left his backpack leaning against a wall, unopened. His dark red sweat-soaked shirt was spread out on the floor next to it and didn't look very dry. He sauntered over to the pack and squatted down, opening it to consider a change of clothing, which reminded him that Home had threatened him with a bath at some point. Not that he minded getting clean, but if she was going to start acting like Marina . . .

Dirt grinned and pulled off his pants. Might as well get properly filthy first, then. It'd be nice to get a good coating of *his* dirt, since it might be a while before he got another chance. Baring his legs quickly made him a lot colder than before, but he wouldn't give up that easily. He snapped his fingers to summon a light, then changed it to a hot ember to hover nearby.

Then he took the magical primer and sat down against a wall, shivering at the cool stone. He almost laughed at himself. How weak was he starting to get? A few weeks wearing clothing most of the time, and here he was unable to handle a typical morning in his own villa.

The second thing he noticed was how strange it felt to be sitting on the floor. It was hardly the same room anymore from down here. He really needed to make some chairs. Now that he thought about it, he wondered if he could get the dryads to bring some from Ogena with root travel. He had gold now, so he could buy them. Perhaps some other time.

He unrolled the scroll and skimmed through the important parts, reading over the diagrams for the hundredth time. After yesterday he had more to compare it to and was impressed by its quality. All diagrams were good, drawn perfectly under an exacting hand. The enchantment even preserved the little pinprick from the compass at the center of all the circles.

Dirt practiced looking past each design to see the truth behind it, the reality hidden away in the magic world. He drew them one by one with his mana body, isolated and disconnected so they wouldn't do anything, and watched them resolve into a true image. Sometimes it worked, giving him a better glimpse into a world his mind was the wrong shape for. Mostly the simpler sigils, signs of modification or those dealing with simple elements, like the heat of his ember.

The diagrams of several kinds of warm and cold sparked a memory, and he jumped to his feet, eager to chase it before it faded. He had something for hot and cold already! He raced out of the room and down the hallway, risking breaking his toes in the near-perfect darkness where the dim light hadn't reached yet. It had been right there in the atrium, in the corner where he used to sit and read. How had he not seen it?

Dirt switched his warming ember back to a light, since the atrium was black as night. The hovering light hopped and bobbled to follow him as he ran over to the corner, making his shadow jump wildly against the faded frescoes. It was right where expected. The dial! The only one like it anywhere. He gave a little cheer, despite how silly that was all by himself, and his voice echoed in the empty room.

The dial was just as he remembered. Not quite as long as his hand, its leaf shape contained enough gold to make ten necklaces, with the point indicating which enchantment was selected. It had four settings, four complete enchantment circuits that would adjust the temperature in the entire villa at once. Such magic was shockingly expensive, since you had to keep someone on regular retainer to keep refueling it, usually hourly. Even if a rich citizen paid to have one drawn, they'd only hire a wizard to give it mana for special occasions.

But his was special. Avitus had been a genius among geniuses, or so he'd fancied himself before meeting the wolves or trees. He'd laid the enchantment himself, overseeing the engraving of each line in each stone throughout the whole villa to an unprecedented level of precision. A single charge of mana would heat or cool the entire building for ten hours or more, and he could fill it up himself.

That by itself would have been enough for his name to be spoken all across the Sunset Empire, but he'd gone further than that by overlaying all four enchantments in the same spot, to be selected with this very dial. The underside would complete only one enchantment at a time when turned.

Dirt set it to "mild warm" as gently as he could, holding his breath for fear it would snap off in his hand. It scraped a bit as it turned, but it turned. He touched the dial with a fingertip and pushed some mana into it.

Nothing happened. Nothing even felt like it was trying to happen. He tried not to be too disappointed. After all, this was ancient, and it wouldn't take much to ruin the spell. One stone out of place, one line disturbed by a crack, anything. No, this was just another thing to put on his growing list of projects. Maybe he could trace out the patterns and see how it worked, but it wouldn't be easy, since he'd have to pull the stones apart to look between them. A project for another day.

He took the scroll and stepped out into the fresh morning air, fog swirling around him. Droplets of water fell like rain from any disturbed ferns as he walked where his garden used to be. The little iron fences were gone, as were all the flowers he'd had planted in each space. And the tree in the middle of the intersecting pathways. It had been a small one, some kind of fruit, with a little bench to sit on. Nothing of that remained either, but he sat on the smooth paving stones where the bench once rested and resumed reading the primer.

All in all, it contained around fifteen basic spells and enchantments, and thirty-six different magic words to make them up. He rested his chin in his hands and set the primer aside, wondering what he could say with thirty-six words. They weren't even words in the usual sense. Certainly not "hello." How could there be a magic word for hello in the first place? Hello wasn't an operation. It wasn't a function of the world that needed to be powered. It was just an idea. Well, ideas were a function of a mind, and the elementals and trees had those, so there must be more to it.

Wondering if the trees were waking yet, he rolled the scroll closed and stood, shivering slightly from the chill. He walked down the stone pathway to the gate, where only dark smudges of rust remained of the hinges. The dryads outside were still sleeping, standing straight, staring at nothing. Empty dolls.

If one of them had been Callius, Dirt might have been tempted to shape his dryad into something else, or remove the eyes or something, just as a prank. Just to see what he'd do. But he wasn't as familiar with these ones and couldn't have picked them out of the crowd. The last thing he wanted to do was offend a tree.

With nothing better to do until the dryads started waking up, Dirt wandered from building to building, checking the interiors and gardens to see what else had survived. Anything wooden was long gone, as was most of the metal, but that left plenty still to find. Statues and other carvings, for one, largely in excellent shape after being buried for so long and protected from the weather. No skeletons. If any of those had survived, the trees left them buried.

One small home in a row of apartments had a bronze lockbox as tall as his knee, which the dryads had probably thought was furniture. The rusted-out hinges shattered when he opened it and the inside contained only a thick layer of rock-hard black material. But if *this* chest hadn't been opened by the dryads, that meant there were probably plenty more out there that *also* hadn't been opened, and that piqued his curiosity so hard he was tempted to put off speaking to the elemental until tomorrow.

Further searching was not to be, however, because the trees woke up and came looking for him. Four of them, all girls he didn't recognize, stood at the door of the apartment home and waited for him to come out. He pointedly ignored the fact that all four of them had short, rough tunics on, and he wore nothing.

"Good morning," he said.

"Good morning, friend Dirt," said one. Her voice was an inhuman, breathy groan that made him smile slightly. She still needed practice.

They had nothing more to say, staring at him with pleasant but wooden expressions.

He scratched his stomach and asked, "How is the new tree doing? The one I planted by Ogena? Is she healthy?"

"She is well," said the same dryad. "They call her *la Petita Mestressa.*" The Little Mistress.

"I like it. Is she growing fast?"

"Compared to what?" asked the second dryad, her voice sounding a bit too deep.

"Good question. Never mind. I hope she's happy, at least."

"We are all happy," said the fourth dryad on the far end. Her voice was normal, but her eyes didn't move.

"I guess that's true," said Dirt. He hoped he wasn't too obvious about looking over their shoulders to see if anyone else was coming. So far, they weren't. "So, are you nearby? Where are you?"

Each of the dryads paused for a moment, then turned and pointed in different directions. As he suspected, they were the four closest trees, still several hundred paces away.

"Good. I need one of you to show me something. Do you mind making a space in your thoughts for me? Any of you is fine, if you're up for it. So here's what I'm wondering. When you speak in the world of magic, how do you share an idea like 'hello'? Do you have words of magic that represent other things, like my words do?"

"We do not say hello," said the breathy-voiced one.

The third dryad, who had yet to speak, silently extended her hand. He took it, and she led him out of the apartment and into the street. The other three dryads went still for a moment, communicating with each other through their roots, then followed.

"What are we doing?" he asked, but she gave no reply. She made her face the perfect image of friendliness but didn't bother to keep it looking very alive. Her limbs moved like a human's, though, and her hand felt fleshy enough.

They stopped in the center of the street, a well-preserved section of road that fit together handsomely. All it needed was a good rain to wash the black soil off, but that would never happen.

The dryad stood in the pose that Hèctor had when he'd taught Dirt his very first dance. Side by side, arms extended. Dirt grinned and assumed the proper position as the other three dryads clapped a steady rhythm. Perfectly steady. Their three sets of hands sounded like one pair.

She put an eager smile on her face, and the dance began, starting out just how he remembered. She knew it better than he did, it turned out, even though he'd had more chances to practice. Each foot landed in just the right place, one motion leading into another. Anytime he was about to go astray, a gentle tug on his hand in this direction or that got him back on track.

Then another dryad joined, holding his other hand, and the dance became a different one altogether, even though the steps were similar. The same dance, even, just modified to keep in a line and dance with more people. He learned it quickly and started humming a little tune to accompany them.

The dance changed again when the two dryads joined hands to form a circle. Dirt stopped humming until he saw how it was going to go. They rotated instead of going side by side or back and forth, and once he could keep up, they added new steps to the mix, expanding the dance.

"Oh!" he said, stopping. "I get it now! Okay. Yeah. That makes sense."

"What have you understood?" asked the deep-voiced girl.

"How you talk. I think I could have figured this out from what I saw yesterday, but I really get it now. You don't talk. You play together, and that's how you express yourselves," he said.

All four of them giggled politely, and none of them got the sounds quite right. It sounded horrible, which made him chuckle as well. "Close enough," said the breathy one.

"I'm ready to try again. Can you take me back up? Or should we wait for everyone else to wake up? Or, actually, are you going to make me climb up like yesterday?" said Dirt, walking off the street and into the ferns where the root travel could reach him.

In answer, he found himself flung upward, a sensation becoming more familiar each time. When he was thrown out, there was no ground to hit, and in the instant of disorientation he reached desperately for the nearest branch and missed it. A hand grabbed his and pulled him back up. Callius.

"Good morning, Dirt. Good thing you came out close enough for me to catch," he said.

Dirt swallowed against the riotous pounding in his chest. It was a long, long way down. He couldn't even see the ground through the slowly dispersing fog. With mana protecting him, he might survive that fall. Maybe. Except he might not hit soft ground. He might land on a road.

"Next time, put a net for me to land in," he said.

"How do you know there isn't one down there already?" replied Callius.

"It should be up here."

"But if it's down there, you'll have time to reflect on your mistakes before it catches you," said Callius.

"I think I'd have other things on my mind," said Dirt.

"We will not drop you," said Home, emerging halfway from a leaf. Dawn joined her, a girl with a woman. They held hands.

"Not on purpose, anyway," said Dawn, eyes gleaming in the morning sunlight.

And the sunlight was finally here, just breaking above the horizon. Rays of light ignited the dust and humidity where they pierced between the leaves, filling the landscape with lines of glory. Bright golden light, clear greens, and the flawless blue sky above. Maybe he should build a little space to visit up here. A platform to sit on, with a bed for warm afternoon naps.

Socks would never see this, he realized with a bit of regret. The pup was simply too big for these light branches to support him. There was nowhere for him to stand even if he *could* get up here somehow. Dirt would have to share the image mentally, so he took care to experience it as fully as possible with all his senses.

The air was calm and cold but began to warm and move with the rising sun. Gusts of air blew in, and soon after came the elementals, dancing among the tangled treetops as they traveled. He sent them all a mental idea of greeting, warm and friendly, which they seemed to understand, if not reciprocate.

Then an even, steady gust of wind bent the treetop several paces and calmed again to let it sway back into place. Over and over it repeated, until finally Dirt saw the great elemental's mind appear and grow to its previous size as she got closer and closer.

A dance. A dance, he thought. He closed his eyes and said, "Can you tell her she doesn't need to try and make a face unless she wants to? I see her just fine. I know where she is."

He didn't open his eyes again to look and see the result. Instead, he turned his eye inward and placed his thoughts as firmly in his mana body as he could. The sensation of air on his skin was impossible to ignore, but he let it happen, observing instead of resisting.

Dirt spoke words of magic, partial ones, with no power behind them. Motion, motion from stillness into activity, motion continuing until complete. Wind, a word he knew well. Moving wind, rising into being.

The great elemental responded, and Dirt felt new words emerge and build around his own, enlivening and enhancing them. Some he recognized, like sparks and light. Ideas of physical shapes pressed themselves into his mana body not as themselves, but as the space created by the motion around them.

He couldn't simply listen to her speak, though. The dance required two. Dirt struggled to watch the patterns, to feel and experience what she told him, and strained to react with his own limited vocabulary.

Dirt felt the air on his skin from her perspective even as he experienced it from his own. She depicted it in magic, and he responded by sharing the word for "calling into being." She colored that with the shape of cloth, which rotated around the whole as if trying to find a spot to integrate.

Accompanying that magical concept, her mind had a question in it, curiosity. Just the emotion of it. No words, of course, but he could tell that much. *"Why are you naked?"* she was asking.

Dirt grinned and swung his free arm and leg, letting the rushing air wash over him. He ran his hand through his hair, feeling the wind tug that too. How should he answer? Motion, was all he could think. He sent her the mental feeling of freedom, and she drew a new word, a complicated one that his mana body struggled to accept all at once. Release from restraint. That was it. Release from restraint.

He drew the same word, sharing his happiness mentally. His excitement. It was possible! They could really talk! He could learn so much, and all he needed was practice. He drew freedom from restraint again, and this time, decorated it with motion and the shape of wind as it moved around him.

The elemental's mind flashed, nearly from one end to the other, in pure excitement. The wind suddenly increased, going from a steady gust to a strong gale that bent the treetop a dozen paces. The air pressed hard against his skin and his closed eyes. He had to breathe with his mouth nearly closed. Fear gripped, and his mind raced to think how to tell her to slow down.

She did not slow down. The wind grew yet again, and all at once, it tore him from his perch and flung him upward like a leaf in a thunderstorm.

CHAPTER EIGHT

Dirt screamed as the roaring wind tore him from the treetops and threw him high into the air. He rotated to see the ground, but the constant stream of air was so fierce that it brutalized his eyes and forced them closed.

He blindly felt the acceleration, which he recognized from Socks jumping thousands of times, but there was no fur to hold on to. Nothing but a powerful cushion of wind and empty air.

Dirt panicked as his worst nightmare came true. He was going to be tossed into whatever the sky was made of and fall upward forever. The ground below him would fade to nothing, and it would be like the void all over again, except this time he'd starve to death, and his body would never come back down.

He strengthened his eyes with mana and tried to keep them open. The mana kept them from being harmed, but the ferocity of the wind pushed them out of shape and made them water so terribly that all he could see was an indistinct field of green down below, and featureless blue above. He couldn't even tell how high up he was, since he couldn't get them to focus on anything.

The wind didn't carry him in any sort of smooth flight, either. It tossed him like a leaf, first one direction, then the next. It flipped and spun him before suddenly letting him drop a hundred paces, then blew him in a different direction. Each time it dropped him, Dirt was sure it was the last and he was about to fall.

Dirt wanted to scream, but if he opened his mouth toward the wind, the air rushed in so hard he was sure he swallowed some. The roaring air in his ears was so loud he couldn't hear any screams anyway. He tried to compose himself and turn again to his mana body, but his physical one was so discombobulated that it was impossible to focus.

The wind rushed merrily along, playing with him like a child kicking a ball. It tossed him high again, straight upward, higher than thunderclouds or birds. At least it felt that high. It hadn't been summer-warm to begin with, and it got colder very quickly, which surprised him. He thought it would be warmer where the sun was.

It blew him ever higher, then higher again, and the rushing air slowly faded into nothing, leaving him floating for the briefest instant. He could see properly again and found himself impossibly high above the trees. The frigid air bit his fingers and toes and burned his nostrils. He had just long enough to wonder if the trees kept themselves warm all year before he started falling again. The roar again filled his ears, and the wind pressed his eyes shut.

Dirt looked out with his mind-sight, since that took less concentration, and found the elemental's mind no longer remaining constantly nearby, choosing instead to race the great distances she covered in her vastness, returning her attention only briefly to check on him. He saw himself in her perception, a tiny speck in a space otherwise unhindered by obstacle or restraint. He saw thoughts form in her mind in the shape of magic as she tried to speak with him, but he couldn't respond, and off she went again.

He rolled to his back again and held his arms out wide, and the force of the wind doubled and doubled again as it pushed to lift him, keeping him out of the reach of the trees and an almost certain fall to his death.

Despite the panic flooding his veins, as the initial shock wore off, he was able to gather his thoughts. He could guess what had happened. He'd told her 'freedom from restraint' in a way that made her think this was what he wanted, and until he said otherwise she might just keep tossing him around. So now what? What magical sigils for 'stop' could he remember and reproduce? And what was the likelihood they would simply get him dropped the long, long distance to the black soil beneath the trees? If he was lucky and didn't hit a branch or two on the way down. The trees might catch him, but he couldn't be certain.

He kept his eyes closed and looked only with his mind-sight so he could gauge what she intended, but he found no plans in the vastness of her mind. All her thoughts were either mere observations of shapes and sounds and whatever else she encountered, or magic. All her mind and world were magic, and it was still beyond him.

"Hello?" he shouted aloud, and the word made only the tiniest ripple in her awareness. It seemed to become part of her memory without ever touching her consciousness.

Although, now that he'd had a moment to calm down, was it really so bad? Yes it was, he decided. It might be tolerable if he could see, but the wind couldn't carry him as easily as a pup could. It had to blow harder than he thought possible just to keep him aloft.

He put both hands over his eyes, trying to block some of the wind. It worked but only partially; he had to keep his fingers tightly together because a small crack turned the air into a knife. But if he did that and reinforced his eyes with mana, he was finally able to see. The cold made his eyes water terribly no matter how much he blinked, and the wind got to them no matter where he put his hands, but he could finally see.

It did nothing to calm his terror. The wind was carrying him over the edge of the forest, and his heart sank. Nothing could catch him now if the wind dropped him.

Below was the vast grassland he'd crossed early in the summer, and from so high up, the river cut a long, curving line across the landscape. And there, the basin. It was a lot closer than he expected, at least from this perspective. No wonder Father had thought him capable of making his own way back.

The grasslands hid other ruins he'd never known about. Just shapes now, walls and roads, probably. A few stones still standing, likely too short to find amongst all that tall grass. And regardless, that was a concern for another time. He needed to land somewhere safer than that.

So far, the wind was showing no signs of dropping him. He was freezing so badly his bones ached in places there wasn't enough flesh on them, like his hands. He flexed them, but they were getting stiff. So were his feet.

It occurred to him that he might truly freeze to death. The middle
of the sky was no place for a human. No warming ember would help
him here. Maybe he should have started the day dressed after all, but
how could he have expected this? The trees probably hadn't thought of
it either, or they would have warned him.

If he were to survive the fall with all his bones intact, getting back
to the forest would only be a short run, now that he could run with
mana. So how much would the grass cushion his fall? He knew from
experience with Socks that there was a limit to how much damage he
could prevent.

Dirt closed his eyes again and focused on his mana body. Only desperation helped him find the necessary calm. He was under a genuine
threat of death, but it was not the first time. He'd kept his wits in front
of the Mother and Father of Wolves. He could discipline himself now.

He forced his mind to calmness and clarity the rest of his body
refused, but it was enough. Time to tell her to put him down. He'd have
to do his best with the sigils he knew, so which ones? The two best were
"diminishing," which the primer had included as part of a spell for simple fire to make sure it didn't burn out of control, and "termination at
the end of a process," which was part of a spell to lift heavy objects. He
could work with that.

Dirt watched the elemental's mind and waited until she turned her
attention to him again. He saw her speak into the world of magic, drawing complex sigils to manifest into reality. It was as easy for her as flex-
ing his toes.

He sent her a mental image of gratitude, just the feeling of warmth
and appreciation, to make sure he had her attention. Once he was sure
he did, he drew the signs as carefully as he could. He connected "diminishing," with the simple sigil for "wind," and closed them both with
"terminating at the completion of a process."

Once he'd drawn those, just to make sure she got the idea, he sent a
mental image of himself as that little spot in the sky slowly descending.
"Diminishing," he repeated. His heart begged her to understand and
not simply drop him.

She drew another sign over his, a new one that tugged at his memory until he recognized it as "slowly." Right. Avitus had known that one,
too. He mirrored it back to her. "Slowly."

Then, in preparation for catastrophic failure, he filled himself with mana and reinforced his insides and outside as much as he could. He held his hands before his eyes again to better see the ground.

Thank Grace, the elemental didn't drop him. Instead, she simply didn't lift him up as high on the next bounce. He descended slowly, although still moving forward at high speed. She tugged him along with her in the direction she'd been going anyway, no longer tossing him playfully about. Just enough force to keep him bobbing along, lower each time.

They crossed over the river, and Dirt watched with increasing worry as the trees grew smaller and smaller in the distance. The farther they got from the forest, the faster the wind was at ground level. When he was only a few dozen paces up, he saw it pressing the grass down in great waves that stretched farther than he could see.

Her mind stayed nearer him now, and she kept trying to speak to him in words of magic that he hardly understood. His frozen skin made it so he could only barely feel them in the first place, one sense overwriting the other. When he didn't reply, she'd switch to something else, usually too fast for him to even grasp the entirety of the previous thing.

Dirt sent her a mental puff of gratitude, unable to focus enough for anything else. He drew closer and closer to the ground. Any moment, the wind would release him, and he would fall and hit the ground moving forward as fast as Socks could run. He'd have to roll and control it the best he could.

He was glad they were over the plains instead of in the forest, because if he hit a tree going this fast he'd leave nothing but a bloody splotch on the bark. Lower and lower he drooped, watching the speeding grass approach him. He wasn't sure if Socks had *ever* run this fast. This was probably going to hurt.

Dirt slipped beneath the grasp of the wind and fell. The tufts atop the grass whipped him painfully, and just a bit lower, he hit the stalks and skipped back up into the air like a stone. The second time he came down, he crashed and left a trail of swaying, damaged grass twenty paces long.

He lay for a moment, stunned, and felt the mana sizzling in his skin. His extremities were numb from the cold, and all the rest of him stung, but he lifted his hands, and they looked fine. He flexed his fingers, which were stiff, but they moved. He shifted his legs and felt nothing broken.

Dirt grinned as the liquid terror in his blood seeped out his pores. Thank Grace, he was alive! And in one piece. He relaxed into the ground like a puddle and waited for the relief in his soul to make its way to the rest of his body while he panted, heart pounding against his sternum.

How insane that had been! He needed to find a way to meet new creatures that didn't involve mortal peril. He summoned four lights with a snap of his fingers, changed them all into embers, and curled up to let them bake him like a lump of dough.

He watched for the elemental's mind to return, but she never did. He spotted a few small, distant ones that might have been her children, but they never came near. A gentle breeze slowly moved the grasses, waving their dry tufts back and forth. He felt the aftereffects of motion as he lay there, a phantom dizziness that rolled through him as his body imagined itself zipping this way and that.

Fortunately, his fingers and toes seemed fine after they warmed back up, although his face felt a bit sunburned, along with several other spots down his sides. All of him felt raw, and he was ready for some food and water. Rising to his feet, he jumped high enough to see where the forest was, and it wasn't hard to spot. It sure wasn't close, though. Farther than the basin had been, so long ago.

Dirt stretched. Last time it had taken well over a day to get back, but not this time. Not after running with a wolf. And after what he'd just survived, the task seemed pleasant in comparison.

He inhaled mana, fed it to his legs, and ran with one arm forward to keep the grass from whipping his face. He went faster and faster, faster than he strictly should with no visibility, and realized he wasn't done being scared yet. That flight had been harrowing. He wished Socks was around, because a few licks and some nice warm fur to snuggle in would surely help.

Mostly, Dirt wanted to get back where he could rest and feel truly safe. He wanted the reassuring presence of the dryads while he recovered. He paused to check, and he was still going in the right direction. He'd be there soon enough, so he slowed, in part to force his mind to let go of a little more lingering fear.

In fact, now that he thought about it, the worst possible thing had happened, and he'd survived. If she did it again, he could survive again. He had nothing to be afraid of anymore. He would only improve from here until, hopefully, she was as much his friend as the trees or wolves were.

Were there other kinds of elementals? Stone or water or fire or lightning? How many kinds were there? And how bad of an idea was it to try to talk to *them?* Air didn't seem that dangerous, but look what'd happened to him.

With no idea how long until he was returned to Socks, he needed to make sure to optimize his time. He wanted to read more, and he should continue practicing talking to the elementals. It might be wise to start organizing all that treasure, too. And he wanted to ask the dryads how they'd made the cloth they were wearing, so he could replicate it; all his prior efforts had failed. Callius had promised to demonstrate, so maybe that should happen soon.

What else did he want to do? Perhaps the most important thing was to learn how he'd broken the world. The dryads had mentioned once that there was a skin over everything in the world of Law, and that it had been damaged. Somewhere in all that preserved text should be clues about it. Prisca might have some writings about what had happened, if he could find them. He might even find things he'd written himself, amongst all that jumbled mess of a library.

When he got to the river, he jumped right in, thinking it would be refreshing, and immediately regretted it. The frigid water shocked his system so bad he feared he might drown. But his flailing limbs dragged him to shore, where he rolled onto the cold mud and jumped up in a hurry. He stood there shivering and tried to rub the water off.

That was not fair at all! Who knew water could change temperature like that? It was supposed to be warm, and he had a whole summer's worth of experience to prove it. When he finally stopped shivering, he knelt gingerly on the bank and used his cupped hands to drink his fill, not daring to dunk his face like usual.

He paused and scanned the area for minds, looking for anything unusual. This was a big river, so did it have its own elemental? He found plenty of mice, and a vast sea of grass minds. Some bugs nearby, close enough for him to find their tiny pinpricks of light. Some odd things that took him a moment to recognize as fish, swimming down there in the river. But no elementals. Nothing big or complicated. Not any goblins, either.

Dirt stood and made a running leap across the river, strengthening his legs with mana. He almost didn't make it, since the mud slowed him down just a bit.

No sooner had he landed on the far side and resumed running than he felt himself yanked with root travel, blind to the world for an instant until the bright autumn field was replaced by the somber greens and dim lighting of the forest floor. Twenty dryad faces crowded him, all anxious.

"Hello, everyone. Somehow, I'm fine," he said.

CHAPTER NINE

They didn't let him get up right away, of course. Home knelt beside him and placed her hand on his chest. Tiny white threads emerged from it and penetrated his skin to examine his body from the inside.

"I promise I'm fine," said Dirt, but he didn't complain or resist. They'd win if he tried, not that it bothered him anymore. "I don't think she meant me any harm."

"The intent is less concerning than the outcome, friend Dirt," said Callius with a sly half-smile.

A short wave of raindrops fell, only lasting the space of a single breath. One drop of water landed on his nose, making him blink. It dripped down into the corner of one eye and annoyed him terribly. It wasn't the last, either. After a few straggling drops, another wave came, filling the area with the rushing sound of rain for only the briefest moment. High above him, wisps of fog threaded through the branches and drifted between the tree trunks. Clouds? In here?

"You are not fine," said Home, retracting the white threads from Dirt's chest and back into her hand. "The cold has damaged your skin. The damage is worse on your toes and fingertips."

"Is that all? Nothing worse?" His fingertips were a little redder than usual, and they tingled a little, but they seemed fine.

"It will cause you pain," said Home. She didn't seem to know quite which emotion to use, and it left her face uncharacteristically blank.

Dirt grinned. He might be freezing cold, but there was something warming in how upset they all were. "I've had worse. And if it's still bothering me in a few days, I'll have Socks lick me. He probably will anyway, now that I think about it."

Another raindrop landed in his eye, making him blink and squirm involuntarily. Home hastily withdrew the white threads, and doing it faster filled him with more of the tiny little snags and tugs than normal. He tried not to wince in discomfort.

"Okay, why is it raining?" he said, sitting up and finally wiping his face.

An entire leaf appeared right above him, covering him like the awning of a market stall, except much larger. No fewer than eight dryads took hold of the tips and sides to hold it up.

"It's not rain," said Callius. He held out his hand, and Dirt's pants appeared in it. Then in his other hand a shirt appeared, the thicker red one. "It will be cold for a while, and we're concerned about your ability to regulate your temperature."

"What is it if it's not rain?" said Dirt. He took the clothing from Callius, but then he remembered he'd just been lying on the bare soil. His back would be filthy.

"The wind got a little too excited and did a little too much blowing," said Callius. "It's the moisture in the air falling out. Do you want the long explanation, or the short one?"

"Let's start with the short one, or I doubt the long one will make sense," said Dirt. He lowered his arms, letting his clothing dangle. He'd rather be cold than get it filthy on the *inside*.

"Okay," said Callius. "The wind blowing so hard up there moved around a bunch of air down here, and some cold air got in and ruined everything. Everything is ruined. I hope you're happy with yourself."

"Oh no, not air!" said Dirt dramatically. "What was I thinking?"

"Your punishment is to put those clothes on and warm back up before your body's functions are disturbed by a lower internal temperature," said Callius.

"I have a better idea. And it involves hearing the long explanation," said Dirt.

Home decided which expression she wanted to put on. It was the one a woman in the kitchens had given him when she caught him and Màxim stealing a couple spoonfuls of honey. "Dirt, if you do not get dressed, then we will be forced to dress you for your own good."

He couldn't help but grin even as he shivered from the sparse rain-drops dripping all the way down his body from his shoulders. "My idea involves getting warm, I promise. Do you think you can seal my old bath so it can hold water? In my villa? I want to bathe before I get dressed."

"The water will not be warm enough," said Home.

"I'll warm it up with magic. At least I'll try," said Dirt. He suppressed another shiver. Almost.

"Very well. But if our efforts and yours are not fast enough, I truly will force the clothing onto your body," said Home.

"I'll get dressed before you have to, I promise. I don't want to freeze either. It's unpleasant. But a hot bath! I haven't had one of *those* in thousands of years," said Dirt. And it was true. They'd heated up water for bathing in the duke's palace, but they washed by dipping a rag. Some of the ponds he and Socks had come across had been on the warmer side, but that wasn't the same.

The dryads gave no warning, and Dirt was dumped in the garden of his villa before he realized what was happening. Root travel. How come he never landed on his feet when they did that? Now his front was dirty, too.

Dawn was the first to appear alongside him, with a faint popping sound that Dirt wondered if he imagined. She took his hand and lifted him to his feet.

Her eyes sparkled with excitement as she dragged him into through the main entry and into the atrium. Once there, she stopped near the fountain in the middle and said, "This?"

"No, come on, it's this way," he said. Then it was his turn to drag her, not that she resisted. They went down the hall and into the hot bath room. It was one of the larger areas in the house and seemed all the more forlorn as a result. A flat walking area surrounded the bath, which itself was dug into the ground deep enough that Dirt's head would be below water when it was filled, at least in the middle. Dirt thought he remembered something about pipes and machinery, but it escaped him, and he let it go for now. He had other ways to fill it up.

Fortunately, the bath was big enough for Socks to fit into with room to spare, in case the pup ever wanted to. Not deep enough, of course; not even close unless he lay down. But plenty wide.

Two of the decorative pillars had fallen and shattered, which was probably why a good portion of the ceiling had collapsed. Even though the dryads had removed the soil when they'd excavated the house, the bottom of the bath was still full of broken stone and shards of concrete and roof tiles. The decorative arches along the walls and under the intact parts of the ceiling were still there, though, which made him think he should repair the room completely someday. It was a handsome place, not too ornate and not too boring.

Dirt hadn't taken a close look at the baths before, just a glance as he walked past to remind himself what they were. He'd seen the large cracks from the doorway, but up close, they didn't look quite so bad. Most were thinner than his finger; not too wide, but long, and they traced up and down the corners and around the edges.

He and Dawn walked down the steps into the basin and started tossing rocks and things out, clearing the bath's floor the best they could. Six more dryads came through the entryway and jumped in to help, including the two whose trees were the closest to the villa.

Callius and Home watched from the edge, but said nothing, not even when it was done. Dirt had expected one of them to take charge, but no one did. Instead, Dawn and the others made their fingers narrower and began sticking them in all the cracks. Dirt stepped over for a closer look and watched them filling the gaps with a thick, sticky, dark-colored substance that had a peculiar odor he couldn't place.

"This is a temporary solution, dear Dirt, for we are operating with haste," said Home. "Would you like to dress until the bath is ready?"

"I'm fine," said Dirt.

"Do not feign sturdiness you do not possess, dear Dirt. I can see the temperature of your skin," said Home.

He was about to protest when one of the dryads brushed against him and made him shiver, which wasn't fair. She was as cold as the stones and damp with dew.

"I guess there's no reason not to do this now," he said. Dirt snapped his fingers and summoned five little lights, all of which he turned into hot embers. He climbed out of the bath, since he was in the way, and made the embers slowly circle around him while he watched the cracks get filled in.

Once the cracks were stuffed with dark goo, the dryads came up the steps and stood alongside the bath. They extended their arms, and all at once, water poured from their palms, even Callius and Home. Even though they made quite the waterfall, the bath didn't fill quickly.

Dirt sent his embers down in the water to warm it up, which was harder than he expected. The water put pressure on them and did its best to snuff them out, which made him spend twice as much mana and five times as much concentration keeping them going. And making it worse, their absence made him feel twice as cold, and he kept shivering.

When the water was about knee deep, a mist of steam rose from the top and filled the room, mixing with the dew already leaking from the air and making it stuffy. Not much warmer, though. Maybe if the space had been air-tight, but the wall was missing a chunk, and part of the ceiling was just a net of vines.

At least the water wasn't as murky as he expected. All the sand and dirt stayed at the bottom instead of being stirred up too much. And by the time the bath was full, the room was plenty warm and every wall looked soaking wet and had water dripping down it from the dew. Dirt let his embers snuff out, which was a relief because they'd been draining mana as fast as he could inhale it.

He dipped his toe in, and the water was too hot. It stung. He grimaced and looked at Home.

"It's not much warmer than your average internal temperature. It should not cause you any harm," she said.

Dirt gritted his teeth and crept in slowly, hoping he wasn't about to turn into soup. How did Home know the temperature just from looking, after all? And what was her scale for "not much warmer"?

She was right, though. It wasn't too hot. It only stung because he was already cold, and soon the feeling settled into a pleasant heat that soaked in deep. He made his way to a seat along the edge, which he could barely sit on if he lifted his chin out of the water, grinning in pleasure. Truly, he had missed this.

"Well? Was it worth all that effort?" asked Callius.

"Absolutely! It's amazing. You have no idea. Are any of you coming in?"

"Just me," said Dawn. The other dryads stopped moving and watched as she stepped to the edge of the stairs. She untied the bow at the top of her gray-tan tunic to let it fall from her shoulders and crumple to the ground. She stood motionless, and Dirt watched her dryad become more and more realistic. And it was more than just putting skin on her whole body, which itself was unusual. It was a hundred tiny little things, like her ears looking less solid and the dew collecting on tiny hair fibers on her forearms. The muscles above her knees flexed realistically when she took her first step into the water, and the smile growing on her face looked like it came from deep inside her, not something she'd practiced.

Once immersed, Dawn waded slowly, just her head poking above the water, eyes full of wonder. She sat next to him, and even her breathing was realistic.

"What's going on?" he asked.

Her eyes darted to meet his, and he could watch her thinking by the micro expressions on her face. Dirt found himself in awe, almost unable to believe this was still a dryad. He'd been impressed when Callius made himself look human from head to toe, but this was something grander.

"You're focusing everything on your dryad, aren't you? Can you even talk right now?" he asked.

Dawn regarded him with a quizzical expression. She traced a fingertip along his nose, then pinched some of his hair. After that she stood back up and waded around the bath, not seeming to have any destination in mind.

Callius said, "I am faster, but she is more accurate. Right now, she is mimicking human anatomy almost completely, including the function of nerves. Her whole mind is in there. She is cut off from us for a time."

Whether they were watching her through their roots or conversing among themselves, he couldn't tell. But no one moved, indicating the trees were focusing more on their true selves than their little puppets. Dirt got up and followed Dawn around the bath, just to make sure she didn't bump into anything and hurt herself, if that was possible.

She ignored him, aside from periodic glances. Mostly she waved her arms through the water, or made kicking motions, or turned in circles.

Until she suddenly froze. She lurched upward in the water and lay back, rigid, floating like a log. Most of the detail faded from her dryad, skin losing its lifelike suppleness and becoming more wooden. The dryads around the edge of the bath relaxed, and life seeped back into them.

It seemed strange to just leave her floating, so Dirt put his hand on Dawn's shoulder and pushed her toward the edge, where two girls leaned in and pulled her out. They stood her up and dropped the tunic back on her, even tying the bow.

Dirt rested his arms on the edge of the bath and waited for her to wake back up. "Hey, Callius, Home, everyone, why don't you all get in, too? You don't have to do it like Dawn did. Just get in."

"We can't get in," said Callius.

"Why not?"

"Because we are made of wood," said Callius. "We'll float."

"How did Dawn get in?"

"It's complicated," said Callius, "and not worth doing twice."

After that, Dirt relaxed while Callius did his best to explain all about air. Apparently, some air was heavy and some was light, and some was warm and some was cold, and it all held different amounts of water. Dirt was familiar enough with humidity to get the basic idea, since it was so thick in the forest you could taste it after being away for a while. And he wasn't surprised to learn that the trees spent a lot of time and effort keeping the forest just how they liked it, balancing the water levels and temperature perfectly. Some of it was done with magic, but not all. Their leaves and bark did a lot of the work.

When it got truly interesting, however, was when Callius explained how rain was made. Dirt had never wondered, to be honest, but he would never have guessed. It turned out that clouds were made of fog just like on the ground, and fog was a bunch of tiny, tiny little drops of water floating in the air. When the fog droplets bumped into each other and clumped up too much, they fell as rain. Sometimes it was because the air had to move up over an obstacle, like a giant forest, and sometimes it was because the wind slowed down, or a dozen other reasons.

As the discussion progressed, Dirt summoned his embers again to reheat the water, since he detected it cooling slightly. That got him thinking how much effort it would take to make it rain with magic, if he ever wanted to. He could make wind with magic, and if he got practice talking with the elementals, they could help.

"Hey, Callius," interrupted Dirt, halfway through something about pressure zones and elevation. "What's lightning made of? That's a part of storms, too. I remember that it's sparks, but I don't know what those are either."

The dryad paused, his happy chatter fading as his lecture was cut short. He went completely inert, in fact, as did several others, including Home. Dirt chuckled softly, wondering what they were talking about. Was it hard to explain, or did they just not want to say? It's not like he wanted to try to touch any. He just wanted to know what it was.

When Callius started moving again he said, "We will leave the full explanation for another time. The short version is that clouds traveling over the earth can cause a separation of power, and once it becomes too great, it recombines in the form of lightning. That causes it to settle. Another thing I'll say is that violent storms, with high winds and clouds that tower like mountains, often fill with lightning naturally."

"Can you ever have lightning without clouds?" he asked.

"No. Do you know what hail is?"

"No."

Callius resumed the lecture, explaining in great detail what updrafts were and how they were formed. He continued into how weather worked at a larger scale and how one could even predict a storm with enough information. That last bit was particularly useful to the trees, since whenever they saw one coming, they had to divert it or risk having it mess up their air.

And just to make the point, periodically a wave of rain would fall, pattering on the roof except where it fell through the vines. The rain was cold on his face, but Dirt found it pleasant since the rest of him was warm.

By the end of the discussion, Dirt was confident he'd remember most of what he'd been taught. It all fit together once you had the whole picture. Strangely, it seemed like new knowledge to him, not being retold something he'd learned once before. And that made him wonder why Avitus hadn't known any of this. His people had been able to work all sorts of wonders, erecting grand buildings and sculptures and writing philosophy. So how was it even possible they never figured out how weather worked?

Dirt finally dragged himself from the hot bath and stood on the edge, rubbing his body down with his hands to help dry off. The water steamed right off his skin, and he was dry before he knew it, aside from his hair. Or as dry as he was going to get, anyway, in a room so thick with humidity he could cut it with his knife.

He looked back into the water, pleased to see that it hadn't gotten too dirty from having him in it. The primer had a spell for purifying water, and he resolved to try that later.

After he pulled his shirt over his head, he saw Dawn moving, finally having woken up. "Welcome back," he said with an amused smile. "How was it?"

Her voice was breathy, as if part of her was still dreaming. "Strange. I hardly remember it. The others have been working with me to process all the information. But I felt . . . I felt." She waved her hands through the air like she'd done in the water.

"I know what that's like. Sometimes I get caught up in your dreams and dream I'm a tree. The only thing I remember afterward is how strange it was," he said. He'd tied the drawstring on his pants a little too loose, so he redid the knot. He even put his socks and shoes on, promising himself he'd walk on stone as much as possible to keep them from turning black. "Why did you do it?"

"Why should I have a reason?" she replied sweetly. "I did it for its own sake."

Home handed him a big glob of sap, which he greedily ate, hardly chewing before he swallowed. The heated bath had distracted him, but he was famished.

Callius cupped his hands, filled them with clear water, and made Dirt drink a little more than he really wanted, but they insisted he'd done a lot of sweating and needed his fluids.

After that, Home said, "Dear Dirt, I hope you will not mind if we let you read until twilight? We must spend our focus on balancing our environment before it gets much worse. Will you feel neglected if we do not play games?"

Dirt said, "Oh, no, that's fine. I have a lot of reading I want to do anyway. And I understand. Just don't forget and leave me in the library overnight."

"Good," said Home. She leaned down and kissed him on the forehead. "Do not think our affection diminished for our absence. Tomorrow, you may attempt to speak again to the wind."

"Perfect. I want to try again. She seems . . . Well, I think I can figure it out."

"Just try and tell her something else next time, won't you?" said Callius, slapping Dirt on the back.

CHAPTER TEN

Despite the nice long soak in the bath and sweating all his fear out, Dirt found it hard to focus on reading. He was simply too wound up, after the morning he'd had. He could still faintly feel that falling sensation when he sat very still, although he might have been imagining it.

The other thing making it hard to focus was how much of the material began to seem familiar. As he expanded beyond the magical primer, he'd roll to a new sigil or spell and nod to himself, recognizing it immediately. And he'd remember ways it interacted with other sigils, but half of those he hadn't seen yet and couldn't remember.

What worked best was pretending he didn't know any of it, and studying each new sigil like it was the first time. And if he did any imaginary combining to make a new spell, it was only with things he knew. That was a growing list, and he already had a good start. But then the problem was that so many of the descriptions seemed incomplete or simply wrong, and he had to keep rethinking everything.

For example, the sigil for wood, which he was certain about. It was part of the word the dryads had taught him, and he'd used it to shape wood plenty of times. In a text on alchemy, the author thought it meant the color green. In a different text, it was labeled as "to make solid," and in another, "gentleness."

Avitus was sure that last spell would never work. He recognized the name of the author as someone he'd always disrespected. With cause, it seemed. There were a lot of those—spells he didn't think would work. Their effects were always too subtle to detect right away, like making a harvest more bountiful or increasing one's attractiveness to the opposite sex. A spell to light a lamp, well, that had to work right away or everyone would know. But one to redirect the attention of thieves? How would you measure its effectiveness?

Late in the afternoon, hunger got him to wander out of the library and look for a dryad. He'd already memorized another twenty sigils by then, counting only the ones he trusted. He had ten more he made specific note of, because although their descriptions were too often contradictory, they seemed important.

Walking through it on his way outside, the schola felt dead as a tomb, even with his lights and embers bringing life to it. The smothering silence of the forest still got in, and without any dryads watching everything he did, the whole place turned oppressively solitary.

He missed Socks already. They hadn't been apart in months, not since a few times around Ogena. The pup wouldn't be pleased to do this much sitting around and reading, but he probably would've learned how to talk to the elemental right away.

After all, Socks had a window into the world of magic that Dirt's body didn't. A faint, hazy glimpse, as if through a mostly closed eye, but a glimpse nonetheless. To Dirt, the magic world was much more obscured. It was like how he'd first spoken to the trees by sending them the sensation he caused when he sat on their roots, along with hello. They couldn't fully conceptualize what was happening, just enough to know they were touching something. It was like that. And Dirt's brain wasn't nearly large enough to make himself a magic-world dryad to explore in, if he even knew where to start.

So sigils and spells it was. Shapes and shadows and hints, like trying to communicate by watching someone scratching on the opposite side of a paper you were holding. At least he didn't need all the little tools humans used. No wands or gems or chants. None of that.

Home had left her dryad waiting in the schola's garden, sitting on a stone bench next to a grimy statue of a naked woman with one arm extended toward the sky. Her dryad was inert, and her eyes didn't move when he stood in front of her.

Still, worth a try, since he was hungry. "Home?" he asked. "Can you hear me?"

She reacted, fortunately, but only animated her face, which Dirt found amusing. The poor trees must *really* be busy. He didn't feel like it was his fault, though.

"Can I have some sap?"

Home held up one arm, which creaked like bending wood, and a large glob of sap appeared in her palm. Dirt took it and said, "Thanks!" She left her arm up, and her eyes quit following him.

He walked over to the little basin and drank some of the pure water that filled it to wash down the sap. When he stood, a chill wind blew across the ferns, filling the silent forest with its soft sound. It was such a natural sound everywhere else, but here it intruded. Dirt stuck his hands in his pockets and huddled against the chill, glad he had clothes on. The ever-familiar rhythm of tree-magic shuddered in the stone beneath his feet, and after only four slow pulses, the wind stopped dead, and the area fell silent again.

Dirt peered through his mana vessel and caught only glimpses of the great and subtle working of magic all around him. Half-seen patterns of spells greater and more complicated than he could measure drifted past, lighting across his perception only faintly, like drifting cloth. He recognized portions, though. Wind and air and water and others, in spiraling geometric perfection.

He glanced down again at the water in the basin. He knew how to shape wood, right? What would happen if he swapped out the sigils for wood and growth and replaced them with water? Keeping everything else the same.

The word to shape wood couldn't make it fly, so Avitus decided to make the water stand up, like a little pillar. Maybe all of it, standing straight up like a long, thick pole. A backward waterfall.

Avitus held his hands over the basin, made the image clear in his mind, and manifested the spell. The surface of the water rippled until a lump arose in the center. He fed it more and more mana, but it didn't help much. The water was too slippery and didn't want to stay put. He couldn't shape it in sections, he learned. He had to do it all at once.

But it helped if he shaped some sections more strongly, like the outside. Then it'd hold the inside water in place. And rather than lifting the water into shape, he had to push *other* water down, and then it'd rise where he wanted.

He adjusted the spell the more he used it, shaving off useless parts. The water couldn't grow, at least not using this method, so the parts of the spell related to growth and destruction had to go. And there was no communication like with a living plant, so a large chunk of the spell fell away with no effect. He still knew none of the sigils in that part, which was a shame, since they might actually help when talking with elementals.

He added other things to it, one of which he'd learned from the elemental: continual application of force. But after a few more tries, he removed it again. Feeding it a steady flow of mana had the same effect.

No, less was better. He removed more of the spell. Anything he could think of that wasn't active or that wouldn't work on water had to go. More than once the water rejected his magic and collapsed, sloshing back into the basin. But he kept working at it, adjusting the spell's shape and the sigils that comprised it.

He reduced it to only five complete sigils, arranged around a balanced circle. Perfect in its simplicity, but pushing most of the work onto him and requiring serious concentration. It felt like he was trying to dream out loud, with how strongly he had to picture what he wanted to happen.

But it worked. He could play with the water however he wanted. Avitus poked a finger into the basin and drew out a thread of liquid that stuck to his fingertip as he twisted it in the air. After that he scooped out a ball with both hands and held it balanced in place, watching its surface quiver and ripple. He pulled the ball between his fingertips, and it stretched like bladder.

This was as close as he'd ever get to moving things with his mind. If only Socks were here! He'd . . .

The water splashed back into the basin as he froze, eyes wide. He'd seen Socks move things with his mind a million times, but he'd never been able to do it himself, and neither of them could figure out why.

It was so simple. So obvious. So impossible, before this exact moment. He didn't need the spell at all! The sigils were for complicated things, like processes and procedures and spells. But he didn't need them for something so simple. The power was already there. He just had to remove the filter and enact his will directly.

Avitus's fingers trembled as he held them over the water again. He balanced on an edge sharper than his knife. If he tried and failed now, he might never do it again. But if he succeeded . . . if he succeeded!

Move, he commanded the water with a thought. The mana inside him didn't move. Neither did the water. He swallowed the panic that followed, that maybe he'd ruined it. Maybe his failure had introduced doubt and it'd never work.

He cast those ideas away and hardened his mind. Discipline and sincerity, he remembered. That was his true power, and he needed great quantities of each for this. He'd been too hasty.

Avitus pushed away everything that wasn't part of the task at hand. He mastered every inch of himself, quieting even the constant stream of imagery in the deep recesses of thinking.

He tried again. *Move.* He strained his will, exerting it as hard as he could. The water stayed still.

They'd melded their consciousness, he and Socks, countless times. He'd watched the pup move things with his mind, always with such effortlessness that neither of them could even find a mechanism for Dirt to exercise in hopes of learning. Socks had just *done it.*

Avitus had everything in place already. He knew his mana body and was familiar with it and how it worked. He knew his own mind, how to focus his will. And he had run his fingertips across the immeasurable world of power that lay just beyond perceiving. He need only turn his will and the power would obey.

He tried again. *Move.* Nothing. But he got closer. It had to come from deeper. From a place of truth, and not one of mere belief where doubt also resided.

Avitus drifted his hand to the side, slowly passing it over the water. This was it. He held perfectly still. The world would either obey, or it would not.

He drew his hand upward and willed the water to follow. Not with a word, or even imagination, but with will from a place deeper than words could reach.

The water shivered, barely, briefly, and went still again. Avitus cast away any excitement that might distract him. The task was all that existed. He looked intently at the water and made it move.

The water rippled more deeply. It followed as he moved his hand around the basin in a circle until waves formed, sloshing over the edges. He scooped up a handful with his mind, letting it form naturally into a sphere. Then he brought it to his lips and drank it right out of the air.

All the world returned as his mental discipline fell apart. The endless green above and below, the silence other than dripping water. The feeling of his own clothing on his skin. He jumped up and cheered as loud as he could, mind wild with joy.

"SOCKS, I CAN MOVE THINGS WITH MY MIND!" he screamed mentally. Countless tiny minds around him reacted, first in surprise, then confusion, then forgetting him entirely. Except the trees, who had to stop what they were doing for a moment to figure out what he'd said.

"Sorry," he sent the nearest ones. *"Ignore that."*

They obliged without any reply, resuming their calculations. Any other time, it might be fascinating to watch them all working together so furiously, but Dirt had other things to do. Avitus had never done this. He was sure of that. No one had. Maybe no human ever.

It was so quiet, so solitary, that Dirt's exultation was almost ruined by silence. There was no one to show, no one to tell. Just the empty forest, full of trees too busy to pay any attention to the mighty thing he'd just done.

Although . . . that meant it would be a surprise. Socks hadn't replied, so he was probably too far away to be watching. Dirt would wait until they were back together again and say nothing. He'd move things casually and see how long it took Socks to notice. That would have to do.

He pulled out his knife and lifted it from his palm with his mind, then made it slowly circle around him. First while he stood still, then as he walked slowly, practicing. The hardest part was not thinking about what he was doing, but simply doing it. If he thought about it too much, the dagger got slippery and fell to the ground.

Dirt tried lifting a cylindrical pillar stone, but it was way too large for him. The mere attempt put enough pressure on him that he almost fell to his knees. Since there weren't any little rocks to practice with, he ran to the schola to look for smaller objects. He lifted the lid of a chest with his mind, curious at the feeling of weight it put on his knees.

But the lid slammed shut, and Dirt realized he needed to take a break for a moment. It was getting harder to grab things, and a feeling of weariness was creeping into his brain. This had been quite a day already. He'd spent the morning sure he was about to die. Why push it?

Well, because, what else was he going to do? He'd done enough reading for the day, and the trees were busy, so what else was there?

Dirt poked around among the piles and boxes and chests, all the pots and baskets of gold and silver and whatever else had been preserved. He avoided the ones with little figurines, though, not wanting to be distracted by suffering gods. He used his shirt sleeve to wipe the front of a silver platter and looked at the decoration around the edge. It showed a hunting scene, he guessed, with several dogs chasing a deer. And a person's head, for some reason, with mid-length hair that could be a man or woman.

There was a lot of that, it turned out. Just about anything fine enough to be made of silver or gold was worth decorating. That was fun for a while, looking at all the people and animals and trees. Scenes of battle or street life, bathing and eating, cattle and sheep and fearsome monsters. All of those, he knew the names of, which surprised him. No goblins or gryphons, no lumbering tentacle monsters sliding out of pools. But there were fauns and satyrs dancing in meadows, upside-down striges, centaurs with spears and bows, several kinds of gorgons tormenting and frightening men.

Dirt almost walked out to find Home and ask her if she knew of any fauns or satyrs. Were those real? He and Socks had seen a lot of forests and never found any.

They'd seen some large birds that could perhaps have been striges, but probably not. What else did they feed on, other than human babies? And actually, he remembered something about witches being involved, so maybe they weren't proper monsters in the first place. Maybe one of the scrolls would clarify.

"Witches" was a word that had never entered his head before, but now that it did, Avitus could only think of it with disdain. Sorcery, not proper magic. Beastly frauds with a few tricks. Market charlatans and scammers. Unwashed women in ragged robes who promised to rid a woman of her pregnancy for a price, or skinny men rattling bones at passersby, threatening them with dire fates if they didn't appease the dark powers. For only a few coins, so why take the risk?

The more he thought about it, the more indignant it made him. Wives of rich politicians scrawling curses on lead plates, thinking they were causing their husband's success. A hundred other such things. Sorcery.

Dirt laughed softly at himself, finding it silly how upset he was getting. He must have really hated them, if there was a separate word for the magic they did. If they did any at all. No, even that old anger was a kind of nostalgia. And if the idea still bothered him this much after so long, that was rather funny. Avitus was so proud of his mental discipline and maturity, and here he was losing his composure over street chanters. Dirt's grin stayed on his face for quite a while after.

He found a die carved from ivory, now yellow-brown with age, which might be the smallest thing the dryads had bothered to dig up. Màxim had a few that he kept safely hidden. He'd told Dirt that he wasn't supposed to know about them, and if the duke found out, he'd surely get in trouble. They were used for gambling, and Màxim had learned about it by watching soldiers who hadn't noticed he was around.

Dirt shook the die in his hand and rolled it on the stone floor. Four. He lifted it with his mind, rotated it, and set it down showing six instead. Now there was an idea! He spent the next little while practicing throwing the die and making it land on the number he wanted. All it took was a little nudge with his mind, but the hard part was doing it too subtly to notice.

He practiced, then read some more, then picked through the gold again and looked at the images. After a while, Home fetched him, moving stiffly and saying little. She gave him a bit more sap, encouraged him to drink a little water, and then sent him back to his villa.

It was empty, no dryads standing in the garden or at the gate. Not even inert ones. Dirt watched the minds of the nearby trees for a moment, their minds still fully engrossed in their task. He was reminded again just how immense their thoughts were and wondered why it was so complicated just to smooth out the weather. Who knew what else they might be up to, though. He could ask them tomorrow, if they weren't still at it. Or the day after.

As soon as Dirt lay in his bed of soft fibers and closed his eyes, he knew he was going to have nightmares. Just lying in the dark with his eyes closed reminded him of flying, and he could almost feel his body in motion from it. The fibers folded themselves around him almost like the air did.

But he was being silly. He was tired. Dirt calmed his mind as well as he could and drifted off to sleep.

The night was indeed fitful, and he had three separate falling dreams, waking right when he hit the ground. The first time, he was with Socks walking alongside a cliff. The second time he was climbing up the stairs along a tree and slipped and fell. The third time, the wind snatched him again.

Each time he woke he was sure he felt the impact, and as he calmed his racing heart, he wondered if he'd been hovering above his bed and then dropped into it. That didn't seem likely, though.

The fourth dream, he was fully conscious. He knew he was dreaming but didn't wake up. He stood upon hard, bare soil, with nothing but a blackness devoid of stars in every direction. He tried to dream of something else instead, but the dream resisted. He tried to wake up and couldn't do that either.

Dirt scowled at nobody. He was going to be tired and grumpy all day tomorrow, if this was how badly he was sleeping. He couldn't even dream properly!

Eyes opened in the distance, glowing red and yellow like midnight fire. The shape was familiar, and he said, "Father? Mother? Is that one of you?"

It wasn't Father or Mother, though. It was no wolf he recognized. Or even a wolf at all, perhaps, because it was inferno-filled eyes and bared fangs floating in blackness with no other features visible. No outline of black fur, no scars, no claws. If it had a body, it would have been mostly in the ground. The monstrous face glided silently toward him, eyes focused and never wavering.

It came closer and Dirt turned to flee as dread ignited into terror. The inferno in its eyes cast shadows in front of him as he went, which grew more distinct as he ran. It was catching up. It was getting closer.

Suddenly he was facing it again, unable to move. He felt hard dirt like a road under his toes, but his legs would not obey him. He looked up at the eyes filling the black sky, and the slavering fangs whose saliva sizzled and hissed when it hit the ground.

It spoke to him without words, instead using the images and scents of the thoughts of wolves. *-You have my son's scent upon you,-* it said, and Dirt recognized Father's scent in the bundle of ideas.

-You have encountered my grandchildren.- That included Socks and the other living pups. Dirt knew their scents.

The eyes and fangs drifted slowly backward, but never turned their focus from Dirt. He caught a glimpse of its hunger, its need. It had *his* scent now, Dirt knew, and would follow him. He was prey, but not the meal himself.

The dream erupted violently in a flash of chaotic light and fell apart. Dirt saw countless trees in their dream-shapes building a tree dream around him in its place. The eyes vanished, and the teeth. And the scent, and the memory, and Dirt dreamed he was one of them until morning.

irt woke with a pervading sense of being hunted and only slowly came into wakefulness. For a time, he lay perfectly still, sure that something in the room would hear him and pounce if he wasn't careful. When he finally came to, the fog was already brightening with the day, but he almost rolled over and went back to sleep in protest.

Until he remembered the dream about the wolf. It was the worst of a night full of nightmares, and he could recall every detail as if he'd been awake for it.

He quickly realized what it was. The Devourer. It had to have been the Devourer, and now Mother was going to kill him. She'd do it instantly, from wherever she was, the moment she realized. Dirt wouldn't even see it coming. He'd just be alive one moment and dead the next.

You'd think I'd be used to this, he thought to himself, putting on a half-smile in the empty room with no mirth behind it. It was a feeble attempt to smooth over his panic. *I'm always about to die.*

Dirt rolled out of bed and stood, but too much fear made it feel like he was swimming. Lingering terror from the nightmares and fresh dread of Mother. He straightened out his shirt and fidgeted with the die, which he didn't remember leaving in his pocket, and hoping he wasn't going to throw up from worry. He felt sick, and it wasn't going to go away. He was going to be like this all morning, maybe all day, if he lived that long. The dryads would notice right away and ask him, and he wouldn't be able to say anything because Mother would hear it.

He'd probably live until he returned to Socks and the pup saw it in his mind. A few days, maybe? Could he escape? Maybe he could make himself forget permanently. And then when he had the same dream again, since the Devourer had his scent, it'd be right back to this. Maybe he'd already done it once.

No, he thought with a coldly rational kind of despair, it wasn't worth it. There was no escape from Mother. Never. Best to get it over with now, before the trees learned what had killed him. They would remember him, but they wouldn't be very sad about it. They weren't capable.

And if there was one thing he trusted, it was that Mother and Father would do the best for their pups. They were never wrong, so maybe it was for the best. And maybe he deserved it for breaking the world and all those twisted, suffering gods could finally rest. He thought those things to try to gather courage, but couldn't completely make himself believe them. He wanted to live.

"Mother of Wolves," he whispered, voice scratchy and quavering, before he'd even fully committed himself in his heart. "Can you hear me? I . . ."

The words got stuck in his throat. He couldn't speak. What kind of fool *asks* to be killed? What was he thinking?

WHAT DO YOU WANT, HUMAN? ANSWER QUICKLY.

Her voice filled his head, feeling like it was squeezing his brain. This was how she'd kill him. She'd squeeze it out his ears.

"I . . ." he started, but still couldn't speak. He cleared his throat, but that just made it dry, and he coughed. Then he had no voice at all, so he whispered, "I dreamed of the Devourer. I know what he is now. He's Father's father. Please don't kill me."

I SAID I WOULD KILL YOU WHEN YOU LEARNED WHY I EAT MY CUBS. HAVE YOU LEARNED?

"No," he said, and remembered. That's what she'd said. Not just what the Devourer was—why. Why, was the important thing. He didn't know why. Relief pushed out the dread in the form of cold sweat.

THEN WHY DO YOU PESTER ME?

"I know I can't escape you. You're keeping an eye on me, even though Socks isn't around, or you wouldn't have answered," he said, the words coming easier now that he was still alive. Gods in glory, he was still alive.

"The trees gave a me clue that it was related to the Devourer and they wouldn't tell me what he was, so I thought if I ever found out—"

THE DEVOURER IS MY MATE'S SIRE. HE IS LONG DEAD, BUT NOT GONE. HE HUNTS HIS DESCENDANTS. I EAT MY PUPS BEFORE HE GETS THEM. THE ADULTS ARE TOO STRONG FOR HIM.

Dirt nodded. That was reasonable. Now that Mother said it, several things fell quickly into place, all things he would have realized before mid-morning. That was why they were so concerned about being as strong as possible. If they weren't, they'd be prey. They were prey anyway, actually, until they grew up.

HE EATS THEM TO TRY TO RETURN TO LIFE. HE MUST BE PREVENTED. YOU WOULD HAVE FIGURED THIS OUT.

The fear that had slipped away when Mother didn't annihilate him where he stood started coming back. Why was she explaining? Was she going to—

THERE IS ONE MISSING ELEMENT, AND THAT IS WHAT YOU ARE NOT ALLOWED TO KNOW. PERHAPS SOMEDAY, IF YOU EARN MY TRUST BY YOUR MERIT, YOU MAY LEARN. BUT IF YOU DO, YOU WILL NOT VIEW SOCKS THE SAME WAY. YOUR RELATIONSHIP MAY CHANGE FOR THE WORSE, AND I MIGHT CHANGE MY MIND AND KILL YOU ANYWAY. NOW GO THINK ABOUT SOMETHING ELSE.

Dirt didn't bother to thank her since she didn't want his gratitude. Just his compliance, which he was eager to offer. He raced out of his room, down the hall, and into the atrium, where he hunched over and tried not to throw up. He was still alive! Dirt had faced death too many times already, but never like this. He'd been afraid he'd starve, or bleed out, or suffocate, or get eaten. But never just that he would *die*. Never death itself, and it wasn't the same. He leaned against the wall to keep his balance until it returned, then sat on the edge of the fountain for a moment to rest and recover.

It passed soon enough, as it always did. He was safe and alive, and before long his courage returned.

Actually, Mother hadn't said, but was he in danger from the Devourer now? Or—and this seemed more likely—was Socks in greater danger of being found now that the Devourer knew to watch Dirt as well?

There were signs when the Devourer was getting close, like unnatural storms. He and Socks would be fine. Dirt would just make sure Socks didn't waste time before running away. So why would "devouring" the pups help bring a dead wolf back to life? What did they have that—

Dirt shook his head and forced himself to stop following that line of reasoning. Best not to figure it out. He knew what was going on now, and that would have to be enough.

He knew of a task that would distract him. He stopped by his room and grabbed the magical primer, then turned around and headed for the hot bath.

The bath water was still and dark, the air heavy and colder than elsewhere in the villa. That seemed inappropriate for a room like this one, where people were supposed to gather and relax. Maybe someday he could bring Ignasi and Hèctor and the duke, along with Màxim and any other people who were curious. The bath would probably seat twenty, if not more. And now that he thought about it, did men and women bathe together? He couldn't picture it. At least not with a crowd. Maybe just a few. Perhaps only families did that.

Dirt snapped his fingers to summon a light and sent it down into the water so he could see. Then he reached down with his mind and pulled out a small chunk of roof tile that had been missed, which he set aside. There were a few more, and he grabbed them one by one, feeling the curious tug of water resistance as he drew them out.

Content nothing bigger than a fingernail was left in there, he rolled through the primer until he found the water purification spell. Looking over it, it turned out he didn't need the primer anymore, since he remembered all the parts. The tricky one would be "exclude," which had to be joined to several other things to push everything that wasn't water, out of the water. Still, nothing serious.

What he wanted to try was doing the whole spell without any of the drawings, or the chalk and wand and candles or gem, and still direct it at the correct water. It was more complex than his little light, or the wood-shaping spell, but the accessories were just to help the wizard's mind. They surely had no effect themselves, although Avitus might not have known that. Or anyone else. They thought putting pure chalk in the middle of the "exclude" sigil told the spell to act on elemental earth. At least that's what the primer said. Dirt knew better.

He focused, and the whole spell came to his mind, long-forgotten training making itself useful again, coupled with recent practice. He pressed it onto his mana vessel, manifesting it into the world of magic. Once everything was ready, he squatted down and dipped his finger into the water, in place of the wand he was supposed to use. He filled the spell with mana and directed the effect into the bath.

The spell worked perfectly, which surprised him. It was a complex one, but ultimately it hadn't been hard at all! Maybe he shouldn't have been surprised after doing the spell that made all the grain grow, although that had been largely intuition.

The grime and dirt and rotting fern leaves and everything else floated to the top and gathered into a dark, repulsive, brownish-gray foam. Larger bits, like pebbles and sand, leaped out of the water like it was spitting them. If they landed back in the bath, they bounced along the surface until they stuck to the foam. Dirt kept mana channeling through it until no more bubbles rose from the bottom and the water quit reacting.

He scooped the filth from the top of the water with his mind and tossed it out through the gaps in the roof. His little light swimming through the water showed it to be clean and pure. Even the grime stuck to the bottom surface was gone now, leaving it bright as fresh marble.

Dirt rolled the scroll up, quite pleased with himself. Then an idea struck him and he left the villa at a run. He went a few houses up the street and entered the empty gateway, and sure enough, a dingy statue stood in the garden. It depicted a hunter with a drawn bow, muscles in his back and legs as taut as the long-vanished string. Even the bow was gone, probably rusted into nothing, but the marble was in good condition.

He made a minor adjustment to the water purification spell, replacing the sigil for "water" with "stone." From there, he improvised adding modifications he hoped would clear the surface, not the interior. Naturally, it wouldn't do to try this on *his* statues first. It might make them explode, for all he knew.

The spell worked exactly like he imagined it, although the mana had trouble flowing properly at first until he made some adjustments. But a single tap was all it took to get every last bit of dirt to flake off and fall to the ground. Very little mana, in fact. The statue's surface was flawless now, clear and bright as the day it was carved. All he needed was someone to paint it, and—

Dirt paused and stepped back. They used to paint these, didn't they? He had to pick through Prisca's memories, but it didn't take long to find the answer. They were indeed painted. Even the carvings on buildings were. Everything was painted, colorful and vibrant.

Peering around with fresh eyes, the remains of the city looked even more barren than before. The stately buildings and fine stonework, straight roads and charming symmetry, the pale gray concrete and faded frescoes, it all just looked like bones now. A grave of a place with all the flesh rotted away, like a tomb.

Well, that's what it was. Maybe someday people would live here again and he could get them to start painting things. But for now, Dirt rather liked the unobtrusiveness of the bone-white buildings everywhere. Color would be out of place here. And it wouldn't look right without any sunlight anyway.

Dirt felt a tap on his shoulder and jumped about ten feet in the air, since he still had leftover mana in him. He was laughing before he landed, though, and so was Callius, as naturally as ever.

"Are you alright, friend Dirt? Not nervous about anything?" asked the dryad.

"No, I'm fine. Can I have some sap? And then, do you have any tips on what I should say to the elemental? What do you and she talk about?" said Dirt, checking behind him for Dawn sneaking up to get him again, since it was something she'd do.

Callius held his hand out, and a healthy glob of sap appeared, which Dirt took and ate a bit more quickly than was probably good for him, but he couldn't help himself. He needed to eat. "Tell me, friend Dirt, did you have any strange dreams last night?"

Dirt stopped chewing, then chewed faster and swallowed so he could speak. "Oh, you know about that?"

"Tell me what you dreamed of," said Callius, his voice a bit more urgent than usual, despite his impish, easy demeanor.

"I was visited by the Devourer, so I know what he is now. He said he had my scent. I already spoke to Mother about it, and she said she wasn't going to kill me because that wasn't the secret."

Callius scowled, perhaps the first time Dirt had ever seen him make that face. Or any of them, for that matter. He looked upset.

"Why do you ask?" said Dirt.

"Because we normally keep things like him out, but in our haste to regulate the environment, our defenses were lax. We didn't realize until we sensed your distress in the dream," said Callius.

"Well, I'm fine now, so thanks for rescuing me once you realized. It was not a fun dream to have," said Dirt. Then he took another big bite of sap.

"Did the Mother of Wolves say anything else to you?"

"She said that the Devourer wants to eat the pups so he can come back to life, but there's a secret about that, and that's what I can't ever find out. So if you know, don't tell me," said Dirt.

"We know," said Callius. "And we will not tell you. We judge that the Mother of Wolves was correct, and it is a secret best left kept for now."

"Well, I'm doing my best not to think about it. Other than, I hope someday I can get rid of the Devourer somehow, like I chased off those ghosts in Llovella. So how's the weather fixing going? Do you have it back under control? Everything seems normal now," said Dirt.

"We're getting close. It would not do to allow a disruption so close to winter. A freeze would be destructive here. But do not fret over that, little Dirt. There is nothing you can do to help."

"What do you do in the winter, anyway? Do you use magic to generate heat to stay warm?"

"I think that would be a more complicated answer than you are expecting," said Callius. "We can spend all morning on it if you wish."

Dirt did not wish. "Where is everyone else, by the way? Still working?"

"Still working."

"Okay. Can you take me back up to talk to the elemental again?"

"Yes. We have spoken with her in the meantime, and she regrets the distress she caused you. Sort of. Her relation to emotion is different from ours, and yours. But she will not lift you up again unless you ask very clearly," said Callius. "We told her you will do more listening than speaking, so pay attention."

He reached forward to take Dirt's hand and pull him with root travel, but Dirt caught his wrist first. "One quick question. Is she just like you, happy all the time?"

Callius tilted his head, sort of like Socks did when he was curious about something. "Not exactly. We do not understand loss or pain, since we have no natural faculty to experience those things. But she understands them and is not affected. She remembers everything she touches. Any time a word is spoken in her wind, any time her breeze passes over a hunter and his prey, everything. She knows and understands it all. She can tell you nearly anything you wish to learn, if you know how to ask."

The dryad stretched out his arms and let his fingers drift over Dirt's face, and the nearby ferns, and even the statue. He moved gracefully, like a dance, which carried him all around the garden. "She is like the Father of Wolves—older than this world. Over countless years, she has seen all there is to see, but no matter what, she must keep moving. The wind must always blow. She cannot be slowed by grief or pleasure. That's what she is. She can never stop."

"So," said Callius, slowing to stillness, "she just doesn't let it affect her when something happens, good or bad. Most of her mind isn't even here. The physical is more like a dream to her than anything. She knows it all, sees it all, remembers everything. But her true self is not in the physical. The elementals live in the world of magic."

Then Callius did an impressive backward cartwheel, and Dirt suspected he wasn't really trying to demonstrate, just that he liked to move. Which he did.

"I suppose I should tell you one last thing. If you speak aloud, she will hear your words and know them, but she will never think about them. They will become part of her memory, but her relation to memory is not like yours, and you cannot measure her using yourself as a metric. You must speak to her in her world, in terms of the process and the power. That she will understand. Now, are you ready?" said Callius, his face lighting up like Màxim's did when he proposed a new game. Exactly like it, in fact.

Dirt shoved the last of the sap in his mouth, chewed hard, and said, "Let's go."

Root travel carried them to the top of a tree, but Dirt wasn't quite sure which one until he looked at her mind. Starwatcher again. He wondered if they kept picking her because she was closer friends with the great elemental than the others. She was only barely aware of him, focused instead on the great work of the forest.

The elemental was there waiting, as much as she was anywhere. But no wind reached the leaves—it was all higher, blowing overhead. Dirt couldn't even hear it, and if not for his mind-sight he might not know she was here at all.

A new branch grew where Dirt was perched, just wide enough for him to stand on. He ducked down to keep his balance until it stopped moving, a dozen paces above the treetops. It felt precarious, but Callius was watching intently and would probably catch him if he fell.

Dirt carefully got back up, and only once he was fully standing did he feel the breeze. The trees had lifted him just high enough to feel it gently in his hair. He felt nothing on his pants.

He sent her a warm emotion of greeting, directly to her mind, accompanied by her perception of his face in her air. Her attention increased, and Dirt got the impression that the entire sky had perked up in curiosity, which was an amusing picture.

Dirt closed his eyes and looked with his mind-sight and mana body. He manifested the sigil for "beginning a new process," but left it open and unpowered.

The elemental grabbed hold of it immediately and drew more in countless, expanding patterns. Sigils rotated around each other, and tiny flares of mana caused brief sensations that tickled his awareness. He saw much that he recognized, although far from all. But here was "wind" and there was "increase" and . . .

Oh, she was talking about carrying him away! Now that he knew what she meant, it was easier to follow. Her story was a recitation of a continual process, describing how it happened more than why. This section described how much wind power it took to lift him, with a portion dedicated to the wind sliding off his skinny body and smooth skin, which made it harder. Then over here, she was telling him what direction they'd gone, and he learned several new sigils related to navigation.

With his mind-sight, he could sense some of her emotion, which turned out to be more like nostalgia than novelty, which surprised him. Was he not the first human she'd talked to? There was a sense of familiarity that had no other explanation.

Her story continued, and he saw how she recognized that he was freezing and the cold was hurting his skin. From that, he learned four new sigils related to temperature and a new configuration of sigils that would indicate skin, by how it naturally functioned.

By the time she was done, Dirt was sure he'd missed more than he'd learned, but even so, he had learned quite a bit. He sent her a poof of gratitude, since he had no other way to say thank you. She drew a new sigil for him, two of them. "Gainful" and "closure at the end of an increase." He repeated them back to her. Now that, at least, was simple. Magical thank you.

Other elementals gathered all the while, small gusts and zephyrs that reminded Dirt of puppies racing around their mother. Mostly they played with each other, but always returned their attention to her and what she was doing.

The great elemental drew "beginning a new process" for him, and he hesitated while trying to figure out what to do with it. What should he say? He pictured the towers of the palace in Ogena, tall and thin as they reached up into the sky. Then he tried to draw them for her, carefully describing them with sigils in terms of how the air would flow around them.

He was just starting to feel like he'd gotten the hang of it when she picked up on what he was doing and started filling in the details with dazzling accuracy and complexity. She drew much of the city, including the walls, in a greater array of sigils and shapes than his poor little mind could take in. But if he looked carefully, he could see the people moving along the streets by the disturbance they made in the air. Not well enough to tell them apart, but it was captivating nonetheless.

Dirt tried something else and began describing Socks, showing his shape and his shaggy fur. Even his color, since Dirt knew sigils that could get pretty close. Once again, she understood and filled in the rest, and Dirt recognized his big friend perfectly. He knew every detail already, from the shape of his nose to the length of his snout, to the size of the scratches his claws left when he ran. Everything. And so did she.

She left the array open, waiting for him to act on it somehow and explain what he wanted. Dirt puzzled over it for a moment and then grinned mischievously. He drew the sigils for motion and air and said, "Hello Socks! You're not imagining this. See you soon!"

It took her quite a bit of analysis, which he could only weakly help with, to understand what he meant. He suspected she never considered the meaning of the words, just the way they affected the air. But once she got the idea, she answered with only a few simple sigils: "delay" and "distant" and "pass between separate segments." Her mind grew distant, the vast light of it that stretched from horizon to horizon fading.

The air went still as she and all the little elementals withdrew. Dirt waited for a bit, wondering if it was over. He counted to a hundred before he started looking around and thinking about how he was going to get down. Should he yell to Callius, or just jump down there to be caught?

But then she came rushing back, a strong gust that almost tipped him over. He drew the opening sigil again and awaited her explanation, which came quickly. Then Dirt laughed, loud and hard. He'd startled Socks so bad the pup had jumped in the air and yelped. That was it, just the pup leaping up into the breeze and the pathetic sound he made. Serves him right, after doing that to Dirt so many times!

Dirt thanked her and ended the conversation. He'd want to do this more and learn all he could and become her friend, but for now, he had to tell someone about the prank he'd just pulled. That couldn't wait.

CHAPTER TWELVE

Callius listened to the story with patient humor and laughed along convincingly when Dirt mimicked the sound Socks made and how he jumped in the air. Dirt was unconvinced he found it as funny as he acted, but without Callius's tree nearby to see his mind, there was no way to be sure.

After that, the trees sent him back to the schola while they resumed fixing the climate, which was perfect, since that gave him the whole rest of the day for his plans.

First, he rummaged through the scrolls in the library until he found blank paper in usable condition. It was only barely holding together, but it would be good enough for this, and he could show it to the trees and have them make more, once they were done with their work.

He sorted through the boxes in the main hall until he found a compass and ruler. After that, a pen made of ivory and brass, which he placed atop one of the ancient tables.

With everything else in place, he went from table to table until he found the last thing he needed: an inkwell. Only when he found one did he finally realize the problem. The ink was dry. Of course it was. He checked several more, and obviously, they were all dry.

He took one out to the garden and added a few drops of water from the basin, but the ink was beyond saving.

Dirt stood there for a moment, staring at nothing. How was he supposed to write down everything he'd just learned to make sure he remembered it? He'd probably remember most of it regardless, but still, he wanted to try drawing the sigils.

Should he use blood? No, probably not. He might need a lot, and the trees would get mad at him. That, and Socks wasn't around to lick his cuts, and it would hurt. So, what else could he use? Ferns? Mud?

Ferns would work. Dirt knew ink could be made from plants like flowers and berries. He just didn't know how. So then it was back to the library to see if he could find the method written down somewhere. And if not that, then maybe someone knew in Ogena, and he could go visit by root travel and ask around. It'd been several weeks since he'd left, so they might be happy to see him.

He didn't find the answer, though, because he soon got distracted reading other things. Someone had left a text on history open to a part about a war, which quickly captured his interest.

It told of Emperor Hostilius and his battles against the horsemen of the vast western plains, the Ceremisian tribes. The Sunset Empire lost every battle because the horsemen never properly lined up to fight, pre-ferring instead to ride by on their horses and shoot arrows from their clever bows. Twice, the losses were so bad the empire had to leave and come back next year with fresh troops. The war lasted fifteen years, and the most interesting thing was how it ended:

That was the last battle the emperor fought against the plainsmen, for no further conflict was required despite the indecisive outcome. For Hostilius had seen farther than they and planned more cleverly, with greater wisdom than all their elders possessed. Our armies never once truly bested theirs, but it was our preparations that brought about their defeat.

I told you of the fortifications he built at Quintus and Septus, at Terraco and Scalabis and Sorviodurum. He built many more walled towns besides, all the first settled places on these stretches of earth. Each town was given supplies sufficient to outlast any sieges until the armies could return, and their walls were high, proof against horsemen and arrows. I spoke also of the roads he laid down at great expense. Aqueducts were built, and irrigation dug.

Beside these, I told you of the groves of olives and grapes, the fruits of which he let be sold very cheaply to the barbarians, even at a loss, to give them a taste of civilization. But for this foresight, the gods would not have had opportunity to give us their blessing in the death of the first khan, whose brother ordered the groves be untouched so he could gather their fruit for himself.

Hostilius decreed that despite ongoing bloodshed, the gates were open to any Ceremisians who came unarmed in small numbers, and instructed the citizens to welcome them with friendly hands and words of respect for their virility and prowess in battle. He let it be known that any barbarian who wished to become a citizen would be welcomed, and his wives and children be retained as his own. By this, he led the barbarians to believe that our empire was not worried about them, and that they were perhaps not truly a threat to us.

When the horsemen came to graze upon the land they previously held, even if they encircled the walls of a city, they were unmolested if they did no harm to the citizens. The emperor provided gifts to be given out by free men, to make it seem to the barbarians that our people lived easily, surrounded by all the riches they themselves desired to take by force, with such abundance that every man could afford to give away a portion with no regard for repayment.

Should any hostility be shown, the citizens summoned men with bows and armor to drive them off, focusing on killing their horses and capturing the riders for sale as slaves. If no sufficient number of soldiers could be called, the citizens took their goods inside the town and shut the gates. They were then made to be seen atop the walls, feasting and singing and laughing.

Those Ceremisians who knelt before our glorious emperor were given education, particularly their children, at public expense. They were given shelter and food for their horses and praised for their husbandry. Thus they were made comfortable and pliable. They were made harmless by telling them they need never hunt again, in token of which they should give up their bows. Additionally, they were not allowed to live together in numbers greater than fifty, instead being quietly distributed throughout the empire, some given lands, others not. In this manner, if a Ceremisian proved himself intractable or unsuited, he could be slain or enslaved without his kinsmen coming to know of it.

Only slowly did the independent Ceremisians come to understand how thoroughly they were defeated. Thousands defected each year for a better life, or what they were led to believe would be better. Great portions of their plains had already become ours, despite our inability to conquer them in battle. They allowed this to happen because they focused on what remained—not what they had lost—and measured it sufficient for their current needs.

Never again did a great khan rise to gather them to war. Every further action against us was a raid of little significance. Now our empire stretches across the entirety of the plains to the far coast. The Ceremisians have ceased to be a people, their language seldom heard.

Had they come at first in their full strength to the center of the Sunset Empire, with armies full of men and stomachs full of meat, they could have defeated us. Had they other neighbors to conquer first and thus overwhelm us with numbers, we might have been totally overrun. Indeed, had they focused their efforts on preventing resupply instead of capturing wealth, we might still be at war centuries later.

I suggest that the true cause of their downfall was not the greater appeal our culture held. Nor was it the decay of their martial prowess as the available grazing lands for their horses diminished. Nor was it their inability to push us thoroughly beyond their borders during those fifteen years of constant warfare.

It was this: They lost their conquering spirit, because they believed they had more to gain without it. Our lands remain vulnerable even now to a foe such as they were—mobile, with equal willingness to slaughter a defeated population as to subdue them, and no reliance on complex infrastructure.

For many centuries before these wars, our civilization paid them bribes to assuage their greed and bloodlust, even though they seldom united into anything truly formidable. The belief that a khan *might* arise among them was sufficient to open our pockets. And it was never a false belief. Their outlook and practices remained unchanged from the time the gods first led them into those grasslands and gave them their first horses, until Hostilius.

I shall demur rather than say more on this at this time. The reader has sufficient insight to shake out what further wisdom may be gleaned from these events.

Dirt quietly rolled the two halves of the scroll together again, leaving it in the same spot so he could reread it later. He set it down and stared at it for a time, contemplating what there was to learn. It was certainly relevant, even if it wasn't the same as what was happening now. But losing their conquering spirit? That sounded exactly like what Dirt had observed. If any remained, it was a fading ember. A few sparks drifting on the night air.

Sparks named Hèctor, Marina, and to a smaller degree, Ignasi. And the duke, now that he'd ridden into battle himself. And Dirt, for what it was worth. Little Dirt, the spark, because a part of him still remembered what humans were capable of.

Perhaps a conquering spirit would match well with a wolf. Dirt wasn't a predator—that was silly; he didn't even have claws—but human greatness was something different. Socks, the great hunter, and Dirt, the conqueror. The spark.

Dirt slid off the chair and rummaged around until he found the basket of toy soldiers. There were nine of them, just shorter than his hand, and one charioteer with two horses. They were tin and brass, and if they'd even been used as toys, the boy had been wealthy. It was just as likely they were table decorations, but Dirt didn't care.

He lined them up, giving the chariot to the Ceremisian side since they were horsemen, and staged a little battle. This one was the emperor, and he stepped forward and gave a speech about giving up their warfare and becoming citizens. The one in the chariot was the khan, who replied with a passionate speech of his own about respecting their lands and traditions.

Then they fought, and Dirt stepped through each swing of the sword for each pair of fighters, resolving them separately while considering how it affected the battle overall. The Ceremisians won, of course, but the emperor got away and vowed to come back with another army. "Come back, then!" shouted Dirt, loud enough to echo in the hall. His voice startled him. He hadn't realized he'd been talking out loud.

Well, it wasn't like anyone was around to hear him. After that he reenacted each battle he could remember from the text, taking plenty of liberties. Some of which because he had almost no idea how either side actually waged war, having only the Camayan knights to draw on, and some of which because it was a game and he could do as he pleased.

The game was even more realistic when he stopped using his hands and started using his mind to move them around, such as sliding them on the ground and imagining them walking. It was hard to move two at once, no matter how easy Socks made it look, but he managed where necessary.

After that, he wasted the rest of the day in pleasant distraction. He spent some time playing with the toys he could find among the treasure or reading things that weren't magic and didn't count as studying. Home was still sitting out in the schola's immense garden, on the same stone bench, and he asked her for meals twice before the day ended.

He took another hot bath before bed that night, soaking long enough for his fingers to pickle, long enough for the trees to sleep. Once he crawled out, it took him a while to dry off, just standing there with one of his little lights to keep him company. Dirt resolved to remember to ask them for a towel in the morning, since they knew how to make cloth now. Thank Grace, once he slept, there were no nightmares. Just snippets of dreams that fled faster than the morning dew.

The next day passed much like that one, talking to the wind in the morning and learning a bit more, then wandering the ruins and looking at the murals and sculptures, then reading in the schola, then taking another long bath.

The following day was much the same, and Dirt was starting to itch from too much time alone. He kept thinking about Socks, too, hoping he was all right. The lack of news bothered him, even though it shouldn't. Where could Socks be safer than running around with Father?

But the day after that, the trees all woke with him in the morning, filling his garden and the road in front of it with their dryads before he even rolled out of bed. He wasn't expecting their faces peering in the doorway and startled when he saw them, then broke into a wide smile.

"Hello, everyone! Looks like you fixed the weather?" he said, arms outstretched to welcome them.

Home stood taller than the rest and stepped forward to gather him to her bosom in a motherly way. She hugged him gently and said, "Our work is complete. The oncoming winter will pass us by. We hope you do not feel too neglected. Are you still in good spirits, dear Dirt?"

She was putting a lot of effort into her dryad at the moment, even mimicking the layer of fat under the skin of her back when Dirt returned her hug. Only the fact that she was the same temperature as the ground gave it away.

"I'm fine. I had a lot to do, and I know you were busy. I'd hate to visit in the winter and find the ground frozen and all the ferns dead. And the grubs. Whatever happened to them? I haven't seen them in a while," said Dirt.

"You'll find out in the spring. We don't want to ruin the surprise," said Callius.

"What's surprising about a grub?" asked Dirt. But he got no answer. Home released him, and then it was Sunset's turn for a hug, then Dawn's, then Chaser's, and after that, Dirt got passed around for quite a while, since every last dryad was here. By the end, Dirt wished he'd thought to count so he'd know how many there were.

They played hide and hunt after that, dodging in and out of the buildings and ducking beneath the ferns alongside the roads or in gardens. When it was the trees' turn to hunt, they all hunted, and when it was his, he had to find ten of them, which wasn't easy. The only advantage he had was that not all of them understood perspective and didn't realize when part of them was still visible. Jumping from stone to stone and roof to roof made it hard to track him by the ferns, but they often did the same thing. They even caught him lying flat on a roof, and Dirt had to wonder if someone had put eyes on their tree trunk to find him from above.

Around midday, a sudden bout of anxiety hit him and ruined the fun. He didn't let on, since his mind couldn't make sense of it. He knew he was being silly but ended the game anyway, claiming hunger as an excuse. He ate a hearty meal of sap while sitting in an area that had been a circular park once, not far from his villa. The dryads sat around him in crowded rings, all trying to act leisurely while watching everything he did.

Dirt ate slowly, waiting for whatever was bothering him to manifest. One thing occurred to him, and he asked, "Hey, Home, is Socks by your staff we left behind? Do you know what he's up to?"

"I have not seen him since the first day. The pack left the area, and I have not tracked them. The Father of Wolves will return him when it is time to reunite you."

"Yeah. I was just thinking about him. We're going to travel south soon, where there's a desert. So that's exciting. I hope we find more humans there, and fewer monsters," said Dirt.

The dryads nodded politely, and Dirt wondered if they'd known. Father spoke directly to his mind, and Home's staff couldn't read that. He explained, "Father gave Socks the choice to go north for the winter, or south, and he picked south so I could come. Winter in the north is too cold, and I'd probably freeze, so I wouldn't have been able to go. Hopefully after winter, we'll be allowed to go wherever we want again, because I think we were getting close to the Camayan kingdom's capital before we had to go meet Father."

Dirt took another bite, which he chewed more slowly, trying not to feel worried without a good reason. "We weren't really hurrying, though."

Even so, he felt increasingly uneasy the longer he sat. It wasn't restlessness anymore. Something was wrong, and there was no telling what it was. He could simply feel it. "Are you sure Socks isn't there? Is he okay?"

"I am sure that I do not know, dear Dirt. I will let—" said Home, pausing. She went inert, all the life vanishing and turning her dryad back into unmoving wood. She was thinking, Dirt knew. Focusing harder than usual.

She came back to life and put a worried look on her face. "Socks has found my staff, and he looks frantic. I will send you to him. How did you know?"

Dirt nodded, steeling himself. "I just knew somehow. Send me now."

The world vanished, and he shot forward at impossible speed. A moment later, he tumbled hard onto lumpy ground, and a blast of cold air hit him. He groaned, dazed, and opened his eyes. It was dimmer than last time, sky overcast with low, heavy clouds. Which

Dirt appreciated, since sudden bright light would have given him a headache.

Socks stepped back and forth, indeed frantic. His siblings were nowhere to be seen. As soon as he smelled Dirt, he practically leaped on him, stopping with his nose inches from his face. His mental voice came scared and small, full of worry. *-Help!-*

CHAPTER THIRTEEN

-Get up. Hurry! You need to come.-

"I don't know what help I'll be, but I'll try my best," said Dirt. He knelt and picked up the Home-staff, still in the shape of an arm brace, slipped it on, and patted it fondly. He'd ask her to change shapes later, when it was more convenient.

-Get on. We can't find Father. And Big Sister is gone,- said Socks. *-We don't know what to do.-*

The pup turned around, and Dirt used mana to jump on just in time to grab the harness for a run. Socks was certainly not wasting any time. Dirt hunkered down, and Socks left at a full sprint. The rushing wind and sheer speed reminded him of flying with the elemental, which revived a physical memory of terror that he had to push down.

-Why are your fingertips sore? And your toes, too. What have you been doing with the trees?- asked Socks. He slowed slightly, but sped back up once he noticed.

"*They had me try to learn to speak with an air elemental, a big one that I think is a mother of smaller winds. I'm getting the hang of it, but, well . . .*" said Dirt. "*We had a little misunderstanding that resulted in her lifting me into the sky and tossing me around. She thought I wanted to fly. But anyway, it was cold up there, and I wasn't dressed, and the cold got to me. But it's not bad. I'm fine.*"

-It seems like every time you visit them, something horrible happens,- said Socks.

Dirt chuckled into Socks's fur, enjoying the fact he could keep his eyes closed and not be terrified he was about to hit something and die. *"It really does. But I still love them. I'm glad I went. I can't wait to show you . . . Oh! Okay, don't look at this. I want it to be a surprise. I have something really, really great to show you."* He did his best to lock away the disinterred city, all its handsome buildings and roads restored to their proper places. And in particular, he buried the memory of his hot bath so tightly he almost forgot about it himself. *"You're gonna love it."*

-*I'm not in the mood to love anything right now. I am too worried.*-

"Sorry. So what's going on? Where are we going?"

-*There's an old place that Father said he hasn't seen in a long time, and he said all sorts of old things are coming back now, like little Dirt from ancient days. So he decided to show us. He was in a good mood because his pups are strong. But then he disappeared. And so did Big Sister, who followed right after him.*-

"What do you mean he disappeared? He ran away, or he fell in a hole, or something like that?"

-*I mean just what I said,*- snapped Socks. Then he felt chagrined for speaking sharply, but Dirt sent him a puff of reassurance. He understood perfectly; there was no need to explain.

Socks shared the rest with images instead of words. He saw Father from the pup's perspective, slightly smaller but not by much. And Big Sister walking like all the other pups did—mostly following, but stepping this way or that to smell something interesting or look behind a rock. Sometimes ahead, sometimes rushing to catch up. But for now, she was only a few steps behind her sire, and was the closest.

The great black wolf stepped lightly between two square monoliths that guarded the entrance. Inside was a perfectly circular valley nestled up in an expanse of sharp, rocky hills. A great wind went before him and threw several millennia's worth of drifted sand and weeds into a towering cloud that drifted out of sight. A faint dome of light covered the circular valley, and ripples of disturbed force spread like waves on water wherever anything larger than a mouse passed through it.

Father spoke to his children without words, sending pictures and scents and emotions instead. His voice sounded very different from Socks's perspective. It was warm and strong and not the least threatening. The meaning was perfectly clear: *HUMANS DID NOT BUILD*

THIS. OLDER CREATURES DID, AND THEY WERE NO FRIENDS TO OUR KIND. BUT WE REMAIN, AND THEY DO NOT. THEY WERE HUMAN SIZE, SO THIS PLACE IS SMALL.

It didn't look small to Socks. It looked as big as a city, a great big circular one, with sections containing an exciting variety of things. The buildings were so old they hardly looked like buildings anymore, with solitary pillars of lichen-painted stone standing here and there, amongst piles of debris so decayed they might never have been part of anything at all.

Underneath it all, the roads were still intact. Or perhaps the entire city was built on a stone platform. Either way, it was more impressive than any of the human roads and might have put their fine buildings to shame if everything was all still standing. The architectural style was bizarre, with long, exact lines and curves tracing across great distances of unbroken roadway. The ground was all intact, one single piece.

Socks sniffed at the old dust and smelled traces of little mammals and birds, larval insects, and drifted leaves. Nothing big, though. Not even a curious wolf.

THIS PLACE HASN'T BEEN ACTIVE FOR—

And then he was gone. Father vanished without a trace except a whiff of air that smelled like it came from somewhere else. Not even a scent of surprise left behind. Big Sister, in shock, stepped over to where he had been and disappeared as well.

Socks looked at his siblings—Big Brother, Brother, and Sister—and they were as stunned as he was.

-And that was what happened. I was the farthest away, so I told them to sit down and wait while I went to get my human. Only one of us should risk moving, and I was the only one with somewhere to go. We have tried to speak to Mother, but she is resting now and does not hear us,- said Socks. *-I came to get you because I don't know what else to do.-*

"*I can't imagine anything happening to Father that he didn't want to have happen,*" said Dirt.

-Me neither,- said Socks, his voice full of worry, which floated across a deeper cavern of quietly rumbling terror. Dirt recognized it. That's what had been nagging at him earlier, that feeling. It had belonged to Socks after all.

They left the rest unsaid. Dirt sent puffs of encouragement to Socks, but they just made him feel worse, because neither of them truly had much hope. Instead, the idea of Father being gone sank in more and more, and the world became an empty, terrifying, hostile place. How was that even possible? It was more likely they'd wake up and the sky would be green, than that Father could disappear.

It was a long run from there, a cold one through an icy wind that smelled like snow. Dirt stayed warm by hunkering down, his fingers dug into Socks's fur. What few shaggy late-autumn leaves still clung to the trees and brush looked wilted now, wind-blown and tired. The grasses, once yellow and stiff, were gray and sagging.

Socks ran over a high and rocky landscape, through hills and along the foothills of long mountains with crests of brown rock. Twice the pup became so distraught that he forgot to cycle mana and suddenly found himself too tired to run until he caught his breath.

Dusk arrived too quickly, but not before they arrived. Socks's siblings sensed his coming and sent their worried greetings, just thoughts at first in the way of wolves, then adding words for Dirt's benefit.

-YOU WERE GONE A LONG TIME-, said Big Brother.

-I'm back now, though,- replied Socks. He approached the two obsidian pillars, a material Dirt recognized but had never thought about before, and smelled the crosswind before stepping through the gap.

That gave Dirt just long enough to see the markings, which none of the wolves had cared enough to look at, including Socks. It might have been writing, but if it was, the script was ridiculous. Instead of nice, clean, separate lines to draw a letter, these markings were far too flowing, too flowery, like cursive that had gotten out of control. They swooped decoratively and had too many curves and stray dots, all of which would make it hard to read or to carve them. But if not writing, Dirt couldn't guess what it could be instead.

From the outside, there wasn't much else to see. The rocky hills rose steeply beside either pillar, quickly becoming taller than even Father, and the gap shimmered, like seeing through fog so faint that Dirt might not have noticed if he hadn't been looking for it.

Socks didn't smell any approaching danger, so in they went. The inside was just as Socks had shown him, a city not quite as large as Ogena with its walls, but larger than Llovella. The stone inside wasn't black obsidian like the entrance pillars—it was all a neutral gray, granite probably, dirty and lichen-covered with age.

Looking around, Dirt wasn't convinced that anyone had ever lived here. Rough gray monoliths dotted the area, surrounded by piles of rubble and broken stone. It seemed more like a wasteland than a ruined city. Nothing even looked like a building anymore. The area was strangely dry, the air quiet and unmoving, and despite the cold wind just a moment before, it was warmer here. The sky was blue and barren overhead, the sun already sunken past the ring of hills that made up the horizon.

The most notable thing to see was the three other wolves, Big Brother and the other two who were Socks's size. They looked a lot less confident than when he'd seen them last.

Dirt sent the other pups a quick mental greeting, then slid off Socks and walked back to the two obsidian pillars to take a closer look. He turned his gaze inward, onto his mana body.

Just as he suspected, something was happening with the pillars. They were an active working of magic, almost certainly tied to others around the perimeter; but what their precise purpose was, he couldn't tell. Something about the air, that was part of it. Holding it steady and keeping it clean, which made sense. But still letting it . . . talk, maybe? Exchange something? With the air outside the dome.

That part of the spell probably anchored it into the pillars, and a carefully balanced array of sigils drew a perfect stream of power to keep it going. There were plenty of new ones, but the strangest thing about them was how they were only partially anchored in the stone. From what he knew, if you wanted a spell to stay there, you had to draw the whole thing, and there was no way for it to gather any mana on its own. If Dirt could learn how this worked, then his bath would stay warm forever, all by itself!

Socks nudged him anxiously from behind, and Dirt said, *"Sorry. I was just trying to figure out what magic is happening here. How close do you think we can get to where Father and Sister disappeared without disappearing ourselves?"*

The pup picked Dirt up with his mind and put him on his back, then headed toward the center of the circular town at a jog.

-WHAT CAN DIRT DO THAT WILL HELP?- asked Big Brother.

-My little human is clever, and we have no one else to ask. We will see together if he can help,- said Socks.

-Do not disappear,- said Sister, and Dirt could tell she was sick to watch Socks risking everything by running around. Dirt realized that's why the others were all just sitting there—they didn't dare move and in so doing, disappear like Father had.

What could Dirt say to comfort any of them? They weren't stupid. Dirt and Socks would be no match for anything that could surprise Father. But neither should they give in to despair, not until they saw a corpse.

He watched the lines on the street as they ran, long and perfect. Somehow, none of the ground had been damaged while everything else decayed. Dirt looked with his mana body and saw nothing. If there was some great working engraved here, it was either broken or too large for him to perceive.

Still, he suspected there was something going on, because the lines themselves looked like an artistic rendering of the kind of enchantment he was familiar with. At their scale, the entire *city* might be a spell. It might not even be a city at all. Maybe no one had ever lived here in the first place.

Although that didn't make sense. They were clearly on a road, one very similar in width to any from the Sunset Empire. And those monoliths might have supported wooden constructions that decayed in the eons since they were abandoned. Who could tell? Was that gap a doorway? Socks wasn't about to stop and let him poke around and think about it.

Dirt could believe, however, that it wasn't a human place. It might not have occurred to him if Father hadn't said so, but something about it seemed to unnerve him. Something about how it was laid out bothered him, like a triangle with one corner not quite joined. He wished there was even a single statue to see what the creatures who built it looked like.

The spot where Father and Sister disappeared was on the far third of the circle, and along the way, they crossed the center of the city, an array of joining sigils decorating a great plaza. The creatures probably walked all over it with impunity, if the stone was still in such good shape even now. Father's wind had cleaned all the dust out of the grooves, and Dirt recognized a few sigils for direction. The spell here had no power in it, though. There was nothing to see with his mana body beyond the faint and subtle workings of regular physical existence.

They stopped at the edge of another plaza, this one square, with a clear area large enough for Father to lie down in. The stone was bare except a wide U shape inside an indented border.

-*Here. I think it was here,*- said Socks. He sniffed around and told Dirt and his siblings what scents he found. Father, Big Sister, and hints of plants Socks didn't recognize, so faint he could only barely perceive them.

Dirt wondered if the wolves got turned into plants, but that wasn't it. There weren't any here. So where did that smell come from?

There were no other traces. No bones, blood, or fur. Not even a scent of pain or fear from Father or Big Sister.

Socks keened softly, his fear growing after finding not a single clue about what had happened. Dirt slid down again and the pup put a wall of mental force in front of him to keep his pet from taking even one step forward. Dirt patted Socks's foreleg. He wasn't going anywhere.

The enchantment surely had something to do with it, even if it was inactive. Even if he knew all the sigils that comprised it, it was too large for Dirt to see all of. Or even most of it. Just a few sigils joining a larger working to this spot. And most of those were only half-manifested and unreadable; they contained a little mana, but it was weak and sputtering, exhausted and unable to renew itself.

Dirt told everyone, *"My guess is, whatever happened probably took a very, very long time to charge up. Father might not have known this was here or that it would do anything, if he wasn't actively looking. It's also possible he knew and did it on purpose. You should all be safe if you don't step anywhere that has a symbol like this. You can come out if you want."*

The other pups gingerly stepped out from where they'd been perched for hours, stretching and shaking their fur as they did. Once they were convinced nothing would happen, they visibly cheered up.

He and Socks looked at each other, and Dirt smiled and jerked his head in their direction. Socks left at a run to go comfort his siblings. They met in the plaza in the center and began licking each other's snouts and rubbing their faces and shoulders together as if they had all escaped grave peril. Which they might have.

Dirt picked a line and followed it, wondering where it would end up. Only a few spaces over amongst the rubble, he saw a partially buried sigil. He tried lifting some of the shattered stone that covered it, but it was too heavy, even with mana strengthening his body.

Well, he just needed to get an idea what it did. Was Father still alive? Maybe he'd been carried somewhere like with root travel. Hopefully that, and not shunted out into the void. Dirt was not keen to return there.

He leaned down and touched the edge of the sigil with his finger and gave it a little puff of mana. It manifested in the magic world, and Dirt recognized it. This sigil didn't have its own specific function; it modified other sigils to lengthen their effects. Well, that was good. At least he didn't start a fire seeing what it was.

It got dark before Dirt had much chance to trace the lines and figure out what the whole spell was for, and tracing the spell out under his little lights was rather slow. There was no moon yet, and the stars in the blackening sky didn't do much for his vision like they did for the pups.

He considered stopping for the night, but the pups were too restless. They could still smell each other's fear, and it kept any of them from relaxing, or stopping being afraid. None of them wanted to face the night without getting any answers. Not in this place.

So Dirt did the only thing he could think of and started pumping mana into the spell. Nothing visible happened, but the world of magic ignited into activity as the swirling magical combinations sucked up power faster than he could provide it. It was easily as sophisticated as a full expression from the elemental.

"No one move for a bit. I'm trying to figure out what this does, and I might accidentally turn it on," Dirt told the pups.

The four of them froze and sent him wordless panic. He replied with a feeling of reassurance and said, *"Don't worry. I'm just looking. I won't use it."*

They were not much reassured. Socks couldn't help himself and padded silently over to stand right over Dirt, watching warily to make sure he didn't do anything foolish. The other pups stayed away, which was probably wise.

He sighed and refocused. Okay, what was this for? He could only keep part of it going at a time, and he didn't get to pick which part. That was a sigil for stone, one which had been modified and expanded in a way that probably meant a particular type of stone, or even a specific stone. Around that, sigils for motion and power, an array that might filter things out? It acted on air, and Dirt was pretty sure it excluded it. But not always—there was a reverse in there, if something else activated.

Dirt stood and hurried back over to the square plaza with the U shape in it. This was the center of it, and whatever the spell did happened here. Well, obviously. But not *just* here. He noticed the mana he fed in wasn't draining out—it was being retained. The enchantment wanted to be full, but whatever powered it was too slow and anemic to do so quickly. At the imperceptible rate that the mana trickled in on its own . . . Well, Dirt had already guessed that part too.

Against his own better judgment, Socks provided the remaining mana the spell needed in a steady, monstrous flow, until finally Dirt could see the whole thing at once.

Just as he'd suspected, once it was fully powered, a connection formed that stretched far, far beyond sight. Which wasn't that far in the dark, but that was all Dirt needed to be sure.

"It's like root travel. It carries people somewhere else. But, I think only living things. And maybe their clothes. It's hard to tell. Father probably drained almost all of its power, and Sister emptied the rest. Anyone else who stepped here wouldn't have gone anywhere," said Dirt.

-WHERE DID IT PUT HIM? IN THE BOTTOM OF THE SEA? INSIDE SOLID STONE? WHY CAN'T HE HEAR US?- said Big Brother, insistent and impatient from worry.

"I have no idea, but probably somewhere very, very far away. And I think that plant smell was because it replaced Father and Sister with the air on the other side. So not water, and not rock. They're fine. I'm sure they're alive. In fact, I'm certain," said Dirt.

-When will they come back?- asked Sister.

-And why haven't they already, I would also like to know,- said Socks. *-But see, I told you my human would be useful.-*

Dirt sat at the edge of the square plaza, just out of range of the spell. Socks sat beside him, hovering protectively to make sure Dirt didn't get any ideas.

"I guess we should wait here for the night and see if they come back. I think if he wants to, Father can just power up the other side, and it'll bring him across."

They were amenable to that and gathered nearby to lie down and rest. None of them wanted to get this close to the plaza, though, and Dirt couldn't blame them. But he did know something that would help them feel better.

He stood and stepped out from under Socks. It was time to show off one of his new tricks. The pup lay down and blocked the road into the plaza, keeping a wary eye on him.

Dirt carefully hid his thoughts and lifted the rake from Socks's harness with his mind. It floated down toward his hand, and no sooner did Socks see it than he yelped in surprise and jumped all the way in the air, instinctively trying to get away. Dirt reached out to grab the rake, laughter forming in his throat.

Then Socks landed with three paws in the plaza. And vanished.

CHAPTER FOURTEEN

Dirt stared in shock for a moment, until he was interrupted by the scraping of claws on stone behind him. He spun and saw Socks's siblings rising to their feet with growls in their throats.

Perhaps he might have waited to see if Socks came back on his own, or if Father reached out and spoke to him. Or if, perhaps, he could discern more about the destination before he tried it himself. It was one thing to *say* it landed somewhere safe, and quite another to find out firsthand. But seeing the pups' lingering fear turn to anger dramatically limited his options.

"I better go make sure he's all right. We'll charge up the other side and come back if we can," Dirt told them. *"Maybe you should hunt instead of waiting around, though, just in case."*

Then, before any of them could do something hasty, he held his breath, steeled himself, and raced into the plaza. His foot landed on the engraved border in the stonework, and all the world twisted away.

White chaos clawed at him, and Dirt knew he was in the void. The eternal abyss outside all existence, which held so much suffering and so little else. He was there just long enough to start to panic, to think maybe he would remain here and return to his original fate. And he'd deserve it twice over, once for breaking the world and once for putting Socks here.

But then gravity took hold of him, and he felt himself pulled gently back into existence. The void scattered with a faint sound like breaking glass.

He stood in snow up to his knees, and it was freezing. Thank the gods he'd gotten dressed this morning. Why had he put shoes on? Just lucky, he supposed.

It was night here as well, and heavy snow was falling. Even after summoning a light, the quiet storm was so deep that it hid anything more than a dozen paces away in any direction. The falling snow clung to him, sticking to his sleeves and hair and threatening to bury him if he let it. There was no wind, no motion except the plummeting clumps of snow, and no sound.

"Socks? Socks! Hello?!" Dirt shouted mentally. Then, just in case, he shouted with his voice as well, giving a high, shrieking howl, hoping the pup's hearing might catch it.

No reply came, at least not that he could hear. The snow seemed to muffle even the sound of his breathing.

So where were the ruins? There should at least be fallen stones and things around. All he could see were some indistinct lumps, none taller than his waist. The ground was otherwise perfectly smooth and white.

Dirt bent down and dug into the snow and found not stone, but grass. Flattened, yellow grass with long, thin stalks and ragged tufts on the end. He took three steps sideways, which got snow up under the hem of his pants and into his shoes, and tried digging again. No stone. No ruins. He'd landed nowhere. Right in the middle of nowhere, with nothing around but snow.

"Home? Can you hear me?" he asked the forearm brace. For a moment, there was no response at all. Nothing happened, until finally, there was a slight tremor. But that was all. Just a tremor. She must be *really* far away, and he probably couldn't rely on her for much. Maybe not for anything. But at least she was still connected to this part of herself.

"You might be too far to hear this, but don't try to bring me back with root travel until I've had a chance to look for Socks. Okay? Don't bring me back yet," he said. The brace gave no response, and Dirt sighed.

So now what? He was just starting to feel the cold now, especially in his wet fingers after digging in the snow. It wasn't as bad as he suspected, but that was likely because there wasn't any wind, and he was still dry. For now.

He trudged forward and quickly became annoyed with how hard it was to walk in deep snow. Even grass as tall as he was hadn't been this tiring, since he could push that apart with his hands.

After thirty steps, he realized his shoes and pants were already as snow-covered as they were going to get and gave up trying to step in and out of the snow, preferring to kick through it instead. He made a wide circle around his landing spot, looking for any sign of anything at all.

Dirt scattered the snow off one lump on the ground and it was just a bush, not a corpse. So that was good. There were more of those around, and if they'd all been corpses, he might have been in danger from whatever killed them. But after walking in a complete circle, he was more sure than before that there weren't any ruins here.

He couldn't see very far, but it wasn't as bad as the forest fog. If he brightened his lights and watched carefully through the heavy, falling snow, he could see the outlines of anything twenty or thirty steps away. Just well enough he was sure there wasn't a huge building nearby, or any trees.

Just to be sure, he dug one last time in the snow and found grass, and a single old brown leaf. This time, he put some mana in his fingers and pulled up the grass by the roots, despite the freezing ground not wanting to let go. He dug a bit, hoping he'd find stonework under a thin layer of earth, but he did not. No ruins here.

So maybe nearby? That was the best he could hope for. And if not ruins, at least somewhere to take shelter. Even just a tree to curl up under and warm himself with an ember. The cold was setting in, and he wasn't sure if he could stay warm in snow up to his knees unless something changed. He started walking.

He went far enough for his starting point to disappear and kept going. Far enough to wonder if he was even going in a straight line. There was still nothing to see, not anything. Not one tree, no rises of hills or anything else. Just a few lumps that were probably more bushes.

The snow got thicker, though. It piled up on his hair and shoulders, first an inch, then two. He shook it off from time to time but eventually just ignored it. He balled his fists to keep them warm, and when that stopped working, he held the end of his sleeves shut. The cold got in the hem around his neck, and the snow melted against his skin and ran down his back.

The snow that had been up to his knees deepened inch by inch as well. Slower than it stacked up on top of him, since it was probably packing down the more there was on the ground, but still it rose.

By the time it was halfway up his thighs, he wasn't sure how far he'd come. It didn't feel like it had been that long, but maybe his focus on moving made an hour feel like minutes. If he looked back, the trail he made seemed straight, but was it really? How long until he actually found something?

There, off to his left, was a small hill, the first thing he'd seen that was taller than him. The snow had let up enough that he could see a bit farther now, but it was just a big snow-covered lump the size of a barn. Instead of unbroken white, bits of gray showed through, which blended well enough he wasn't sure if they were real. What was that thing? He looked around, wondering if there were others.

It didn't look like shelter, though, and his toes were getting unacceptably cold. Dirt did his best to stomp out an open area where he could get the snow off his legs, which was harder than it looked.

When Dirt turned again to look at whatever that big lump was, it had gotten closer. Had it? No, surely not. It was completely still. The real shape of it was almost impossible to make out. Just lumpy white atop dashes of pale gray, and there near the ground a bit of dark. It moved, lifting slightly to creep one step closer.

He laughed. "Socks!" he shouted, running over. Then with his mind he said, *"You almost snuck up on me. If you'd only had a little more snow on you, you would've gotten me."*

The pup stopped hiding his mind and stood to full height. He shook off the snow that had accumulated atop his fur, which had the effect of looking like he was materializing out of nothing. *-I thought you would spot my nose or eyes first, so I kept my nose in the snow and my eyes closed.-*

Dirt sent the mental image of exactly what he'd seen, which gratified the pup. He was better camouflaged than he'd thought.

"Are you mad at me?" asked Dirt. *"Because I'm sorry I startled you and sent us here."*

-I might have been mad if you hadn't followed. Get on. It is late, but let's go find shelter, if there is any, so it's easier to get you warm.-

"Aren't you cold?" asked Dirt.

-No, not at all. My fur is thick. I like it. Now get on.-

"But you're covered in snow."

-So are you.-

Well, that was true. Dirt took a little breath of mana and jumped up, where he cleared the snow off his usual spot. He lay down and dug his fingers in, relieved at the warmth he found buried in the fur. His toes still ached, though. He'd need to get his shoes off and warm them up before long.

Socks moved at a run, watching with ghost sight instead of his eyes. There was still snow on the ground in that world of gray shadows, almost transparent, shimmering and faint enough to see the flattened grass underneath. But he saw none in the air, revealing a flat landscape several hundred paces around them.

They were indeed a long way from anywhere. Socks widened his ghost sight so far it gave Dirt a secondhand headache, and still there was nothing to see. All flat everywhere, although they found a slow-moving river that was frozen over.

Its ice was thin, and Socks cracked it with a heavy paw to drink his fill. Dirt slid down to do the same and immediately regretted it. He was soaking wet now from all the melting snow, and dunking his face in ice-temperature water didn't help. But maybe it was for the best. Home might not be able to give them food or water right now. He'd have to find out later.

-We are not lost, so do not worry about that. I never get lost. But we are very far away. Here, look,- said Socks. He was thinking about his direction sense, focusing on it so Dirt got the idea. Neither of them knew how to express the distance, neither physically nor in days of travel, but between here and Mother's den was quite far. Much farther than they had ever traveled before. It seemed a dizzying distance, an impossible length of ground to cover.

-Father landed even farther away than this, but he still noticed when I came through,- said Socks. *-That old transporter is broken and sent us to random places. He didn't know it was still functional. He did not think we would follow him.-*

"You could have figured out how to use it on your own, I bet," said Dirt.

-Maybe, but we didn't,- said Socks. *-Father thought it was funny. He will talk to me later.-*

"Are we going to meet up with him?" asked Dirt.

Socks replied with a mental image of his direction sense, this time indicating how far away Father was. Dirt took that to mean "probably not."

After that, the pup decided that was enough running. He rolled on the snow to flatten a big section of it, upon which he lay down. *-We may as well sleep here so we can drink water in the morning. I don't think we'll find anywhere better.-*

"Probably not. I hope we do eventually, though, because I didn't even bring my pack. All I have is what I'm wearing. I'm not made to sleep out in the open," said Dirt.

The pup curled into a circle, and Dirt climbed in. He lay against Socks's front leg, nestled into the fur under his ear. Then he took his shoes off so his feet would warm up faster.

-Stop squirming,-

"I'm not."

-Take the rest of it off, and we will dry it in the morning,- said Socks.

Dirt hesitated, but once he got his shirt off and nestled deep into the fur to make sure, it was warmer than when he had it on. He tossed his clothing out to get snowed on and relaxed deeply into the pup's thick fur. *"Don't forget I'm here and get up and toss me into the snow."*

-We'll see about that,- replied Socks playfully. *-So what have you been doing with the trees the last few days, other than getting carried off by the wind?-* asked Socks, not quite ready to sleep yet.

Dirt said, *"You first."*

Socks grumbled in feigned annoyance. *-Fine. Father said I was getting influenced by you too much after you found the magic primer. He said that wolves do not do magic that way, and we don't have to, and all those little lines and drawings aren't real in the first place. That's a human thing, even if it works when I try it. He made me try standing on one paw. A front paw.-*

"I've never seen you . . . hmm. Now that I think about it, your body isn't really designed for that, is it? So could you do it?"

-No. But Father says if I can learn how, then I'll just be one step away from changing my shape.-

"Wolves can change their shape?" said Dirt, almost shouting with his mental voice. *"Into what?"*

-Into whatever we want. But only for a little while because we get tired. Father showed us by turning into a bear.-

"A big one?"

-Yes.-

"Can he turn into a small one?"

-Why would he want to?-

"I'm asking if you can learn to turn into something human sized, obviously," said Dirt.

Socks huffed his amusement and changed the topic, which excited Dirt terribly. If Socks was being coy, then the answer was yes, and they both knew it. The rest of what Father taught him was things about hunting—pack strategies, now that there were enough pups together to learn, and clever details about using scenery and their natural coloring to hide. Socks had been trying that with the snow, in fact, and almost pulled it off.

Although the hunting methods were more interesting than Socks had promised, Dirt kept getting distracted by his own imagination. If Socks could turn human size, then he wouldn't scare anyone the next time they found humans. And he would be easier to feed. And if he could stay that size all night, then he could learn what it's like to sleep in a bed. And what if he could turn into human shape, not just a different animal? What would he look like?

Each time Dirt's mind wandered, he expected Socks to interrupt him and confirm or deny it, but the pup stayed coy and let Dirt's mind wander. In fact, Socks was probably letting him do it so he'd have more ideas to try once he figured out the trick.

Then it was Dirt's turn to explain what he'd been up to, but there wasn't much else to say without giving away the raised city, and he didn't want to do that because it might give away his villa, and if Socks learned about *that,* then he'd be able to pry up the secret of the hot bath. So Dirt mostly talked about the schola and the texts there and what he'd read. And all the gold and silver the trees had collected.

I SEE YOUR PET FOLLOWED YOU, said Father, his voice rumbling in their minds like thunder. Dirt grinned, and Socks sent back a wordless mental shout of affection. *I SUPPOSE YOU ARE NOT GOING TO THE DESERT AFTER ALL. GO HERE AND KILL EVERY-THING. AND AFTER THAT, GO HERE. THERE IS SOMETHING THERE FOR DIRT. I WAS WAITING UNTIL HE WAS GROWN TO TELL HIM ABOUT IT, BUT IT'S ON THE WAY. AND IF YOU*

WANT TO, YOU CAN FIND HUMANS HERE AND HERE AND HERE. FINALLY, YOU CAN MEET TWO OF YOUR RELATIVES HERE. THEY WILL BE PLEASED TO MEET YOU, IF YOU DO NOT STAY LONG.

Father sent impressions of each location in direction-sense, which Socks took care to remember.

FLEE THE DEVOURER. CAUSE HAVOC. DIG HARROWS IN THE EARTH. TURN RIVERS FROM THEIR COURSES. LEAVE FIELDS OF BONES BEHIND YOU. EXPLORE AND RETURN WITH EXPERIENCE, MY SON.

And that was all. Father said nothing further. Socks missed him already and sniffed his own shoulder where the faintest hint of Father's scent remained.

CHAPTER FIFTEEN

The night was windless and quiet, and neither Dirt nor Socks had any trouble sleeping there, huddled together in the open plain. Despite the snow that fell and tickled his nose, Dirt stayed pleasantly warm, even when it melted and dripped down his chest.

The storm passed, and morning came slowly, with Dirt waking early and not wanting to move because the moment he did, the cold air would get in. His hair was soaking, and his face was damp, but huddled below the breezes, it gave him no chill. It would, though, the moment Socks woke up and stretched.

Socks didn't stretch first thing when he woke, fortunately. He dug Dirt's clothing out of the snow and lifted it with his mind where the boy could see. Dirt summoned hot embers to circle and dry them off, but it took quite a while. Long enough that they both started feeling hungry and wondering if there was anything to eat but grass and snow.

Once Dirt's clothing was dry, Socks finally uncurled and stretched. Dirt landed feet-first in the snow and got dressed faster than he ever had in his life, before even the leftover heat had faded from the cloth. Socks licked him, then said, *-Oops, I will get you wet if I do that.-*

"If you only lick me a little it's fine," said Dirt. The pup's tongue had been warm, actually. The thin layer of saliva, a little less so.

-No, I must take good care of you, or you will freeze. You stayed warm last night, didn't you?-

"Yep, plenty warm. It was comfortable, too. Did I make your front leg sore by sitting on it all night?"

-A little, but you are not very heavy, and it is already fading.- Socks raised his head and looked around. There wasn't much to see, though. Just flat fields of snow. Then he happily lolled his huge tongue out and said, *-So when did you learn to move things with your mind?-*

"Just a couple days ago. I haven't even had a lot of time to practice."

-I wonder if you're the first human to ever do that.-

"Probably not, but I'm not sure how anyone else would have figured it out. I only did because I watched you so much. I was just playing around with a spell when I thought of it."

-We'll have to think of some new games to play, now that you can do it too,- said Socks, his mind already rolling to come up with ideas.

"You'll be way better at it. At first, anyway!" said Dirt, implying a challenge.

Socks looked back to give him a disbelieving glance with one eye, then snorted. Dirt grinned.

There was a pause, so Dirt asked aloud, "Home, can you make me any sap? Or are you too far away?" Several breaths later, the brace trembled slightly. Just a few tremors, and that was all. So that was a no.

-Did you not eat much yesterday?- asked Socks.

"Not really. I had some sap in the morning, before the trees sent me over. That was a really long day," said Dirt.

-Then we shall hunt along the way.-

"Where are we going first?"

-The place Father said to kill everything. Perhaps we can eat whatever is there, if it is not disgusting,- said Socks, thinking of the abominations they'd been facing.

"I'm not hungry enough to eat tentacles yet," said Dirt. *"And by the way, once the fight starts, you know I won't be able to use the staff, right? Just my knife. So we'll have to be careful."*

-I know. Do not fret, little Dirt. You are useful in a fight but seldom necessary. Now back up because I am going to shake all this snow off me.-

Dirt stood up and hurried a short distance away through the snow, which was up to his waist now.

Socks rose lumbering to his feet, clumps of snow bigger than Dirt falling away and hitting the ground with a thump. The big pup shook from nose to tail and flung off all the rest, sending some of it flying quite a distance. Then he wagged his tail, pleased with himself.

Dirt nodded appreciatively and said, *"It looks like that works better with snow than water."*

-I can fling the water off, too,- said Socks.

"But not as well."

Socks examined his harness, making sure the flaps were closed and everything was in good order. He pulled this way and that, adjusting it into just the right position. Then he surprised Dirt by grabbing him and lifting him up for a lick. *-Do you want to ride curled up in one of the pockets? I bet you could fit.-*

"Maybe if I get too cold. But I like my spot."

-It feels weird not having you there. When I was with Father and my siblings I kept feeling like I dropped something.-

The pup deposited Dirt on his back, and Dirt lay down and snuggled in for a run. The clouds were breaking up, making the landscape an uncanny contrast. Unbroken, perfectly flat white ground as far as he could see, even from up here, ending in a horizon so flat he could've drawn it with a ruler. Above, startlingly blue sky where the clouds withdrew into white clumps and floated away.

-Keep an eye out for birds. I'll let you know if I smell anything worth hunting.-

Socks left at a good run, then picked it up bit by bit until Dirt said the wind was getting too cold. Then he slowed slightly, and that was the pace. Dirt mostly lay there, enjoying the warmth and the smell of the pup's fur. He watched the land and sky out of the corner of his eye, but there wasn't much to see.

They spent the morning chatting with each other and playing imagination games. Dirt showed more of the elemental and explained how he'd talked with her, and Socks talked about some of the adventures his siblings had been on. Big Brother had found a turtle as big as he was, and Sister had dug up some bones that were bigger even than Father, which were too large for her to put them back together to see what they'd belonged to. Father refused to say.

In his eagerness, Socks kept running faster and faster, which made the wind on Dirt unbearable until the pup finally decided a mental shield to block the air was worth the effort.

It worked far better than he expected, once he realized he should curve it. Instead of all the added weight of the air against the shield holding him back, it softened the air his body ran through and allowed him to go even faster with less effort. *That* was a delightful discovery, and he raced faster than Dirt was strictly comfortable with from sheer joy.

Dirt lay on his back the whole time and watched for birds, as instructed. The storm must have scared them off, though, because there wasn't a single one anywhere for several hours. When he finally spotted one, he almost forgot he was supposed to be paying attention.

Dirt watched eagerly as it flew closer and got bigger, hoping it would turn out to be big enough to eat. Even just a snack would be nice.

But it kept getting bigger, and Dirt realized it wasn't a regular bird. It was far too large for that, and it was carrying something. Not a gryphon, either, which was the largest flying thing he'd ever seen. This might be even bigger, all black, or so it looked from down here.

"Hey, Socks, what is that?" he asked.

The pup slid to a stop and looked up, but he couldn't see as well at a distance and had no answer. They waited until it passed by, not quite overhead, and headed roughly the same direction they'd been going. It came in range of their mind-sight, and its mind was very bird-like, but awfully clever. It lacked that "almost smart enough" quality the gryphons had, its thoughts complex and colorful. It was probably as smart as Dirt was.

It saw them with perfect clarity despite the distance, and it knew what a wolf was. Once it was confident that Socks was watching it, it cycled its thoughts between several images of nests, each in different directions and found in different scenery.

-It doesn't want me to know where it's going,- said Socks. *-It must be going home to eat.-*

The trick didn't work, of course; Dirt and Socks both had way too much experience prying hidden thoughts open. The problem was that they had no idea where anything was, so seeing its true nest atop some sort of rocky place didn't help much.

"Can we chase it?" asked Dirt, hunger gnawing at him. He *really* needed to learn how to make his own sap.

As if in reply, the bird angled sharply in a different direction, its huge black form cutting the air like an enormous knife. It glided low to the ground and flapped hard, sending it racing forward.

-Want to? I think whatever it was carrying is alive. I didn't get a good look at its mind because it was too far. But maybe it's food, and we can steal it.-

"Well, we haven't seen anything else to eat. Let's go!"

Dirt rolled to his stomach and grabbed on to the harness, so at least he wouldn't pull Socks's fur if he was about to get tossed.

The pup raced forward with a surge of mana, so fast that Dirt's feet floated in the air until he got himself back under control. Socks kept the round wall of force in front of him and gave chase.

The bird certainly didn't make itself easy prey. Flying low was almost enough to lose them—if they'd been just a bit slower, it would have escaped out of view over the horizon. Even so, Socks had a hard time keeping up. It kept turning, hoping to lose them, and flew so low to the ground that it left feather marks in the snow in some places.

Suddenly Socks stopped and sniffed the air. *-I'm going to let it think it got away, and follow by scent. If it stays low, I can follow right to its nest, and if it flies high, you can spot it.-*

"And maybe if it realizes we're still chasing it after that, it'll drop its food and we can eat it."

-You will not want to eat it.-

"Why not?"

-Because it's carrying a human female. I can smell her. Young. An adolescent. She is not well.-

That changed the whole mood of the hunt in an instant. For Dirt, at least. Socks wasn't too concerned, which was understandable. *"Where did it find a human?"*

-Father showed us where to find human places, but none of them are close. I wonder.-

Dirt sent a mental nod and sat up so he could watch the skies, keeping a firm grip on the harness. Humans were pretty far down the list of priorities, but if they found one, they'd have to take her back, wouldn't they? If she was alive in the first place, which seemed unlikely.

Socks waited a bit longer than Dirt thought was necessary, then ran forward again. Not as fast this time, because he had to make sure he didn't lose the scent, and that also kept him from using the mental shield to block the air. Which made Dirt's face awfully cold. Dirt changed his mind about keeping a constant eye upward and chose instead to just peer around every now and then so he could keep his nose out of the wind.

The first scenery came into view. Socks ran past a group of ragged trees with no leaves. The snow melted in the sunlight and dripped down from them like rain, but there was still plenty in the branches. It'd be a few more days until they were bare again. After seeing those trees, they found more. A few pines here, a few tall, bare ones there. And some hills, finally, to break up the landscape. Some dips and curves. With all the snow, though, it was hard to get a sense of what the area looked like normally.

A row of short mountains came into view, slowly rising from the horizon like a pale bubble as they got closer. Socks lost the scent, but there was no doubt anymore where their prey had ended up.

It was really just a few large hills, perhaps too small to be called proper mountains. Three or four of them in one clump, all with flat tops of differing heights. Trees grew up and down the sides but left the tops bare.

-This is where Father told us to go kill everything,- said Socks, taking stock of his direction sense.

"I guess we got lucky, then. We should probably go slow and sneak up on them, but I want to go fast and see if we can save that girl," said Dirt.

-It's probably already eating her. I bet it fed her to its young, if it has any.-
"Then we'll surprise it mid-meal."
-Perhaps. Hold tight.-

Dirt didn't need to be told, but he gripped the harness even harder anyway. He filled himself with mana, sending it to strengthen his skin and bones until he needed it for something else. Socks filled himself with mana as well and ran forward in a wild flurry, kicking up snow ten paces in the air behind him.

They spotted the great bird's mind at the same time, and it wasn't alone. There were four more, and from their minds, it seemed none were hatchlings. Socks dashed up the canyon between the two closest flat mountaintops, which was really more of a long, sloping hillside with plenty of open area devoid of trees. He slowed once he realized the ground was all boulders under the snow. He looked with ghost sight to keep from slipping and snapping a leg, and that's when the birds noticed their approach.

All five of them flapped and flew upward into view, shrieking at deafening volume. To Dirt's eyes, they were hideous. They weren't all black like he'd thought; their feathers were only black at the tips and lightened to a dingy yellow-gray near their bodies, with bulbous lumps of red flesh around their necks and ankles. Their heads were bare of any feathers at all, showing skin that was the blackest part of them. Their eyes were quick and sharp, with beaks like gryphons. The girl was on the ground somewhere farther in, if she wasn't in their stomachs already. Probably just one stomach, since any of them looked big enough to eat Dirt whole. Just one wing was longer than Socks's body, including his tail.

One shrieked, facing them directly, and Dirt saw a wave of force shoot from its mouth faster than a slingshot. It knocked him clear off Socks's back and twenty paces back down the boulder-strewn canyon, where he bounced twice before landing against something hard and stopping.

He picked himself up piece by piece, making sure nothing important was broken. The mana he'd stored up only moments before had saved him, but it had been close. He was almost completely drained of it now. Just enough to strengthen one arm and pull himself out from between the boulders where he'd landed.

Socks was more than they could handle, though, at least so far. He ripped all the feathers from the wings of that closest one, yanking so hard with his mind that his body shook, and they almost didn't come out even then. But when they tore free, Socks leaped on it and twisted its neck so hard its massive head came off in his teeth. He spat it out and growled.

A giant bird dove at him, beak first until the last second when it extended its black claws. A second bird dove in from another angle, and only when Socks jumped away from the first one did Dirt see why. It was a trap.

Dirt yanked his dagger free and flung it at the second bird, straightening the throw and pushing it faster with his mind. Despite the blade spinning wildly, Dirt scored a lucky hit on its neck near the breast. The dagger sank in past the pommel, and Dirt lost sight of it, but it startled the bird enough to disrupt its dive, right for where Socks landed.

Socks struck it with his mind, using that tree-piercer that Father had shown him. Despite the bird's bulk, it was flung upward and to the side but not killed. Punctured and bleeding, but not harmed enough to slow it down. Dirt could feel it—they used mana to protect themselves.

The other two birds staggered attacks at Socks, one coming on the tail of the other, but this time Socks was ready for them and jumped out of the way each time. One of them did another percussive shout, striking Socks full in the side and knocking him over. He rolled sideways once, landed on his feet, and snarled.

The other bird tried the same attack, but Socks deflected it with his mental shield. He picked up a boulder from under the snow and tossed it upward. It struck its target, but the bird just pushed off with its claws and was flung higher, unharmed. The boulder crashed down so hard it shattered.

The one with Dirt's dagger in its neck struggled to get airborne again, so perhaps Dirt had done more damage than he thought. The bloody wound made finding his dagger impossible anymore, so there was no chance of getting it back until the thing died. *"I'll kill this one,"* said Dirt, indicating mentally which one he meant.

Socks turned his attention back to the other three, two of which were repeating the staggered dives.

Dirt bounced up the canyon like a bug, filling himself with more mana as he went. The injured bird saw him coming, but it wasn't expecting the sudden explosion of speed. Dirt planted both feet on a boulder and jumped with all the force the mana would give him, and he shot like an arrow right past Socks and hit it near its injury.

He grabbed a flap of red, bulbous skin with one hand and poked his fingers into the wound with the other. The bird shrieked and hopped, unable to get its talons high enough to get him off. It reached down with its beak to bite him, but Dirt pushed the sharp tip away and made it bite itself.

Dirt dug his teeth into the skin around the gash and tore it wider open with his other hand, then reached into the wound. His arm went in all the way to the elbow before he found his dagger.

Thank Grace, he found the hilt first and not the blade. He closed his fingers around it, turned the blade outward, and yanked it out, slicing as he went. The ancient dagger cut a wide gash, slicing through the flesh like it was hardly even there.

The bird collapsed to the ground, trying to crush him beneath its bulk, but Dirt knew that trick as well from playing with Socks. He dove away and was lucky to land on a hidden boulder big enough for both feet.

The bird struggled to get back up, largely due to its bulk and the unwieldiness of its wings. Dirt tossed the dagger and mentally directed it right into the creature's black eye, then pushed with all his mental might. He felt the rebound force driving him down with such power that his feet started slipping out from under him, but not before the dagger exploded out the other side of the bird's head. It fell dead.

Socks was having a bit more trouble with the other three. They'd taken to attacking him all at once, and although they hadn't gotten away unscathed, neither had he. They'd managed to get at least one talon past his fur, up near his spine, leaving a spot of blood the size of Dirt's fist.

Dirt pulled the dagger back with his mind, then grabbed it out of the air and hopped like a bug over to where Socks was fighting. The pup saw him coming and tossed him high into the air, above even the birds circling for another dive.

Taking careful aim, Dirt threw the dagger downward toward the back of one's head. He steered with his mind, but Socks saw it as well and yanked it downward so hard it went right through its target and vanished in the snow.

Dirt pointed at a different bird, and Socks pushed him that direction. Dirt landed on its back, knocking it a bit lower in its flight. He started punching and biting and ripping out feathers, doing all the damage he could with his bare hands and teeth. It wasn't much, but it probably hurt, because the bird twisted in the air to fling him off.

Socks saw his chance and grabbed its beak with his mind and twisted its head the other direction. Dirt heard more than one loud pop, and they fell to the ground together. It didn't move after that.

Fed up, Socks called an enormous swarm of sparks around the remaining one, focusing so intently that he held his breath and stopped moving. It sensed the danger it was in, but it was too late. With a flare of heat that stung on Dirt's face, Socks enflamed the sparks into a booming inferno. It only burned for a few seconds, but that was enough. The last bird fell, and the pup finished it off by snapping its neck.

The two of them paused for a moment, both panting hard. Before he forgot, Dirt retrieved his dagger, finding it by the hole it made in the snow. The tip was buried three inches into a stone, but fortunately it slid out with no trouble.

-We have plenty to eat now,- said Socks. *-We can leave the bodies in the snow until we want to eat them. Cold preserves meat. Father taught me that.-*

The big pup would be smiling if that was a thing wolves did. It had been a great hunt. A long one, over a great distance, with a fight at the end against a new enemy.

Dirt hopped over and hugged Socks around the snout and patted his forehead. They nuzzled their heads together, despite the hilarious size difference.

They noticed at the same time—that girl was still alive. The faint light of her mind was still glowing, although she was unconscious.

-Don't get too excited. She probably won't last long.-

"*I know. Come on,*" said Dirt. Socks picked him up and leaped nimbly across the boulders, and a short distance farther they saw down into the circular-shaped depression between the flat hills.

It contained almost no snow, strewn instead with endless heaps of logs and branches and great quantities of packing material, like grass and old feathers. The whole thing was a nest, a single big one the giant birds all shared. It was far too large for all of them together, but Dirt supposed his villa was bigger than he needed, so who was he to judge?

They only found her by scent, since she'd been placed in a little gap that was invisible until they were about to step on it.

She was dressed far more warmly than Dirt, bundled in thick furs almost from head to toe. They hid her shape so well that if Socks couldn't smell that she was a girl, Dirt might not have known. She was taller than him, and thicker. Probably at least Èlia's age.

The poor girl was injured, too; that much was obvious. The bird had carried her by digging in its talons so she couldn't wriggle away. Deep puncture wounds on her legs and torso oozed blood, which dripped down through the tangle of branches beneath her and disappeared. Her breathing was raspy and wet and quick.

-Take her clothes off so I can lick her wounds. Hurry, while she's still alive,- said Socks. He lifted her gently from the nest and held her in the air, carefully turning her while Dirt struggled to figure out what to untie

to get her coat off. Finally, he gave up and just started cutting the cords with his knife. Soon enough the front opened, revealing a much thinner undershirt.

Socks pushed that out of the way with his tongue and licked her wounds. There was a bad one on her stomach, deep enough to show purple guts inside, and the punctures near her shoulders were no less deep. After Socks was satisfied her skin would hold together, they closed her coat to keep her warm.

Her pants were easier to remove, since belts were straightforward. Both legs had been stabbed right through, in the meaty part of the thigh. When Socks rotated her, blood poured from them rather than dripped or spurted. It was a wonder she hadn't bled out already.

After her wounds were closed and starting to heal, Socks lay down and kept her floating in the air. The ground here didn't look particularly comfortable. Dirt sat down atop the pup's front paws and surrounded her with embers to warm her back up. Then they waited.

And waited.

She lived. The girl opened her dry eyes and didn't seem to see Socks at all. She saw Dirt, though, and whispered, *"Stammi luntanu da mè. Sò maleditu."*

Dirt grinned. Another language. He should have seen that coming. In mild exasperation, he told Socks, *"Uh oh. We're doing this again?"*

CHAPTER SIXTEEN

Socks wasn't concerned about her strange language. Mostly he was amused by the fact that she hadn't spotted him, despite being right there. He said, *-I want to hold very still and see how long it takes for her to notice me. You distract her.-*

Dirt schooled his face to keep from grinning. He peeked at her mind, and she thought Socks's legs were part of a building, or something like that. Pillars, maybe. Fuzzy ones. Her thoughts were jumbled and confused, which made sense. She was barely conscious. But even so, all she had to do was turn and look up to see Socks leaning over her, and she hadn't yet.

She seemed to think she was lying on the ground, or maybe on a bed, and not floating in midair held up by Socks's mind. Dirt couldn't blame her for that. It wasn't the sort of thing one expected. To keep it going, Dirt made sure all his warming embers stayed out of her field of vision, just in case.

He smiled kindly and patted her head, then gently pushed a few loose strands of pale brown hair out of her face and back under her soft fur hood.

"How are you feeling?" he asked, in his language.

She scrunched her face a little, perplexed. *"Chì avete dettu? Quale si?"* She shifted restlessly, squinting her eyes in pain. *"Induve sò?"*

"Hold still," said Dirt gently. "You're safe now. The birds are dead."

The young woman squirmed and turned to look upward. Dirt quickly covered her eyes with his hand and said, "Rest. Sleep."

Socks almost snorted in amusement but stopped himself. That had been close. She'd almost seen him.

She tried to raise her arm to push his hand away, but it was the arm with the shoulder injured from the bird's talon, and it was still too sore inside, so she gave up.

"Take it easy. Just relax for a little while. If you want to, you can sleep."

"*Dorme?*" she said, catching the last word he said. "*Cumu possu dorme avà?*"

It was almost the same word in his language, which was a relief. Maybe it wouldn't be so hard to learn to talk with her after all.

"Dormi, sì," he said. "Dormi." *Sleep.*

"*Siete in periculu sè site cun mè,*" she protested, her big brown eyes turning back to him and getting a bit more spark. They held fear. "*Per piacè, scappate.*"

Her voice was so cracked and dry it was almost a rasp. It probably hurt to even speak, so why wouldn't she relax? Dirt decided he'd had enough guessing and looked at her mind.

He found that it wasn't herself she was worried about—she thought he was in danger from being around her, which was silly. She wanted him to run away before she caused his death somehow. She'd already resigned herself to dying, and if there was any one emotion she felt more than the others, it was guilt. He could learn some of her words later, but that was the general idea.

"Listen," said Dirt, a bit more sternly. Not unfriendly or domineering, he hoped, just sternly. "You need to stop complaining and trying to get up."

He poked her injuries to help make the point. Each of them, one by one. She squirmed again, and he wagged his finger at her. She seemed to resent being scolded by a little boy, even in her state, but she got the idea and relaxed with an air of consignment to her fate. And Dirt's fate, she presumed.

Dirt continued. "You're warm, and you're safe. You need to rest. You'll heal because Socks licked you, but that doesn't mean you're healed yet. So just lie there for a while and get better. You look thirsty. Water?" asked Dirt. He made a drinking motion, and the girl nodded slightly.

She licked her dry, cracked lips. It did no good. Her tongue was too dry. She said, "*Acqua . . .*" which was the same word as Dirt's language. Water.

"Aqua," he said. Knowing there were two words he recognized was a bit of a relief. That meant she was descended from his people, and he was still within the old bounds of the Sunset Empire. Which, now that he thought about it, must have been huge. He'd known it was, but not really. It was one thing to know a fact and quite another to experience it.

She nodded and repeated it. *"Acqua, per piacè."*

Dirt smiled and nodded, saying, "Okay, some water coming right up. Now just relax, please."

She forced a half-smile of eager gratitude but couldn't very well without cracking her lips more. Poor thing.

-I'll lick her lips after she notices me. I didn't think of those because she wasn't bleeding there,- said Socks, remaining silent as a statue. He still sounded amused. *-I bet she screams when she sees me.-*

"I bet she doesn't. I bet she doesn't believe her eyes and ignores you," said Dirt.

The girl shifted again on her bed of nothing and gave a quiet groan of pain. Dirt glanced at her mind again, and it was her legs that hurt. Socks subtly adjusted his grip to take some of the pressure off, and that helped. She didn't notice the bed moving, but it reduced her discomfort.

Dirt watched her for a moment to make sure she wasn't about to try to get up. She finally closed her eyes and relaxed in a more convincing manner. Glancing at her mind, she was sure she'd die before she opened them again. She still felt bad for Dirt, even while wondering where he'd come from. She kept thinking of the giant birds, expecting them to come back. And remembering a tall female figure standing on something, menacing and beckoning at the same time. She shied away from the image.

Now that she wasn't looking, he picked up some snow with his mind to keep from freezing his fingers. He gathered a respectable ball of it while Socks watched, impressed at Dirt's control, and put an ember in the middle to melt it. To his dismay, it melted down to about one tenth of its prior size. That didn't seem right. Snow was ten times more poofy than water?

Well, it was a start. He wasn't trying to drown her. Now, how to get it into her mouth? She'd probably be concerned if he made it float in front of her face. He pulled his arm brace off, and decided it looked enough like a cup. He put the water inside and held the thinner end closed with his mind.

Dirt lifted the girl's head slightly and slowly poured the water across her parched lips. She let it trickle in without complaint, understanding the need to drink it slowly. He looked at her mind again, and while he couldn't understand any of the words racing through it, he saw enough to know what she was thinking of. She was just beginning to realize that she was warm, and so was the water. But it was so bright! Where was she, and why wasn't she dead yet?

She opened her eyes and squinted against the brightness of the sky. Her mind struggled to make sense of the giant dark shadow over her, until she saw the pup's eyes. Terror filled her, but she shut her eyes again and made no sound. Her face scrunched up, and her chest shook, and Dirt realized she was about to cry. Her courage had failed her.

He patted her head and said, "There, there, it's okay. Nothing's going to happen. He's friendly. You don't even know what you were looking at, do you? Here, drink a little more water."

When he held the cup to her lips, she resisted and tried to speak, but Dirt tightened his grip and poured anyway. He didn't stop until she finished the cup.

Once he pulled it away, she shook her head and said, *"Morte. Era a morte. Aghju vistu l'ochji di a morte in u celu. Hè quì per noi."*

From her thoughts, it seemed she was sure she was about to be carried off into the world of the dead any second now. She had a mental image of how that would happen: giant fingers grabbing her and pulling her spirit into the ground, leaving her dead body behind. Her imagination was taking Socks's eyes and filling in a giant spirit in the shape of a man, rising out of the ground to collect her soul.

Well, now Dirt was starting to feel bad. It had been a funny thought, tricking her and seeing what happened, but it wasn't going well.

-I guess you were closer to correct than I was,- said Socks. He leaned down and licked the girl's face, startling her terribly.

When he stopped and pulled back up, her eyes focused, and she finally realized what she was looking at. She screamed, and it was a hopeless, miserable sound that tugged painfully at Dirt's heart.

Socks huffed and pushed her mind, forcing her to sleep. Then he gave Dirt a little lick and said, *-Don't feel bad. There is no right way for a human to see me for the first time. It would have gone poorly no matter what we did. At least this was kind of fun.-*

"That's true, but look at her. Poor thing."

-If she gets mad at us later, we will remind her that we killed the birds and saved her life, and then she will stop.-

Dirt and Socks watched her sleep for a moment. Socks had only given her a nudge, and her natural exhaustion had done the rest. The stress and pain faded from her countenance as she sank deeper and deeper into her rest, and soon her face relaxed into a relieved peace.

"I'm going to wake her up and give her more water before too long. She didn't drink enough."

-Melt this for me. I want some now,- said Socks. He gathered a pile of snow as tall as Dirt with his mind and rolled it into a ball. Dirt obliged him and melted it, resulting again in a disappointing amount of water. But it was enough, and after Socks drank what he wanted there was some left for Dirt to finish off.

-Now let's go have some food. I know you're hungry, and you've waited long enough.-

Socks headed down out of the nest, lifting the girl with great care so as not to disturb her. Dirt followed over the edge and down the hillside, hopping from boulder to boulder and sliding where he could. He made his way across the messy battlefield, carefully stepping around the blood and viscera to keep his pants from getting any dirtier.

The area truly was a mess. Broad splashes of blood, black feathers everywhere, snow churned to reveal the brown rocks beneath. It looked every bit as messy as the fight had been. And, of course, the ruined bodies of the giant birds. They looked even larger now than they had in life, with their wings all splayed out and broken.

The pup plucked Dirt's knife from its sheath and got to work slashing the birds. He pulled the skin away with his teeth, eager to smell and taste the pale flesh beneath, but after only a nibble, he sliced away huge strips of meat with the dagger and set them nearby in the snow.

Socks tossed Dirt a nice chunk of pale meat, which he turned over in his hands before taking a huge bite. Too bad they had no salt.

-You are getting spoiled,- said Socks, teasing him.

"I am getting civilized," said Dirt. Hunger made him dig in with relish. It tasted milder than some of the other bird meat he'd had but wasn't as soft. Not quite stringy or tough, but tougher than he'd expected. Maybe in a bit, he'd try some of the blood and see how it compared to other things.

Waving the knife through the air, Socks resumed cutting whatever meat he could from the birds, and in the process, dug his snout in to eat anything he found tasty. The hearts were good, and he liked the livers. Intestines less so, unless he was particularly hungry. Dirt didn't like those either. Too hard to chew.

Socks lifted a slab of meat longer than Dirt was tall, probably the entire breast. He tossed it onto a clean spot of snow and said, *-Can you cover that up while I keep cutting?-*

Dirt nodded and scarfed down the rest of the meat he was holding. Then he braced his feet and used his mind to toss as much snow as he could pick up at once. He made a big scoop with his mental fingers and lifted more snow than his arms would have been able to handle, but bracing his feet and back solidly kept the recoil weight from knocking him down.

He threw clump after clump, and each time it sent a poof of powdery snow floating on the air that stuck to his face and made him shiver. When it was done, the effort left him panting and the muscles in his back stiff and tight. He turned back to Socks, groaning at the soreness gathering in his muscles. That was more work than it looked like. His body hadn't even been moving.

Dirt stretched with a groan and turned to watch Socks continue his butchering. He sniffled and realized he was leaking water out his nose again. That had been happening a lot, ever since he got here. That had to be normal, right? Something that happened in the cold? He looked at the girl to see if she was doing it too, and she was watching him.

The girl was awake, her face dripping wet. The rest of her clothing was coated in a layer of powder snow. Dirt kicked himself mentally, realizing he'd been the one to wake her up.

She didn't speak. Now that she had his attention, she raised her good arm and made the same drinking motion he'd done before. Dirt nodded and picked up a bunch of snow, then melted it with an ember.

After that, he floated it over to her face and let her drink it right out of the air. No point hiding anything now. She tilted her head and shifted her eyes downward, looking at the nothing she was lying on. Then she pointedly looked back at Dirt. Are you holding me up, she seemed to be asking.

Dirt shook his head and pointed at Socks.

She glanced back at the giant pup, and he hopped twice through the snow to land nearby and licked the melted water off her face. She shivered again, but a shy smile appeared on her face.

-She is handling this better now,- said Socks.

Dirt snorted in amusement and replied, *"It probably helps that she can't run away. But you're right."*

-Are you going to let her find out you can see her mind? Since she knows you can do magic already,- asked Socks.

Dirt pondered that for a moment and replied, *"Not yet. I'd still have to learn her language for that to do much good. Maybe we'll find an air elemental later on, and I can try asking for it to teach me."*

Socks tossed a slice of flesh over, and Dirt caught it and showed her. He held it to her lips, but she went a little pale and shook her head.

Wasn't she hungry? Dirt looked at her mind and gathered that she thought raw meat would make her sick. He chuckled at that. Sick was the least of her worries. He caught her eyes and took a bite himself, then nodded and held it back toward her mouth. She gingerly took a nibble, managing to hold down the revulsion he saw on her face. Oh well. She'd learn.

When it didn't kill her, she took another bite, and another, and by the end she was able to eat without gagging.

-I guess our next stop is some of the human places around until we find out where she belongs, so we can give her back.-

"Yep. I wonder how she ended up like this."

-I suppose we'll find out,- said Socks. Then he went back to butchering.

CHAPTER SEVENTEEN

The sunlight failed to provide any warmth, except where it fell long and undisturbed on Dirt's clothing, if he held still. That was not enough, and he found himself wishing those dead birds had fur so he could wear that. His clothing was too thin.

The girl was doing well and looked more relaxed now. She'd made peace with hovering in the air and although her meal of raw meat wasn't sitting well in her stomach, the water Dirt gave her had already caused a positive change. Her cheeks and lips remained pale from having lost too much blood, but when he looked at her mind, she could feel the water helping.

In fact, right now, she was thinking of other ways to melt water. She'd started out on her travels eating snow, but it took a lot of snow and made her too cold. Perhaps if she had a big dark cloth, it would get hot in the sun and melt snow that would then drip into a pan? If she had a pan. But if she had a pan, then she could light a fire and melt it in *that,* but to light a fire she'd need . . . Her throat was dry again.

She turned her head to catch Dirt's eye, then looked deliberately at some snow. She tried bringing her good arm up to mimic drinking again, but it caused twinges of pain in her torso, and she let it rest, hoping Dirt would just figure it out.

Well, he did, because he could see her thoughts. Dirt nodded and gathered another big ball of snow and melted it down for her, then let it trickle into her mouth while she slowly drank.

The blood on her clothing was still partially wet. It clung to her skin and made her feel even the softest breeze. Truthfully, she looked awfully ragged, and her clothing would be hard to clean. The cloth parts of her clothing could be soaked in cool water to get the blood out, but what about the fur? Would that work? Maybe.

Cleanliness aside, with that many holes, her furs probably did about as much good as Dirt's linen. Too bad the trees hadn't had time to show him how they made cloth. Or taught him how to ask the elementals for language.

Socks was having a great time slicing up the corpses, though, and he was getting better at it as he went. There was only a short rest before the next piece was ready for Dirt to bury, and even shorter for the piece after that. From that point on, Socks sliced the meat away faster than Dirt could cover it.

After tossing a prodigious amount of snow, Dirt realized he was sweating. Lifting so much with his mind was still hard work, even if he did it in small chunks now instead of big ones. It was strange—he felt warm under his armpits, and his legs were fine, but the air chilled the sweat on his brow, and his back where his shirt was damp.

Finally it was done, and Socks helped cover the rest of the meat. Afterward Dirt sighed and stretched, trying to absorb as much sunlight as he could against the cold, which was already starting to seep in through his sweaty shirt. Socks made him and the girl eat another helping of pale bird flesh, more than they were strictly interested in, because who knew when they'd eat again? They couldn't just carry the meat around forever. It would go bad. But it would be here, frozen, if they wanted to come back another time.

Socks stepped down the slope a bit to admire his handiwork and take in the stench of butchery that sat heavily on the still air. They had truly made a mess, an enormous one that put battlefields to shame. The pup liked the smell, and Dirt had learned to appreciate it from him, but the girl preferred the wind to be blowing in the other direction. After a few moments of self-pride, it was time to go.

"I have one more thing first. Hold on for a moment," said Dirt.

-What is it?-

"I want a staff, so I'm going to make one while there's some wood around. They're useful, and Home can't manage it right now because we're too far away." Dirt stumbled his way back up the mountainside and into the nest, where he dug for a likely chunk of wood to use.

He found one the right weight and gathered a few good puffs of mana, then spoke the magic into the hidden world and commanded the wood to transform. Despite being dry and dead and old, it creaked and cracked and slowly responded. *Straighten,* he told it, and *condense.* He left it a hand's length shorter than he was, then ended the spell.

Dirt swung it a few times, thumping through the snow and smacking it against exposed branches. It seemed solid enough. He stuck it in Socks's harness.

He and Socks both regarded the young woman, who kept thinking the same thing over and over: *Hè un diu? Deve esse un diu.*

Dirt recognized one word, *diu,* as being similar to his word for "god." Rather than awe, it seemed to evoke feelings of dread inside her. Her thoughts about Dirt's potential godhood were complicated and rapid, as if she couldn't decide if it was a good thing or a bad thing that he might be one. She was leaning toward bad thing.

"Why does she think I might be a god, but not you?" Dirt asked Socks.

-Aren't gods all human shaped?-

"Are they?"

-All the ones you showed me are. But you better not say anything, if you don't want her to think you are one. If she finds out you can see her mind you'll never convince her otherwise.-

"That's probably true. I think I'm just going to let her think she's really good at body language."

Socks dropped his jaw open and panted, eyes sparkling with amusement. He looked at the girl, then back at Dirt. *-Me too.-*

"Well, I'm ready to go if you are."

-Should I let her stand up and move around a bit first?-

"No, not yet. I think she's still too sore. Eventually she's going to have to pee, and we can let her walk then," said Dirt. He inhaled a puff of mana and jumped up onto Socks's back, then wondered where they were going to put the girl.

Socks had it all figured out, though. He lifted the young woman and laid her down on his back, with her head resting where Dirt usually sat. *-Pat her head and make sure she's ready, then you can lie on my neck and head. It'll be fine that way for a while.-*

"That works. Just let me know when your neck starts getting sore."

Careful not to step wrong and tug at Socks's fur, Dirt stepped around where she could see him.

The girl had a look of trepidation on her face. She knew what was about to happen, but not quite what to expect. And who could blame her? How many people had been privileged to ride a wolf, in all of history?

Dirt smiled and mimicked holding still, then nodded at her.

She lifted her hands a little, then acted like she was dumping something off to the side. Herself, he gathered. He looked at her mind, and she was indeed concerned about being dropped along the way.

Dirt shook his head and pointed at Socks, then at her, and made a holding-on motion. She panicked and tried to get a handful of the pup's fur, so he had to correct himself. He pointed at Socks first, *then* made the holding motion, *then* pointed at her. After that, he pointed at her again, then smiled and made a pillow with his arms, and relaxed into it.

She got the idea. She kept a grip on Socks's fur, though. Dirt knelt and made her unclench her fists so she wouldn't pull any out, then guided her hand to show her she could stick it in there and keep it warm.

Once that was all taken care of, she looked at him with something important on her face that she couldn't figure out how to express. He looked at her mind again, and it was easy to see: *Where are we going?*

He had no good way to tell her, so he didn't try. He just patted her on the head and lay against Socks's neck, resting his arms on the pup's head, and his chin on those.

Socks weighed his bearing against his direction sense, then turned back around and headed down the mountain in the direction they'd come. *-The bird was carrying her in almost a straight line from a human place. It's the closest one, too.-*

The pup picked up speed bit by bit instead of all at once to keep from terrifying his cargo, but it scared her anyway. Even with Socks's curved mental shield in front to direct most of the cold wind away and nothing to look at but the sky, she could sense how fast they were moving. She felt the motion of the pup's muscles below her and caught glimpses of the snow he kicked up behind him, and she spent the next while in a state of mild emotional distress.

Dirt and Socks had little to do other than watch her thoughts, which were easy enough to understand if they didn't struggle to learn each word. She kept having loud, imaginary arguments with people, and not always the same ones. Two who must have been her parents, a man and a woman. And an old man and woman, who seemed to be the leaders since they seemed to be giving orders.

She wasn't supposed to go back, but if the wolf was taking her home, then there was nothing she could do about it. She was worried in part for Dirt and Socks, fearing they might be attacked, which Socks found amusing. Her mental picture of that attack was four large men with spears.

They learned her name. Biandina. She kept picturing people yelling it in anger or surprise, calling it while they pleaded with her to leave, or sentencing her to death.

And she was certain they were going to kill her for returning. That was clear. She was deciding what to say before that happened. Some of it seemed conciliatory and apologetic, and some was harsh invective. Curses upon them, for letting her get too far in. For letting her do what she'd done.

She struggled to fight against the bud of hope that had grown inside her. The odd little boy-god and the wolf had saved her when she thought she was dead. She should be dead right now. Perhaps the gods were real after all, and not evil.

The girl got some sleep once she finally got used to Socks's speed and convinced herself she wasn't going to fall off. Dirt took the liberty of tapping her with his foot any time she started having a nightmare. She slept for well over an hour, which was rather impressive considering the circumstances.

There was less day left than they thought, since the sun raced across the sky much faster in winter than it did in summer. Twilight came before they'd reached their destination, requiring them to stop near a small hillock, which was the only shelter they could find nearby. Perhaps they should have stopped at the trees they'd passed a while back, but it was too late now.

Biandina was feeling quite a bit better, and once they let her stand up, she poked at her wounds in amazement to find them closed. Still sore inside and out, but the bleeding was done, and she could move around.

Her good health gave her a bit of spark, brightening her eyes. She gestured at the snow, trying to convey that Dirt and Socks should make a shelter like she had in mind, which was a round embankment, tall enough to keep the worst of the wind off them.

They obliged, piling up snow in a ring tall enough for Socks to lie inside of and not be seen. It took an absurd amount of snow, but there was plenty to work with.

After that, they dug through the snow to pull up grass to sit on. Biandina kept wincing and hissing every time she bent over, so Dirt made her stop and just watch. It didn't take long to gather enough, especially with Socks helping. The grass under the snow here was long and sturdy and thick and reminded him of the grain that grew around Ogena. They pulled up more than they needed and turned their little snow-bowl into another nest.

Miraculously, it ended up exactly like Biandina envisioned, which made her quite proud of herself. She gave Dirt a nervous hug and accepted Dirt's invitation to pat Socks on the snout. Socks somehow managed to restrain himself from huffing and startling her, but only barely. He'd been tempted.

Socks curled up in the shelter, and Dirt and Biandina crawled in afterward to make themselves comfortable against his fur. The grass was much better than sitting on the bare snow, and once Dirt summoned a few embers, the shelter held in a surprising amount of warmth.

Biandina did a lot of squirming as she tried to find a position that didn't put pressure on her injured insides, and Dirt was sure she fell asleep long after he and Socks did. All that digging in the snow had made him tired, and so had being cold. Being cold all day was exhausting. And now that he was warm, Dirt sank quickly into sleep, relishing it.

Once during the night, Socks gave a low growl, which woke Dirt up. Socks said, -*It's nothing. Go back to sleep.*- So he did.

The night was long, and they all woke before dawn, at the earliest light. Since Dirt and Socks held still and rested in case they fell back asleep, as they so often did, Biandina thought she was the only one awake. She sat in silence, feeling forlorn and miserable and scared about return-ing home again. The same faces kept swirling in her mind, the same conversations. Her thoughts cycled between that, and wondering how her wounds were healing so quickly and so well. She was still sore inside and out, but not nearly as bad as yesterday.

When Socks finally decided it was time to get up, Dirt and Biandina were surprised to find countless pawprints in the snow around the shelter, all larger than Dirt's foot but smaller than Socks's. Each print bore the claws of a predator.

-They smelled the scent of human, and they smelled me, and they thought I had killed some and they could scavenge. I think they believed I was something else. Smaller. Maybe a dog.-

Dirt found that somewhat ludicrous, since he'd smelled both dogs and wolves through Socks's nose, and they were nothing alike. But he was not one himself, so what did he know?

After seeing the tracks, Biandina was a lot more nervous than Dirt was, since she knew what the tracks belonged to. Her mental picture was something canine, but with a hunched torso and a short tail. They were a bit taller than adult humans and hunted in packs. She gazed around warily, watching the horizon with fidgety agitation while Dirt melted enough snow for everyone to get a drink. Socks needed three batches.

Even after that she was still nervous, so Dirt picked up a snowball with his hands and shaped it somewhat like the beast she was picturing. He pointed at it, then at the tracks.

She nodded, curious.

Dirt put it on the ground, pointed at Socks, and then smashed it under his heel. That got a chuckle out of her, followed by a wince. Her stomach muscles still needed more time, it seemed. But it was nice to see her smile. Color was coming back to her cheeks, too.

They were not far from the settlement and saw it on the horizon a few hours later. It was perfectly square with intact walls, but no buildings peeking up over them. It was small, too, smaller than Llovella, and the word that came to Dirt's mind for it was "outpost." A military place. A fortification where soldiers went. Dirt was sure his people had made it.

Biandina felt Socks slowing and sat up, rotating around to sit and face forward. Dirt slid down to sit right in front of her, and she draped her arms over his shoulders, which eased the pressure on her guts.

A group of horsemen charged out from around the walls, and Dirt imagined the gate must be on the other side. Six men, each with spears, rode their horses hard through the deep snow, as if they thought they'd make a charge. Dirt rose to his feet and hopped up onto Socks's head and waved, hoping to stop them before they did something that would get them killed.

-Look closer. They are not coming to attack me. They know what a wolf is,- said Socks, his voice tinged with curiosity.

Well, that got Dirt's attention. He looked at some of the closer minds. Farther away were a few hundred more, he estimated. And Socks was right. They were terrified out of their minds, but intended to welcome the giant pup, of all things.

Biandina stood on wobbly feet and held her hand out to Dirt. She pleaded, *"Sò chì ùn mi pudete micca capisce, ma per piacè, ùn li attaccate micca s'ellu pudete evitari."* Don't attack them, was the gist of it. That much he could tell.

Aloud, Dirt said, "Socks won't attack them unless they do something stupid."

The horses stopped thirty paces away, not daring to get any closer no matter how their riders urged them forward. The men had their spears pointed up, not forward, in a way that reminded Dirt of the duke's palace guards. They had no armor, though, just thick furs like Biandina had on, including the tight hood around their bearded faces.

Dirt hopped down and trudged through the snow to greet them. It was only thigh-deep here, not waist deep, but that was still too deep to traverse gracefully. Once he got reasonably close for talking, he waved and said, "Hello, I'm Dirt. Nice to meet you. We brought back a person of yours."

At this, Biandina rose from Socks's back and sailed gracefully through the air, to the horrified gasps of the riders. Dirt saw confusion in their minds, in part because they didn't recognize her, and in part because her torn and bloody clothing made them think Socks was returning a corpse.

But she landed gently on her feet and kept her balance after Socks let go. She slowly raised her face. She stood straight and pulled her hood back. She turned to the rider on the left and said, "Salutu, Babbu."

The man's face hardened like ice, and he slid quickly from his horse. Two steps brought him into range, and he stabbed directly for her heart. She closed her eyes and didn't flinch.

Dirt was ready, though. He already had the mana. He stepped over and grabbed the spearpoint right before it went in, bringing the spear and the man to a jolting stop. He snapped the spearhead off and threw it to the ground. "Let's not do this, okay?" he said.

The men screamed. Their fear made them lose the last of their control over the horses, and each bolted in a different direction. Four men were tossed into the snow. Those got up and ran back toward the fort. The other rider went off in completely the wrong direction and didn't stop.

Socks huffed in amusement. *-That's more like I was expecting. Come, little Dirt. Let us go make some friends.-*

CHAPTER EIGHTEEN

Looking at the minds of the fleeing men, they didn't think Socks was just a big scary wolf, or Dirt was a mysterious boy. *Hè un diu!* they shouted in their thoughts. He's a god, Dirt assumed. Or it's a god, something like that.

The images that accompanied those thoughts were of Dirt commanding Socks to attack, and much more besides. Torture and painful death, of wicked beasts that could not keep their shapes but changed with each lurching step. Of great rents in the earth out of which enormous spiders crawled; of strikes of lightning that deposited screaming human skeletons that walked and bit the living, all driven by some great and terrible thing just over the horizon. A god.

One man fled toward a barn somewhere, hoping to protect his sheep. Another struggled to regain control of his horse and rode for the walls, thinking only of his mate, who smiled beneath a halo of candlelit reddish-brown hair in his memory.

What a mess. So where to start? Socks was already walking toward the fort, sauntering with an amused air about him. He was planning on peeking over the wall and seeing what was in there and what everyone was doing.

Dirt looked back at the girl, though, still standing silently where she'd been. She gazed forward unseeing, her thoughts so conflicted she couldn't think what to do. Her mind and emotions were the most tangled jumble Dirt had ever seen.

He stepped over and gave her a hug, patting her sincerely on the back. She raised her arms and returned it limply, her mind elsewhere. Nowhere, really. Lost.

Well, that wasn't going to work. He stepped away and waved his hand in front of her eyes to get her attention. It took several tries. Then he pointed at the fleeing man who'd tried to stab her and said, "That's your father? *Babbu?* Papa? *Pare?*" Dirt hadn't even gotten a good look at him, with little to see other than his warm fur clothing.

"*Sì, hè u mo babbu,*" she said. "*Ùn duverebbe micca purtatumi quì.*"

"Okay, well, wait here for a moment. I'll go get him, and you can talk," said Dirt. He patted her arm and gave his best reassuring smile. She looked more miserable than reassured.

Dirt filled himself with mana and charged after the man, running right through the snow like a horse. He tackled him from behind, nearly missing because he wasn't very quiet about it and the babbu stepped to the side to dodge. But Dirt still got one arm around the man's waist and was able to spin him to the ground. After that, Dirt caught one of his fists and pushed it awkwardly against his chest so he couldn't go for a second punch.

The babbu squirmed and fought with such terrified abandon that Dirt couldn't help but laugh in sympathy, but a mana-infused Dirt was too strong for him. "Good human! Nice human," he said, putting on his most beatific half-smile. "It's okay. Calm down. Calm down. There you go. Good human. Good *babbu.*"

Either there was a word or two in there that the man understood, or he got the point some other way. His mind still contained despair, and below that, a fiery revulsion for Biandina. But he stopped struggling and gazed up at Dirt, his darting brown eyes only half-lucid, as if merely watching for an opening, not truly seeing anything.

"Better. Okay. Are you going to behave yourself? Good babbu?" asked Dirt.

"*Bonu . . . babbu,*" said the man. He wasn't sure what Dirt was getting at with that. His thoughts grew a bit more coherent, but that didn't help much. Instead it resulted in a steady stream of words that Dirt couldn't understand. Biandina's face flashed in his memory, but without context.

Dirt pointed at himself and said, "Dirt. My name is Dirt. Dirt."

"Nomen . . . nome? Dirt?"

"Dirt. Nome Dirt," said Dirt, nodding in approval. Then he pointed at Socks, who had changed his mind and turned around to watch, and said, "Nome Socks."

The man nodded. "Socks." More than anything, he seemed surprised to still be alive, and hearing human speech from the terrifying little monster.

Dirt pointed at the girl and said, "Nome Biandina?" He accentuated the question in his voice.

"*E . . . Etiam, id est Biandina,*" said the man, "*figliola mia.*"

"She's my friend," said Dirt, in his language.

"*Amica . . . amicu? U vostru amicu?*" said the father.

Dirt was pleased to discover more and more words that were similar to his language, although it was strange that it was all different ones from the language of the Camayans. "Yes, she's my friend."

He let go of the man's arm and gently got off him, then held out a hand to pull him up. The father rolled and jumped to his feet, expecting to sprint toward the fort now that he had an opening.

Except he didn't. No sooner had he turned around than he nearly bumped into Socks's snout. The pup gave a low growl. Just the hint of one. The barest hint, but it was enough.

Dirt took the man's cold, rough hand and led him over to Biandina, who hadn't moved from that spot.

"Your daughter," he said. "My friend. Although I really don't know her very well, since we speak two different languages. But I guess that doesn't matter, does it? Daughter. Friend," said Dirt, pointing, just to make sure the father understood.

She spoke, her voice timid and resigned. "*Aghju purtatu un diu, Babbu. Mi dispiace.*"

"No," said Dirt sternly. "I'm not a god. Not a *diu!* A boy. I'm a boy, and my name is Dirt."

Two of the other horsemen had gotten their beasts under control by now and were watching from a distance. They expected to have to charge in to save their human but didn't want to make the first move.

"*Avete da vultà à a tomba. Ùn ci perseguite micca, figliola,*" said the father, his voice containing not fear, but revulsion and despair.

"*Ùn sò micca mortu. U picculu diu m'hà salvatu. Ùn sò micca mortu, ma ùn sò micca perchè,*" she said, almost a whisper. Her eyes were wide now, fearful as her father was.

Mortu? That sounded like his word for death. So that's what the father had in mind. It made sense, now that Dirt understood it. The revulsion was because he thought this was a walking corpse.

Dirt sighed and lifted her ragged, bloody shirt to show the healing wounds in her abdomen, still red and sore but no longer open and oozing. "Look, see? She got hurt by that bird, but she'll get better now. She won't die."

He pointed at the talon-holes in her pants, then at her shoulder, showing all the places she'd been injured.

Socks decided he'd had enough and spoke with his mind, loud and clearly for them all to hear. The image he sent was of Biandina dying and limp in the great bird's talons, then Socks licking her wounds, then her wounds healing and her recovering. At the end, he showed his cute little Dirt patting her head, making very clear that Dirt was *his* pet, not the other way around, and not anything but a human.

The babbu was stunned but recovered his wits quickly. He only needed a glance at Socks to figure out what had happened, and Socks hadn't exactly made it difficult. The bundle of thought was very clear about whom it belonged to. And just like that, everything changed in his mental world. No longer was Dirt a god here to destroy them, but he was a stray human that a wolf was keeping as a pet.

His relief was obvious, but not complete. His body seemed to deflate as he relaxed and breathed out a heavy sigh. He retained a hint of ice in his eyes, his mind considering far-off implications more serious than a curious wolf, but he waved to the others to come nearer.

Biandina muttered, *"Mi salvavanu senza sapè ciò chì passava."*

Babbu nodded and bowed his head, closing his eyes. He thought very, very loudly, which got a little grin from Dirt. He knew at once why the man did it—closing his eyes and thinking loudly made it easy to tell who was talking. He couldn't exactly indicate with his own scent like the wolves did.

He did his best to think only in images and emotions, but didn't quite pull it off. He pictured Biandina wandering off, going a separate direction from Socks. He added some explanation in a hasty stream of sentences that neither boy nor wolf understood, but the general meaning was clear. *Please get rid of her.*

Socks growled, and the man went pale and froze. The horses stepped back and their riders had to pat them on the necks to keep them calm. The pup sent an image of putting Biandina in her sire's arms as a gift, and the man spurning it by tossing her into the snow.

"Maledetta," said the man softly, struggling to think how to explain without words.

"Oh, *maledicta*?" said Dirt. The word was almost the same as his: cursed. They were saying she was cursed. He felt a whiff of disgust. Sorcery. Nonsense. Wasn't it? That was a lingering opinion from old Avitus.

"*Iè, hè maledetta! Hà datu un sacrifiziu è pricava à un diu,*" said the babbu, his voice pleading.

Socks huffed in amusement. *-These humans are silly,-* he told Dirt. *-Why are they worried about something like a curse, when nothing here is trying to kill them?-*

"*I'm starting to think silliness is a hallmark of my species,*" replied Dirt. "*Are curses even real?*"

-I don't know, but Mother never told us about them if they are,- said Socks. Then he sent another mental image, loud enough that everyone in the fort probably heard it. It showed Socks and Dirt wandering around looking for something to do, then spotting her being carried, then fighting and killing the birds. Then finding her alive, and himself licking Biandina's near-fatal wounds. Then Dirt giving her water, and her recovery. The message was similar to his last one, but the meaning was different. He was saying, "She is incredibly lucky for someone who is cursed."

Babbu and Biandina had the same reaction, as did the men nearby: None of them wanted to argue with Socks, but they still thought she was cursed. All of them resolved simultaneously to make the pup happy and give him what he wanted until he left. After that, Biandina would leave again, and hopefully it wouldn't be too late.

-My siblings must visit every now and then, for these humans to know what I am and how to talk to me,- said Socks. *-It makes me wonder if this is their territory and they are letting the humans live here, or if they leave their territory every now and then when they want to go see new things.-*

"*I hope they aren't farming the people to eat,*" said Dirt.

-I doubt it. Humans take too long to grow up, and you don't have enough meat to make good livestock,- said Socks, which was honestly one of the more reassuring things he'd ever said.

"I don't think they have much experience with wolves, or they wouldn't have thought you belonged to me in the first place. I suspect they just have old stories that tell them what to do. If we ever learn to talk to them, we can ask," said Dirt.

Now the men were considering their stocks of food and wondering if they had enough to feed the wolf, while Biandina was trying to decide whether she even dared enter the fort and face the people inside. Her mother was there, and her siblings and friends, and the old man and woman who were probably in charge.

Socks's belly was still full after glutting himself on bird meat yesterday, but he sent them a mental image of giving Dirt a piece of bread to eat, and of Dirt greeting other children.

"Pensu chì avete a fame," said the father to Dirt and Biandina. He waved for them to follow and politely stepped around Socks to make his way back to the fort.

Socks figured out which horse-mind belonged to the man's horse and told it to come back, which it did, to the surprise of the other riders. Babbu took it by the reins, choosing to walk instead.

Only Biandina hadn't moved. She was trying to keep her face blank, but it wasn't working. The conflict in her heart was plain to see, even without knowing her thoughts, which Dirt mostly did.

And so did her father, apparently, because he said, *"Torna à mezu à noi, figliola. Sembra chì ùn semu micca scappà di u nostru destinu, tuttu ciò chì pò esse."*

She nodded, but hesitated, so Dirt grabbed her hand and pulled her forward. The jolt caused little twinges of pain up and down her body, since she wasn't completely healed yet.

-I'll carry you,- said Socks. *-Your little legs can't handle this snow.-* He lifted Dirt and Biandina onto his back and led the way, growing impatient. Dirt saw in his mind that he was getting whiffs of things he wanted to examine from inside the outpost walls.

The girl glanced down at her father, hoping in her mind that he wouldn't be frightened to see it, but he was past being surprised by anything at this point. He mounted his horse and mumbled to one of the other riders. That one sped on ahead, probably to warn everyone they were coming.

The party was somber and joyless as they made their way into the fort, which wasn't what Dirt had envisioned at all. He'd expected mostly terror, since Socks was here, or joy, since they'd brought Biandina back. But neither was the case. Just brooding quiet. Unease.

Hardly anyone had been outside the walls since the snowstorm, as evinced by the lack of trails through the deep snow. Socks kicked a nice trail for them to follow, cleaner and easier than the one left by the horses a few moments before, until they found the gate.

A large door of crisscrossing iron bars swung outward, and a thick wooden one swung inward to grant access. Both looked monstrously ancient. The opening was about the size of the doorway to the duke's palace, only big enough to let a wagon through. It was nothing like the gates of Ogena, which were wide enough to let an army march out.

To Dirt's surprise, when he peeked in, the inside was shadowy and dim, despite the cloudless sky and sunlight. It was not until Socks ducked down and shimmied through that they saw the reason why— the entire outpost was covered with a mesh netting. It sagged precariously beneath the weight of melting snow, even though the spaces in the mesh were half an inch wide.

Regularly spaced poles held it all up, and those spots had holes to let smoke out, which is also where most of the light inside came from. Those spots shone brighter than lamps. The snow on the netting blocked most of the sunlight, leaving only a dim, lumpy glow where it peeked through.

The heat from inside the fort had already started the snow melting, resulting in steadily dripping rain everywhere. Most of the water dripped from the centers of the sags, under which strange water basins made of hide and bone slowly filled, but everything was nonetheless damp and cold.

As his eyes adjusted, he quickly found the people. Men, women, and children, all with curious expressions and suntanned faces. They stood or sat on thick pillows to keep their bottoms off the wet pavement, and with so many people huddled together it was somewhat warm. No one inside wore those big fluffy leather coats with fur lining, preferring simpler attire indoors. They wore clothing reminiscent of the Camayans, but with more wool than linen, and which favored zig-zag patterns for decoration.

There were no roads. The outpost wasn't large enough to need any. Instead, narrow pathways wove between the tangled mess of shacks and tents covering every available spot of ground. The smell of the place was as strong as an Ogena market square at midday, with so many bodies living in such close proximity.

As with Ogena, the light of so many minds made it difficult to tell them apart. But unlike Ogena, if he dimmed his own thoughts as if to hide them, the overlaps dimmed as well, and he could tell them apart. The close ones, anyway. Mostly, they contained a mixture of curiosity and awe, but Socks could smell plenty of acidic fear in the air. Dirt sniffed and wondered if he could smell it too, or if he was imagining things.

-This place is too crowded. There is nowhere for me to lie down without crushing a human or a little house,- complained Socks.

The big pup was right. There was hardly any room at all, anywhere, at least not by the gate. Dirt stood and stepped up onto Sock's head and could touch the low parts of the ceiling cloth. But from up here, he saw an open area about a hundred paces farther in. That would do. Socks headed in that direction, stepping carefully as he went.

Even when the pup's giant claws landed only a foot or two away, no one made a sound. The crowd stayed seated and quiet, except for a few babies and toddlers that screamed, or a young child who asked questions only to be quickly hushed by a parent. Dirt found it truly unsettling. It seemed the archers attacking them in Ogena had been more welcoming than *this*. What was everyone doing?

-They are making sure not to annoy or startle me. Wolves do not like it where there is too much sound or commotion, unless we're making it. I am an exception because I am used to you, but if a different wolf were here, this would be smart,- explained Socks. *-They spread the word quickly. I wonder how.-*

"I wonder how we're going to get them to agree to keep Biandina. Do you think they have any other problems we can solve while we're here?" asked

Dirt. Looking around, it didn't seem like they would be very forthcoming, but maybe that would change after they got to know each other.

-I don't know, but there aren't very many of them. They would be foolish to refuse us,- said Socks.

"Hopefully something will come up that we can fix before we have to leave again," said Dirt.

He eventually made his way past the crowd and into an open area in front of the Principia, still standing despite the centuries. Any façade or decoration the building once bore was gone and many of the stones had been replaced by much shoddier brick, but the shape was right. It was the only proper building in the place, the only thing not assembled from whatever spare parts the locals could stick haphazardly together.

The granary that should be next to it was missing, as was the commander's quarters, which served to remind Dirt that the Sunset Empire was still gone. This was the corpse of a place inhabited by people who didn't understand it, not an island of old culture that had endured.

There was enough open space in front of the Principia for Socks to sit down, and he finally did, slumping down to rest with false tiredness that was intended to put the humans at ease. If it helped, it only did slightly.

Dirt slid off and helped Biandina down, and once her feet were both on the ground, she practically hid behind Dirt in a way that reminded him of how Màxim would always stand behind Èlia until he'd gotten familiar with Socks. Dirt smiled softly at that. Would Èlia and Biandina ever meet, he wondered?

The crowd near the gate were shuffling into the area and sitting again, all quietly so as not to give offense. It made Dirt feel like he was at a funeral, the boring part of one. Which was a curious thought. What happened at a funeral?

Biandina's father rode past, taking his horse to a nearby stable, leaving her and Dirt to stand there blankly and stare at the crowd.

Dirt looked with his mind-sight and took it all in, trying to gather the general mood of the people and see what he could learn. Very little, beyond what he could tell with his eyes. Curiosity, nervousness, and so on.

But there was one mind that stood out among the rest. Not because it was brighter, but something about its shape or contents grabbed his attention. He focused on it, wondering what it was, and recognized an unnatural emptiness. A familiar one, belonging only to the most wretched of things.

"*Hey, Socks,*" said Dirt in his mind, "*one of these people is dead.*"

CHAPTER NINETEEN

Socks startled slightly, then stuck his nose up to sniff the air. He looked with his own mind-sight and found it quickly. *-You are right. Half dead, and I wasn't looking. What do you want to do about it? Shall we merge our minds and kill it right now?-*

Dirt looked at all the people staring at him and grew self-aware and went about straightening his shirt and smacking stray dust from his pants, even though there wasn't any. *"I don't know. Let's see what they want to do with us first. I'm not sure it'd be a good idea to rip one of their people in half right away. They probably don't know what it is, since it's not attacking anyone."*

-But we are going to rip it in half, right?-

"Oh, of course."

-Good.-

The half-corpse mind had no thoughts in it, no reasoning of any kind, but the living part of its face still functioned. Its eyes took in light so it could see, and its ears still heard. Right now, it was somewhere near the back of the crowd, watching Socks. The end of the pup's tail twitched, eager to go destroy it. Soon enough.

Shortly after, an older man emerged from the Principia, which pleased Dirt; at least they were using the building somewhat correctly. The duke or Father or whatever they called him belonged there. He approached carrying two slices of dried meat the size of his forearm on a handsome ceramic platter with patterns in blue glaze.

If that was all he was bringing out for something the size of Socks, food must be scarce, even this early in the winter. Why they were short on supplies, Dirt could easily speculate. Perhaps the giant birds, or local goblins, or those big wolfy creatures, but it didn't really matter. That was just the fate of humans.

The old man had a spry step, though, and a vigor that didn't match his wrinkly, spotted old face or head with more bare skin than hair. His simple gray woolen shirt did little to distinguish him, but the way people moved out of the way and lifted their palms for him made it clear he was in charge. That palm lifting was a strange gesture, but Dirt figured it symbolized upholding his leadership, or his health, or some such thing.

His age showed when he winced as he bent down to place the ceramic platter on the ground before Socks. He had a sore back, like so many of the aged men of Ogena. Socks and Dirt were able to pick out his mind in the crowd when he thought very loudly that Socks should eat. Mostly in pictures, but a few words snuck in. *Per piacè, manghja.* "Per piacè" was "please," so manghja must be "eat."

Socks replied with an image of himself glutting on bird flesh, enjoying the blood that got all over his nose and the fur of his face, and the feeling of his stomach getting full to bursting. Even now he felt full. But his little human and their new friend had gotten no breakfast. Socks ended it with Dirt and Biandina tearing away some dried meat and taking a bite.

Dirt had no interest in waiting around and hopped over to grab some. Biandina didn't follow, so Dirt tore off a strip for her as well, then grabbed her cheeks like he was going to force-feed her, unable to suppress a giggle. She got upset and considered smacking him, which made it even funnier, but chose to eat instead, shyly looking at anything but the crowd while she wolfed it down.

It wasn't bad. It was fine, just not good enough to bother sharing his sense of taste with Socks. Nothing delicious about it, just meat and almost enough salt. They probably saved the good stuff for creatures with more discerning palates than Socks and his kind.

Still, it was food, and Dirt couldn't go for a week on a full belly like Socks. He had a much smaller belly, and it emptied out in less than a day, no matter the size of the meal.

So he smiled and repeated the palm-up gesture at the old Father and said, "Thank you. Can I keep the rest of this?"

The old man gave Socks an inquisitive glance, hoping for an explanation, and Socks replied with an image of Dirt putting the leftover meat in a harness pocket to eat later. The old man smiled genially and nodded, then picked up the leftovers and reached up to drop them into the pocket himself. Then he patted the pocket and stepped back.

After that, no one was quite sure what to do. It quickly became apparent that they were hoping Socks would either tell them what he wanted, or leave.

-What should I tell them? And even better, how?- Socks asked Dirt. A mild sensation of frustration accompanied his thoughts.

"You're overthinking it. Just talk like a wolf. Tell them like you'd tell Brother and let them figure it out. Knowing how to talk in my language is making it seem harder than it is," said Dirt.

-Fine,- said Socks, visibly relieved. He shifted his weight and settled in, then crossed his front paws and rested his head on them. It was a restful position, but not a sleepy one, and Socks's eyes were still high enough to keep watch on the surroundings.

When he spoke again, his thoughts filled the gathering like the scent of incense in a temple, calming an already quiet crowd of curious humans. He spoke calmly, without any of the harshness or pressure that Father or Mother or Big Brother had. Like when the pups spoke amongst each other, scent and impression conveyed more than images or sounds did.

He began by introducing himself, sharing his own scent that revealed his sex and age, still a pup on the verge of getting his adult fur and coloring. He showed Mother, stronger than the roots of the earth, his nurturer and teacher and judge, sending him to explore, and how he found Dirt on one of his very first forays into the wilds away from the den.

Socks skipped a lot of details that Dirt thought were important, like the order things happened in, but instead he focused on the things he thought were interesting. Sights and smells, interesting places. Bugs and birds and all manner of prey, the flavor of blood of a dozen creatures.

Human places they'd found and explored. Goblins they'd fought. Those digger creatures in the mountains, the tentacle beast. Socks hid as much as he revealed, always keeping Dirt's role in the background, perhaps to keep him from seeming superhuman.

He showed them the white tower of Llovella stained with soot and the empty town around it. To Socks, it was a place of startling variety, more things than he could take in everywhere he looked. Smells in a wild, heady confusion; old wood and paint and cloth and rotting grain; new plants growing, traces of passing animals, much more. Always some fascinating thing to spot in a window, or Dirt showing him some new artifice intended to make up for natural human inadequacy.

After that, Socks showed the walled city of Ogena and all its bustling little humans crammed in together, some wearing metal and others cloth, and now his little Dirt felt like he should wear clothes too. Socks found it all very fascinating and communicated it with how the materials smelled and how humans smelled while wearing them, with only flashes of images as if what it looked like didn't matter.

The humans in the crowd paid rapt attention, even the infants and small children. Dirt had an easier time picking their little minds out, since they were both simple and full of light. The little ones took in what Socks was telling them and processed it at a primal level, more completely than any of the adults. The older a human was, the more he had to struggle to figure out what it all meant.

A woman just as old as the city's Father came out of the Principia wearing a thick woolen dress that went down to her ankles and looked pleasantly warm. She had a big pot of water over one shoulder, which seemed more than she should be able to carry. She set it down in front of Socks and handed Dirt a ladle to drink out of, then Biandina. Finally, she gestured for Socks to finish off the rest. His tongue was too wide to fit into the opening, so he lifted it with his mind and emptied it into his mouth in one splash. It might be plenty of water for a human, but it was no more than a gulp or two for Socks.

Dirt wondered if they were bringing out only small amounts on purpose, intending to give the pup the idea that they were not a reliable source of food, but by the time Dirt picked out her mind amongst all the lights in the crowd, it was too late to tell.

After that, Socks went back to when they first met Ignasi and Marina and Hèctor and how frightened they'd been because they couldn't recognize Dirt for what he obviously was: a normal little human.

He skipped to watching Dirt learn to dance and being thoroughly confused, since the rhythm and sounds of music didn't have the effect on Socks that it did on humans. Socks's best guess was that it made up for having incredibly dull senses of smell and hearing and losing all the pleasure that came with them. But Dirt liked it, so Socks could appreciate it by proxy.

After that, Socks showed the ruins of Ocriculum, and Dirt being sad about losing his human civilization. Dirt, despite being tiny, had exuded more of the scent of misery than Socks had thought possible for a living creature, standing alone in a half-collapsed room howling at the sky while his eyes leaked water. His own heart had ached in sympathy, and they'd become even closer because of it.

Dirt, aside from being adorable, was a wellspring of novelty. Each time Socks thought he was beginning to fully grasp human behavior, something new happened.

From there the story wandered as they explored over the rest of the summer and much of the autumn, of plants and games and the scents found only on the tops of mountains. Of hunting with Father and his siblings, of the bracing vigor that came with the cold weather, and how it energized him.

Socks left out the magical device that transported them here, preferring to leave it vague, but showed how they spotted Biandina being carried by the bird and rescued her. He showed the fight, mixing in the scents of terror and pain from the birds, and sharing information Dirt hadn't noticed—three of the birds were old, and two were young, but they weren't parents and children to each other. That meant there must be lots more of them around.

The pup's tale ended with what would happen if the humans harmed Biandina or cast her out again: Dirt would be sad, and that would make Socks angry. And just to make the point, he raised his head again to give Dirt a little lick on the side of his face, then glared possessively at the crowd before resting his head again.

It seemed half the crowd didn't know what had happened with the girl and were confused, and the half that knew got rather uncomfortable. All at once, dozens of children asked their mothers what Socks meant and who Biandina was. In reply came just as many hushed responses, short ones that probably didn't explain much.

The tribe's Father seemed nonplussed and wiped his hand across his head as if he still had hair to straighten. Biandina's babbu approached and muttered something in the old man's ear that Dirt didn't quite catch.

The old man then leaned down to repeat it into his mate's ear, and the old woman's face smoothed immediately into a gentle smile. So she *was* like the duchess, after all.

She leaned down slightly toward Dirt, just enough to give him her full attention but not seem condescending, and said, slowly and clearly, "*Tù è u lupu pudete capiscenu, nò?*"

"Tu" and "lupu" were close enough to Dirt's words to tell she was asking about him and Socks, but the rest was obscure. She saw his hesitancy on his face and mimicked puppets with her hands, one talking to the other.

Dirt grinned and said, "Perfectly."

His word for that must have been close to hers, because she gave him a friendly nod and pointed at his eyes, then turned her hand outward, gesturing for him to come see something. Then the puppet hands talking again. Come see this, then tell the wolf.

Dirt nodded and took the staff he made from Socks's halter, then reached for her hand. She took it and gave a polite little bow to Socks.

-Don't let her trick you. Put mana in your skin now, just in case,- said Socks.

"*They don't know I'm dangerous, but there's no doubt that you are. They wouldn't dare. Want to share our sight?*" replied Dirt.

-Yes.-

So they did. Dirt opened his mind to Socks, and that portion slid together, easily as ever. There was a moment of disorientation before Socks closed his eyes, but the pup had to give one last glare at the woman just to make sure she didn't get any ideas. The pup rested his head on his paws again afterward, but his ears kept flicking to listen to everything, indicating he was still awake.

The woman led him through the crowd, which only parted enough to let them walk past. The old man followed, and behind him, Biandina's babbu and the girl herself, shyly trying to keep out of sight. As they snaked through the people, Dirt did as Socks instructed and inhaled enough mana to toughen his skin from head to toe. If anyone tried to hurt him, they'd be in for a surprise.

They walked right to the Principia, which was the thing Dirt most wanted to see anyway. The door was long gone, leaving just an empty frame that Socks might not be able to fit through if he tried. Dirt's missing memories twitched as they entered the Great Hall, and for just an instant he expected to find hanging banners and flags, spears and swords and shields decorating the walls. Bright lamps and colorful decorations.

But there was none of that, and it confused him until his eyes adjusted to the dimmer light. Even with the snow dimming the area outside, they burned no lamps or candles during the day here, and it was dark as a cave. The old woman led him very slowly, keeping him from stepping on anything, and it wasn't long before he could make out his new surroundings.

The Principia's Great Hall was missing nearly everything that should have defined it. Instead, the spacious room was merely filled with tents and shacks of slightly better construction than outside. At least there were weapons stacked along the near wall, mostly long wooden spears, but clearly not as decoration. He had to suppress the scowl his face wanted to put on, but Dirt reminded himself that this was not a place of *his* people anymore.

His eyes were drawn to the door across the way, straight opposite the entrance. That was the part of the Principia he most wanted to see, even while he was certain he'd regret it. Something drew him, a sense of familiarity and duty. That was the place he would have gone first, he knew, back when he was Avitus. Through that door, and into . . . something.

Before they could enter, though, the men had to move a heavy wooden frame they'd set there to block the way. It didn't quite go all the way up, as anyone could see by the light shining over, and Dirt could have climbed up and squeezed through if he wanted. And he found it encouraging—if no one went in there, maybe it would be untouched after all these years.

The room was much brighter inside, due to a big hole in the roof through which the snow had fallen. It lay in a big round clump, spotless. The sunlight reflecting on it was so bright that Dirt had to squint to see anything else, but then he saw an outline and rushed in, to the dismay of the old woman who couldn't quite keep a hold on his hand.

In the center of the room, under the pinnacle of the arched roof, was a statue of Melodia, the Mistress of Song, Watcher over Travelers. An unusual goddess for an army outpost to worship, but not unheard of, especially if troops were regularly moving in and out.

And just like every other image of the gods that Dirt had seen, she was injured and suffering. A gash ripped her open from one shoulder to the opposite thigh. Blood of carved marble ran down her leg and pooled around her feet, then dripped from the plinth and gathered in a small pool on the floor. Her dress hung ragged, and one hand tried to hold her guts in, though they bulged around it. The other arm was broken at the elbow, turning the wrong way and dangling uselessly, and one foot was turned and lame. Her face bore such miserable pain that Dirt felt sick to his stomach.

The old woman noticed Dirt's dismay and placed a comforting hand on his back. But there was little comfort in her voice as she explained, *"Biandina hà fattu un sacrifiziu à stu dea. Hè per quessa ch'ella hè maledetta è perchè deve lascià."*

Dirt caught the words for sacrifice, goddess, and curse, and mulled it over for a moment. Then his eyes got wide, and he made a motion of slitting a throat, then pointed at Biandina. They'd tried to sacrifice her? Over a stupid curse? And she'd gotten away, somehow, maybe?

The old woman saw the anger on his face and shook her hands to indicate "no." She pointed at a carved stone rabbit in part of the decoration along the faux pillars lining the walls. Dirt nodded and made rabbit ears with his fingers to show he understood.

She mimicked holding up the animal by its ears and carrying it toward the statue, then ending its life with the slash of a blade. She pointed at a dark stain on the plinth, which Dirt realized must be the animal's blood. "She sacrificed a rabbit?" Dirt asked.

First off, she'd done it wrong. The blood was supposed to go on the altar, and there wasn't one here. And second . . . did Melodia accept rabbits? He didn't know. It might be written down somewhere. But more importantly than that, who cared? What could a god that looked like that do, for good or evil? And besides that, were there even still gods in the world? It didn't seem that way to Dirt. Either they were helpless, or they were gone.

Thinking about it made the old guilt resurface. He was partially responsible for all of this. He was a living sacrilege himself, so why should he be upset about Biandina doing something useless?

Dirt sighed like a tired old man. He looked up at the statue, and she seemed to be staring down at him, imploring him to end her pain. "I really do keep coming back to this, don't I? I'm sorry, Melodia, for whatever I did."

He placed his hand on her good foot, palm resting on her tightly curled toes, and bowed his head for a moment. There was something he should be doing or saying, something he had done a thousand times, but he couldn't remember what. He had lost it forever.

The other humans were dismayed by his behavior, and Dirt glanced at their minds to find out why. To them, it looked like Dirt was familiar with the gods, and that seemed such a blasphemy that they were wondering if they should somehow warn the wolf, or if the wolf was part of it.

Biandina's babbu's heart was pained and unsettled, and he was strongly considering killing Dirt and his daughter right here, then trying to talk himself out of it. He wasn't a fool; it was simply a matter of which bad outcome would be worse. The attention of that god—the embodiment of suffering and evil—or the ire of the wolf.

Dirt stepped back and sighed, shrugging. He looked at the old woman with a look on his face as if to say, what now?

"*Cumu cunnosce u so nome? Cumu cunnosce u nome di a dea?*" asked the old woman.

Dirt heard the word for "name" and "goddess." "Oh, what's her name? That's Melodia. Melodia," he said.

Well, that was the wrong thing to say. The old woman recoiled, and the old man let out a quiet hiss. Biandina's babbu saw their reaction and considered trying to stab Dirt, but remembered what Dirt had done to his spear.

"What's wrong? What did I say?" he asked.

But before he could get an answer, Socks severed their shared sight. The pup had heard something and wanted to see what it was, and soon told him, -*Watch out, Dirt. That half-dead human just snuck in the doorway. I think he's coming to you. I only caught a glimpse but he looks like this.*-

The pup sent an image of a man from behind, wide-shouldered and hood down, revealing a head of short, curly hair and a pale neck. *-Need me to come?-*

"Not yet. Let me see if I can smooth this out first. Otherwise we might be leaving in a hurry," said Dirt.

He raised his hands apologetically, trying to look chagrined. He pointed at himself, then mimicked sacrificing a rabbit just as the old woman had done, then emphatically waved his hands in an X shape, hoping to communicate that it was something he'd never do. He gestured twice, just to make the point.

A pair of eyes flashed deep inside the doorway, back in the dark of the Great Hall. Dirt looked at the minds and found the half-corpse. It was hiding there, silently and thoughtlessly watching him.

Dirt pointed and said, "Who's that?"

The others looked just as it crept backward to hide. The old man had seen motion, though, and stepped back into the Great Hall to see who it was. Dirt heard him conversing with someone else, a gruff male voice with a gravelly quality. Then the old man and the half-dead corpse walked in, both squinting in the sunlight.

He looked perfectly normal. Even his mannerisms seemed average. He had a short, dark beard to match his dark hair and wore the same woolen clothing everyone else had on. If anything distinguished him at all, it was his skin, just a shade paler than average.

The man-shaped monster gave Dirt a polite wave. With a hint of apology in his voice, he muttered something to the old man that Dirt didn't quite catch.

Dirt assessed him carefully, looking for anything he could accuse the man with. Dirt would prefer to kill him before he realized he was in danger, but he didn't want to fight half the tribe on his way out.

The man smiled, flashing his teeth in a way that made Dirt think of hunger. The old man muttered something else, and the monster snorted.

Dirt decided it was time to make a move. Better to strike first than wait and react. He smiled and stepped over to the man, then reached forward to offer him a handshake. The man accepted, and his hand was cold and strong, barely moving. Dirt suddenly tugged the man's shirt up with his mind, since there was no way all of him looked normal. Dirt just had to expose him.

The man's clothing went tight, but surprisingly, his shirt was sewn to his pants to prevent exactly this.

"Got you now," said Dirt with a predatory grin of his own. Strengthening both his arms, he dropped his staff and caught the other man's wrists to hold him in place. Then with his mind, he yanked the knife out of its sheath and sliced a circle around the man's shirt.

It fell open and revealed a mass of pulsing gray flesh covering two-thirds of his torso. Under his armpit was a woman's face from the nose down, chin jutting two inches out from where the rib cage should be. Dirt held him there for long enough for the others to see it, then swung the knife back around for a stab.

The monstrous human gave Dirt a brutal kick in the stomach that lifted both feet off the floor. It was so vicious that a tiny bit of pain made it through Dirt's mana protection, but Dirt kept hold of his wrists, strengthening his fingers with more and more mana.

The others realized what they were seeing and screamed. Biandina's babbu reacted first and stabbed the half-corpse right through his gray, pulsating chest, spearpoint coming a handspan out his front.

It didn't affect him in the slightest. The only reaction was that the monstrosity quit pretending to have human emotions and let his face go slack. The woman's face under his right arm jawed its mouth, reaching with its teeth.

The creature leaned in with its male head to take a bite of Dirt's face, but Dirt threw the dagger straight into the monster's forehead with his mind. He braced his feet and mentally pushed it deeper. Then he yanked it out with a wet smacking sound and went for the neck.

At the same time, some of the twisting flesh on the man's torso unwound and became a long arm with three joints and a single clawed finger on the end. It stabbed over and over at Dirt, hard enough to sound a solid thump in his chest, but Dirt's mana didn't let it puncture him.

Dirt still refused to let go, strengthening his fingers to iron. He stabbed over and over with the knife, yanking sideways each time to leave huge gashes, only some of which bled. The man fell apart, losing an arm, then a leg, then his head, and then finally dying all the way. Rotting black blood pooled on the floor and raised an incredible stench, and all was still.

Into the shocked silence that followed came a scratch, scratch, scratch, gentle and rhythmic, from under the stone floor.

CHAPTER TWENTY

The humans must not have heard the scratching, or if they did, they chose to ignore it. The shock of the sudden fight filled the air with emotional sparks. Biandina's babbu pulled her away from the spreading black blood while the old woman hastily wiped some splattered drops from the old man's face. Other than that, everyone stared in horror and disgust at the brutally mangled corpse of their corrupted kinsman.

Dirt was filthy, blood all up and down his front, but thank Grace he'd had the good sense to keep his mouth shut. He never wanted to taste anything worse than tentacle slime, and this smelled like it would be.

He stepped over to the untouched pile of snow and pushed his face in as far as it would go, then turned his head left and right to try to clean it. That turned out to be painful, since the snow scraped like sand, and the icy cold wasn't pleasant either. And on top of that, it didn't work very well.

Oh well. He'd borrow a rag and use that. First, though, he retrieved his dagger and cleaned it thoroughly in the snow by wetting it down, wiping it with his fingers, and finishing with the back of his pants where they were still clean. The sheath was untouched, fortunately.

By then, Socks had squeezed into the Great Hall somehow and stuck his head through the doorway of the Aedes, as close as he could get without ruining the building. *-Everyone, hold still,-* he commanded in the way of wolves, then shared his sense of hearing with Dirt. The humans looked at the wolf, trying to assess how angry he was and didn't seem to know how to tell. They hushed and held still.

With Dirt's human ears, the scratching had been faint and distant, but now it echoed clearly in a hollow space under the front of the statue. It was a metallic sound, unlike the scratching under Ocriculum. Giving the floor a closer examination, he saw that the spot where the altar should have gone had two half-stones instead of a full one, and the altar would have hidden the line.

"What do you think that is?" asked Dirt.

-It's not a bone. But other than that, I don't know. I can't see under the floor with ghost sight. I wish I could get closer,- said Socks. *-It doesn't sound like the empty space is very large.-*

"No, I was just thinking that. The sound is reverberating in there, and I can almost hear the shape. Oh, I know what that is. It's the treasury," said Dirt. He stepped over and knelt, then leaned down and rested his human ear directly on the stone. Even doing that, Socks's ears heard it better than his did.

-What do you put in a treasury? Dead things?-

"I don't remember that much. Just the name of it, and that it's hiding in the Aedes."

-The Aedes?-

"That's what this room is called. I guess you would come in here to see the god when you wanted to. Or to make a sacrifice."

-And there's a place underneath called the treasury? Is that because there's treasure in it?-

"Probably. Although I bet there isn't anymore, after so long. People have been living here the whole time. I'm surprised the stone covering it never broke."

-They probably don't like to come in here because of the god.-

"Yeah, but three thousand years is a long time," said Dirt. He stood back up. The pool of blood didn't look like it would spread this far and drip into the treasury, but that made Dirt wonder how well it was sealed. Although if it wasn't well-sealed, it would have been full of water by now.

He looked at the humans, wondering what he should ask them, and more importantly, how. Biandina's mind showed she could hear the sound, and wondered what it was, since she hadn't noticed it before. She had a memory of coming here late at night, before the snowfall. Sneaking silently, kneeling before the statue with a rabbit in her hand. She hadn't noticed the sound then.

Her babbu thought perhaps Dirt was making it, but mostly he was interested in the flying dagger. He kept thinking of how he'd get Dirt to let him examine it.

The old woman was filled with dread that seemed unrelated to the reeking corpse only a few steps away. No, she was concerned that Dirt had noticed something.

Dirt watched more closely. She had been young when it happened—it was an old memory, hazy and half-full of imagined details. She'd watched as they'd tied him up, screaming all the while, begging for mercy. They'd plunged a knife into his stomach, then buried him alive right where Dirt was standing. The large paving stone was pushed back into place, and his pained groans were muffled to nothing. Almost. Almost to nothing. She'd stood there, as had they all, until he was silent.

He was silent no longer, however. After so long, he was scratching at the underside of his tomb.

"Hey, Socks, she—"

-I saw it. The old man is thinking about it, too,- said Socks.

Biandina was the first to move, being the least afraid of the giant pup. She gingerly stepped over to Dirt, pointed at the monstrous corpse only a few paces from the hidden tomb, then at herself, and made the sacrificing motion again. She was trying to tell him it was her fault, but Dirt just shook his head and shrugged. He doubted messing up a sacrifice to a missing god would bring a half-dead person to live in their city, but how should he go about explaining that to her?

Socks said, *-Make a light. I want to lift the stone and see what's in there. It should be a dead person, and we will take care of him.-*

Dirt patted Biandina on the back in a way he hoped was comforting, then gripped her shirt and pulled her a couple steps back. He snapped his fingers to call a little light into being, then picked up the staff.

The two old people stepped forward at once, arms out to stop him, but Socks held them in place with his mind and gave a low growl. They immediately quit resisting, and he slid them back a few paces before letting them go again. Biandina's babbu held his spear ready, but wasn't sure what the threat might be. He must not know about the burial.

Dirt gripped his staff in both hands, then raised it over one shoulder for a swing just in case.

The old man held his hands out toward Socks in a gesture of pleading. *"Per piacè, ùn apre micca. Ùn sapete micca ciò chì fate,"* he said, and the meaning was clear enough, from his nervous glances at Dirt and the stone floor. *Please don't open it. "Per piacè."*

Socks could hardly move his head with it stuck in the doorway like that, but he glared at the old man out of the corner of his eye.

Dirt asked, "What's in there, do you think?" and pointed at the cover stone with his staff.

"Una maledizione," said the old man, his voice full and desperate. *"Una vechja maledizione."* A curse.

A curse like on Biandina, Dirt wondered? Too bad curses probably weren't real. Dead things that moved, though, those were real, and they needed to be taken care of.

Dirt nodded and told Socks, *"Okay, I have enough mana again. Open it, but be ready to smash whatever's in there."*

-Of course. In fact . . . - said Socks, and with that, he lifted Dirt up and brought him safely back alongside his snout. -*Your job is to keep it from poking my nose.*-

Before finally lifting the stone, however, Socks sent out another message to everyone, and this time, it was his sense of annoyance at the humans behind him that were trying to squeeze around him and see in the doorway. *Stay back, you are bothering me,* he was saying. Biandina's babbu tried to peek over the pup's head to see who it was, but there wasn't a gap big enough with all that fur.

"If anyone steps on your tail, you have my permission to knock them over with it."

Socks huffed in mild amusement. -*As if anyone's tall enough to do that. Ready?*-

"Ready," said Dirt. He raised the staff again, ready for a swing, and brightened the light he had hovering over the stone.

Socks lifted the whole lid at once, raising the stone straight up higher than human height. Beneath was a small chamber, just a box, really. A small whiff of purple smoke drifted out and dissipated completely, before Dirt even remembered what Father had said about burning that stuff away. The smoke's vanishing revealed an old corpse, mostly skeletal, with one yellow, fleshless arm extended upward. It held a ruined dagger worn all the way down to the hilt, and waved it to scratch exactly where the lid had been, eternally mimicking the victim's dying hope.

The rest of the corpse lay still, bony face clearly visible, with the rest of him concealed beneath what remained of his clothing.

Seeing the moving corpse caused the old couple to moan in horror and shrink away. Their minds filled with guilt and despair, and their capacity for reason shrank beneath the weight of what they were witnessing.

The corpse pushed its arm upward, as if slowly recognizing the lack of resistance, and hung motionless in the air for a moment. Then, with the sound of ancient cracking joints and crumbling flesh, the dead man rose from his grave, standing up almost as if being lifted rather than rising under his own power.

Its head was the last part of him to snap into place, and his empty skeletal gaze fixed on the old couple, ignoring the bloody child and giant wolf completely. Its mouth clacked in mimicry of speech as it shot an accusatory finger forward, just bone, but with flaps of old flesh hanging beneath it.

The old couple whimpered and clutched each other. The old man shouted something at it, something desperate and stuttering, which sounded more like a plea than a command.

The decaying skeleton lifted its knee and stepped from its grave, arm still pointing. Its shoes, surprisingly, were in good condition, and its soft footfalls made no sound.

Once both its feet were out of the box and it started shambling forward, Socks smashed it. He crushed it from above with a wall of mental force, and from one instant to the next, it was gone.

Dirt wondered if there might have been some trace of the purple smoke monster on it like Father had warned about, but it was too late. Nothing remained but a wide, flat spot of dried jerky, bone dust, and tattered furs, mingling along the edges with the slowly spreading pool of blood.

Dirt seemed more relieved than the rest of them. He hadn't realized he was nervous until the nervousness left him, but he had been. Perhaps something of his fear of Prisca remained, but thank the gods, this was nothing like *her*. And hopefully, nothing ever would be again.

He stepped over to peek into the treasury and said, "That's too bad. It's all empty." Biandina's father stood at his side, gazing in briefly with a dark demeanor. He toed the corpse dust and smeared it a little, as if having a hard time believing what he'd just seen.

The old couple shuffled toward Socks, indicating by their body language that they wanted his head out of the doorway. There was a sense of urgency in the air, and Dirt figured the humans had had enough insanity and danger and wanted to go somewhere less intimidating. He patted Socks on the nose and told him, *"May as well put the lid back on."*

The stone floated down until Socks was sure it was lined up perfectly, then dropped a few inches into place. After that, with a resigned snort, he pulled his head out the door and almost instantly armed men rushed in, first five, and then twenty. The Aedes was spacious, but not *that* spacious, and with a pool of blood and a pile of snow taking up so much of the floor space, it quickly became crowded.

The fighting men saw the mangled corpse and the blood all over Dirt, with him standing here holding a staff, and jumped to the obvious conclusion. They lowered their spears and shouted at him, anger and fear in their eyes.

But only for a moment. With a cry of alarm, the old man hurried into the group of soldiers and started pushing their spears to the side. He shouted as well, and hearing him, they quieted. Dirt could guess the meaning well enough—*Don't attack the boy.*

Other humans started creeping in past Socks, eyes wide and necks stretched to see what was going on. First a couple women, then a man with no weapon who walked tall like he should have one and hoped no one noticed. He stood amongst the fighters.

Then, of all things, a child, younger than Dirt. A little girl. Dirt was terrible at guessing the ages of humans, and pretty much everything else except for wolves, but she was old enough to talk without difficulty and still young enough her mother was almost certainly nearby. She wore no shoes, despite the chilly stone floor, but had the same long woolen dress that most women wore.

The little girl snuck behind the adults, and Dirt realized he was the only one who'd seen her. Well, best not to give it away, if she was that sneaky. He couldn't blame her for wanting to look.

But she wasn't here to look. Once she spotted Biandina, she ran straight for her and clapped her arms around her waist and held her tightly. "Eudossia?" said Biandina, startled.

Babbu saw the little one too late to stop her, and now he didn't want to pull them apart, even though he reached out a hand to do so before changing his mind.

Biandina knelt and spoke sharply to the little girl, wagging a finger. It didn't last, not against the pleading eyes the little one gave her. This, of all things, was too much for Biandina, and she looked helplessly at her father as tears began streaming down her face. Her chest shook with a sob, then a second one, both of which she suppressed. Her hand hovered over the tiny girl, and Dirt saw she wanted to return the hug but didn't dare.

So he pushed her arms with his mind and made her. Glancing at her mind, Biandina didn't realize it was him who did it. She thought it was an involuntary reflex and gave up resisting.

Then another girl just a bit older and a boy about Dirt's height snuck into the room as well, far less effectively. No one stopped them, though, and they rushed right to Biandina as well, hugging her.

Right behind them came an older boy with a stern, wary gaze and a spear of his own. He stood near Biandina and planted the butt of his spear nearby. He looked down at her, then looked sharply away when she looked back up to meet his eyes. Still, judging by how he stood, he was there to protect her rather than keep her in line.

"Look, Socks, she has siblings! They must have been sad about her," said Dirt, his own pity awakening. Socks had been stoic about losing so many of his own siblings, seldom dwelling on it, but it made Dirt melancholy any time he thought about it. They had been so precious, and now they were gone.

Another child, smaller than the first, with hair so messy Dirt wasn't sure what sex it was, and an older girl came rushing in and went straight for their sister. Another little one followed shortly after, a boy. Seeing them all together, the similarity was so obvious that even Dirt could see it, and he had very little experience telling humans apart.

But that wasn't all. Last came a woman with a tiny child in her arms, too small to walk but big enough to sit up, and started calling sharply to the children to come back, each of them by name. She refused to look

Biandina in the eyes, and it took Dirt a minute to find her mind. Once he did, he found a soul as hard as flint. Whatever emotions she had in there were locked away so tightly they might never come back out. A hard woman, and a hard life.

The room was too full of commotion for anything productive to happen, other than all the adults pointedly looking at anything other than Biandina, suppressing sobs, and the smaller children wailing without making the attempt. She had been dead to them, and was alive again.

Pity burned hotter in Dirt's heart, sympathy that enkindled righteous anger. What stupid humans they were, to have a perfectly good human and get rid of her over some stupid rabbit! And an absent god! Didn't they know how rare humans were these days?

It was the old woman who did what no one else wanted to and finally started peeling away the children and pushing them toward the mother. The mother yanked them commandingly toward the door, but with so many and only one arm, she couldn't force them all out. The boy with the spear, in particular, resisted just as sharply, even lowering his spear in a way that was almost, but not quite, threatening. Several of the men yelled at him, but he didn't budge.

That was more than Dirt could handle, and he nearly started shouting at them to stop, but didn't. They couldn't understand him. He could shout all day long, and they might understand no more than five words of it.

"I am getting really sick of not knowing their language!" said Dirt, practically shouting to Socks.

-I can see. I would pull you over and give you a lick, but you have that blood all over you, and I don't want to taste it either,- said Socks. His voice was gentle and tinged with his own sympathy. Not necessarily for Biandina, but for Dirt, whose current anger was a kind of suffering.

"They are so dumb! What are they doing? Can't they see the siblings want their sister?"

One of the littlest ones chose to fall on his bottom rather than get ushered toward the door. He cried and reached his little hand for her, tiny fingers grabbing. Dirt wanted to scream.

Socks growled, and the low rumble cut through the noise, causing the men to stop speaking loudly to each other and the children to stare back through the shadowed doorway in fear. The pup's yellow eyes glowed with reflected light, adding to the effect. There was a predator here, and they were not behaving themselves. He sent out a mental image, showing his displeasure that they were making Dirt sad.

Shockingly, Biandina's mother spun and stomped out to face him. She stopped three paces from Socks's face and shook her finger at him. *"Ùn capite nunda. Biandina deve andà. Nimu li piace, ma deve succede. Capisci? Ella deve lascià."*

Neither Dirt nor Socks understood her words, but her mind was still easy to find. She was the only one staring a giant wolf in the face. In her heart, she'd already given up, and this was just another miserable task. Like burying a loved one or slaughtering a pet for food. That's what her emotions felt like. Hard and bitter, resigned.

"Okay, you know what?" said Dirt. Hardly anyone was listening to him, though, since they were all fixated on the wolf, who was probably about to eat their woman. "This is stupid. Something insane is going on here, and I'll never figure it out this way. I'm going to go learn how to talk your language. Nobody do anything stupid! Like kick Biandina out again!"

By the end, most of them had at least turned to see what he was ranting about, not that they understood.

"Okay, Socks, toss me up on the roof, right through that hole."

-Are you going to call the wind? You will be cold up there.-

"Yep, I'm going to call the wind, and once it gets here, I'm going to ask for the language. Up I go, please."

A chorus of startled gasps followed Dirt up through the hole in the roof. He landed atop the dome and grabbed on to the crumbling crest-work, where once a spire had stood.

Satisfied he was secure, he raised his staff and spoke magic into the world, summoning a gust of wind. He called more, and more.

CHAPTER TWENTY-ONE

The icy wind blew right through his clothing like it wasn't there, and the fact that it was still wet with blood made it worse. The wet spots stuck to his skin and got so cold it stung. He gritted his teeth and flexed the muscles in his chest to keep from shivering, then did his best to focus. His anger was slow to fade and helped keep him warm. Stupid humans.

The dome he stood on wasn't high enough to get a good view of the full scenery, and the netting covering the rest of the outpost took up most of his field of vision. It made a wide, uneven grid of dark edges containing white squares of melting snow; a view he found rather remarkable. Entirely unlike anything he'd seen before, but now wasn't the time to enjoy it.

Instead, he looked for minds. Socks's glowed brightly, brighter than anything else, since he was so close. The cluster of humans below were turbulent and troubled. Dimmer human minds filled his view beyond those ones. Nothing like the blinding glow of Ogena, but still too many to tell them apart without serious effort. It was impossible to look away from some and see others, since there wasn't any directionality in the mental world. Just bright and dim, near and far.

But wind elementals weren't humans, and it should be easy to pick them out if he watched, so watch he did, with both his mind-sight and mana body.

There wasn't any natural wind now, but if enough air moved, they had to start showing up, right? The wind Dirt made typically didn't go far, which he knew from watching the ferns when he first learned how. Maybe it would help if he made the wind longer, since true wind stretched quite far.

Rather than improvise how to make that work, he aimed it in different directions. Upward had the greatest effect. The rising wind caused an updraft that lifted air from all around and rose like a tree, far, far overhead, until it spread out like branches and faded. Here below, the rushing air whistled softly in any exposed netting and would have made the whole place whip and shake without snow to hold it down.

Surprisingly, at the very top of Dirt's wind-pillar, fog appeared and grew into a thin, wispy cloud. He looked harder with his mana body, wondering if he was missing something, or if another creature was nearby doing magic at the same time, but he found nothing unusual.

He went to ask Socks about it, but the pup was as surprised as he was, and as curious. He'd stuck his head back through the door, blocking it again, and had just the right angle to watch. Perhaps they could ask Father someday. Or the wind itself, for that matter. If he could figure out how.

Dirt decided to see how much cloud he could make before a wind elemental showed up. He poured in more and more mana, calling as much wind into being as he could. He even tried lifting the air with his mind to make it go faster, but that proved impossible—there was nothing for him to grab on to, and he hadn't figured out how to make a whole wall like Socks did.

Overhead, the cloud stretched and drifted away from the updraft and never grew into anything big enough to cause shade, but it was interesting to watch. Dirt tried drawing with the wind to make it different shapes, but if he didn't direct the wind straight up, it didn't go as high and wouldn't make any cloud.

A massive gust of wind burst out of the hole in the roof, creating a momentary roar that vanished faster than it arose. Dirt peeked down and saw Socks with his chin on the ground and his eyes turned upward, looking almost guilty.

-I wanted to try,- the pup told him. But it implied more than that; he'd tried doing magic naturally, instinctively, in the manner of wolves. Not with all the sigils and preparation of humans.

"Well, you didn't break anything, so try as much as you want," said Dirt. *"Good job, too."*

The humans down there were standing as close to Socks as they dared get, which wasn't that close other than Biandina, to peer up through the roof and watch. The armed men let their weapons sag, and larger children held up the smaller ones so they could see.

Well, he didn't have much of a show to put on. He couldn't call lightning or play music. He went back to his task, raising his staff again and regenerating the upward pillar of air. Another burst of wind fired out of the hole like an arrow, though, only a moment later.

-Sorry. It's harder than it seems. I keep wanting to move the air with my mind, but that's not the same,- said Socks, just to him.

Dirt replied with a puff of amusement, then one of affection. After that he added, *"Just make sure to catch me if you break the dome."*

-Maybe, if I think of it in time,- said Socks slyly. *-Remember to yell.-*

Grinning, Dirt went back to making his air pillar. That much motion and a little cloud was sure to attract the wind's attention eventually, right? How did the wind decide where it wanted to go, and when?

There was a little squeal from down below, and Dirt peeked over the edge again to see that Socks had picked up two of Biandina's smallest siblings and put them on his head, right between his ears, so they wouldn't be underfoot as the humans began to ignore the wolf and the blood on the ground and pack more tightly together. The little ones clung to each other like chicks in a nest, eyes wide, and Biandina did her best to comfort them with a wave and soothing words. Dirt found her mind, mostly by familiarity, and saw that she was worried Socks might try to keep them. She was already imagining how to gesture to convince him they needed to stay here.

Dirt's idea of making wind to summon more wind worked. When he looked back up to resume his task, he saw the cloud being pushed in half by a gentle crosswind, and soon he found the mind of a wind elemental. Just a small one, but the shape of its mind was unmistakable when compared with all the humans. Its perceptions stretched from near to far, but nothing like the wind-mother's.

He formed the opening of a conversation in the world of magic, drawing the sigil for "beginning of a new process," like he'd been taught. The little wind caught sight of it immediately, and Dirt felt a slight increase in the breeze as it descended to see what he was. He watched the shape of his body and clothing passing through the twisting tangles of its mind, before it began drawing its reply.

This one's mind was small enough he could grasp more of it than the big one, and he verified something the dryads had told him. They said the physical world was like a dream to the elementals, and from what Dirt saw, that wasn't far off. Only a small portion of its awareness took any note of him.

In dreams, other than those shared with Socks, Dirt acted and moved and spoke, but it was hard to say he had any control. It was just things that happened. Conversations that seemed real but upon waking seemed garbled and incoherent, emotions that were performative and often unrelated to whatever was going on. Humans only drifted across that world, awake or asleep, and made ripples but never saw the depths.

That's what the elemental seemed like to Dirt. He was talking to its dream, a part distant from the core of its reality. In fact, its presence in the world of dreams was probably more concrete than it was here.

The elemental took hold of his "beginning a new process" sigil and began to speak. The words it formed were more familiar than Dirt expected, which made him wonder if the small ones had a simpler vocabulary. It drew Dirt's air pillar, described it by its natural process—a system of incoming pressures with lower pressure above, squeezing the air upward. The elemental's mind was tinged with curiosity, although the object of its curiosity wasn't clear. What was he doing, perhaps, or why.

Dirt learned a new sigil: "cloud," which was a variation of "water." That appeared when the elemental drew it plainly, almost by itself, with the sigil for "small." Why was he making a small cloud?

He thought about that for a moment, then redrew the opening sigil, as if to start a new conversation. In the places where the conversation might begin, he drew the sigil for "empty" and sent a mental puff of desire.

From there they began a mostly pointless artistic dance, drawing sigils for each other in combinations Dirt had never considered, and might not have any effect if powered. He and the elemental tossed ideas back and forth, making one change each time; it was just like the imagination games he and Socks played, although he was worse at this. Was this elemental truly a child? Did that word even apply here?

Dirt tried to steer the conversation toward something productive, since he was really starting to get cold up here, but if the little elemental understood, it disagreed. Finally Dirt said, aloud, "Okay, this is fun, but let's try something else."

The elemental processed the words as vibrations in the air, which Dirt could see in its mind. He sent a purely mental image of that perception, along with the idea of a question. Something similar had worked on the trees, so maybe?

The elemental floundered for only a moment before figuring it out. There was a moment of greater clarity, a brightness in its mind that made Dirt wonder if perhaps he'd done something to wake it up. But that faded, and afterward it drew a series of complex symbols, each modifying the others in a dazzling array.

Dirt worked his way through it, doing his best to decipher what the little wind was saying. That sigil looked like an overlay of "motion" and "small" but was its own thing, and soon he realized that was the sigil for "vibration." As for the others, some of what he saw appeared to have no meaning at all, except for how they fit together. They looked incomplete, but not in a way that anticipated he would have more to add.

He traced the process with his mind and felt a rhythm there, something familiar, on the edge of recognizability.

Socks interrupted, *-Let me try.-* Dirt watched as his mind withdrew from words and concrete thought into a more primal mode, one of impression and sensation and instinct. Something purely wolf, with no human influence at all. Except that wasn't quite it, because the rhythm of speech, the sounds and cadence of Dirt talking, remained in his mind, but without meaning behind them.

A new magical array spread before them, Socks interposing his own magic between Dirt and the elemental. The pup was rigid with concentration, ridding himself of most of his ideas of magic. It had been too human, Father had told him. Wolves had different magic, and for complicated things, he'd been copying Dirt. Not this time.

The elemental's intent became clear, now that he could see what Socks was doing. The little wind had drawn a single pattern that described an entire language at once. Not each word, or even any meaning, but its name in the world of magic. The pattern of it, the process and rhythm. Socks could feel it in a way Dirt couldn't and spoke it clearly for the elemental to see.

Dirt understood it, now that he could see it in Socks's mind. That was *his* language, its name, and it was beautiful. He felt its grammatical accuracy, its ease and fluidity, its stateliness and poetic lyricism, all circumscribed into an expression that no tongue could communicate. He would never forget it. Indeed, if this was all he learned today, it would be worth all the effort.

He did his best not to admire it too much, though, lest he risk missing something else important. The pup was describing a mind now—Dirt's mind—by imprinting his impressions themselves on the world of magic directly. It caused a dizzying amount of new signs and symbols to flash into being. The mind, Socks said, belonged to the little boy-shape there atop the dome.

Next to it, Socks drew his own mind, vast and pure and primal, and set the two symbolic constructions together in a way that indicated unity of purpose.

Then he created a new magical array, one that indicated many humans huddling sheltered below, out of the reach of the wind. But their voices still rose into the air, and he depicted the rhythm and sounds of their speech from the perspective of a total outsider, which he was. A different language, the one spoken here, and the one the little elemental had first mentioned. Dirt watched eagerly to see how it differed from or matched his own.

Then, finally, Socks created an opening and imprinted a language-impression into the two minds he'd drawn, but in an incomplete way. A hollow where a new language needed to go. *Give us their tongue,* Socks was saying, in the pure processes of magic.

But such efforts were still a struggle for poor Socks, and his concentration couldn't keep it going forever. Not without more practice. Having mostly accomplished what he wanted to do, he let out a tiny whimper as his concentration broke. The magical images vanished. He huffed wearily, the gusts of his breath rippling the clothing of the small crowd.

The elemental paused, pondering, its mind chasing inscrutable things across the vast winding tunnels of its thought. Then it vanished, winking out of existence entirely. The area settled into a silence that made Dirt's ears ring.

He leaned over the edge to look at Socks, but his friend had nothing to say after such intense concentration. The small crowd of humans peered back up at him through the hole in the roof, eyes curious. The little ones on Socks's head had each grabbed an ear and seemed less scared now.

Behind him, the sky opened, and a new wind rushed out, chill and menacing. It whipped at Dirt, causing his clothes to flutter violently and his eyes to water so bad he had to close them. Before he could look again with his mind-sight and see what it was, a stunning shock of energy lit into him, forcing him rigid. He heard an audible buzzing sound, and he lost all sense of balance, even forgetting where he was, and drifted emptily, nearly unconscious.

Dirt shook himself to keep from falling asleep, but he was on the cold, hard ground of the outpost now. Socks whined over him, squeaking him back into full consciousness.

"Is he alive?" asked an old man, his voice rising from the muttered whisperings of a large crowd.

"Ow," said Dirt. He tried to sit up and got a screaming headache for his efforts. "I'm alive, but I wish I wasn't awake."

He whimpered in pain as the headache refused to abate. The gasps of the crowd did nothing to alleviate it. He clutched his head and rolled onto his side, moaning.

-Do you want me to make you go to sleep?- asked Socks.

"Maybe, if it doesn't go away soon. This really hurts. Did I fall and crack my skull?"

"Child, did you speak? Can you say that again?" asked the old man.

"Say what again? Oh, I can speak your language now. That's good. Can you be quiet for a moment?" said Dirt.

-Everyone be quiet,- commanded Socks in the new language, his mental voice filling every head in the outpost.

Soon enough, the headache abated, and Dirt rolled onto his back with a sigh of relief.

The moment he did, Socks relaxed and lowered his head to the ground, nose touching Dirt. The little ones atop his head held on for dear life, not knowing that was the safest place they could possibly be.

Dirt patted his friend's nose and climbed to his feet gingerly, fearful the headache might come back. It did not, thank the gods. Then he thought, *"I'd hug you but I'm still filthy. But you did it! I think I learned more watching you than the whole time with the trees. How did you figure that out?"*

-Only by watching you. I closed off my mind-sight and just watched with magic and saw how it felt, and everything you two were saying started to make sense,- said Socks. He was feeling quite proud of himself, and justifiably so.

Dirt grinned and sent him another puff of affection, then patted his nose.

The old woman clutched his shoulder with a firm hand to get his attention. "You can speak our language? Why did you not before?"

"Because I couldn't before, silly. I learned just now by asking the wind," he said. Perhaps he wasn't being quite fair, but she'd reminded him he was still somewhat angry with their tribe. "What did you think I was doing up there?"

The old woman stared back at him, struggling to find a reply.

Dirt gave her to the count of three before pushing past her to get to the girl. He didn't have to squeeze through to get to her, since the crowd parted to let him by. Except the older boy with the spear, who gave him a serious look before stepping aside.

"Hello, Biandina. My name is Dirt. It means *dirt* in your language. And that is my best friend, Socks. His name means *socks,* which some people think is funny."

"Your name is . . . Dirt?"

"Yep! And I know you think you're cursed, but you're probably the second luckiest human alive, because Socks and I were there to save you. How likely do you think that is? Socks is the only wolf anywhere who has a pet human. I doubt anyone else would have thought about saving you, even if they could," said Dirt.

She stared, struggling to find a way to answer. Her siblings crowded her, and she was trying to rest her hands on all of them at the same time, and that strange little boy was *talking*! She didn't know where to begin.

Dirt said, "Anyway, you're saved, and we brought you back, so everything should be fine now. You're obviously not cursed."

"I did something I can't take back," said Biandina. "Even if you saved me once, it doesn't change that."

"This old woman told me. You sacrificed a rabbit to the goddess. But so what? Look at that statue. Do you think she's in a position to do anything about it? I did some—er, I know of someone who did something way, way, worse than that," said Dirt. "And that person is fine. Curses aren't real."

"And who would that be?" said Biandina's babbu, stepping between Dirt and three of his children.

"Probably no one you've ever heard of, unless you've been to Turicum," said Dirt. "But don't you have bigger problems? Like that half-dead man I killed? Did you know what he was, or was that a surprise? And how about the actual corpse?"

"He is the reason—!" began the old woman.

Socks interrupted her, saying, *-Do not raise your voice at my little Dirt when he has done nothing wrong.-*

To her credit, she exhaled and calmed down. Then she said, "I apologize, great one. Corruptions like Iliaru are the reason she must leave. She begged the Murderous Lady for strength and will soon end up like him. We are fortunate we caught her before she turned into . . . that."

Dirt nodded. "Well, first off, that statue is Melodia, the Mistress of Song, not the Murderous Lady. And second, the gods are gone from the world. I have that on good authority. So begging her won't get you anything, good or bad. And third, there aren't enough humans left to just throw one away, when she seems perfectly fine to me. And let's be honest, after that thing with the skeleton, you're not in a position to be criticizing *anybody*."

The old woman went pale and tried not to show her discomfort. Still, it drew a few eyes.

Not Biandina's, though. She said, "No, Dirt, Gnese is right. I saw it." She spoke with eyes downcast and inner turmoil in her voice. She looked up and continued. "I thought maybe . . . I just wanted . . . I knew what would happen, but . . . I know something saw me. I know it did. That's why I confessed instead of hiding. I need to leave. I need to die." The last word came out a whisper.

Her siblings' faces were ashen and fearful, the same misery that Dirt saw on so many others. Stoic, perhaps, but suffering.

Dirt asked, "What did you see?" Was Melodia not truly gone? Did he dare get his hopes up?

She pointed at the hole in the ceiling and said, "The moment the rabbit's blood touched her feet, I looked up and saw a . . . giant eye. It was right up there, through the hole. Then it blinked itself away, leaving empty sky."

Socks raised his head and looked at Dirt. Dirt looked back. Both of them were thinking the same thing.

"What? Are you two talking again?" asked Biandina.

"No. But I guess I was wrong. I guess it is a big deal after all," said Dirt.

CHAPTER TWENTY-TWO

Dirt's agreement made Biandina wilt just a bit further, which made him regret saying anything. She avoided the gazes of the children clinging to her and said, "I still feel that eye up there in the sky, watching me always. Even right now. I know it's there."

"It's not," said Dirt.

-It's not,- said Socks. *-We can tell, and it is not in the sky.-*

Dirt felt bad, so he stepped over and patted her on the shoulder, mindful of his still-filthy clothing. "If it's any consolation, I would never have guessed that would happen either, and I have seen a lot of things."

Socks perked his ears up a bit and said, *-I wonder, humans. Why do you tell your progeny about this, if you don't want them to do it anymore? The wise thing would be to forget entirely. No one would invent the idea of sacrificing an animal if no one told them about doing that.-*

Biandina's babbu answered, "Because we sacrifice to other things. The sky and wind, the earth and water. Our ancestors. We tell our children they must never sacrifice to any gods."

"Why not?" asked Dirt. "Do you think they're bad?"

"They are the Seven Destroyers," answered the old man. "The ones who bring calamity and suffering. They cannot be slain, but they are not part of the true order, and that is why they are gods."

"Seven Destroyers? What are you talking about?" Dirt asked.

"Why don't you answer that, girl?" said the old woman. She kept glancing back at the empty treasury and the mummy dust left by its inhabitant, and from the set of her shoulders it looked to Dirt like she was trying to direct attention away from it.

Biandina swallowed in embarrassment and said, "The seven gods are the whirlwind that eradicates, the wildfire that consumes, the blizzard that buries, the earthquake that shatters, the lightning that stops the heart, the hail that destroys, and finally, the murderer in the shape of a woman, who gives birth to death."

"To them you must never sacrifice, for they regard only wickedness and deliver only misery," said the old woman.

"That's a list, not an explanation. So they're elementals, I guess? Like the wind?" said Dirt, growing more confused. Why would they think a god *was* a storm, instead of a being great enough to create one? And the gods weren't evil, they were . . .

He paused. In his heart, he felt the old rumblings of piety and worship, but those feelings had no object and never explained themselves. The gods couldn't be evil, though. That was ridiculous.

The old man gave him a tired look, one with some anger behind it, and said, "The gods are the gods. You are too young to understand."

"No, I recognize a god. I just don't think you have the right idea about them," said Dirt. If they were evil, he wouldn't feel such yearning for them. He recognized Melodia, even in this state, and they did not. That was all there was to it. But if sacrificing to them caught the attention of that thing in the sky, then their beliefs were wrong, but certainly not foolish.

Socks said, just to him, *-Are you sure they're wrong? Are you sure it's not a god up there? Something happened to them, after all. Maybe it made them harmful. Like what happened to the Devourer.-*

Dirt felt a chill that had nothing to do with the cold air drifting down from the hole in the dome. The very *idea* that something as great and marvelous as a god could turn into something like the Eye was too horrific to contemplate. Even considering it felt like blasphemy.

"I didn't make the gods evil, Socks," said Dirt, trying to convince himself more than his friend. His fingertips trembled against the cloth of his pants, and he clenched his forearms to make them stop. *"That can't be right. They used to help and protect mankind, so they couldn't . . . well . . ."*

-It was just a thought. Do not be upset, little Dirt. There is no way for us to find out right now, so you don't have to think that if you don't want to. Someday we will learn the truth, and you can believe that instead,- said Socks. He sent Dirt a puff of warm reassurance, and it helped.

Dirt cleared his throat and said aloud, "Actually, Socks and I know what that eye is that Biandina saw. We fought it once, but I can't say we won, exactly. I think it just gave up and left. The Father of Wolves called it the Great Enemy of Mankind. We just call it the Eye, even though it's a lot more than just an eye. It wants to get rid of every human. Eradicate us."

"What you are saying is not too far off from the truth," said the old woman. Gnese, if Dirt remembered what Biandina had called her. Gnese. "It is the Murderous Lady, and like all the gods, she takes many forms. Some she kills directly, but often she corrupts and watches for harm to be done."

Dirt tried to keep from scowling and probably failed. He was never going to win the argument about Melodia. And frankly, he was afraid he was wrong and it *was* her. What she had become.

Socks said, *-Want me to get rid of the statue? I can carry it away and smash it, and then no one could sacrifice to it.-*

Gnese, the old woman, replied, unsuccessfully swallowing the sharpness on her tongue. "We can't get rid of it. We've tried."

The old man said, "Our tribe has been here for thousands of years. I could tell you the names of a hundred generations of my fathers, most of whom dwelled right here between these walls. All of them have wished to be rid of the burden of its presence. If there was any way to be rid of the Murderous Lady, we would have found it."

"So," said Dirt, pausing to reformulate his question and not seem like a dullard, "what happens when someone tries to break it apart and carry away the pieces?"

Gnese answered, "She returns to her place during the night, in the first moment no one is watching, perfectly whole and reformed, with no hint of a crack in the stone. We have tried everything."

"Wait, really? If you break her all up and carry the pieces away, she just reappears when no one is looking? And I guess you tried having someone watch, and it only worked for so long."

"That is correct," said Gnese. "We have an old story about a family who was tasked with watching the plinth night and day. They made it a year."

-*Then why not dig yourselves a new den somewhere else?*- asked Socks.

"Even with her here, there is nowhere safer than inside these walls," said the old man.

"Oh," said Dirt. From what he'd seen of the rest of the world, he could believe that was the case. If nothing else, the netting would keep the birds from carrying people away.

-*I have a question, and then I will move so people can use the doorway. Biandina, what did you want from the goddess?*- asked Socks, turning his head slightly to fix his fearsome yellow eyes on her.

The room went silent, and Dirt wondered whether it was because they all knew and it was shameful, or because they didn't. The silence was long enough that Dirt started glancing in random minds nearby, and it turned out, almost no one knew. He held his breath in anticipation right along with the rest of them.

-*Dirt wants to help humans, so you should tell us,*- coaxed Socks.

Biandina hesitated to answer. "I . . ." She looked at her father.

"We really should not say, great one," said the babbu.

-*Answer or I will pry it from your minds,*- said Socks, sternly.

"Can he do that?" whispered Biandina, mostly toward Dirt.

"Yep, easily." In fact . . . "*You already know, don't you?*" said Dirt, just to Socks.

-*Yes. You will think it is interesting,*- replied the pup, with just a hint of a twitch in his ears. Dirt was sure that on the other side of the door, Socks was wagging his tail.

Babbu was close enough to hear Dirt's reply, of course, and he swallowed dryness then answered with hesitation in his voice. "A *rucca* carried off her brother two weeks ago, right as the bad weather hit. All our efforts were spent gathering inside the walls for winter, and we had no one to spare. I told her we could not send out the riders to bring him back, and she did not forgive me. She sacrificed to the Lady for revenge. For power to kill the *rucce*."

"What's a *rucca?*" asked Dirt.

"*Rucce* are the great birds you rescued her from," said the babbu, as if admitting to a crime.

Dirt's eyes widened as he realized why they didn't want to say. The sacrifice had *worked*! Out of nowhere, Socks and Dirt had come along and not only rescued Biandina, but killed the bird that took her and all the ones that shared its nest. Her brother's bones might be among the others they'd seen.

Well, now Dirt had a million questions, none of which they were likely to get answered. What sorts of requests did the "Murderous Lady" grant, and how often? Was there any sort of pattern they knew? Did it always attract the attention of the Eye? What specific harms could result from a sacrifice? Did something bad always happen to the supplicant? Or was it secretly banned because the bad things happened to other people, at the supplicant's request? Dirt had no idea what to make of it, and Socks didn't weigh in either.

The same realization—that Biandina's sacrifice had *worked*—spread through the crowd. Dirt could watch their faces and see each person figure it out. No one spoke, not even the little ones. He looked at the statue, wounded and suffering, standing silently above them all. Melodia . . . could she still be there? Faint, but still aware? And if so, was her suffering genuine?

"All we are waiting for now is the disaster she called down. She must leave before it finds her," said the old man. He seemed pale now; frail, after so many terrors had come and gone in a few short hours.

Dirt expected everyone to start talking all at once, but they didn't. No one spoke, and when Dirt glanced at Socks's mind, the pup smelled the twin scents of awe and horror.

With nothing left to discuss, Socks finally pulled his head out of the doorway, and a new crowd of people tried to push their way in. Some peered around like they were simply curious, but one of them was Biandina's mother, who must have been outside when Socks stuck his head through. She rolled through the crowd like a boulder until she made it to her brood. The infant in one arm limited how much she could do, but with her spare arm, she tried to shoo the rest away from their sister. They refused to comply, and she gave a mean glance at her mate, who stood by and didn't help.

With the new crowd came a hundred questions, not all of them quiet. The old man and woman glared around, but not convincingly; too many people had seen their terror and helplessness during the fight earlier. The rumor broke like water from a dam, and the room quickly filled with speech and commotion.

"How long will you be staying?" asked the old man over the sound of the crowd. His tone of voice conveyed that he hoped it would not be very long.

"We should probably stay for a few days so that if anything dangerous comes around, Socks and I can kill it for you," said Dirt, pretending not to catch his intent. "Oh, you should probably burn that dead body instead of burying it. You can guess why."

"It is not easy to spare so much wood," said the old man.

"Then carry him out, and Socks can burn him later."

"Do not ask us for wood. We must spare it for the coldest nights."

"Socks can make fire with magic. We won't need any wood," said Dirt.

"Then burn your clothes. The blood of the corrupted can cause disease, even if you wash them," said the old man.

"But I don't have anything else to wear," said Dirt.

"Then go naked! It's not my problem. I am simply warning you. Do as you wish," said the old man, almost succeeding at not raising his voice. And with that, he joined the throng pressing their way back out the door.

Dirt pulled his shirt off, kicked off his leather shoes, and then removed his pants. He tossed shirt and pants on the dead body and examined his shoes. They were blood-free, so he put them back on. His actions caught a few surprised glances, but he paid them no mind. They'd probably stare no matter what he did, and it was too late to worry about fitting in and acting like a regular human. Ideally, he'd be able to get some of *their* clothes somehow. Those furs looked plenty warm. Even the thick woolen clothing they wore inside was warmer than what he'd owned.

He summoned a few embers to float nearby and keep him warm, then went back to Biandina's family. The older children, the boy and the girl closest to her age, gave Dirt sideways grins that looked slightly embarrassed, the boy leaning his spear away. The younger children furrowed their brows in concern. Dirt found the mind of the girl named Eudossia, who'd first snuck in to find her sister, and she was mostly concerned that Dirt would be cold. He stood a little closer to her and held one hand up, then made an ember hover over it. He showed it to her and let her feel the warmth on her face, and all seven of the other children leaned in to inspect it themselves.

"As long as it's not windy, and I'm not wet, I won't get cold. I should probably wash all this blood off, though," said Dirt, taking note of how much had seeped through to stain his skin. "Does anyone know where I can get a rag?"

The mother and father ceased their angry, whispered conversation and looked over at him. He stood so naturally amidst their offspring that they weren't sure what to say.

"And some water. But I already know where I can find some of that," said Dirt.

The babbu gave a resigned sigh and scratched his beard, putting on body language of relaxing, ceasing his wariness. He said, "Are you one of ours, now?"

Dirt grinned. "No, not unless you can beat Socks."

"What's your plan, then?"

"Well, first, I need to wash off. But after that, I'd like to come see your house and learn all your names, if you'll have me," said Dirt.

The mother had not softened in the slightest. Her face was still hard as flint. "We don't have room," she said.

"Oh, Socks will stay out, obviously, but he won't mind. He can see through walls. When he gets bored, I'll leave you alone and go do something else for a while," said Dirt.

"The girl is not welcome back," said the mother, with finality in her voice. "Do not toy with us like this."

"What makes you think I'm toying with you?"

"You take after your wolf. Find a curiosity, sniff at it, poke it, maybe dig a little hole, and then move along without any mind for the mess you've made," she said. "We have to live here. My daughter is dead. She died the day she prayed to the Murderous Lady. Do you think to just leave her in our arms and all will be well? Go run along, little boy."

"She's alive. She's right there, face pale as ashes and heart so full of guilt she might just die of nothing. Look at her," said Dirt, pointing.

The mother stared down at him and did not look.

He pointed more insistently, and the woman just stared even harder, widening her forceful eyes. Dirt, who had once deliberately met the eyes of the Mother of Wolves, was not intimidated.

They stared and stared at each other, long past when it made every-one else uncomfortable. Dirt had to admit she had a respectable amount of willpower, but he was Avitus.

Eventually, she looked away first, even glancing involuntarily at her daughter. She said, "You don't know what you're doing. But fine. Come visit. She may come as well. We still have her things, and perhaps she'll need them."

Dirt nodded and said, "Thanks. And don't worry too much. I know what I'm doing; it's you who doesn't. But maybe once you do, you'll feel better about it."

-Come out of there already,- said Socks, leaning down to peer through the doorway with one eye. *-I found a rag, and you stink.-*

Dirt smiled at the woman, whose face still failed to soften. He said, "Guess I'd better go."

"Because he's terrifying and you have to obey him?"

"No, silly, because he's my best friend."

CHAPTER TWENTY-THREE

Socks held aloft a square bit of cloth he'd found somewhere, and Dirt followed him out of the Principia and into the main courtyard. They found the nearest water basin, and Dirt warmed it up with an ember, then washed himself until Socks was satisfied. The pup affirmed his cleanliness with a thorough licking, which left the familiar film of dry saliva all over him. He rinsed that off, too. After that, he followed Biandina's family to their home, about halfway through the mass of tents toward the wall.

They lived like everyone else in their tribe: in an unstable tent supported by carved, interlocking lengths of bone tied together into longer poles. Wood truly did seem scarce, which Dirt should have expected after seeing so much flat landscape. It wasn't like there was none at all, just that things he expected to be wooden often weren't.

The tent was tall enough for the adults to walk in without ducking, and the flap that served as a door was tied to the interior ceiling. The covering that made up the tent was a mixture of leather and cloth, but striped and deliberate instead of patchy and random, giving it at least that much appearance of civilization. Patterns of green, red, and white colored all of it, so at least it wasn't plain.

Socks chose to rest nearby and chat with the swarm of curious onlookers rather than stand and peek in through the light-holes in the tent roof, so with nothing else to sort out, Dirt was the last to enter.

It was darker inside, so the first thing he did was snap his fingers to make a light, which he made hover in the center, near the top. All the humans gawked at it, but what truly impressed them was summoning a couple embers to warm the tent up quicker.

The inside felt roomier and more comfortable than he expected. A rich carpet of furs covered the entirety of the stone floor, several layers deep and soft. Woven baskets hung by coarse threads tied to the frame and contained whatever a family like this kept handy. Food, extra clothing, and tools. Stuff like that, judging by what Dirt could see from this angle. Half of the baskets were up out of his reach, and since at least four of the children were younger than him, that made sense. They probably put the oil up there, or the knives.

The children were much better behaved than the raucous crowds of them in Ogena. They sat calmly instead of running around and fighting and causing chaos like he'd expected. There was no room next to Biandina, since her siblings sat protectively close to her, and the littlest one climbed into her lap. Dirt sat near the boy who looked closest to his own age. They sat somewhat in a circle, and it looked like the room had been arranged that way. Everyone had their own spot with their own bedding, although it looked like most of it was shared. As it should be, especially in winter.

Eight children, one infant, and two adults wore varied expressions, either staring at Dirt, peering up at his magical light, or watching the magical embers lazily float around and warm up the tent. Even with so much ventilation, the temperature was quickly becoming bearable.

Dirt settled in and looked around, wondering what was going to happen next. No one said anything, so he spoke first. "I guess you already know, but my name is Dirt. The Mother of Wolves says I'm eight years old. Socks named me Dirt because when he found me, I was covered from head to toe in dirt. Dirt means 'dirt' in my language. Some people laugh, but I like it. I was born in a forest of trees that go all the way up to the sky, and they're alive and can turn into people called dryads. This is a part of one of them, named Home," he said, holding up the arm with the brace on it. "She was the first tree I made friends with, but Socks was my first friend overall. He was the first thing I ever talked to."

He paused, not sure what else to say, and no one jumped in to get things going. They looked at him and each other silently. The children curious and nervous, the mother stony and mad. The father scowled, but Dirt got the impression he was more conflicted than angry.

Dirt said, "Right now, Socks and I are traveling around the world exploring, and helping out humans whenever we can because there aren't many left. I guess I have some stories I could tell, since Socks didn't tell everything earlier. But first I want to hear all your names. And can you tell me something about yourself? Anything at all. I've spent, maybe, ten or fifteen days around humans in my whole life."

Biandina nodded, seeming happier already. There was still tightness in her lips and posture, but the frown was gone and her eyes had lost their despair. "I'll go first. Let's go oldest to youngest. We had an older brother, Prosperu, but he was taken by a *rucca*. I'm Biandina, and I'm in my fifteenth year, and . . ."

She bit her lip and glanced down. She had no idea what to say about herself, poor thing, now that she was an outcast.

Her father said, "When she was a little girl, she found a snake and picked it right up, then carried it around showing everybody. It was deadly venomous, and no one dared get close enough to snatch it away from her. It caused quite a panic. We didn't want to scare her in case she dropped it or let it bite her. She finally took it outside and put it down, and it slithered away." He had a hint of warmth in his eyes that faded as soon as he was done speaking.

"I'm Antelmu, and I'm in my thirteenth year," said the oldest of the boys, the protective one who'd had the spear earlier. He was a muscular lad with the same build as his father, but not the beard. "I'm training to be a horseman to fight for the tribe. I already broke my own colt. We're not going to geld him because he's even handsomer than his sire. His name is Boulder."

Dirt nodded, smiling slightly. "I'd like to meet him," he said, honestly. He had seen horses, but never really interacted with them. Socks scared them too much, and Dirt had been too busy to seek them out.

"I'm Lavisa and I'm in my twelfth year," said the next girl. Her hair was darker than the rest, closer to black than the brown of the rest of the children, and she wore it pulled back tight. "I'm the best dancer in the family."

Mother almost—almost—cracked a smile at that. She had to force it back. Dirt saw her twitch, and he could tell.

"I'm Gnaziu," said the boy sitting next to Dirt, the one closest to his age. He wore neat clothing and combed hair. "I'm in my tenth year. I made my own bow. Do you wanna see it?"

"I do. I've never shot one. Is there a trick to it?"

"Just show it to him," said the mother, her voice flat. "Don't shoot it in here. Don't even pretend."

"I know," said the boy, fake annoyance in his voice. He stood and took a bow off a hook, which Dirt hadn't noticed before. Now that he looked, there were several more like it, and quivers of arrows as well. This one was as long as the boy's torso and decorated with feathers at the top and bottom. "I found the wood myself, and the bones on the end for the notching were carved from a *ragnulì*."

"What's a ragnulì?" asked Dirt.

"It's those big dog-beasts with the arched backs," said Gnaziu.

"Oh, Socks smelled some of those, but I didn't see them," said Dirt. "I like that bow. It looks great. And you know what? Your name sounds like Ignasi, who is one of the first humans I ever met. He's a Camayan. And in my language, that name is Ignatius. That makes it a very, very old name."

"What do you mean by that?" asked the father.

Dirt hesitated, unsure how much to reveal. Maybe not so much after all. He said, "My language is the oldest one, and every other language descended from it. I'm probably the only person who speaks it anymore."

"How can you possibly know that, if you don't know any other humans?" asked Antelmu, the twelve-year-old.

Dirt grinned mischievously and said, "Let's save the other stories until we're done. Who's next?"

"Me," said a girl shyer than the others, about his same size. Maybe just a little younger, but it was hard to tell. She watched him steadily, but with clear distrust. "I'm Lisea, and I'm in my eighth year. I have a cat."

"You have a cat?" asked Dirt, almost standing. "Can I see it?"

"She's not here right now, but she'll come back later," said Lisea.

"I've never seen a cat, even though Socks has smelled them. The trees teased me once saying I'll learn about cats when I'm ready. I told

Socks that, and now he won't show me what they are either. It's a little animal, right?"

The shy girl cracked a smile and didn't say anything. After she saw Dirt's exaggerated disappointment, she giggled.

"Your turn," said Biandina, nodding at Eudossia, whose name he'd learned earlier.

The squirrely little girl loudly whispered, "What do I say?"

"Your name and how old you are," replied three different children.

"I'm Eudossia and I'm in my sixth year," she said. She clamped her mouth shut and acted shy, indicating she was done.

"She likes to sing, especially at night when I'm trying to sleep," said Lavisa, the eleven-year-old girl.

Everyone ignored that.

"This is Miliu. He's in his sixth year. Say hello, Miliu," said the father.

"Hello," said the little boy. "How come you're naked?"

The whole family reacted, some shifting nervously, others grinning. One girl shushed the little boy like he'd done something improper. Dirt said, "The old people said I had to burn my clothes, and I don't have any more with me. But I'm used to it. I spent most of my life like this."

The boy he was sitting next to, Gnaziu, said, "Do you want to borrow something? Nobody goes naked inside the walls."

Dirt nodded. "If you have anything, sure. I'll give it back before I leave, unless I think of something good to trade for it." Judging from how they lived, Dirt didn't think they had much to spare. Lisea, the next youngest girl, would probably be wearing anything Gnaziu grew out of.

Gnaziu stood up and dug under the skins for a bundle of cloth, all rolled up. It was a thick woolen pair of pants, much like he had on now, except those were baggy and rolled up on the cuffs for him to grow into. Dirt stood and put them on. They were a bit tight, even though Dirt was a smaller. He immediately felt warmer, and when Gnaziu handed him a long woolen shirt to go with it, he wondered if he should make one of his embers wink out.

"What kind of stuff would you want to trade for this?" Dirt asked, adjusting the shirt. It was a little tight as well, but it would do for now. If it had been warmer, he might have declined.

Gnaziu said, "Um, wood, or meat, or good bones. Arrows. Anything silver. Or other clothes, maybe."

The father said, "Those are too small for you. If you think of anything to trade, we'll find you bigger ones."

"I'll see what Socks has in his harness later," said Dirt. He sat down again, carefully so he wouldn't rip the tight pants.

The youngest boy climbed off Biandina's lap and started pulling off his long woolen gown. "Oh, no you don't," she said, trying to prevent him. The child laughed and struggled to get away.

"That is Oraziu," said the father, gesturing at the squirming, noisy boy. "He's in his fourth year, but only barely."

"He's cute," said Dirt.

Little Oraziu shrieked in dismay and said "No! My do it!" as he squirmed and tried to get free of Biandina's interference. Finally, she let him go and he got his gown almost off, up around his head, before one of the other girls grabbed him. Several children laughed, and Dirt joined them.

"What's the infant's name? Is it a boy or a girl?"

"It's a girl, and we haven't named her yet," said the father.

"Just don't name her Prisca," said Dirt, wishing Socks was around to share in the joke. Judging from the shrieks and laughter he heard outside, the pup was enjoying himself.

"I know of a Priscilla, but no Priscas," said the father. "What's a Prisca?"

"She was a magical skeleton who tried to kill me," said Dirt. Every member of the family glanced at Dirt, wondering if they'd heard correctly. Except for little Oraziu, who struggled his way free again and ran to the other side of the tent, where he resumed pulling off his gown with a look of pure enjoyment on his chubby face.

-Dirt, there is a crying infant nearby, and it is his mouth that hurts. Go see if you can help him,- said Socks, just to him.

He looked again at the minds nearby, picking out the children easily. Adult minds had more thoughts, but children had more light in them, and Dirt's best guess was that it was their spirits waiting for their brains to grow in. The infants were the clearest, just impressions, a single sight or smell or touch at a time, although their emotions were just as vivid as anyone else's.

One infant was sleeping, and that must be the girl in the tent. Another was resting and tasting milk, so that wasn't the one Socks meant. Dirt looked around until he found it—a tiny boy who was screaming and thinking of nothing but inescapable pain, coming from his tongue.

Dirt got up and said, "I'll be right back. Socks found a crying baby he wants me to go check on."

"I'll come with you," said Gnaziu.

"Me too," said Biandina.

"And me," said Antelmu, the oldest boy. Once that was declared, all five of the others wanted to come, except for Oraziu, who was now screeching about being unable to get his gown up over his head. It was stuck around his neck, and he fell over and howled about it.

Dirt led the procession out to where Socks was, only to find about fifty children of all ages crowding around him. Some were petting him, others trying to climb up, and a handful more were laughing and shrieking at the top of their lungs as Socks held them all a few feet off the ground. Dirt sent the pup a puff of amusement and affection, then asked, *"I don't hear it. Which way?"*

Socks gave him the direction, and he squeezed first through the crowd, then between the tents and shacks until he heard it himself. The poor baby's cries were ragged and weary, and Dirt hurried as fast as he could without leaving Biandina behind, since her guts were still sore and she couldn't move very fast.

He slid into the tent without asking first and found a lonely mother with tears streaming down her face, holding her offspring and rocking, at a total loss of what to do.

"Hello," said Dirt. "Can I see him?" In came the rest of the children.

"Who are you?" she asked. "What do you want?"

"I'm Dirt. And I want to look at his mouth," said Dirt. He stepped over as politely as he could and looked in. It was a normal baby mouth, with four handsome little teeth.

"Whose child are you? Did someone send you? I could use some water, if you want to help," said the mother. She was young, now that Dirt got a good look at her. This was probably her first.

Dirt said, "I guess you missed all the excitement. I came with the wolf."

Then, instead of waiting for her to say anything else, Dirt lifted the tiny boy's tongue up with a finger and examined it. Right away he saw the problem. A briar. The little one had a small briar under his tongue. Dirt pulled it out, and the baby stopped crying almost immediately, resorting to an exhausted half whine while he calmed down.

Dirt held it up and showed the mother, whose eyes widened in horror. "I can't believe it. He's been crying all day!"

He checked all the adult minds until he found hers, which only took a moment. She was thinking over and over, *"I'm such a terrible mother, why didn't I check?"* Things like that. She was relieved and yet, at the same time, somehow felt even worse.

"You're not a terrible mother," said Dirt, patting her on the head. "I bet you won't even eat him if he's weak. Do you want to keep the briar?"

"What? No, please get it out of my tent. Who are you again?"

"I'm Dirt. Maybe I'll come visit you later. You probably both need a nap," he said. He handed Lisea the briar, since she was the closest, and stepped back out.

Biandina's siblings regarded him with something close to awe, and he just grinned and beckoned them to follow again. He hurried back to Socks, quite pleased with everything, and when he got there, the pup had a new task for him. There was a youth who had dropped an arrowhead into a crack between the paving stones and couldn't get it out. Socks had heard the scratching of his attempts to fish it out.

Dirt found him and peered down into the crack, then simply yanked the arrowhead out with his mind and snatched it from the air, then handed it to the startled young man. "Are there any more, or just that one?" Dirt asked.

"Just that one. Who . . . ?" The young man sat up, confused.

Dirt turned to Biandina and said, "I bet no one is going to recognize me without my old clothes. I look like one of you now, except my hair is darker than average."

"You really don't look like one of us," she said. But Dirt just smiled and made his way back to Socks, parade of children following behind him.

Socks sent him on all sorts of errands after that, which Dirt thoroughly enjoyed. He helped a very surprised man lift a heavy barrel of presumably very precious wood back onto a shelf. A child Oraziu's age was fighting her parents, who wanted her to take a nap because she was sick and had slept poorly, and they were all exhausted. Dirt pushed her mind to sleep very, very gently.

He found a tent with an old couple, older than the elders, who were shivering and unable to keep warm. With his knife, Dirt scrawled a heating sigil into the stone beneath their furs and filled it with mana, enough to last a day or two. It wasn't perfect, but it didn't have to be. No one but him could refill it anyway.

Biandina and her siblings were quite impressed by all of it, and they followed with eager eyes, taking in miracle after miracle. Dirt could tell they were warming up to him. Standing a bit closer, smiling more, things like that.

After that they split up, sending the girls back while they went to go feed Antelmu's horse, Boulder. The older boy was as proud of his pet as Dirt had ever seen anyone, as proud as the duke was of his children. And it was a fine horse, shining brown with a black mane. From its mind, it recognized Antelmu and was happy to see him, in part because there was a good chance he'd get a treat.

Antelmu brushed and fed his horse with every bit as much affection as Dirt showed Socks, and during that time the three boys chatted so naturally Dirt felt almost at home. They told him the snow this year was unusual; it usually came weeks later, and seldom this thick. The tribe didn't stay in the fort all the time—when the weather was better, they ventured out to farm the surrounding area or tend herds of sheep. Many of these tents would disappear when spring came.

Dirt learned they hadn't been told why Biandina had disappeared, just that she was leaving and never coming back. Antelmu had suspected his parents had something to do with it, since it seemed their mother wasn't very endearing, but he couldn't prove anything. "I'm not going to let anything happen to her this time," Antelmu insisted resolutely. He glanced across the outpost toward his tent, wondering if something was currently happening that he should be trying to stop.

"Socks won't let anything happen to her," said Dirt.

"He can't watch everything," said Antelmu.

"He's just an animal," said Gnaziu, although he wasn't very sure about it.

Dirt smirked. "Socks isn't just an animal. He's smarter than me."

Both boys gave him quizzical looks, then their eyes drifted while they thought about the things they'd seen and heard already. The giant pup could talk with his mind, so maybe being animal-shaped was deceptive.

Dirt said, "He doesn't think faster than I do, and he's not really better at figuring out a riddle, that sort of thing. We're the same in that way. But he has a huge mind, and he can pay attention to more things at once than I can. Right now, he's probably watching me, keeping track of Biandina, and playing with all those children at the same time. He can think bigger thoughts, but I guess that's hard to explain, isn't it? He's still just a pup, though. You should see what the grown ones look like."

"I wish Boulder could talk," said Antelmu. "Sometimes he's rebellious, and I never know why. Stupid animal. Dumbest thing around, aren't you? Yes you are." He spoke with an affectionate tone of voice the horse responded positively to and made a kissing motion. Boulder rubbed his huge lips on Antelmu's cheek, which made Dirt and Gnaziu grin.

After the boys were done with their chores, Dirt followed them back home. He checked the local minds, and Socks was still nearby, although he'd gone out of the fort for a bit. Hopefully he wasn't bored. It was a shame the place wasn't a bit bigger and less crowded, so he could come along.

They fed Dirt along with the rest of the children, and then it was time to start putting the little ones down and getting ready for the night. Babbu and the mother didn't exactly kick him out, but they did leave him plenty of opportunities to volunteer, and he eventually got the hint.

He slept outside the fort that night, cuddled up with Socks. Which Socks preferred, of course, since he didn't quite trust this batch of humans yet, and it wasn't so cramped outside.

As they waited for sleep to come, Dirt said, *"I know we can't stick around very long, but I don't feel like we've done anything real to help yet. Just little things, which was fun, but it's not going to save their people. It's too bad I don't have a good way to teach them any magic. I wonder if we should find one child, just one, and you could open his mind like you did to me, so he can see thoughts."*

-It would not be hard, but that would only be helpful sometimes.-

"And I'm still not sure how people would react. No one knows I can do it. I don't know if it would make them afraid, or glad," said Dirt. *"Maybe I can ask the elders."*

-You can ask them, but you should be careful. I don't trust them,- said Socks.

"I guess I don't either, now that you mention it. Good night, Socks. Thanks for helping with the elemental earlier."

-We are both growing stronger. I am glad. Good night, Dirt. Perhaps you will think of something helpful in the morning.-

The next morning, Socks said, *-I want to go hunting. I will not be long. Do you want to come, or go spend time with the humans?-*
"I can hunt with you anytime. I'll stay here."
-Good. You should learn what you can. I just didn't want you to be sad that I left you.- The pup gave Dirt an affectionate lick and bounded off across the snow.

Dirt headed into the fort and spent a while simply poking around, seeing what everyone was up to. Although he'd spent a few days in Ogena after the battle, it had been a wild, busy time, usually spent getting into trouble with Màxim. He had seen almost nothing of typical domesticity, and now he was curious.

First, he crept close enough to Biandina's family to make sure they hadn't done anything to her, and everyone was fine. All the little ones were competing for her attention, and the mother was helpless to stop them. After that, he quietly snuck around everywhere he could fit to see what there was to see. Mothers scolding little ones, fathers and older children out and about on various chores. Working with strips of hide set out on frames, checking on the stores of charcoal, taking horses to go ride somewhere, all sorts of things.

People stopped to chat wherever they met. Some mentioned the giant wolf, wondering if he was still around, and marveled that nothing awful had happened. Apparently not all the stories about giant wolves had happy endings, and if Dirt stayed here long enough, he wanted to hear them all.

Word was also spreading about the events in the Aedes yesterday, too. The accounts all conflicted, with some saying that the wolf had killed a man in anger, and some that the guards had killed someone who attacked the wolf's pet boy. Only a few of them mentioned half-dead Iliaru's true nature, and those were typically recited and received with skepticism. No one mentioned the moving skeleton.

The general atmosphere was festive, in a subdued way. This tribe had only been gathered back together like this for a short time, only since the bad weather started not too long ago, and they were still in good spirits about it.

Dirt didn't always manage to stay out of sight, which limited how much he could observe. He stood out too much in his unusually tight clothing. One woman carrying a heavy waterskin on a rope, waved him over and quietly said, "Boy, come here. Were you Mettodiu's son?"

"Nope," said Dirt.

"Whose son are you?"

"Nobody's," said Dirt.

"Who are you staying with, then?"

"I'm staying with the giant wolf," said Dirt. "I'm the little human he brought along."

She looked visibly relieved, then gave a friendly little chuckle. "You need to ask him for some new pants. I thought you were an orphan the tribe was neglecting."

"Oh. Well, thanks for checking. Do your people always take care of orphans?"

"Of course. We have more work than hands. We can't spare a single pair," she said. Then she nodded, readjusted the rope holding the big waterskin, and continued on.

Dirt was growing fonder of the tribe already. No one had shot an arrow at him yet, for one. It seemed like they took care of each other and everyone got along. If they didn't, they wouldn't all cram in here together every winter.

The tribe had its problems, surely. The giant birds and hulking canines that hunted them, and who knew what else was out there. And that statue in the Aedes. That was another problem. Exiling Biandina over it was a problem, too. And he wasn't even sure where to *start* with the elders murdering a man by stabbing him and burying him alive in the treasury. Should Dirt punish them? What if they'd been justified somehow?

Now that he thought about it, the poorer it sat with him. Here they were sending Biandina to her fate for killing a rabbit, and they'd killed a human in the exact same place and hidden it from everybody. The part of him that was Dirt viewed the action with innocent ignorance, having very little idea of what was appropriate for humans. But the part of him that was Avitus squirmed at the idea. It revolted him, even. There should be *laws*. Especially if they had sacrificed him to Avitus's dear Melodia. That would be a sacrilege.

A short while later, he decided it was time to go find the elders. He needed to ask more about the statue and test the waters on teaching someone to see minds. They'd probably say it was a terrible idea, since that person would learn their secret, but he still wanted to see what they thought about it. He'd just have to be coy about it.

Once inside, he wondered why the tents were nicer in here, under the ancient roof where it would be dark day and night. He understood wanting to have a roof over his head, but it would be like living completely underground. Perhaps they liked it because it kept the rain off. So how did they decide who got to live here? He'd have to ask later.

They hadn't yet replaced the heavy wooden frame that blocked the entrance to the Aedes, fortunately, and Dirt walked right in.

The corpse and Dirt's bloody clothing were gone now, and the elders were kneeling next to the bloodstain and discussing between each other in hushed tones. They held wet washcloths in their hands and judging by the heavy leather waterskin, they had been cleaning. They'd even made some progress, it looked like.

No one else was in here besides them. Dirt suspected that typically, no one was allowed in, and they were the ones who decided. They looked over as he entered and gave him unpleasant glares.

Well, no reason to waste their time if they were busy. Best to get right to it. Dirt asked the old man, "I don't mean to interrupt, but I have a quick question for you. I know Gnese's name, but not yours. That's not the question, though."

The old man's face stayed cold, but he answered. "Fidelu."

"Fidelu. That's another old name. Huh. Thanks. Well, the question is, you know how Socks can see your thoughts, and that's how you were talking to him at first? What would happen if a human in your tribe suddenly learned how to do that? Hear people's thoughts," said Dirt. He stood awkwardly, not sure what posture he should take. He landed somewhere between friendly and dignified, he hoped.

The answer was not quick in coming. Dirt watched as they thought it over, glaring at him all the while. They glanced at each other, then back at Dirt.

"What are you saying?" said Gnese, carefully.

Dirt's eyes went to the uncovered treasury. The corpse dust in front of it had already been swept up and disposed of, and the lid put back to hide the opening. Melodia herself stood suffering, just as she'd been before.

His lack of a quick answer made them both grow more hostile in the set of their shoulders. Their faces hardened, but the sense Dirt got was more of fear than anger. He wondered if he should find their minds; it wouldn't be too difficult. But that might give away something he wasn't ready to reveal yet.

"What am I saying? I was just thinking about it," said Dirt, trying to sound oblivious. "I'm curious what would happen if a normal human, just some random person, suddenly started to know everyone's thoughts. I'm asking you because you're the elders so you must know the most. So how would they be treated? What would happen to them?"

"That person would never be trusted," said Fidelu hastily.

"Why not? It can be really handy, if, for example, you want to know why a baby is crying. Wouldn't people be happy?" asked Dirt.

"That would be useful, but there's more to it than that," said Gnese.

"Like what?" asked Dirt. He'd expected this, honestly, but it was still disappointing. Humans were naturally wary and skittish, but he'd been hoping for a different reaction.

Fidelu got his wariness under control and let his face and posture smooth out into something more grandfatherly. He sat up to relax and put on a warmer half-smile. "My boy, have you ever made a mistake?" he asked.

"Sure, probably. Like what?"

"It doesn't matter what. But as you grow, you will find yourself making more and more of them. Some will be big mistakes, and some will be small. Let me explain it this way. That wolf is your only friend, right?" asked Fidelu.

Gnese had picked up on the change of tone and lost all the harshness in her demeanor as well. Dirt did his best not to let on he knew they were putting on airs, since he was interested in their explanation.

"No, he's not my only friend at all. I have a bunch of friends that are trees, and some humans. My best human friend is Màxim, the duke's son from Ogena," said Dirt.

"Fine. Good. So imagine that one day, you got angry with Màxim and said something cruel to him. Something truly unacceptable, and then, because you are human and we all make mistakes, you didn't apologize. And it got worse and worse, until you weren't friends anymore. Now, I'm sure that won't happen, but imagine with me for a moment, hmm?" said Fidelu. His wrinkly old face lent itself well to being warm and grandfatherly.

"Okay," said Dirt.

"You have done something that he will not forgive, and now you are no longer friends. You regret what you did, and you know it was your fault, but it is too late," said Fidelu.

Even though the situation was imaginary and extremely unlikely, Dirt found himself bothered. He briefly pictured an angry Màxim telling Dirt never to talk to him again and didn't like it. Dirt had to admit they were good at teaching.

"Now let's take a step back. Suppose that instead of *saying* those cruel things, you only *thought* about saying them. But you realized that it would be horrible to say them and what Màxim would think, so you didn't. In fact, you didn't even really mean those things, so you're glad you didn't say them," said Fidelu. "Instead of a disaster and losing a friend, nothing happened."

"I see," said Dirt. "So, if Màxim could read my mind, then he'd know what it was I thought about and get offended anyway, even though I didn't want that to happen."

"Exactly. There are many things a man wishes to keep hidden, child. Some are mistakes he wishes to move past. Some are things he can never say, but still thinks of. Some are desires he must keep under control, but struggles with. Everyone who has lived long enough has things they don't want others to know. Even you, I bet. Can you think of anything like that?" asked Fidelu, gesturing with his hand for Dirt to answer.

The first thing that came to Dirt's mind was that he, Avitus, had broken the world and ruined the gods and sent humanity into an extinction spiral. Everybody didn't need to know that. "I guess," he replied.

Gnese put on a grandmother's friendliness, although the hardness in her face made it less convincing than her mate's. She said, "Now, imagine there's one person in the tribe that everyone knows can see all their thoughts. All the things they need to keep hidden. Things that aren't truly themselves, or things they're trying to overcome. That one person knows all their secrets. How do you think they'll be treated? They will always be outcasts, right?"

"Also, they would not *want* to be close to anyone else. They would know that the others fear them, and they would hear those thoughts that were never meant to be spoken aloud, and be unable to stop knowing them," said Fidelu.

Dirt nodded, thinking that over. They had a good argument. They were completely wrong about what it would be like to know everyone's thoughts, but it was their perspective he was after. He suspected they were correct, which is why he'd wanted to make sure before having Socks open someone's mind-eye.

He'd be creating an outcast. Even if that person was useful, like helping babies. And there were other things, too, like telling the rats in the granary to come out where they could be captured. Or helping a horse calm down. Or knowing there was a half-dead person among the tribe.

If he was honest with himself, Dirt had known before asking what the answer would be. They'd say not to do it, or they'd ask for it to be done to themselves, secretly. He'd intuited from the moment he first met Marina and her party that it was not something others should know.

The elders waited patiently while he thought, and finally he said, "I guess that makes sense. And they'd probably be in danger, too."

"Yes, they might be. From what?" asked Gnese.

"Say someone did something horrible, like a murder, and they didn't want anyone to find out about it. But they knew that *that* person knew. They might want to kill them too, before the secret is revealed," said Dirt, furrowing his brow to look like a little boy deep in thought.

Both of them faltered for the briefest instant, searching his face for any sign of duplicity, but quickly regained their composure. Gnese, however, gave him an intent look, and Dirt knew what she was thinking without even looking at her mind. She was almost certainly thinking something loudly to see his reaction. Perhaps, *"Child, can you see my thoughts?"* Something like that.

Dirt gave no reaction, of course. They were amateurs. His best friend was Socks, and they wanted to win a thought game?

It made him feel a little guilty, manipulating them like this. He preferred honesty and forthrightness, and, as he often reminded himself, discipline and sincerity were his true power.

But he doubted this was information they would easily part with. Murder, if that's what it was, was something that should not be tolerated. He knew the word "justice," even if he couldn't say how it should play out. And he also knew the word "execution," which was what happened to criminals like murderers. Maybe he could get them to let something slip, and it would be exonerating instead of condemnatory.

"I'm not reading your minds, so you can stop looking at me funny. Tell you what. Let's do a bargain. I'll answer any one question from you, even if the answer is a secret, and you do the same for me. What do you think?" said Dirt.

"I decline," said Gnese, without hesitation.

"As do I," said Fidelu.

Dirt scowled. He should have seen that coming. He thought they might want some answers themselves, but all they wanted from him was his departure.

He searched out their minds then, taking only a moment to find them. They were easy to find, being the closest, and they were both looking at him. And they had fear in them that was tied to watching his face, to his voice. They were afraid of what he'd say.

Dirt made sure to watch so he could get his answer, whether they wanted to give it or not. "Fine. Oh well. Suppose instead that for no reason at all, I just randomly asked you whether you had a good reason for killing that guy and stuffing him in there," he said.

It wasn't easy watching both of their minds at the same time—that was one thing he didn't have much practice with. In Gnese's mind flashed an image of tendrils creeping through the hole in the roof, of dark

whispers and darker fears. In Fidelu's, memories of envy and lust. He'd
wanted to mate with Gnese, and that was related somehow. In both
cases, they quickly tried to think of something else.

"Don't think about it, whatever you do. Don't think about why you
killed him. Stop! Think about something other than why you killed
him!" said Dirt, making it impossible. "Aaaahhh, not that! Not why you
killed him and stuffed him in there!"

Fidelu and Gnese had a similar idea, that they needed to propitiate
the Murderous Lady. For Fidelu, it was an excuse, an opportunity,
and for Gnese, a solemn obligation. She was pregnant now, and the
tribe would be secure. How could she ask anyone else to suffer in her
place? How could she make some other woman a widow, or bereft of
her child?

In the few seconds before they managed to start thinking of other
things, albeit imperfectly, Dirt put the story together, at least in simple
fashion. Fidelu had desired Gnese for his mate, and Gnese had known
that, but she was already paired to Ghjacumu. They had slaughtered
him for the Murderous Lady, hoping to calm her curse, and it had
worked. Gnese's nightmares and daydream visions had ceased, and
the two of them became a mated pair and married, and raised
Ghjacumu's baby.

"So how'd you get away with it? Why didn't anyone . . . Oh, the previous elders covered for you?" asked Dirt, finding the answer in their
thoughts. "So they were in on it? I guess they must have told you about
it, but hardly anyone else, or people would have checked the treasury
the moment Ghjacumu disappeared."

"Don't speak that name here," hissed Gnese.

"What do you want?" asked Fidelu, cold and hard. Hard as Biandina's
mother. From how his mind felt, this was more natural for him than
anything else he'd been doing.

"What I want changes all the time. First, I wanted to meet more
humans. Then I wanted Biandina to live safely with her family, but only
her siblings want that right now, not even her. Now what I want, is . . .
I guess I don't know. What do I want?" said Dirt. "No, I do know. I
want you to be free of this."

He pushed past the two of them, and they gave him no resistance.
He stepped over the dead body without looking at it. He stopped in

front of Melodia, Goddess of Song. The Murderous Lady. Which was correct anymore?

Frankly, the whole situation disgusted him. He gathered that the Eye was using the goddess to manipulate humans to their detriment, to whittle them down generation by generation. Fear, mistrust, deception, death. Was it simply toying with them, or had it not made enough horrible monstrosities in this region to annihilate them yet? It'd had three thousand years to work on it, so either it preferred slower methods or was generally incapable of anything else. But still, to manipulate them using something so bright and beautiful as the memory of a goddess?

"Are you still there, Melodia?" he asked, in his language. He didn't expect an answer, and she gave none. She stared past him, wounded and dying.

Behind him, Fidelu had risen to his feet and was looking for something to smash Dirt's skull open with. There wasn't much, but perhaps he could pull a paving stone up. He was even trying to hide his thoughts while he debated it, the poor fool. Without turning around, Dirt said, "Socks is nearby, Fidelu, and even if you managed to hurt me, which you won't, you'd only outlive me by a heartbeat."

The message was heard and understood, and the elders struggled to think of what else to do. They wanted Dirt to leave so badly it was going to give them a headache. Everything was about to fall apart. *Everything.*

Dirt quit watching their minds so he could concentrate and filled himself with mana. He stared up at the statue, old marble still smooth and bright, even if every trace of the paint was gone. She had been glorious once.

Well, if the Eye would rebuild the statue every time it was destroyed, then destroying it wasn't the answer. He knew what he had to do.

Dirt hadn't tried this on stone yet, but he knew the sigil for it. There was no reason it shouldn't work. He used it to shape wood all the time. It didn't work very well on water, but that was water.

Dirt took the wood-shaping magic the dryads had taught him and replaced the sigil for "wood" with the one for "stone." After considering a few more changes, like replacing "grow" with "reform," he spoke the magic into existence.

He started with her broken arm, the one twisted the wrong way at the elbow and hanging limp, and by Grace, it worked. The stone lost its solidity, and Dirt gently reshaped it. He turned her forearm back the right way, doing his best to make sure it looked right, and did an acceptable job. He felt his own elbow to remind himself of the shape of the bones there, and it seemed to match.

Then he made her marble innards suck back up into her stomach. The stone slid upward, losing its shape and becoming just a solid mass, but it was exactly the right amount to fill the cavity. He made the arm that had been holding her intestines extend away a little, then smoothed over her stomach and reshaped it to be a dress again. Fortunately not all of the stone fabric was ruined, which gave him plenty of places to copy, as he filled in all the rips and tears.

He straightened her club foot by making it look like a mirror of the other one, and straightened her posture to balance out.

Finally, he had the confidence to fix her face and get rid of that horrible expression of pain. Despite all his practice making wooden toys, the finer details were beyond him, so he left her expressionless. Still human-looking, but blank. It was good enough. He turned her palms forward in a gesture of welcoming, cleaned up a few other details like the drips of marble blood on the plinth, and then he was done.

The mana left him, and he stepped back. His eye found a dozen mistakes, but they were all minor. If he wanted to master this, he needed to spend a lot more time wandering around Turicum looking at the statues the dryads had recovered, and get a lot more practice. But despite the flaws, there was no mistaking this for anything other than Melodia. It was not a statue of a tortured, suffering woman any longer. It was an imperious woman in a full-length dress, gazing forward at a horizon only she could see.

Dirt decided there was one last detail he wasn't willing to leave overlooked, so he created the magic again and tilted her head downward slightly, turning her gaze onto the people in the room. Only then did he turn around to see what the elders thought.

They watched in silence, eyes wide, completely unsure what to think. What they had just seen was too impossible to process.

Before anyone spoke, a shadow came over the hole in the roof and plunged the Aedes into darkness. Gnese and Fidelu both cried out in alarm, but Dirt snapped his fingers and summoned a light.

The whole gap was covered in white flesh, the flesh of the Eye and the things that emerged from it. A sinuous tendril drooped down and flopped around like it was looking for something to grab.

Dirt heard motion behind him and spun to see all his work being undone. The statue of the goddess was moving just like a real person, her dress ripping away to expose long gashes that opened on her thighs and chest. She moved an arm forward as if pleading for mercy, and it broke at the elbow, the one Dirt had fixed. Her gaze turned down to him, terror and pain coming alive in her marble features, and then she froze again, and fell from the plinth. It broke apart when it hit the ground, and all the pieces slid back together.

-COME, DIRT,- yelled Socks. -COME NOW!-

Dirt's heart ached to see what had happened yet again to poor Melodia, but he had no time to spend on grief. He waved a hand in front of Fidelu's face to get his attention and said, "There's going to be a fight. Go get ready."

Then he ran out of the Aedes and Principia, with the stray thought that he probably shouldn't be calling it that anymore. It was not a Principia at all, just the skeleton of one.

Outside in the main courtyard, the chaos had already begun. Monstrous shapes in the sky were seen imperfectly through the edges of the netting, and the tribe's attention was rapidly turning upward. Cries of alarm rang out each time flashes of white flesh crossed the narrow gaps. The Eye, or whatever shape it had taken this time, swam through the air above the outpost, but it was impossible to get a good look at it. Some screamed and froze; others called out names and raced to find them. Men took up spears and gazed upward warily, hoping nothing would come through the ceiling.

It did. An arm with four joints and two pincer-like fingers at the end burst from a drooping snow-dip in the canopy, sending wet slush everywhere in an explosive burst. It tore away a tent and grabbed two humans, a young man and a child, and began to raise them upward.

Dirt sprinted toward them and inhaled mana, then jumped to catch the arm. He was going so fast that he slammed into the two humans with a crushing thud and then almost failed to grab on. The child screamed in pain, but Dirt hadn't felt anything break, so hopefully it was fine. He climbed around like a squirrel until he got both hands around one of the giant fingers and pulled with all his might, opening the claw's grip.

The two humans tumbled out, awkwardly, headfirst, and for an instant Dirt was sure they'd smash their skulls, but Socks caught them with his mind and set them down. The pup was already back inside the fort, thank Grace. Socks grabbed him and yanked him halfway across the courtyard.

-We should go outside and fight it there,- was all Socks said, and Dirt agreed. But before they even turned to go, another monstrous arm ripped open the netting not far from where they stood and reached down to toss a tent aside. It clutched a woman holding a babe in her arms and lifted her up. In a desperate moment of good judgment, she tossed the little one to someone nearby.

-I can't grab it!- said Socks, meaning the giant arm. It was certain, then—this was the same thing they'd fought outside Ogena. Socks hadn't been able to grab that one with his mind either.

Dirt pulled out his knife and threw it forward for Socks, and the pup snatched it with his mind and sent it shooting forward faster than an arrow. It was too late, however, and the woman gave one desperate shriek of helplessness as she was pulled up through the hole in the netting. Socks returned the knife to Dirt.

"Pull it all down!" shouted Dirt in his mind, and Socks complied. The netting began to tear and collapse everywhere, burying hapless humans under piles of snow and fabric that proved near impossible to get out of.

Nearby children raced toward Socks, hundreds of them, but not all. Dirt made sure that none were caught under the falling netting by pulling them to safety with his own mind. The rebounding momentum caused him to slide this way and that on the floor, and he fell more than once, but soon enough, a good portion of the sky was exposed and with it, the Eye.

But it was more than just an eye this time, peeking through its rip in the sky. Other holes opened in the air through which long, gangly limbs emerged, waving as they looked for their next target. The captured woman was nowhere to be seen, but Dirt suspected that she was inside a bulging mass hovering near the eye, one that added a shade of tumorous red to its sickly white flesh.

Everyone was screaming now, complete chaos having taken hold. Fortunately, nearly every child in the tribe was close to Socks, so none of them got crushed in the wild stampede for the exits.

Socks took his iron ball from its pocket in his harness and braced himself for a throw.

"Get the arms first so no one else gets grabbed," said Dirt.

The iron ball flew like a lightning strike, with so much force that even Socks's paws slipped on the bare stone. Above, a monstrous arm exploded in a spray of blood and flesh and crashed through a place where the netting hadn't yet fallen.

Dirt focused and called a few sparks up near the Eye itself, which he caused to burst into flame to serve as a distraction. The Eye gave no indication that it had been harmed, but it rotated in its slimy socket to find him and Socks standing below. It began to glide silently through the air toward them.

Socks obliterated another arm, then another, swinging the ball too fast to see as his giant body swayed from the rebounding momentum.

The Eye seemed to pay its injuries little heed. It stopped before it got to them and turned its gaze downward toward a cluster of humans.

Biandina. She was down there, arms spread protectively over several of her little siblings, and it was looking right at her. Her father stood next to her, pointing his spear boldly upward, ready to strike at whatever came. The mother was nowhere to be seen, fortunately, and Dirt hoped she was safe somewhere with the infant.

Having fixed on her, the Eye floated upward and withdrew the stubs of its ruined arms back into the sky.

The cluster of humans below broke apart, and everyone ran in a different direction. Half of them fell, stumbling over collapsed tents or getting tangled in cloth and rope from the netting. Anyone who fell was picked up instead of stepped on.

Antelmu, the oldest boy, had little Oraziu and Miliu under his arms when he successfully broke from the crowd. His face was set with determination and purpose, and he ran with greater strength than Dirt expected, darting nimbly between tents until he got far enough away and chose to hide. It wouldn't help much; Dirt could hear Oraziu's shrill screaming all the way from here, even over the cacophony of the crowd. Lavisa, the girl just younger than Biandina who'd mentioned dancing, was not too far behind.

That left Biandina and three others unable to get away in time. The Eye filled with a hissing red liquid and blinked, dropping a single tear right on them. Her father yanked Gnaziu back so hard he tumbled head over heels, then shoved Lisea out of the way. But Eudossia clung to Biandina's legs and kept her from moving out of danger. With no time to spare, Biandina folded her arms over her sister and bowed protectively.

Dirt sprinted that direction as fast as his mana-infused legs could carry him, but it was too far. Socks tried grabbing the red drip, but his mind wouldn't close around it. That left him only an instant, in which the pup flung a bundle of cloth—probably part of a tent—into the drip's path.

The tent cloth caught most of the liquid, but not all. A splash made it past and fell across Biandina's arm and shoulder, with a few drops on her back.

Everything the liquid touched was destroyed, evaporating into bitter, reeking smoke in an instant. The tent cloth became mere tangled strips, and the stone's surface was pitted where the splash fell. Biandina's arm severed completely at the shoulder and fell to the ground. The wounds in her back dug deep, exposing ribs and the things beneath them. Her clothing had been torn and ruined already, but now it was ribbons as ragged as the goddess wore.

It was no longer possible to tell who was or wasn't screaming. Biandina fell to her knees, popping Eudossia out to the side. Her father grabbed the smaller girl and carried her a safe distance away, eyeing the smoking pits in the floor in distress.

Dirt reached her then, too late. She huddled, gasping, unable to handle the damage done to her body, to say nothing of the pain. Her injuries quickly welled with blood, and Dirt wasted no time. He lifted her by her thigh and armpit, sparing not even an instant to worry about her comfort, and raced toward Socks.

Mana-infused leaps carried him over ruined tents and clustered garbage, and the Eye followed them. Dirt heard another drip only a few steps behind and felt a burning puncture wound on his calf from a splash, but it was not enough to stop him. He made it back to Socks before his eyes even started watering from the pain.

The crowd of children around Socks had broken, with most of them running off toward their homes, or at least hiding somewhere else. Socks gently swept the few remaining stragglers aside, most of them landing a bit roughly, but unharmed.

He tore away the tatters of Biandina's ruined shirt, and for the second time, licked her wounds to save her life. This time she was awake for it, and she choked and gasped and twisted in revulsion at how it felt, which made Dirt feel miserable himself.

But they had no time. Not even enough time to completely lick her wounds before the Eye was overhead and another drop rained down. Socks got everyone to safety, but only barely—one tiny girl ran out at the last instant and nearly took the full brunt of it. Socks and Dirt both pushed her to safety with their minds so hard the sudden acceleration knocked her unconscious. No minds winked out, thank Grace.

Dirt looked up just in time to see a four-jointed arm press a flailing man into the bulging red mass of flesh hovering near the eye. He was absorbed into it almost instantly.

Socks said, -*What do we do?*- The pup sounded panicked.

"Fire! Burn the whole sky!" screamed Dirt mentally. *"Mind meld first."*

Their minds slid together, and an instant later, the blue sky filled with bright sparks that spread across as wide an area as their combined consciousness could handle.

Socks and Dirt flooded the sky with another wave of sparks to reinforce the first, watching with two sets of eyes to keep them burning, and ignited them all with a deafening roar. A blast wave of scalding heat ripped through the outpost, so hot the boy's body had to shut his eyes and turn away.

Flames hotter and brighter than the sun filled the sky, orange and red and white bursts of flaming rolling and crashing. The half-dead mind of the Eye quickly withdrew, closed, and disappeared.

Socks and Dirt kept the flames burning for a bit longer, a count of three, until even the wolf ran out of mana and couldn't keep up with the demand. The flames died, the sky dimming as the blue returned.

Only a few steps away, the bulbous, squirming mass fell and burst open. Inside were the remains of three humans—the people who'd been snatched up. They were halfway through the process of being reshaped into something else, something revolting and incomplete. Their heads were exposed, dead faces and eyes staring at nothing, but their torsos were melted together. Half of their limbs had already been absorbed.

Socks and Dirt beheld the sight with utter disgust, and the wolf tossed it with all his mental might out of the fort. The wolf lifted the boy high into the air so they could scout for further danger, but there was nothing from horizon to horizon, nor could they find any dangerous minds. Just the minds of a crowd of humans in a state beyond terror, and the horses, who had somehow been insulated from the entire affair.

Still, they kept watch for a moment longer just to make sure before bringing the boy down and separating the mind meld.

There was no hush in the crowd once the danger was gone. Cries of terror turned to cries of anguish or pain or calls for help. Dirt felt sick inside. He hadn't intended for this, nor should he have seen it coming. But here it was, in response to something he'd done.

Socks resumed licking Biandina while Dirt took in the devastation all around them. In the few short moments the conflict had lasted, the tribe had lost its net ceiling, and half or more of their tents had been destroyed. The entire area was laid to waste, leaving everything in soggy heaps. Mothers raced around, desperately looking for their children, and men stood ready with spears to stab the sky, unable to believe it was already over.

And maybe it wasn't over. The Eye had focused on Biandina, so did that mean it was keeping track of her somehow? Maybe she'd been right all along. Maybe she was cursed, or at least its functional equivalent.

The gouge in his calf *really* needed licking, and Dirt felt the blood making the bottom of his heel sticky. But he wasn't ready to be rid of the pain, not yet.

He felt a chill where he wasn't expecting it and peeked back to find that his pants really *had* been too tight, and the seam was torn open on the rear. Further inspection showed similar damage to both armpits. He scowled. Looking around, it seemed unlikely that anyone would be interested in giving him a new set of clothes anymore. They had their own messes to deal with. It was going to be a long, cold winter for them.

-What do we do with her now?- asked Socks. *-If we leave her, they will throw her out again, and now she only has one arm. Oh, I forgot your calf. Come here, and do not argue.-*

Dirt thought about it while Socks healed him, but ultimately, it wasn't his decision to make, was it? Biandina was kneeling, hissing and crying softly while she covered her breasts with her remaining arm. Her wounds were clean, but the skin had only barely begun to regrow and still looked like ground meat. Her head was bowed, but she kept glancing all around, unable to keep her eyes off the destruction.

He glanced at her thoughts and found what he expected. Bitter, painful emotion that sparked sharply amongst every thought. Thoughts that rang with self-pity and guilt over the poor state of her tribe. She'd brought this upon them. She had brought the Eye with her sacrifice.

In fact, she was already planning how to leave. She'd tell the boy she had to pee, tell the wolf not to follow her, and then run away and never come back. Better to fall in the snow and die out there than face the consequences. She was supposed to leave and die, but had returned, and this was the result.

Dirt squatted down next to her and patted her on the back, on an undamaged part of her skin. "I know what you're thinking, and it's not your fault," he said. He tried to smile, but couldn't force one onto his face.

"What would you know?" she said, voice croaking. She could hardly speak. Dirt looked in her mind and even her lungs hurt.

"This was one of my mistakes, not yours. I tried to fix the statue, and it brought out the Eye," he said. The words almost stuck in his chest. Socks had started helping the other humans, untangling them from the netting or whatever else, and Dirt would help soon. When he could bring himself to stand and face all the humans whose home he helped wreck.

She said, "I hate this. I hate being alive. Everyone just accepts misfortune. We shouldn't have to live like this. You know what I thought, Dirt?" Her voice was weak and broken by shivers of pain. "If everyone just did what they knew was right but didn't dare, it wouldn't be like this. I just wanted to stop that *rucca* that took Prosperu so it wouldn't take anyone else, but look what I've done now."

Dirt nodded. "So, you thought maybe humans should be fighting back instead of just dying out?"

"Don't make fun of me," she said.

"I'm not. I tried the same thing here. Was I wrong? I don't know. I really don't. What do you think?"

"What do I think?" she said. She finally turned her head and looked at him. Her eyes were puffy and red, and she shuddered every time she moved. But there was a bit of life in her yet, he was relieved to see. "What did you do, exactly?"

"The gods weren't always like that. They're supposed to be beautiful and benevolent. Something happened to them a very long time ago, and I thought maybe . . . well, I don't know if this was stupid or not. But I thought if I fixed the statue, Melodia would come back," said Dirt, his voice soft. Embarrassed, perhaps. The admission didn't want to escape his lips, and he had to push it out. "I hoped she was still involved in the world somehow, and the other gods. Guiding things, trying to save us. But I don't know. Probably not."

"Gods are evil. Everyone . . ." She coughed and spat a lump of something bloody on the ground. She looked at it and said, "That's not a good sign."

"Socks licked you, so you'll recover."

"If you say so," said Biandina.

"You will," said Dirt.

"Honestly, Dirt, I'm in a lot of pain right now. Can we talk later?" said Biandina.

"Before or after you run away to go die in the snow?" he replied.

"I'm not going to go die in the snow," she said, a bit of fire in her eyes. Her mind revealed she was lying, but offended he'd think that. And . . . she wasn't so sure she wanted to die. She'd almost done that several times. Maybe . . .

"Oh? Good to know you're staying here, then," said Dirt. Then he grinned, despite himself.

"What?" she said. "What's funny?"

"I don't know a lot of humans yet, but you remind me of Marina. She wanted to save her people, just like you. Same thing—if no one does anything, nothing will change, and everyone will die out. She found Hèctor and Ignasi, and they were the first humans I ever saw. They succeeded, so far. They found the duke, and he promised to help their town," said Dirt. "They still have a lot of work to do, but she's the one who got it moving."

"What about you?" said Biandina.

"I'm trying to save all the humans, not just one tribe." He ruefully added, "This was not my best moment."

-You are going to bring her with us, aren't you?- asked Socks.

"Only if that's okay with you."

-I suppose I'm fine with what you have in mind,- said the pup, adding a mental sigh to his words that he didn't truly feel. He couldn't quite hide the protective feelings he was developing for the poor little human whose blood he still tasted on his tongue.

Dirt said, "So, wanna come with us?"

"To where?"

"To meet Marina. And to help me save every tribe, including yours."

"I'm useless now," said Biandina, but in her mind, she didn't believe her own words. She was already thinking of how she'd tie a knot with one hand, and other things. She'd lost her right arm, and she was right-handed, but she could still manage. She'd have to.

"You were useless before. Wasn't that your problem? But I think some of my friends might be able to grow you a new arm," said Dirt. "And I really want you to meet them. And along the way, you can teach me more about humans, since I'm an amateur. And one very important reason is, I need more people like you. I don't know what I'll do with them all, but I can't save the humans on my own. Not even with Socks."

She nodded, and Dirt watched in her mind as her resolve grew and settled. She had felt the need for a long time and still felt it now. The world was wrong, and someone had to do something. Her parents heard her complaints and called her silly and childish, saying it was the whims of a naive girl. But she had known, deep in her heart. She dwelled on that feeling, savoring it, and turned it into hope instead of regret or fear. The wolf was *strong*, and so was the boy. Startlingly so. Perhaps, maybe . . .

Biandina stood, wincing painfully and struggling to keep her breasts covered with her remaining arm. She grimaced when she straightened her back, then coughed again. Then harder, loudly, until she spat out another loose wad of flesh from inside her lungs. The Eye's tear really had gotten deep inside there, hadn't it?

"Let me get another shirt," she said shyly, growing embarrassed now that she was up where everyone could see. "And help clean up a little, if they'll let me. And say goodbye properly this time."

CHAPTER TWENTY-SIX

Leaving, it turned out, was no simple matter. The tribe's people had gone mostly unharmed, but their homes hadn't, and a tremendous amount of work was required to make the fort livable again. Everyone was cold, everything was wet and in disarray, and night was still expected to arrive at the regular time.

The three people who'd been captured and melded together were the only deaths, as far as Dirt or Socks could determine, but a dozens of others had been injured in some way, with injuries ranging from scrapes to broken bones.

In short, there was more work than able-bodied humans around, so Dirt jumped in the first place he saw a need. A nearby family was trying to stand their tent back up, a middle-aged couple with two boys older than Biandina. Dirt took the fourth corner and lifted. Once they got it up, the mother went inside. She immediately gave a cry of dismay and yelled, "The pole is broken!"

The others scowled or looked at the floor. The man said, "How broken is it?"

Dirt let his corner sag and stepped around to the entrance to see. The center pole that held most of the tent's weight was in pieces, and not just from the leather thongs coming untied. Dirt guessed that it had been stepped on after falling over, crushing one of the larger bones into jagged shards. It was fixable, but the tent ceiling would be shorter by at least a foot as a result, and it wasn't very tall to begin with.

"Do you have any wood around?" he asked innocently.

The woman gave him a half-hearted glare, and the man mirrored it almost perfectly. The shorter of their two sons said, "If we had enough wood, we wouldn't be using bone for everything, would we?" The sarcasm in his voice was unmistakable, arising from bitterness.

"No, I mean, any at all. Even just a little," said Dirt.

Dirt spotted a wooden ladle, old and worn, lying near the next tent over, which a different mated pair were struggling to put back up. He hopped over and snatched it, then held it out. Inhaling a fresh helping of mana, he spoke the magic to reshape it. In his hands, it straightened, grew thick as his fist so it would be nice and sturdy, and then began to extend in both directions. "How long do you want it?" he asked.

The youth's sarcasm vanished in an instant, and he gave a low whistle that sounded impressed, eyes eager. The mother climbed back out of the sagging tent and froze when she saw what Dirt was holding.

"How long? About like this? Or do you want it taller?" Dirt asked for the second time. It seemed about as tall as the broken one, and would probably be sturdier.

"Taller. How did you do that?" asked the man, trying to act less excited than he felt.

"I was raised by trees and wolves. Actually, you over there, do you want one too?" said Dirt, toward the next family over. When they nodded the affirmative, he extended it long enough for two, then made it sever in half. The top section clanked loudly on the stone floor.

The second son, taller than the first, reached down to pick it up, but he wasn't expecting the weight, and it slipped from his fingers. "It's real," he said, somewhat embarrassed. The second time he picked it up, he used both hands.

"So is this the right length, then?" Dirt asked, standing his pole straight up.

"Yes," said one father. "That's fine," said the other.

"Is everybody going to want one this tall?"

One of the boys said, "If anyone wants a shorter one, they can just cut it. A little extra wood—"

"Yeah, we can just cut it shorter and use the extra for other things," interrupted the brother.

Neither brother seemed upset, so Dirt supposed that speaking over each other was normal for them. He nodded and channeled mana again, but this time instead of growing the extra length out the top, he had it grow sideways and then split down the middle the long way. The third pole was caught before it hit the floor. Dirt did it again, and again, and then word started getting around.

It turned out that wood was more valuable to them than anything he'd been offering before. Maybe if he could produce sap or those energizing berries, they might want those instead, but he couldn't. After repeated assurances that Dirt could make enough for everyone to get one, they formed a line and Dirt learned from direct experience that two hundred was a lot of times to do something.

The first few lengths of wood were trivial, but after about thirty he started getting distracted, which made it harder. After another fifty, his mana vessel seemed to tighten and wouldn't gather as much mana at once, slowing him down. But he couldn't stop, not until everyone had what they needed. Where else were they going to get it? And he owed them.

People stood in line with broken arms hastily strapped into slings, or with seeping bandages over cuts that Socks hadn't discovered yet. Neighbors waited with their injured friends and helped them carry theirs back, to ensure everyone had a chance.

Not every pole was used to hold tents up. Some people lived in shacks of stacked bricks with skins draped over the top, for one, and not every tent pole had been broken. A good number of Dirt's new poles were stored outside, leaning up against something for later use.

While Dirt tended to that, Socks collected the monster's fallen flesh and burned it in midair, then scorched the blood off the stone when he saw people trying to scrub it. Anything its blood had touched had to be burned, and one of the things that kept distracting Dirt was watching Socks being led to this or that spot to pick something up with his mind and ignite it in searing flame, high overhead.

Cleanup took less time than Dirt expected. He was sure it'd be a multi-day affair, but most of it just had to be picked up and set back in its place. Spilled things were wiped or swept up, and whatever was torn or broken was either repurposed or tossed in a heap of refuse near the front doorway.

Biandina came with her mother and the oldest brother, Antelmu, at the very end of the line to get their pole. The girl had a fresh shirt on, a baggy one that probably belonged to her mother. Her face had been washed to remove Socks's dried spittle and her hair fixed, and she looked far more presentable now. There was no ignoring the way her shoulder sagged and the sleeve dangled uselessly, however.

Antelmu walked tall behind her, almost hovering protectively with his dark eyes sharp and fierce. It seemed as if he was daring anyone to insult his sister.

The mother said, "We talked about bartering yesterday. Make me three poles like that, and I'll give you clothing that fits you." She had the same hardened face as always, perhaps even more so now that Biandina's return had indeed accompanied a disaster. She glanced at Dirt's bottom hanging out his torn pants and gave him a disapproving look. He wasn't sure if it was for being exposed, or damaging something he was borrowing.

"What are you going to use the poles for?" asked Dirt.

"It's none of your business. Biandina will be leaving by nightfall, and I expect you'll want to go with her," said the mother.

"I'm asking because I can make them any shape I want," said Dirt, growing indignant.

"We'll carve them as needed. I don't know everything I want yet," she replied. Her arms stayed folded as she glowered down at him.

"I haven't told Biandina this yet, but I'm going to take her somewhere she'll be safe. You know that forest I mentioned before, where I'm from? It's a place the Eye won't dare offend. She'll be safe and happy there. There will be people to meet, both humans and trees. Dryads," said Dirt.

The mother's glare didn't soften, but some of the tightness in her posture did. Dirt might not have noticed if he wasn't used to watching Socks's subtle body language. He continued. "The trees there are so tall the clouds have to go around them, and it never rains. There are ruins everywhere from the same empire that built this outpost, long ago. There's even an entire library to read. It's never too cold or too hot, and the trees give you food and water, or even clothing if you want any."

The boy, Antelmu, stepped up closer to listen. He might be almost thirteen, but that was still too young to keep his expression from giving away his thoughts. All the fierceness in his demeanor was being replaced by curiosity. The boy's mind spun as he imagined it all.

"Sometimes wolves like Socks come, and they have to be on good behavior because the trees are too powerful to offend. That's how I met

Socks. He was just wandering around and found me. But that's not all. There will be humans there too, starting with Marina. The trees fixed her womb, so she's looking for a mate, and then she'll live in the forest for a while to have her babies. But if you want to see something other than a forest, the trees can send you to Ogena."

"What's Ogena?" asked Biandina.

Dirt had been talking mostly at the mother, trying to win her over somewhat, but now he looked apologetically at Biandina, whose fate they were discussing. "I mentioned that before, and so did Socks. It's a city so grand it puts this fort to shame. There are, what, five hundred people in the tribe here? Ogena has over three thousand but they could fit plenty more. They have metal and stone and all the wood they need, and in the center is a giant palace so beautiful I can't even describe it. The duke lives there with his family, and they're my friends."

The mother hesitated, but she shifted her weight as if she was trying to decide what to say. Finally, she muttered, "That's all none of my business."

"Oh, I know. I'm just telling you for no reason at all. Biandina will be safe and happy and healthy and see amazing things. She might even come back one day. Who knows? But never mind. Here you go." Dirt handed them their poles, but during the short talk a few more people had gotten in line, so he would be staying here for a bit longer.

Neither Biandina nor her mother seemed completely convinced, but Antelmu certainly was. The young man was bubbling over with questions he wanted to ask but had to restrain himself until later.

"I'll come get my clothes in a minute. You should go pack up, if we're leaving today," said Dirt. Biandina nodded. Her mother didn't. They turned to go, and Antelmu dragged behind, glancing backward and bumping his pole into something, almost dropping it.

The last few people in line weren't the elders, and Dirt assumed he wasn't going to see them again. He couldn't blame them for not coming to bid him farewell.

First was a mated couple, and then a tall, lanky boy with a scruff of dark hair on his chin, and a few others.

Very last in line was a man holding a babe in his arms, and both of them were crying. The man wept quietly, tears streaming down his face, but the babe screamed with its pitiable, tiny voice.

Dirt's throat tightened. The man was sadder than he'd ever seen any-one, truly deep in despair, and Dirt's heart reached out in sympathy. "What's the matter?" he asked lamely.

"My wife is gone," said the man. He did nothing to hide his crying or summon any dignity. The mourning he felt radiated from him with nothing to veil it. "It took her, and she is gone, and now I cannot feed my son. I fear he will starve."

"I'm sorry. I was too late," said Dirt. He knew exactly which woman that was. He'd watched her toss that very baby to safety before being pulled up to her doom. Guilt crept up from the floor and twisted its pointed claws into his stomach.

"It is an evil day. An evil, evil day," said the man. The baby wailed louder, and the man's face tightened. He had to close his eyes as sobs shook him. A moment later he opened them again and said, "Please give me a pole, if you don't mind."

Dirt handed him the last pole, the one he'd been using to make all the others. He racked his brain trying to think if there was anything else he could do. Home was too far away to give them any sap, and Dirt didn't know the spell for it. The people here had plenty of water and didn't need more. The baby couldn't eat meat; it didn't even have teeth. Dirt had no gold to give. There was nothing. Nothing at all.

The man turned to go, carrying his pole in one arm and the hungry babe in the other. Dirt looked down at the floor, and their cries filled his ears as they drifted back toward their tent. The babe's, and the man's. He pictured that woman's last moments, the courage she had shown. She hadn't screamed for rescue; she'd saved her baby instead.

Dirt had mourned his forgotten past more than once, and that was only impressions and faded memories. This man had a real memory, a real face and name, a real person he could never touch again. Dirt felt dissatisfied if he went more than a couple days without touching puppy fur, so how much worse would it be if it was a mate, not just a best friend?

He didn't cry, but that didn't mean he wasn't miserable. He walked stony and ashen-faced, unable to step out of the puddle of guilt he was sinking into. Did Dirt's hope and good intentions matter to the little baby who missed his mother and might starve to death now? They did not. Hunger and loss until it died. That was all the baby had to look forward to.

Socks nudged him and said, -*Do not be too sad, little Dirt. They can find another woman to nurse him, or feed him mare's milk, or sheep's milk.*-

"*Sheep and horses have milk?*"

-*Of course. What do you think the little ones drink?*-

"*Where are the sheep?*"

-*Not close. I can only smell them sometimes.*-

"*Socks, did I make things worse?*" he asked, guilt and sympathy twisting his insides into knots. He squeezed his eyes shut and quit walking.

-*I am on your side, always,*- said Socks, simply.

"*Is it my fault that woman died?*"

-*I am on your side, always.*-

"*But—*"

-*Let the accusers come!*- said Socks forcefully. He fixed his great yellow eyes on Dirt, giving him the full force of that predatory gaze. But only to strengthen, not intimidate. -*Let them come. Let the accusers come and say what they have been doing that is better than you, if they want to judge you. None will answer. I will tell them that humanity has only one real enemy, and it is not you. And they have only one person who will fight it, and that is you.*-

"*What if this keeps happening? What if I keep making it so people die or get hurt?*"

-*Then let the accusers come! Let them try to condemn you and see what I will do about it. I know your heart, my dear little Dirt. You are not a callous creature, nor one of malice. And what did Father command us?*-

"*Cause havoc. Dig harrows in the earth and turn rivers from their courses. Leave fields of bones behind you. Explore and return with experience. But he was talking to you, not me.*"

-*I am his son, but he was talking to both of us, or you would not have heard him. He did not tell us to be timid and cautious. Do not be sad and scared and give up.*-

"*I wasn't going to give up, I just . . .*" Dirt trailed off, unsure how to finish that thought.

They were already raising some of the roof nets back up, using pulleys and ropes. Most of the netting was still in need of repair, but it seemed it would go back up faster than Dirt expected.

-*I am on your side, silly little Dirt. Always,*- said Socks again. -*And maybe you were incorrect, but I do not think you were wrong.*-

Dirt took that for how it was meant, and let it help. He stood straighter and patted the pup's nose, sending a hefty puff of affection, which the pup returned. After taking a few deep breaths, Socks licked him again, and he felt a lot better.

They stepped their way through the clutter, and Dirt waved at people he recognized, or who waved at him first. It wasn't far to Biandina's family tent, and with so many little hands to help, everything was already cleaned up. Dirt stepped inside and found the father cooking flatbread on a small copper pan. They had a tight basket of dried meat and fruit to put on the bread, and three of the children were already happily munching on their meal. The mother was still settling in, looking through some woolen bags to find things for Biandina to take.

Dirt sat, not wishing to presume he would get any, but to his surprise, the father handed him the next one. He got up and took it, then put a polite amount of the toppings on, and turned to go sit back down. Miliu and Oraziu, the two little boys, both giggled when they noticed his torn pants, and then several of the other children leaned over to see.

After he sat back down, Dirt wondered about the charcoal being used for the fire, since they had very little wood. "Where do you get the charcoal?" he asked.

Gnaziu, the boy just older than Dirt, said, "We make it from grass."

Lavisa, the older sister, was holding the infant to free up her mother's arms. She said, "We cook it, then add water and starch and form it into that shape. Then we just let it dry."

"From grass? Really?" asked Dirt. That didn't seem right, but what did he know? It was right there in front of him.

The mother said, "Why don't you tell them all what you told me, about where you're taking her?" There was a softness beneath the iciness in her eyes that hadn't been there before, and Dirt felt a spark of joy that perhaps he had given her some hope after all.

He sat back and recounted everything, going into a bit more detail. Some of it they'd already seen in Socks's vision, but there were things Dirt had only mentioned and not explained. And either way, this time Dirt placed Biandina there, and that made it all new again. The children listened in wonder, although the older ones had difficulty hiding their regret that she was leaving. Little Eudossia, in particular, clutched Biandina's empty sleeve like a leash.

After telling them all about the forest and Ogena, Dirt said, "There's one more part that I haven't told anyone yet. Socks didn't mention it, and neither did I. We've fought that giant eye in the sky before. Here's a story that only a handful of humans in the entire world know. First, let me ask, have you ever heard the name Avitus?"

None of them reacted to the name, and the parents looked at each other. Dirt was pleased. Perhaps his name wasn't a curse *everywhere* on earth. Yet.

"Three thousand years ago, there was a man named Avitus. He lived in a great empire, so huge it would take months or maybe longer to go from one end to the other. This fort you live in used to be part of it. An army used to operate here. In those days, people worshiped the gods, and they weren't evil. The gods were not the enemies of humans; they were helpful, and people worshiped them sincerely. Not like what you call the gods now. That statue in the Aedes that you call the Murderous Lady used to be Melodia, the Mistress of Song, and she didn't look like that.

"But Avitus did something, and it broke the world. The gods disappeared and the empire fell apart, and for three thousand years, everything has been getting smaller and worse. New kingdoms formed in the remains of the empire, and those broke apart, and then broke up even smaller, until there's hardly anything left. And the thing that made it all happen is the Eye. It wants to destroy all humans forever. I've seen way more of the world than almost anyone, and it's mostly empty now. Ruins of cities, if there's anything left at all. The Eye works slowly most of the time, whittling away, whittling away. No one knows what to do about it, because why should you risk yourself to change things, when life is already hard?"

That was the part where Dirt got their full attention. They instinctively held still to keep from making any sound. The infant squirmed in Lavisa's arms, and she gave him a finger to suck on to keep him quiet.

Dirt continued. "I haven't been here long enough to know what that looks like for you, but what if you all got together and hunted down every last *rucca*? Maybe sometimes you want to, but it's too dangerous, so you don't, and so they keep eating your people. But not every human is like that. One woman named Marina went on a long journey to save her tribe, a dangerous one. She succeeded and convinced the duke that he should fight back against the world falling apart, even though it's always dangerous.

"The duke in Ogena and his people faced an entire army of goblins, and they wore armor of metal and rode horses that sounded like a thunderstorm. They came out with us when Socks and I went to fight, and together we killed and scattered the entire army. The Eye appeared then, and Socks and I fought it and won there just like we did here," said Dirt.

Antelmu asked, first as a mutter but then growing louder when he realized he was speaking out loud, "Humans can fight that stuff? How? Are some people strong like you?"

"Well, not like *me*," said Dirt, "at least not any I know of. But they can be very courageous and strong, and if no one is willing to do that, everyone is going to die out. It's going to happen. That's why I want to take Biandina with me and introduce her to Marina and the others. Maybe it was really stupid, what she did, but the point is she was willing to do something. She dared."

"I didn't know about sacrificing, but I did shoot at the *rucca* with my bow," said Antelmu, somewhat surly. "And I'll do it every time I see one. She's not the only one who has courage."

"Good. Then maybe this tribe has a future after all," said Dirt.

The babbu awkwardly changed the topic of conversation back to something safer, asking about the clothing they wore in Ogena, and more about what dryads looked like. Dirt was content to answer all their questions. He'd said everything that needed to be said.

After that, Dirt was given clothing in better repair, and which was a little loose on him. It was the same wool and fur they wore when they ventured out the fort, heavy and thick, and much better than he was expecting. It was probably Gnaziu's, but Dirt wasn't about to complain if they were feeling generous. He changed into the new attire and immediately noticed how much warmer it was. Even the shoes were warmer than his old ones.

That was about the end of it. It was time for the second farewell, the deliberate one. She'd snuck out on her own before, but this time Biandina was given a pack to carry full of whatever supplies the family could spare. When she stood and put it over her good shoulder and tied it around her waist, the other children knew it was time and looked heartbroken.

One by one she hugged them, messing their hair and kissing them and whispering in their ears. Then it was her father's turn, and her mother's. Dirt had been nervous about that, but the woman's icy face finally broke, and real emotion poured out. She buried her eyes in her daughter's good shoulder, letting out only two sobs before making herself stop. She straightened, face red.

Biandina nodded, sniveling, and failed to keep her own composure as she turned and walked out. She clenched her jaw and from behind, only her chest shaking at her sobs gave her away.

Antelmu didn't cry, but the rest did, louder and louder. Dirt said, "I really do think she'll be back someday. Goodbye."

They left, following her quick march through the town and out the gate. Socks leaped over rather than squeeze through the doorway, since they hadn't put the roof back over that spot yet. Once outside, she hid her regret, but Dirt could tell something about her seemed warmer. She'd gotten a real farewell this time.

She wiped her tears on her sleeves, held her head high. and put her hood up. "So, where to now? Will Socks mind if I ride him?"

The pup simply lifted them both onto his back, with Dirt in front and Biandina behind, holding on. Once they were settled, he left at a run.

-First, the place we left that bird meat to freeze. After that, we will visit the wolves. I want to visit them next,- said Socks to both of them.

That was all they said for quite a while. Dirt left Biandina to her own thoughts, even though with all the other humans out of the way, they were plain as text on a scroll. There wasn't much to say to Socks for a while either.

The day was nearly over already, and the rest of it was windy and cold, which made Dirt glad for his new clothing. It made all the difference, and with Biandina leaning over him to keep warm, the final run was much more pleasant than the last one. They bedded down inside a half-circle heap of snow like before, and after everything that had happened during such a long day, sleep came quickly.

Until the middle of the night, when Socks woke them. A light wobbled in the darkness, following their trail. A horseman. No. He reached them, and it was no man.

Antelmu, on his prized colt Boulder, holding up a small copper lantern. The boy had followed the wolf's trail, trusting his horse to carry him speedily through the darkness. If Dirt and Socks had left any earlier in the day, he never would have found them. The boy had snot and tears frozen to his face from the cold wind, but he looked resolute as a stone.

"I'm coming," he said. "I dare, too."

CHAPTER TWENTY-SEVEN

The next thing Dirt knew, it was morning, and Socks was still asleep. He and Biandina and now Antelmu slept huddled together, lying on a blanket as close to the pup's warm belly as they could get. The horse, Boulder, was bored, standing there with nothing to do and unwilling to go anywhere. Socks must have convinced him not to be afraid, because he had no fear in him beyond the normal fidgetiness of a prey animal. His human was lying there asleep, and that functioned as a tether.

Just as Dirt was settling in to rest and wait, Socks woke with a start and stood. He lifted his nose to the air and said, -*Wake up, you two. Humans are coming.*-

Antelmu practically jumped out of his skin, going from a dream about mice to startled wakefulness in an instant. A single heartbeat later, his face filled with fear, and he rushed to his horse, making sure everything was ready to go. It was. The horse was less than enthused, and Dirt supposed it was probably hungry.

-*We were too tired to talk last night. Dirt was exhausted, and so was I. But if you want to come, you cannot bring your horse. He is too slow,*- said Socks.

"Boulder is fast. We won't slow you down," said Antelmu, checking the various bags and things draped over the horse. He very pointedly didn't look at Socks, just continued being busy getting ready.

-*Boulder is fast, but only for a horse. My legs are much longer than his, and I can use mana,*- said Socks. -*I cannot see their minds from here, but I bet the humans are coming to take you back. Choose now. Ride back to meet them, or send the horse back without you on it. I will tell Boulder to follow the trail until he meets them.-*

Dirt gave a sympathetic little frown. Antelmu probably pictured things starting very differently. He loved his horse, and he was probably as skilled as anyone at riding. And without it, what did he have to offer? Instead of helping, he'd be baggage that eats. Sort of like Biandina, now that Dirt thought about it. That made him smile, which he suppressed before anyone noticed.

Biandina stepped over and placed a gentle hand on her brother's shoulder, which he tried to shake off. "I don't doubt you deserve to come with us, but don't Mother and Father still need you? They lost Prosperu, and they lost me. Who's going to train the new dogs in the spring, and who will teach Oraziu to ride? I have to go. I don't have a choice. But you do, Antelmu. Are you sure you want to come? We might never return."

Dirt had expected her to tell him to go back, but the girl surprised him. He glanced at her mind, and Biandina *did* want her brother to come, out of affection. But she also thought it was probably wrong.

Antelmu continued fussing with his bags. He pulled out a feedbag that Dirt didn't get a look into before putting it over Boulder's head so the horse could eat.

The bright, icy morning was invigorating. Each breath of cold air sparked in Dirt's lungs and energized him. His new clothing held the night's heat in remarkably well, and the cold only touched his face. The snowy landscape was blinding, though, unless he was looking at Socks, who was big enough to block most of the reflection. All in all, it didn't look like the kind of morning that needed to start with a giant flurry of activity. But here they were.

-Horse or us. Decide right now.-

Dirt got the impression that this was a harder decision than coming had been. Looking at Antelmu's mind, the boy was in serious turmoil. Everything he had imagined himself doing had involved the horse. Fighting monsters, exploring, hunting, other great and exciting things. The boy already felt like a hero from a story, but now it might be cut short.

No, this was a test. The ancestors would watch and guide him, as would the seasons and elements and stars, if he showed them his value. He would not stop already, hard as it was to choose.

Antelmu turned toward the big pup and gathered his thoughts. He held both palms upward, as his people had done when Socks first got there, and said, "Great Wolf, will you please carry me as well?"

-Are you sure?-

"Yes."

-Why?-

"Aren't we in a hurry?"

-Then be brief.-

"I want to save my tribe, I want to see everything, and I want to make sure she's okay," he said. Each statement was quieter and more sincere than the previous one.

-Then grab whatever you're bringing.-

The boy took a pack, a waterskin, a small bow, and a quiver of arrows. Then he unstrapped a spear and asked, "Should I bring this?"

The spear leaped out of his hand all on its own and slid into the pup's harness alongside the staff Dirt had made earlier. Then the three children rose up and were deposited hastily on the pup's back. Dirt helped arrange the other two so they could lie down out of the wind and still hold on.

Once everyone was ready to go, Socks told the horse to go back up the other way, largely by associating the ideas of food and warmth with going in that direction. The horse looked around warily, then huffed into its feedbag and started walking.

There was one last thing to do. Socks lifted his leg and peed, a huge amount as always. It melted a bare spot on the grass several feet across.

Dirt told Socks, *"We all have to pee, too. How come only you get to?"*

-Their horses will smell the predator urine, and it will be hard to get them to keep following. We'll stop for you three in a bit, so just hold it.-

"Well, don't jostle us too much or we won't be holding it for long."

-I never jostle,- said Socks, amused. He was tempted to shimmy and give Dirt a good jostling as a joke, but refrained. Barely.

The pup left at an eager run. The snow was denser now but not as deep, and Socks could run almost normally. He did his best not to jostle, but Dirt couldn't take it and made him stop only a short time later. Biandina refused any help with her clothing, which she needed since she only had one arm now and the wounds were still painful, and everyone had to wait until she figured it out. Eventually she did, and got her pants tied to her satisfaction.

After they were moving again, Socks went too fast for the humans to talk easily over the wind, which left everyone to dwell on their thoughts. Dirt couldn't help his curiosity about his new companions, so he watched their minds a bit. Biandina was relieved that she might survive, although she felt hideous and malformed now with her missing arm and all the scars. But aside from that, she kept remembering her family and how they'd clung to her, and how much she loved them. Even her mother, who was usually cold and bitter, had shown real affection there at the end. It was a kinder farewell than she'd dared hope, and a memory that would warm her for years to come.

Antelmu, on the other hand, just felt worse and worse as time went on, although his resolve never wavered. At first he was proud of himself for being hard as iron and not getting sad at all, but the loss of his horse opened the door to the loss of his family and each person added another layer to the lump in his chest. His friends, too, who had been tighter than brothers. They didn't know yet. But someone had to do something, like the strange little boy said. And that was him.

Near nightfall they reached the small group of flat-topped hills and dug up the frozen meat. It was hard as ice, but Dirt's knife was sharp enough to cut it anyway. They fed Socks some, but he didn't like it frozen and still wasn't really hungry yet after gorging himself here a few days ago. They ended up taking six thick strips as long as Dirt's arm, packed in grass the other two dug up. After that, Dirt sliced off some thin strips for dinner, which they ate cooked this time.

"Can I try that knife? How do you keep it so sharp?" asked Antelmu, but Biandina was right over his shoulder.

Dirt grinned and said, "I never have to sharpen it. It's an eternal blade. Ever heard of those?"

"Nope," said Biandina. "Can we see it?"

"Sure," he said. He held it out, and Biandina took it first. "I found it in a crypt buried with a dead man."

She sliced, carefully at first with just the tip, but then her eyes widened, and she sliced off a strip of half-frozen meat as long as her arm. "What . . . ?" she said, unable to believe it. "How is it so sharp?"

Antelmu carefully reached in and plucked it from her hand, unable to wait any longer, and did the same thing. He cried out in amazement, then gave a startled laugh. "You got this in a tomb?" he said, eyes sparkling.

"Yep, underground. It was in the ruins of an old city of my people," said Dirt. "There are probably others."

Dirt didn't have to see their thoughts to watch Antelmu and Biandina decide they needed to explore the ruins now, just like Hèctor and Ignasi had when Dirt told them where he found it.

When night came it got truly cold, and the humans huddled on blankets right up against Socks's belly again. The three of them didn't fit very well on the same one, so Dirt had his own, and the siblings shared the other. They lay on their backs for a while, shoulder to shoulder, whispering quietly to each other. Dirt snuggled in against Socks's fur and summoned a few warming embers, which he shared.

"How far to the wolves' territory, do you think?" asked Dirt, aloud, for the benefit of everyone.

-Just a few days. Maybe three or four. It depends on how fast we go.-

"I hope they're happy to see us."

-We will see. Good night, little humans.-

Antelmu and Biandina said their good nights, then kept whispering to each other. Dirt could still hear it, but only if he listened deliberately and he chose not to. Let them have some time to each other.

Dirt asked Socks mentally, *"What do you think about all this? I feel like we do too many things for me and not enough for you. I wish you could spend more time with your siblings and Father."*

-I do not regret it. I am having fun. Visiting the other wolves next is a thing for me,- said Socks. *-I do miss them, though. I want to roughhouse without worrying I will hurt someone. And Father teaches us different things than I am learning with you, things I need to learn. You cannot teach me how to be a wolf. But I am learning other things that my siblings cannot learn from each other. Someday, Father can teach me the rest, and I will know two sets of things.-*

"Do you think it's a bad idea to keep fighting the Eye? We don't even really know what it is."

-It's too late to think something like that. You have two humans who have joined you expecting to fight.-

"That's true. I just want to know what you think, since we haven't talked about this aspect of it."

-I think that if we can ever find a way to get rid of it, we should. And I hate it. I want to kill it, and I will fight it every time I see it.-

"Good. Me too," said Dirt. "I wonder how things might have been different if these were the first humans I found instead of Marina's party."

-Well, what if the first one you met was the man who shot you with an arrow?-

"True. That really hurt, now that you remind me."

-It would have killed you if I wasn't there to lick it.-

"Also true. You save me in lots of different ways."

-You saved my life, too, remember. And we learned things together that saved my life other times, which I would not have learned alone.-

"Oh, I know. I'm just saying thank you."

-You are welcome, dear little Dirt,- said Socks. He didn't feel like moving, so he sent an image of licking Dirt's face along with a puff of affection.

Dirt smiled and returned the puff of affection twofold. Then he said, "You know what I still wonder? You know how Biandina offered a sacrifice, and then we saved her life and killed those rucce? I wonder if the gods are still listening. I wonder if they guided you to me somehow. Things like that."

-Who can say? Father and Mother don't seem to think the gods matter anymore.-

"I remember Father saying he was less free when the gods were still here. So I worry about two things, sort of. If the gods are still around, are they mad at me for breaking the world? Will they want revenge someday? And if they came back, what would happen to your kind, and to the trees? Do you think they'd put the trees back to when they were ignorant and small?" said Dirt.

-I think,- said Socks, -that the gods are probably gone. But if not, Father is on my side, and the forest is on yours, and we are on each other's side, so even gods would have to be careful.-

"I'm just going to say, so you never have to wonder, that if fixing the world means hurting the wolves and the trees and the elementals, and maybe all the other wonderful things we haven't met yet, then I won't do it. I won't," said Dirt.

-And I am going to say, that to me, the world is not broken. It is a paradise. Everywhere is open, everything is free, and the world is stuffed full of *enemies and prey and new sights and wonders. The fact there are some little humans in it just makes it more wondrous. I love it. I love being alive. And I love you, my own little Dirt, and I am glad you are with me.-*

"I love you too, Socks. I'm glad I'm with you."

-What should we dream tonight?-

"Let's take Biandina and Antelmu and see what the moon is made of."

About the Author

Ryan English is the author of the Land of Broken Roads series, originally released on Royal Road. He was first introduced to fantasy when he read The Hobbit at the age of seven and has been reading and writing in the genre ever since. English currently lives in Utah and works in cybersecurity.

JOIN THE FELLOWSHIP

follow us on our socials

 podiumentertainment.com

 @podiumentertainment

 /podiumentertainment

 @podium_ent

 @podiumentertainment